THE WEIGHT OF OUR SINS

HEATHER DUBREE

To The Book People,

To [illegible], [illegible] the Book

DEDICATION

Dedicated to all the women who have always felt like the world was
not enough.

Copyright © 2023 Heather Dubree All rights reserved.

❀ Created with Vellum

ISLE OF WAVES

DANA

THE OTHERWORLD
Land of the Sidhe

HY-BRASIL

TEMPLE OF DANU

N

THE GORGE

PROLOGUE

When the car hit the water, her world went black. By the time Anna came to, the car was barely staying afloat. The freezing water seeping in through the seam of the door and the spider vein cracks in the windshield. The only thing warm was the blood running over face, blinding her vision in a red haze. She kept wiping at it, confused and disoriented. Not entirely understanding why there was glass embedded in the palm of her hand.

Then, her memory hit her almost as hard as the airbag had. Kate had screamed as they went over the edge of the bridge.

Anna remembered flying. Her coffee cup from that morning hit her as it was thrown from its holder, the bag of groceries crashing into the front window. The can of soup splintering as it hit and the strange way they had been floating. It was as if time had stopped and then unfathomably sped up as they hit the water. Her hands had come up to cover her head as the glass shredded her skin and tendons.

It was dark. And it was so cold.

She felt her arms lift as the water submerged the car. The only thing holding her down was the seatbelt which once was her lifeline but now threatened to be the thing that drowned her. Kate had been screaming. Until she hadn't been.

Anna was warm.

She vaguely remembered thinking that she must have been dying, because isn't that what people said happened before you die? You get so cold, then warm. Anna didn't think it would happen this way, swerving to miss something on the road- whatever it was had just shot in front of her. A white, feathery blur. It was enough for her to lose control. Hit the guardrail going sixty-five in a forty.

The floating sensation disappeared, and she felt the solid ground underneath her, her fingers digging in and feeling pine needles piercing her skin. There was a sound of birds singing, distantly and in a flock.

The air smelled different and lighter. The floral smells were more potent, the scent of the earth so pronounced it was as if she stood in a freshly tilled garden.

Rustling in the grass by her feet, wet sneakers on the forest floor. Movement in the trees. Anna's heart hammered in her chest, panicking as she looked around her in dizzying circles, trying to get her bearings. Was she dead? Was this heaven? She had never really given much thought to heaven and hell, but now, faced with her own mortality, the question of where she stood was at the forefront of her mind. A large shape cloaked in darkness. It whispered as Anna felt herself begin being laid down on the soft, fragrant earth. So she lay there, trembling as warm and bright blood still ran down her face.

Her ears were thrumming, the anxious voices surrounding her without her being able to summon the focus to make out what they were saying.

The warmth of the forest leaked from her, her skin breaking into gooseflesh. She suddenly was overcome with a wave of cold, even with the warm forest air drifting around her. Her heart pounded and skipped, causing her to cry out as something pulled at her chest beneath her breastbone.

Then, the feeling of being ripped off her feet in the most savage way she could imagine, her back hitting the ground that had been so welcoming just moments before. The place that had been filling her lungs with the sweet-smelling air, was replaced with screaming.

Was she screaming?

The bird's song had disappeared. The air now smelled sharp, and something was over her mouth, forcing her to breathe a sickly sterile scent. The beeping was so loud now, replacing the rustling of trees, and her fingers spasmed. Grasping for the floor of pine needles but was only met with pain as her fingernails burrowed into concrete. Anna wasn't floating this time but sailing. Lights flashed over her head as she did, faceless people over her shouting and pushing and running.

Were they for her?

There was a pinch in her arm, and she started to float again. But this time, the birds weren't there.

Kate wasn't there.

That day, Anna left a part of herself in those woods.

1

Since the car accident, Anna Thorne has stayed away from water. She had been lucky, at least, she had been told that repeatedly. A motorcyclist had seen her car careen off of the bridge and was able to get her help in time, but just barely. Anna can't even remember the doctors she had seen over the past few months about it. The scars on her hands never entirely went away, gashed deeply from the splintered glass of the car, causing nerve damage. She had struck her head on the steering wheel hard enough to cause a nasty concussion, which doctors and therapists had used to explain the odd experience she had had when she died.

And she had died for a few seconds. And in those moments, she had lived somewhere else entirely. Her therapists had been as helpful as possible, but it took her months to get back on the road. She had more miles on her ride-sharing app than she should have.

Her father had been her saving grace, bringing her back home and taking her to physical therapy to strengthen her grip again. She knew she was fortunate. Anna had a small scar above her eyebrow from the steering wheel, a few gashes on her palms, and more anxiety issues than before.

Kate wasn't lucky. Kate didn't walk away with a hand that didn't close all the way or a scar that split her eyebrow. Kate was lying in a coma. A coma she would probably never come out of. And every day, Anna had to wake up and remember that. Sleep would have been a refuge and as if the universe knew that, it had constantly evaded her.

Once unconsciousness began to take her, she panicked, grappling with the feeling of being pulled under. Of never waking up. Of Kate's screaming as they went underwater. Her father had stayed with her, even when her nightmares woke him up at night, turning on every light so she didn't think she was underwater. The ever-present heating blanket keeping away the chill of the night, even in summer. Because the moment she became cold, it was like it was happening all over again. The ice cold lake. The smells. The water lapped at her waist while blood rushed into her eyes.

Her therapist had sent her to a psychiatrist who, after giving her a laundry list of anxiety and PTSD medication, had tacked on a sleeping pill. Small and pink. Anna refused to take it, just throwing it in the medicine cabinet despite her friend, Ian insisting it was safe. But Anna had been out of control once and refused to be so again.

Anna refused to respond to the therapist when he had asked if she refused the medication because, perhaps, she didn't feel like she deserved that reprieve.

Sometimes when she did sleep, she was in a different place entirely. The darkening sky with stars far brighter than they held in her noise-polluted metropolis. She could hear the sounds of the nights completely engulfing her as the slow, cool breeze grazed her moon-bathed skin. Even in her dreams of that otherworld, she still was clothed in whatever she had been wearing when she had fallen asleep.

It was peaceful, so unlike her waking hours.

✳✳✳

The hospital looked the same. The months that had passed did little to such a place. And Kate looked the same. The same tubes and wires, the small pale blue gown she had been dressed in for the past year, made even her dark skin look pale. Kate's parents had been by. Fresh pink peonies adorned her bedside table, their sickly sweet aroma filling the small space. Anna sat stiffly in the uncomfortable chair, scooting it across the linoleum floor to take Kate's limp hand in her own.

"Hi, Katie," she whispered, keeping her gaze on her friend's hand, finding it hard to look at her face. The bruises had long healed but Anna swore she could still see them when she closed her eyes. Kate had a scar now, her face had been so unblemished, even in high school her golden brown complexion always seemed to glow. But here, in this place, she looked dull, like her light had been smothered. Like she was simply a breath away from being extinguished.

Kate was soft, whereas Anna was all sharp lines, the yin and yang in physical form.

"I got a job," she continued, stroking the small empty space between IV lines. "It's a stupid job in telemarketing, which is stupid too because you know how much I hate talking on the phone." Her voice shook at the end.

Anna finally allowed herself to look at her friend's face, her mouth slightly agape from where the breathing tube was inserted. The rise and fall of her chest an artificial movement caused by a pump.

The guilt rolled into her like a wave, just as fresh as the day she had woken up in the hospital, but Kate hadn't. Her ruined hand tried to clench into a fist but failed miserably, the deep scars pulling at the shortened skin and taunt ligaments.

"I'm so sorry, Kate," she whispered, a sob welling within her. "I am so sorry that I woke up and you didn't. I am so sorry that I was driving too fast. You should be here. And I should be in this bed." She pressed her forehead against her friend's limp hand, crying earnestly."I will be back to visit you every week. I swear." Anna sniffed hard and wiped her tears on her shirt sleeve quickly as a nurse walked in. The nurse saw the moment, and smiled sympathetically before walking out the way she came. It's not like someone sobbing in a hospital room was something they hadn't heard before

"I love you, Katie," she said, regaining her poise and lightly kissing her friend on the cheek, rubbing her fingers where her lip balm had left a small stain on the brown skin.

Anna straightened, looked at her still friend, and walked out the door.

✳✳✳

The chair was uncomfortable, and Anna shifted her weight for the hundredth time in the past few minutes. Her scuffed flats had god knows what on them from the commute, and with that hot day, she didn't think it was a good idea to take her shoes off to tuck them underneath her.

So she sat. The comings and goings of everyone speaking to their respective callers was a distinctive white noise she had learned to drone out over the past few months. The calls didn't stop today. Being a part of technical help for one of the largest phone companies was not something for the faint of heart. It allowed her her own cubicle, paid leave, and health benefits while still allowing her some free time. So she dealt with endless ringing phones and headaches from the luminescent overhead lights.

Between her 14th call of the day, she sat back heavily in the uncomfortable office chair, leaning her head back and closing her eyes for a moment. Anna took deep breaths, calming her nerves from today's constant barrage of voices.

"Anna," a sharp voice said, far too close for comfort and sharply jarring her out of her reverie. "Your lines are blinking." She started, her stomach dropping at the reprimand as she saw the flashing red lights on her telephone, alerting her to five waiting callers. Anna mumbled an apology, attempted to calm her racing heart, and returned to the fray.

It had been a long day. The commute home was lengthy, and she swore she hit every red light on the way home. Her ancient car was grinding each time she pressed on the brakes scolding her for neglecting to take care of it. At first, the electrical tape she jokingly placed on the dash over the annoyingly bright red engine light was a joke, something to peeve her friend Jessie. But it was out of sight and out of mind at this point.

Anna's small apartment was home. She had carved a bit of herself into the city, leaving the small town in which she grew up. Everything wrong had happened in that town. It was where her mother had died, where her five-year relationship and one year of marriage disintegrated.

After the accident, her remaining love for that small town evaporated, and she was left with Kate's shadow.

She opened the door, keys stuck in the old lock for a moment. The smell of cooking surrounded her, and she smiled. Anna had given her friend Ian a key to the place for safety, and sometimes, when she couldn't sleep, he would come over. They would watch reality tv reruns until she passed out on the couch. She had missed her father, but it was time to be on her own again.

Anna just turned 33, and with the one year of her accident loom, she fled the small town. Tulsa might not be the biggest city in the world, but it was much larger than the small suburb she had grown up in. She had once romanticized the hip coffeeshops and walking to the farmer's markets on Saturdays. She imagined herself lazily sipping on hot tea on a balcony, the scenes of the city below her. That didn't happen.

Of course, the sun did set behind the city buildings, and it was beautiful. That is, the few times she was off work in time to enjoy it. She'd never been to the farmers market, the closest she had come was the organic aisle in the supermarket. There was a lot of hot tea, but her tiny balcony wasn't big enough to hold a chair, let alone an outdoor set.

The world had greyed after Kate had been hurt. She knew, deep down, she didn't deserve to have the happiness of a new apartment. The first time Anna had been on her own since she was nineteen. She dropped out of college and immediately got into a serious relationship with the first guy who was nice to her. Despite the guilt that had ate at her, the apartment was something she was proud of.

Growing up in a frugal household gave her the skills to create a comfortable space without spending a ridiculous amount of money. Though the thrift stores were combed through quickly, she still could find cute furniture and adopted many wilting houseplants from the local supermarket, giving her small space life and color.

"How was work!" Ian's chipper voice sounded from the kitchen as she hung her purse and jacket on the hook near the door. She and Ian had been friends since ninth grade, and there wasn't too much lost between them. Sharing wine and dinner had become routine. It was nice having him there when she got off occasionally. He lived in the apartment beside her and had found her the place and the job.

Anna smiled, walking into the warm cooking space and gladly taking the glass of wine he offered. It was cheap but palpable. She knew it was cheap, because it was hers. Most nights, a small glass of wine helped ease her into unconsciousness, though she would never admit it.

His husband Matt, put out her mismatched dinnerware. So they were having a proper at the table dinner tonight? Not just collapsing in front of the tv? She scrambled to remember if she had forgotten some special occasion.

Spaghetti and wine, white bread with butter smeared over it because garlic bread was too expensive.

"So, how was today?" Ian asked again, twirling his fork in his noodles and bringing it to his mouth in an undignified slurp.

Anna shrugged, tearing a piece of the buttered bread and dipping it into the red sauce, chewing thoughtfully, "It wasn't bad. It was just work, I guess."

"You making friends?" Matt chipped in, suppressing a grin behind a glass of red wine.

Rolling her eyes, Anna emptied her glass before replying sarcastically, "Why yes, thanks, Dad."

"So many new people for Kate to meet when she wakes up," Ian stated, the redhead helping himself to more bread. Anna didn't say anything, just chewed in silence for a moment, ignoring the look Matt had shot to Ian across the table.

She rubbed a fingerprint off her wine glass, the room quiet except for the scraping of forks on cheap plates.

"You don't have to say that, you know," she breathed, swallowing hard against the threat of her food making a reappearance.

"Anna-"

"Ian," she stopped him, setting her fork hard on the table. "You don't have to try to make me feel better. It's sweet, and I know you're trying, but," she stopped, reaching across the table and pouring herself another deep glass of the red liquid. Matt looked like he was going to say something but decided against it. Anna took a deep gulp to steady herself, drowning the guilt in her gut.

"I know it's coming up. The one year anniversary of when it happened. We don't have to pretend she's going to wake up." Ian, the eternal optimist, leaned back and folded his arms against his chest, "She could, Anna."

Choking on a bitter laugh, she drained the glass, her throat burning with the cheap wine.

"Ok, Ian." The rest of the dinner lost its magic. Matt and Ian cleared the table while Anna put the dishes away in the dishwasher. She usually just left them in the sink until she ran out of silverware, but she had to uphold some type of a facade of good mental health while her friends were here.

They hugged, Matt gave her a pointed look as if apologizing for his significant other, but she shooed him away with a small smile.

When they left, it was just her. Alone with her thoughts. It wasn't something she liked before and now, even less. It was dark outside, the creatures of the night making themselves known even over the noise of people shutting their homes down for the night. Tea replaced coffee as her hot beverage, and she was settling into her overstuffed second-hand wingback to watch some tv before bed.

The mindless noise of the television helped dull the roar of the anxiety that still caused her to tremble when it got bad enough.

Every day was the same, like Anna was just waiting for something to happen. But, at the same time, the guilt in deep within her prevented her from doing anything more than predictability. So here she was, collapsed in front of her tv screen once again.

2
_____

It had been dark when she had felt herself being pulled into sleep. And it was dark here too. But a fire crackled in the large hearth, occasionally popping to send bursts of sparks into the air, the sounds comforting in the drafty building. It seemed as cramped as it was dark. Smells of stale beer, body odor, almost overwhelmed her senses and drowned out the sound of muffled speaking. Anna couldn't make out the words, but people, primarily men, were talking.

If she leaned forward a bit more, she could make out what they were saying. It was growing more recognizable the longer she listened. Mixed languages? Anna couldn't put her finger on it. She leaned forward in whatever she was sitting. A chair? A bench? She felt something hard and dug her fingernails into it.

Closer.

Closer.

The talking stopped. Whispers.

Her fingers dug deeper into the wood beneath her. Something brushed past her.

Anna woke with a gasp, her chest feeling like it was caving in as she struggled to get a deep enough breath.

Looking around her room, she grounded herself just like her therapist had taught her months ago. What did she see? Her room.

She was in her room.

What did she feel? Her bed. Her sheets were damp with sweat.

What did she smell? The lemon verbena candle she had accidentally left burning. So she had fallen asleep accidentally.

What did she taste? Smoke. Why did she taste smoke? It was like when she went to her Uncle's for Fourth of July and sat downwind from the fire too long.

Moving a shaky hand to her table side lamp, she carefully turned it on. She blew out the candle in the process, and watched the smoke billow through the room.

Blood. There was blood on the bed, her fingernail had been ripped. Anna brought the broken nail to her lips, staunching the very light flow with the flick of her tongue until she felt something sharp dug underneath her polished pink nail. With the taste of iron in her mouth, she coaxed the offending splinter out with her teeth. She lay in bed, trying to make sense of her dream and the splinter, until her alarm clock startled her to lucidity.

The remaining morning was a blur of coffee, barely brushed hair, and attempting to clean off her makeup from the previous night. Anna's pale skin was only embellished by the deep circles that had made their home under her brown eyes, even the concealer couldn't hide them effectively. Deep down, she knew this would happen. It was nearing the first anniversary of her accident. Her doctors warned her about it, and she desperately tried to push it down.

Having all but sprinted into work after realizing she had failed to stop and get gasoline the night before, she was a mess of tangled hair and muttered apologies as she reached her desk at long last. It wasn't until lunch that she started to perk up a bit, a second wind courtesy of her third cup of coffee.

"You look like hell, Anna," her co-worker Jess remarked, her perfectly arched eyebrows rising slightly at her appearance as she took a seat next to her.

"Hi to you, too," she replied, but smiled slightly to let her know she knew she was kidding. And to be honest, she knew she looked tired because she felt it too.

"Rough night?" Jess asked, pushing around a kale salad with

unmasked disinterest. Anna bobbed her head, downing her cup and taking a sip of water to wash the taste the burnt liquid the office dared to call coffee out of her mouth.

"Weird dreams. Weird night. Probably something I watched." Jess nodded in agreement, pushing aside her salad and going for her main course. Something vegetarian but hearty looking.

"You know," Jess quipped, "Some of us are going out after work tonight if you'd like to join us. Nothing big, just the bar on the corner on Main. It would be nice to see you outside of work for once." Anna quickly did the math - she had been working there for nearly a year, and Jess was one of her closest friends besides Ian. Still, a friend she never actually did anything with outside of work.

She couldn't quite bring herself to go out much, but the thought of not being alone in her apartment did sound appealing. Her therapist warned her that avoiding her feelings simply delayed the healing. But nearly a year later, the wound still felt like a raw scab, and Anna knew it would bleed if she scratched against it. And she wasn't ready for that.

It wasn't that she didn't want to hang out with Jess, she was intelligent, funny, witty, and a gorgeous person inside and out. She just felt so drained after her shift. She felt as if after work and just routine household errands, the precious time she was alone in her own company was too little as it was. Being an introvert but constantly craving the bond of inclusion was a tricky map to navigate.

"Ok," she said resolutely, tearing open a granola bar and instantly wishing she hadn't forgotten the bento box in her fridge. "Ok, I'll go. It'll be fun. I need to get out more." That'll shut her therapist, Dr. Warner, up.

Jess beamed, her smile reaching her eyes in a way that it didn't with many people Anna had encountered, "Fantastic! Ok perfect. Can we carpool? I can pick you up at 8?"Almost instantly regretting her decision when she mentioned the time, Anna swallowed hard and agreed.

She did feel a tad ridiculous being thirty-three, drawing closer and closer to thirty-four years old, and already being tempted by the sweet siren song of her bed at 9 pm every night.

"I'll grab us a red eye," Promised the other girl with a wink as she swallowed the last bit of her meal and took off before Anna could change her mind.

***

It was loud, mostly due to the large neon letters announcing ladies night, with first drinks free. She didn't use to be much of a drinker, but she found more and more that a bottomless glass of wine at night helped lull her to sleep. Anna felt herself becoming a sad stereotype but ignored it.

Swimming through the sea of unrecognizable faces and her already diminishing gumption (not to mention lucidity thanks to her sleepless night beforehand), she took the offered drink from Jess. She didn't even complain about the burn that accompanied it.

The music wasn't as bad after that, and she overlooked the sticky mess of spilled alcohol that clung to her shoes everywhere she stepped. It wasn't a dive bar but nothing too upscale, which she was happy with. She was glad the dress she picked out wasn't too wrinkled for having lived in the back of her closet for so long.

It felt good to get out, the bar's energy was electrifying, and the conversation was good. The laughter was contagious, and though the dark bar offered nothing in the way of entertainment besides a poorly maintained dart board, they had a good time just in each other's company. Anna stuck by Jess's side most of the night, she was the buffer between her co-workers she didn't know well except in passing and random birthday parties that are thrown together in the break room.

Having only downed a few soft drinks when they first arrived, plus some hot dogs from a street vendor out front, Anna offered to drive Jess home - her apartment only a few blocks away.

"Are you sure?" Jess asked, already handing over her keys, her eyes bloodshot. The other girl's smile told her that she had a great time and was feeling no ill effects besides being too inebriated to drive. They drove a couple of miles to Jess's complex, and Anna opened the front door for her to ensure she was safely inside before walking herself home.

The night was clear, crisp, and absolute heaven to walk in. A couple of open restaurants and bars lit the way before she found herself in an older part of the city. Mostly composed of crumbling apartment buildings and historic homes with large gates.

She allowed herself to enjoy the walk in silence. Her mace gripped tightly in her right hand because she wasn't ignorant of what nighttime holds. Even nights as nice as these.

Anna hummed quietly, allowing the air to play with her hair and letting the night capture her imagination as she drew closer to the house.

A rustle to her left drew her away from her thoughts, and she gripped the mace tightly as she froze.

Fuck!

She always knew she would be the one girl in the horror movie that would freeze and get viciously murdered. Her breath came out in short, uncontrolled gasps as she waited to see someone or something waiting for her in the tree line. She jumped back as a small head - no two small heads came slithering out of the bushes beside her, nearly silent save for the grass parting underneath it.

A snake.

Flattened skull with two heads and four gleaming black eyes on one scaled body. With the drumming in her ears, Anna swore she could feel her blood pulsing as it took her back to that night, to that dream when she was knocked out.

That otherworldly feel. Just like the night she had died. Her hands trembled, something her father had spent thousands of dollars in therapy bills to help calm.

It seemed to stop and stare at her more consciously than she would have liked for a reptile to do. The wind picked up at that moment, a smell hitting her. The smell of fresh earth and plants and she swore, she could feel the pine under her fingernails again. She did not scream or pass out. She slowly backed away and ran across to her apartment building, a car honking at her as she nearly missed careening into their oncoming headlights. Her ankles protested as she ran up the stairs in her heels, quickly unlocked her door, and slammed it behind her.

"It's fine, it's fine," she whispered, getting her breathing under control and willing her hands to let the death grip on her mace loosen enough to put it on the hanger near the door. She couldn't stop her hands from shaking as she turned the facet on. The orange pill bottle stared at her on the medicine cabinet. She quickly ripped the top off, grabbed the round medication, and swallowed it back dry.

Anna gripped the sink, the cool porcelain grounding her as she gulped air. Slowly, her breathing regulated the blessed magic of modern science in that pill, staving off her panic attack. She was trembling, but practiced the breathing she had learned over the months of therapy. She wouldn't admit it was enough that the scare took away her peace as she walked home. Her stomach churned. Every time something good, hell, normal, even began, that icy grip of anxiety stole it from her. Her fear turned to anger as she kicked the heels across the floor, her clothing immediately feeling too restrictive.

Anna shook out her hands, breathing deeply over and over as she walked to her small bathroom. She lit a candle with fumbling fingers, the lighter shaking with the effort. She wrapped her arms around her trembling naked body as the bath filled, until realizing the apartment was dark and seemingly closing in on her. Anna ran naked through the small space and shakily turned on every light, pressing back that suffocating darkness.

The feeling of the car floating in the lake, the oppressive cold seeping in. Her therapist suggested night lights, but she scoffed at the suggestion, now silently kicking herself for not listening.

As Anna panted, a sob crept up unbidden as she cranked the tub faucet, the tub filled with steaming water.

"I just need to get warm," Anna thought, her mind racing but trying to pinpoint to that singular task. Something manageable. The hot water soothed her almost bordering on too hot. Anna always got out before the water even began to get too lukewarm.

No pools, no lakes. No cold water.

The water was indeed too hot, steam rising from the shock of cool porcelain it had been poured into. Anna's skin screamed at her, but she ignored it, sitting quickly and wrapping her arms around her legs. Her forehead pressed into her knees while she continued breathing.

The scent of lemon, rosemary, and eucalyptus filled the tiny space, and the candle's shadows danced off the walls around her as she sat, sinking into the shallow tub.

Between the steam rising off her skin and the smell of the candle, Anna took shuddering deep breaths, wringing her hands together and willing the trembling to subside. She allowed her torn hands to soak in the bath, flexing her fingers underneath the clear water and allowing the muscles to relax. And before too long, she was drifting as her fingers danced along the water's surface. She sank into a more relaxed state until the night was cleansed from her body.

It didn't take long for the shaking to subside. Between the wind beating against the aged window pane and the steam rising off Anna's night-kissed skin she felt the effects of the last night's restless sleep catch up with her. Sleeping in the tub might not be the wisest choice, but when on the edge of sleep and the foggy effect of the drugs, she felt unable to resist closing her eyes for just a moment.

Just a moment. And then, she was floating.

It was still raining. And she was in the middle of a forest, deep and lush trees surrounding her. It was like she could breathe again. They towered over her, their trunks too thick to see around with bright green moss climbing them.

Spinning around, she was trying to see the break in the trees above her, just barely peaking a morning sky of pinks and purples. Anna felt something drift around her and looked down slowly to find herself in a pond, just standing while water lilies floated past her lazily, their petals satin soft against her skin. It was warmed by the sun and didn't cause her any panic at being in the open water.

Anna walked out of the pond, still naked, as if from the bath she knew she was in. But she was the only one around; this was her place and her dream.

Her refuge.

The forest was coated with thick vegetation and fallen leaves, cushioning the woodland floor as she walked barefoot over them. Her hair dangled in tentacles around her face and slipped well past her neckline, finally free from the thick braid she had bound it in for the night out.

Anna's skin rose as a slight breeze broke through the thick trees, warm and welcoming. It was fragrant with the dewy morning air. Anna began following a sudden manmade path to her right, dodging errant branches and allowing the passing ferns to tickle her ankles and bare legs.

This place was hers, her dream.

The break in the tree line had her picking up her pace. The sun was rising, and she saw it in all its glory as its rays penetrated the deep thicket. And she stood in awe.

Mountains and rolling hills, all covered with deep, thick trees and a waterfall in the distance. It's roar could be heard now that she was out of the forest. Though it was probably miles away from where she stood.

She stood on a bridge, stepping on the ground cover that had spilled from the forest. The stones looked old and hand-cut, smoothed from hundreds of years of rain and travelers.

The forest's calm was interrupted by a snapping limb that caused her to whirl, heart pounding. Too real. Too fast. Too loud. Anna suddenly felt exposed as she stepped back, the once peaceful forest now seeming a bit more sinister. She realized could barely see the warm pond now that she was on the bridge, her feet backing up into the moss and smooth stones.

The snap became footsteps and quiet conversation as three people came out of the deep forest, as she had just done moments before - and stopped at seeing her.

"You?" A dark haired man whispered in undisguised shock, his eyes fixed on her. He looked confused. Anna stumbled back, feeling her feet hit the edge of the bridge and tip backward.

The man leapt forward, glove-covered fingers reaching for her, but she fell back into the open air.

Water flew around her as she rose from the bottom of the tub, her body reacting to the dream of colliding with the ground. Anna sputtered, dosing a few of the candles out with a hiss as she choked on the bath water. She struggled to get her bearings as she wiped her face with trembling fingers.

Wrapping her arms around her knees, she set her forehead down onto them getting her breathing under control. She must have dozed off, and she hated dreams like that, the feeling of falling still felt all too real in her gut as it turned. Her heart raced no matter how many times she repeated to herself, *"I'm fine, I'm fine."*

Anna wasn't sure how long she sat, trembling fingers gripping the wet porcelain, before finally rising. Steam still rising from her water-warmed body as she quickly toweled off. She pushed the soaked bath rug into the corner to deal with in the morning, leaving her towel in a pile. Turning off her phone almost angrily, mad at herself all over again.

She pushed the heel of her hands into her eyes, feeling tears prickling behind them. They were just nightmares. It happened to others, especially those with similar trauma.

At least, that's what her doctors had said.

Pulling the shower curtain closed, she paused, her brow knitting together as she saw the water not draining very quickly.

"Goddammit," she growled, dropping to her knees hard on the cold tile floor, piercing her skin like a knife. Pushing her fingers into the tub drain, Anna instantly made a face as her fingers collided with something soft. It was wet, sopping wet, and green.

Mushy between Anna's fingers, and she pulled it from the drain. Anna dropped the clump of damp, green moss with a hitch in her breath.

3

Anna didn't sleep. At least not well.

While her dreams were nothing out of the ordinary, the sense of something looming had seeped into her sleep. Flashes of that two-headed snake made her shiver even while making her morning coffee. Her head was pounding from the moderate intake of alcohol from the night prior.

When she went to check her phone, she realized she missed a call from her psychiatrist. Fumbling in her cabinets, she withdrew her tiny bottle of anti-anxiety medication. She was prescribed them after her accident and continued taking it despite her reservations. She didn't deserve the relief it gave her, but she went back, again and again.

"No refills"

was stamped underneath the date. She shook the bottle, feeling she was nearly out. Sure enough, the voicemail reminded her that her 1-month appointment was due. They had a cancellation that day and wondered if she wanted to come in.

"Just what I need today," she mumbled, but accepted the time anyway. She side-eyed the bathroom over the rim of her coffee cup, she hadn't looked at the tub since the night before. She had decided last night that everything that happened was a coincidence. She must have gotten some moss stuck on her while walking home from the club. The subconscious was a weird thing. And to be honest? She wasn't ready to think about it. There wasn't room in her head.

She needed to call her psychiatric office, whether she liked it or not. It was her day off, she couldn't blame putting it off for work. Anna tapped the outside of her mug for a moment, sipping her now lukewarm coffee before she hit the bottom of her cup caked in sugar.

"I'm 33. I can make a fucking doctor's appointment," she grumbled to herself, mentally chiding herself for her laziness. The woman on the other end didn't seem very enthusiastic about her phone call either. The loud nails on a keyboard that seemed to go on forever before she found her chart, informing her that a 4:00pm appointment was open. Anna took it without looking at the time, or her calendar, or even thinking about it.

4 p.m.

Anna tapped her phone, the screen illuminating to show it was only 12:30 p.m. Anna collapsed back in her chair, the ancient velvet molding to her as she sank into it. Her empty coffee cup clutched in hand like a security blanket. She had time to relax, and do some laundry. She always hated evening appointments, watching the time slip by. It was best to get some errands done.

Busy work, but things she had been putting off.

Overcast skies greeted her as she peered out of her glass door, her head resting on the back of the chair. She knew she eventually needed to venture into the bathroom again. Her teeth felt disgusting, and her makeup clung to her skin from the night before. Resolutely, she set down her breakfast and strode to the bathroom, refusing to look into the tub. The lump of moss she knew was still there, where she had flung it the night before.

Or worse, what if it wasn't? What if she had dreamed up the moss as well? Was she finally losing it?

She brushed her teeth. Washed her face. Moisturized her skin and brushed her brunette hair.

Anna still avoided the tub. Avoidance was her superpower, and it worked well enough in her 33 years. Or not, according to her therapists. This was not the day to deal with whatever had happened last night, imagined or real. A mental breakdown would have to wait.

She tossed her hair into a quick ponytail and jumped as her phone sprang to life. Jess's name popped up, her photo illuminating the small screen.

"Hello?" Answered Anna, certain she sounded breathless, but her voice an octave higher as she feigned lightness. "I just woke up," came the muffled voice of her colleague, the shift of her blankets rustling over the phone. Anna smiled, putting her on speaker as she applied the drug store mascara.

"Good morning to you too, sunshine," she grinned, the normalcy immediately soothing her nerves.

"Thank you so much for dropping me off last night," Jess replied, groaning. "I'm a shit friend. I didn't even make sure you got home okay."

Anna smiled, putting the makeup bag back in the cramped cabinet, "You're not a shit friend, and I'm fine. I was more than capable of getting home. But I appreciate you calling." There was no sound from the other end except the pop of a cap.

"How are you feeling?" Asked Anna, though she already knew the answer to that.

"Like shit," grumbled her friend, "So you're good? I'll see you Monday?"

"Yeah, absolutely,'" she paused, gripping the sink in indecision, "Jess, have you ever seen or even heard of anyone seeing snakes in the area?"

Jess snorted a bit, "Um, sometimes. I mean, I know it's the city, but there are parks all around, lots of nature reserves, you know?" She stopped, the sound of Jess downing a glass of water on the other end, "So yeah they make appearances in town once in a while. Why? What did you see one?" Jess sounded excited at the prospect.

It was validation. Anna knew the information but needed to hear from someone other than a search engine. "Yeah, scared the shit out of me, actually," she laughed, grabbing the phone from where it balanced precariously on the sink ledge. "It had two heads, I think?"

"Seriously? Yeah, that is kind of weird," Jess admitted, but her voice held more intrigue than concerned. "The zoo would've probably paid you good money for that."

"Probably. Maybe I was just a bit more tipsy than I thought," Anna admitted, brushing it off. She just needed to say it. Talking to Jess was cheaper than therapy, and this didn't involve her calling her father, which would immediately prompt him to offer her a ride back home.

"Probably, but hey, listen. I'm glad you came out. It was great seeing you outside of the office for once," Though Jess's voice was still rough, she sounded more awake. Anna was more grateful than she could put in words that she had called.

"Yeah, me too," Confessed Anna, smiling despite herself. Anna did have fun, though she thought it might be a few more weeks before she ventured out again. Her social meter needed to be refilled once every few weeks before she felt solitude calling her name.

"Thanks for calling. I'll see you at work." After they hung up, Anna felt better. Picking some of her jeans and boots, she pulled on a thick oversized sweater that she had spent too much on last week. The coffee she drank just had barely touched her exhaustion. With the threat of an evening appointment looming, she headed down to the local coffee shop, a cute place with plants hanging from the tall ceilings. She could breathe when she left the quadplex, the air was brisk but enjoyable. The nip in the air made her feel vibrantly alive, something she desperately needed.

Anna let her feet swing from the bar stools as she enjoyed her coffee and bagel, which was more cream cheese than pastry. It was relaxing and calming. Anna was delighted that she brought a paperback from home as the murmur and flow of the space was a welcome noise as she read.

Today, she was just glad to be out, away from her apartment and her thoughts. That fucking tub. The day continued that way at a steady pace, from the coffee shop to the laundry mat, where she ate stale cheese crackers from the vending machine for lunch.

Anna packed all her laundry in her small trunk before reluctantly driving to her appointment across town. By then, a slow pattering of rain had begun to fall, draping the small city in a thick eerie mist.

✳✳✳

Dr. Warner's office was tucked away in a cramped building, and Anna always forgot the unit number amid the cluster of names on the marquee. It always smelt a bit musty like most old buildings, she was sure the carpet had been there since the 80s, and the ceiling tiles had small spots of water damage where the erratic Oklahoma weather had finally made its way inside.

The lady at the reception desk finally acknowledged her presence to check her in, banishing her to the uncomfortable armchairs next to the expensive tropical fish tank. She was sure her $65 copay helped cover its expense.

"Anna Thorne? I'm ready for you to come back!" came the chipper voice of Dr. Amelia Warner. Anna smiled and stood. Despite her hatred of appointments, doctor's offices, or making appointments in general, she enjoyed Dr. Warner. She was kind, friendly, and got to the point.

The office was a shade of muted green, complimenting nicely with the view outside of the woods. Immediately Anna felt peaceful, which she was sure was the desired effect.

"So Anna, how are you feeling?" Dr. Warner asked after exchanging the required pleasantries, her pen tapping her thick notepad expectantly. Anna looked down, not sure how to respond.

"Honestly, mood-wise, I'm good. Work is fine, I guess. Just normal stuff." The grey-haired woman looked at her expectantly, slight smile as she looked over the rim of her glasses. Dr. Warner never said much in there sessions, instead letting the silence linger, allowing Anna to sort out her thoughts and fill that space.

"But?"

"But," Anna requited, folding her hands in her lap, trying to prevent the nervous picking of her cuticles. She forever felt under a spotlight, like any little thing she did gave away some deeper meaning, showing the physician more than she was comfortable with. "I had an episode again. Fell asleep in the tub. I had nightmares. Disorienting, vivid nightmares."

Saying it all in one breath, she allowed the words to spill out of

25

her before she could keep them back. The doctor pursed her lips, and she wrote quickly in a scroll that Anna knew wasn't meant for a quick read.

"You took a bath?" Nodding, Anna looked out the window as she continued to write. The rain was coming down hard now. "Given the notes your therapist back home had provided, it looks as if this is something you both tackled fairly early on in your treatment," the older woman scanned her file, all of her trauma and treatment tucked neatly into a manilla folder. "I'd like us to reprise some earlier exercises perhaps, even going to the local fountain to sit near the water. Allow yourself near it before you bathe again. Knowing the water is not the enemy and your body's reaction can be treated."

Anna nodded. She knew the exercises that they had worked on before.

"Yeah, I'll try it, whatever you think is best," she replied, smiling quickly and looking out the window.

"Anna," Started Dr. Warner, removing her glasses to clean the lenses with the corner of her blue cardigan, "This is not a step back. This is not failure. Recovery is not linear."

Anna inclined her head, feeling the knot in her stomach as she said goodbye and was ushered to the front desk. More refills, a 3-month check-in visit, and the cordial *"Have a nice days"* were exchanged. She found herself running to her parked car, her sweater the only thing keeping her from getting completely drenched.

Anna sat there, her car on standby, letting the water beat on the vehicle. She wasn't sure how long she had been there before someone slammed a car door next to her, pushing her to leave the small parking lot.

It was nearly 6 p.m. when she returned to her apartment, turning on the small lamp near the sofa. Oklahoma was still in the throws of early spring. She was already tired from the early sunset and the rain practically called her to sleep.

Deciding to skip the shower until tomorrow, she splashed warm water on her face instead. Steadfast, she stalked across the small bathroom. She grabbed the still-damp clump of moss, and tossed it in the waste bin, covering it with bits of tissue. It was done, a stupid dream and stupid dirt. But she stood there a bit longer, feeling cold all of a sudden, and her skin rose with goose flesh. She quickly retreated to her bed, shutting the bathroom door behind her.

Her bed was soft and cozy, her heating blanket warming the soft linen sheets as she sank into the mattress. Anna took the small bottle from her nightstand, her name in bold print across the orange bottle. It was the sleeping pills Ian swore by and set beside her bed.

"Just in case," he had said, not taking no for an answer. She didn't know her enneagram, but Ian told her that her astrology sign had difficulty giving up control. Anna liked that excuse more than being a type A control freak that couldn't stand the thought of being out of control of herself, even for a night.

Getting tipsy was one thing, home alone with a glass of wine or with friends. Anna knew her limits. But for some reason, medications always made her nervous. It probably had something to do with her hippie Aunt who helped raise her, some lingering side effect of child-hood indoctrination that she was sure Dr. Warner would love to dig into the next meeting if she got the chance.

Turning the bottle in her hand, she felt the pills rolling around, the same amount that had been there when prescribed.

Take one at bedtime.

Anna took a deep breath. And another. Emptying the contents of her old water cup, she quickly popped the small pink pill and swallowed before she could overthink it. The tiny pill barely registered as she swallowed, and she turned on her white noise machine so the room was filled with the sound of a crackling fire and soft forest noises. Her warm blanket wrapped around her like a cocoon.

Closing her eyes, she wondered how long it would take. Anna just needed to- *sleep*.

4

The pills were working, but nature's call couldn't be persuaded to wait, even at 2 a.m. Anna padded to the bathroom, bleary-eyed and unwilling to turn on any lights. It caused her to wake more than she already was. She ran her feet on the side of the bed, looking for her house shoes.

The floor felt off. Her damn slippers weren't where they usually were.

Anna swayed a bit, unsteady from the sleep medication. There was a sound, almost like a popping of a crackling fire. Anna swore she could feel the heat against her skin. The occasional pop and hiss of the flames started to rouse her. Had she left on her white noise app that she had downloaded on her phone? She normally had it on a timer.

Shifting, she swore to herself. The pills didn't work, or they were working, and she was sleepwalking. Should Dr. Warner up the dosage? Or perhaps they had sat too long and gone bad? Could that even happen?

Of course, it was the first time she had taken these. There was always trial and error when taking medication right? A gentle breeze brushed her face, causing her to pull her robe closer to her. She startled, a breeze?

She blinked hard, muttering to herself. She was in her bedroom. This was just an effect of the medicine. She was in control. This was a dream.

Anna opened her eyes. It was dark, taking her a minute to adjust to the night. She looked up, but instead of her ceiling, she gazed at the most *glorious blanket of stars above her. Brighter than she had ever seen. Brighter than it should have been, because she was in her bedroom the last time she had checked.*

The sounds of the night seemed to mimic the ones she had left on her phone, the occasional soft sigh of the wood's fallen foliage, the buzz of insects, and the gentle sway of the trees.

The pop of the fire. Was there a fire?

A rustling.

Her body went stiff. Her jaw clenched as she looked through the grouping of trees near her to see the source of the sound and heat. Across a small campfire sat a hooded figure, barely discernible in the dark. The flames cast shadows over the tall man but not able to reveal a face under the guise of the heavy hood worn.

"Where am I?" She whispered, not able to take her eyes off the figure.

"Did you hear that?" A deep voiced asked two companions she had missed before and stood startled. She closed her eyes.

Heavy footsteps accompanied the crunch of the leaves as they got closer to her.

She could hear their breathing, and everything in her told her to run and fight and -

The blaring of her 7 a.m. alarm startled her. She awoke to find her fingers clenched around the robe she was wearing, just like in the dream. Anna shot up violently, her blankets trapping her, heart pounding wildly in her chest as she gulped in the air at the unexpected wake-up call. She swore she could still smell the hint of the outdoors clinging to her nostrils.

Without thinking, she took the pill bottle still perched on the nightstand and threw it across the room, the bottle harmlessly bouncing off the wall. She stood with shaky hands and wrapped her robe around her like a security blanket before grabbing her phone, switching off the alarm that was aggravating her headache.

Anna was tired. She was tired of this happening. Though she had gone through insomnia most of her life, it seemed to be happening more frequently. Anna opened the search engine on her phone, and typed in the prescription name she half hazard taken the night before without asking questions. She had just needed a good night sleep.

Looking at the side effects, she relaxed. They said she could have intense dreams, especially the first few dosages.

Other insomniacs comforted her by proxy, saying they only lasted a few nights and found relief after the fact. She could do this. It was just a few days, and she would call Dr. Warner's if it continued. Her alarm blared again, breaking her focus from the online forum. She took a quick shower (the offending moss now hidden in her trash bin), snagging a granola bar and a coffee before she flung herself to work.

Tonight would be better. Different. It was just a nightmare.

✻✻✻

Work was dull. She probably told at least ten people within the first hour to simply turn their device on and off to fix their issue. Anna tried not to sound smug when her directions worked without fail, leaving the client sputtering embarrassed apologies for the previous vulgarities they spewed at her just moments before hanging up.

"Hey, you okay? Long night?" Jess popped around her corner, water cup in hand, before setting it down. Jess was a good friend, constantly reminding Anna to at least chug a glass of water with her coffee to counteract dehydration.

Taking the offered plastic cup, she nodded, "New meds to help me sleep, messed up my dreams," Anna explained, hoping the pressure settling behind her eyes was not the warning signs of an impending migraine, but rather the lack of rest her body desperately needed.

"You know, you should try this thing I've been reading about," Jess exclaimed, "My brother used to have terrible night terrors, so he tried lucid dreaming."

Anna frowned, "Isn't that kind of an oxymoron?" Jess rolled her eyes and pulled out her phone before typing furiously.

"It's just about controlling and realizing you're dreaming, so that you can wake up or at least control the narrative." A small beep pulled her attention to her phone. Jess had already sent her a link. "It really helped him. Once he got control of his dreaming, he hasn't looked back. The night terrors are gone now."

Anna nodded, taking her phone and tapping the screen, briefly scrolling through the article.

"Ok," she whispered, slightly intrigued if she was being honest with herself. "Yeah, I will give it a go. It is not like anything else is working at this point."

"Thats the spirit," joked Jess, squeezing her shoulder as she left.

Lucid dreaming? Sipping on her water, she scrolled through the article more intently. Some sleep studies have found that this can give the dreamer some control over their somniphobia. Were they nightmares, though? Nothing major had ever happened. Nothing had hurt her, tried to hurt her, or, save for last night, spoken to her. It was just the intensity of the dream. Made it feel... Not like a dream. THAT was what scared her.

Not the dream's contents, but the way it made her feel. It felt real enough that she was beginning to question her sanity.

The phone's wait lines blinked at her.

✳✳✳

The day was beautiful and the sun shone uncharacteristically bright when she took Dr. Warner's advice.

There was a public place, a park, couples walked lazily hand in hand, and children screamed at the brightly colored jungle gym just a few yards away. Dodging bicyclists, she made her way to the relatively large pond. The fountain graced in the middle was turned off due to the cold nightly temperatures. However, there were still a flurry of ducks and water movement, suggesting the fish were feeding on the morning bugs that skimmed the surface.

It was uncharacteristically warm this morning, and people were out in droves enjoying the sunshine and mild temperatures.

Nonetheless, Anna was still wrapped in her hoodie, a beanie sitting firmly on her head.

Seeing the large body of water made her stomach sour, but she squared her jaw and walked past the wooden trail to the water's edge.

There she set her thick blanket and her drive-through order she had grabbed beforehand. Anna sighed, allowing the bright sun to spill over her, letting the gentle breeze play with her hair.

It was time to get this over with and so she can get better and move on with her life. Of course, she wasn't sure where her life was going, but it wasn't going anywhere until she stopped breaking out into a cold sweat near a damn pond. So she sat, and despite the mild temperatures, the ground was cold and uncomfortable. With her legs tucked underneath her, she poured some cream into her coffee cup and unwrapped her breakfast sandwich, chewing thoughtfully.

It wasn't so bad.

The water moved slightly from the movement of the ducks across the way, happily munching on insects on the water's edge. The coffee tasted heavenly in the morning hours. The sun beaming on her through the bare tree branches had her relaxing in its rays.

Brushing crumbs off her lap, she switched her position, crossing her legs and breathing deeply. She closed her eyes, allowing the sounds of the park and water to lull her to a meditative state where she could train her body not to fear water. Even if it was just the park.

Anna stayed long enough for her joints to ache from sitting on the hard ground, her coffee cold before she finally rose and grabbed her belongings. There was a bridge over the pond just a bit from her. She froze momentarily, chewing on her lip before deciding to take that way to her car.

Bridges and overpasses were tricky, especially over bodies of water, but this was safe. She placed herself in an uncomfortable and stressful situation despite being in a controlled environment, just like all those doctors said to do. The boards on the bridge were well up-kept, and bicyclists sped by while she took a spot near the rail that nearly went to her chest. She peered over the water, enjoying the sight of the large fish and turtles swimming underneath her.

Anna stood, staring at the rippling water for a while, watching the pond life beneath her before the wind picked up for a moment. The rippling of water that had once only held the reflection of the sky now distorted.

She paused until the movement on the surface subsided, her

hands gripping the wood on the bridge rail hard enough that one of her fingernails splintered.

Unable to tear her eyes away from the water, she watched the scene unfold before her. The trees swayed in the identical breeze as the one pushing her hair across her face. A picture appeared in the water's surface, a worn road that led to a bridge. Though not the one she was standing on. The same bridge she had fallen off in her dream. It led up to a castle, towering high above the trees, fracturing the blue sky with aggressive spiked towers that framed the palace. Suddenly, a large splash disrupted the image, and she stumbled as if a thread had been cut and released her.

A group of children laughed as they tossed rocks into the pond. Anna stumbled back into an incoming bicyclist's path, nearly getting run over while escaping the water's edge.

"Watch out!" Yelled the cyclist, veering hard to the left to avoid her, and she crashed into the opposite side of the bridge. Her heartbeat was drumming in her ears, and she couldn't quite find her breath. "Sorry, sorry," she muttered in the direction of the long-gone bicyclist. Eyes still glued to the spot that had once held her otherworldly forest, but now, only ducks swam by.

Anna gathered her things, her scarred hand trembling and slipping when she tried to grab the small picnic bag she had brought for the day. She walked to the car swearing the entire time, looking behind her every few steps. Anna knew what she looked like, knew what she felt like. All the way home, she felt a disconnect, like her body and mind weren't quite together. Maybe it was all bleeding together. The trauma, the head injury, her grief.

Maybe she was unraveling.

***

The days went by uneventfully. Anna talked herself out of an emergency room visit by simply laying off the caffeine and switching to decaf for a few days. Dehydration does weird things to a person. Her accident's one year anniversary was approaching, bringing up feelings of dread. Anna's father had already called her twice to remind her how proud he was of her.

She smiled, looking over at the photo she had of her father and herself. She had no recent photos since her father despised being in front of the camera, but this one of his huge smile as she graduated high school had always been her favorite. It traveled with her no matter what apartment or living situation.

The herbal tea was looked upon by Jess with approval as she answered phones for the day. They decided on a dinner together after work, and Anna clung to the plans, desperately needing something normal to counteract the bizarre way she had been feeling for the past week.

"Hibachi or Italian?" Came a sweet voice behind her, jerking her out of her trance.

She smiled. "Well, those are two very different food choices," she observed, sipping the cooling beverage beside her. "There was never anything good back home, so my experiences are few and far between."

Jess agreed, tapping a few buttons on her phone before sending Anna a location. "Well, we're not the food hub that you're used to, but I think you'll like it." Jess said sarcastically, "First drinks on me, but after that, you're on your own."

She smiled, rolling away in her office chair to the other side of the cubicle before anyone could notice she was gone. It was only a few hours later that Anna could finally set down her headset and clock out, rubbing her tired eyes, burning from staring at the computer screen for so long.

It had been hectic, and the withdrawal from her morning coffee had made her cranky, a lingering headache settling behind her eyes. The restaurant had been packed, and they sat with two couples, one obviously on an awkward first date and the other a distant elderly couple who paid no one else at the table any mind. It was bustling, noisy, and distracting.

It was precisely what Anna needed.

Anna laughed with Jess over strong and expensive drinks and ate shrimp cooked in front of them perfectly. The hibachi chef was

34

charming, spinning his utensils with a little extra flair. He cast her a wink when flipping a piece of chicken skillfully on her plate. She responded in kind by eating far too quickly for something hot off the grill, not sure how to react to someone flirting by throwing food at her. To be honest that's better than most men's attempts at flirting in her experience.

"I think he's flirting with you," Jess nudged, probably a bit too loud for the whisper she was seeking, but Anna laughed. The whole experience lasted a bit over an hour, and Anna found herself disappointed when it was over. It was dark and freezing outside when they left the comfort of the restaurant. Jess hugged Anna, the contact making her weirdly emotional.

✳✳✳

She thanked her lucky stars for forgetting to turn down the thermostat when she left for work that morning and she was welcomed by a toasty apartment. The wind was howling outside, rattling her small apartment window. The scratching of the loose branches against them was slightly disconcerting, but not unexpected.

The rent was cheap, which meant it that came with its issues. The building was not correctly up-kept, and the trees hovered over the split-level building. There was always the threat of them breaking the ancient glass with every storm that seemed to sweep through the city in the spring. Anna couldn't be concerned with that tonight. Her body relaxed from the night out, with the meager amount of alcohol she consumed and was full of food. From the cost of the tab, she would be eating instant noodles the rest of the week. Still, it was worth it.

Her hair had become untamed from its braid through the night, small pieces sticking every which way as it attempted to escape from her hair tie. Anna brushed the unkempt locks with her fingers, wincing as she caught a knot or two. When she was satisfied enough to skim through it she placed it in a loose bun at her neck.

Wiping away the day's makeup, a rattle of a branch slapping the window pane beside her made her jump, jostling the mirror precariously perched on the nightstand in front of her. With a gasp, Anna grabbed the side with one hand and pushed against the mirror. Looking up into the glass, it wasn't just her reflection she saw, but the figure out of the corner of her eye. Lingering just out of her field of vision.

Screaming, whirling around and yielding the brush as the only weapon at her disposal, goosebumps raised over her skin.

There was nothing. Her small apartment was as empty as ever.

The brush dropped from her hand as Anna collapsed against her dresser, the shuddering of her sobs the only sounds.

5

Anna wasn't sure how long she had sat there, cradling her knees to her chest before her hips ached. The quiet apartment creaked as she stood, grimacing at her reflection, even as she tried not to look in the mirror again. The little pill bottle sat there, a siren song full of hope and rest on her nightstand.

Fear prickled her. Her nightmare before had been so-

Vivid.

The anger roiled again, pressing against that fear as she grabbed the bottle and swallowed back a tablet. She didn't want her over-thinking to prevent her from, once again, getting a good night's rest. She left the small lamp lit near her, the glow illuminating the small space as Anna wrapped herself in the duvet. Her body protesting as she sat down on the wood floor again. She was vibrating with anxiety, the bed was too constricting.

So she sat. She waited.

Teetering with bated breath for the medication to kick in, praying for it to sweep her away. Even as she shoved back the pinpricks of tears, something dark in the recesses of her mind knew that she didn't want to be here. That she just needed a break. A respite from her racing whirlwind of thoughts and bone-crushing regret that hung on her like perfume. Anna needed, *desperately needed*, rest.

Then, there was the overwhelming smell of pine.

Anna allowed her scarred hand to scan the earth beneath her before opening her eyes. Everything was tilting, and her stomach pitched. She forced herself to draw a deep breath and she opened her eyes.

*****

Anna wasn't in her room anymore. She was back where she had been one year ago. The woods looked the same, with towering trees, massive trunks, tall plants, and the sound of birds in the distance. The pine needles stabbed her palms as she drew herself up.

Grounding. Anna needed to ground herself.

"What do I see?" She whispered to herself, almost inaudibly. "What do I smell? What do I hear? What do I taste?"

Trees. Pine. Birds. Copper. Was that blood in her mouth?

She heard rustling, and she quickly sat up, trying to ignore the pounding in her head as she did so; the forest seemed to tilt for a moment. Anna worried her bottom lip, finding the source of the taste of blood. The rustling came closer. Anna stood, heart pounding, only to realize she was barefoot and clad only in the outfit she had on when she was going to bed, completely defenseless and still had no idea where she was.

Another rustle again to her right, and she spun quickly, her hands forming into fists as a noise slipped through her lips resembling a scream. But she didn't have to wait long because something hard hit her from her left.

Before her body hit the forest floor, an arm tightened around her middle and spun her away from the ground. Anna struggled to breathe as she was pined with her back to the person behind her, their hand wrapped loosely around her throat. They were tall, thick gloves covered their large hands. She could feel the brush of a coat or hood as the figure tightened their grip.

"Where did you come from?" Came a voice, the sound like sandpaper over gravel. He was close enough for Anna to feel his hot breath on her ear. She shook her head, feeling him tighten around her waist. What was she supposed to say?

"This is a dream," she choked out, closing her eyes tightly. "This is a dream."

"I assure you it is not; now tell me where you came from." The hooded man replied gruffly, not letting up on the pressure around her waist. He kept his grip on her throat light enough to breathe and speak, but he was too strong. She felt he could snap her neck if she moved wrong.

Lucid dreaming.

Her eyes snapped open. If this was a dream, a coma, or whatever happened before her accident, she could control it. Nothing could hurt her here.

She took a deep breath and decided to do the one thing her father taught her when she was eleven. *"If someone ever comes up behind you and you can't break free, break their goddamn nose."* With the hand still around her neck, she quickly tightened her core and reeled back into the face behind her. She knew it wouldn't take much force to cause devastating pain to your nasal cavity. She played enough soccer in high school to remember what getting hit in the face felt like.

The blow must have been unexpected as the man behind her was taller and well-built and she was an unarmed barefoot stranger in the forest. He probably didn't find her a threat enough to really restrain her. A howl escaped the man, and his grip loosened enough that Anna used her momentum to push away from him and, in the process, fell to the leaf-littered floor. The man stumbled back, swearing and holding his face. Anna saw the opportunity to run.

And she did.

Scrambling onto her feet, she tried to ignore the pain of stepping on something sharp as she took off through the trees. Anna had no idea where she was going or what direction, just away from him. She couldn't control her breathing, but she swore she heard him behind her. Everything in her screamed to run faster. At that moment, as she dodged an oncoming branch, something caught her ankle. The ground rose to meet her as she once again collapsed. Her breath left her in a rush, her lungs and ribs screaming as she impacted with the unforgiving surface.

She rolled to her back swinging her feet and hands with all of her might, connecting a few satisfying times. Her pulse raced in fear but at the same time in unmitigated fury at the stranger. Her attack wasn't exactly strategic and she quickly found herself pinned with her back to the ground, hands secured to her sides by the man's knees. He effectively sat on her, pinning her down like a wild animal as she squirmed for freedom.

"Let me go!" She yelled, her voice hoarse and breaking. She was on the edge of tears or blood lust, which she could not quite discern yet.

"Not until you tell me why you're following us!" The large man barked back, just as angrily, the hood still low over his face. The crunch of leaves signaled the arrival of at least two others.

She froze, her eyes widening in shock as she looked beside her. A person dressed in white armor with the most flawless, dark skin she had ever seen on a human was closing in, and she couldn't stop staring. The ebony figure had stark white hair and equally dark eyes framed with white eyelashes, eyebrows, and high cheekbones that looked like they could cut her if she dared touch them.

Anna subsequently stopped squirming when the movement behind them made her breathing hitch. They had wings, not unlike bird wings. They had six feathered wings, three jutting from each side. The larger extending from their shoulder blades, shadowing the smaller appendages. They appeared deadly and razor-sharp in the dying light of the sun.

Anna realized she had stopped struggling, her hands going numb from the force of the hooded man's knees on her forearms.

"I can't feel my arms," she spat between gritted teeth, returning her attention to her assailant.

"Well, I can feel my broken nose, and I'd much prefer to be on your end right now," the man's gruff voice was slightly pained this time as he barked in response. Despite this his legs loosened their grip on her sides where her arms lay trapped. Not enough to let her escape but to feel the blood flow begin to return.

"Who is that?" Came a feminine voice this time. Tucked behind the large winged creature emerged a woman who looked around Anna's age. Nothing odd about her. She was pretty, with freckles framing her dark face. She looked young, but when Anna looked long enough, the girls eyes seemed to belong to a much older person.

"The person who has been following us," replied the man, turning his head to spit a wad of blood far too close to Anna's prone form for her liking. "I caught her just up the ridge, probably spying again."

"Maybe," the dark-haired girl said, her soft tone devoid of emotion aside from a bit of curiosity, "You could let her up; she could tell us." The winged creature stared at the woman briefly and then nodded toward them in agreement. The man above her moved so quickly she barely had time to register as he hauled Anna to her feet. He grabbed her wrists and forced them behind her back, though she noticed with chagrin that he kept his head away from the back of hers this time.

"Who are you?" Inquired the creature with wings, the voice soft yet powerful and slightly melodious.

"This is a dream. I am in control," Anna whispered, trying to ignore the tightening of her arms from the gloved man. "This is a dream. I am in control." Anna noticed the confusion on the other's faces as she continued her mantra.

"Perhaps she's sick?" Said the curly haired woman to no one in particular, but her eyes held a type of sadness for Anna's apparent situation at their associate's hands.

"She doesn't hit like she's sick," grunted the man behind her, sniffing harshly and giving no quarter.

"I'm not sick; this is just a dream," she spat angrily but also satisfied that she had hurt the man behind her enough that he was still sniffing blood. "You're not real. None of this is real!"

"You can tell me who you are now," the man in the hood replied, keeping his head close to hers, "Or you can tell me later, and that will be much more unpleasant for you." The winged individual's wings flared slightly, and Anna's eyes darted around when the sound of whispers seemed to come from the creature's corner of the woods. Anna swallowed hard, her head pressed to the man's chest, limiting her movement, and her lungs ached as she was still trying to catch her breath from when she first fell.

"My name is Anna," she whispered, closing her eyes hard and then opening them again as if, perhaps, that would make her appear in her room again.

"Where are you from?" The man behind her growled, shaking her a bit, causing something akin to a whimper to escape her. Anna didn't know what to say. She wasn't built for interrogation, but Anna could honestly say she had no idea where she came from or how she got there.

"I don't even know where I am," she whispered, twisting in his arms and eliciting a strong tug in response stilling her instantly. She felt more than saw the three pairs of eyes on her as if they were sizing her up, trying to figure out what to do with her. Anna had never been more terrified.

"We take her back to the The Golden Keep. Octavia can decide what to do with her." The other two beings looked at each other almost uneasily, and Anna felt a pit in her stomach at their glances. Anna felt herself being pushed out of the way with no tenderness as the man stalked over to a bag that had been left behind a tree.

Picking it up and slinging it over his shoulder, he pushed away his hood from his face, staring directly at Anna, his green eyes intense and angry. Blood was still running down his nose and into the scruff of his slightly bearded face, which he hastily attempted to wipe away with the back of his glove without breaking eye contact.

"You," he breathed, pointing a finger at her, "You're coming with us." Anna backed into a tree placing her hands on the trunk to keep her from falling back and shielding her from any more attacks. Her arms still hurt where he wrenched them behind her.

"Fuck you," she spat, even while her hands trembled around the tree's base, the sharp bark bit into her skin. The birds that had flown away still circled overhead as if they were afraid to land. She didn't expect the man to charge at her, immediately blocking her in, his face dangerously close to hers.

At this close proximity, she could see small scars littered over his tan skin, nicks and cracks that had poorly healed or not tended to, one deep one across his eyebrow.

He was near enough she could smell the iron from the blood she had caused by what she hoped was a broken nose. The red of it was still smeared across his face.

"Listen to me," he growled, his eyes wide and face trembling with emotion, almost like unconfined fury at her lack of obedience. "I don't know who or what you are but I have a job to do, and until I find out why you keep popping up around me and my companions, you," he said the following words with no room for argument, "are coming with us."

And with that, he grabbed her by the upper arm, his grip like iron and his thick gloves pinching the tender skin of her underarm as he pulled her. Her attacker dug in his pocket, pulling out a length of thin linked chain, and before she knew what was happening, it was clasped around her wrist.

"Hey!" Anna cried out, pulling against the cool metal.

The man wore a matching one, just as small and delicate, but as she tugged, it bit into her skin without snapping. No one explained as he raised his hand to signal the others to follow him. She watched the tall creature offer their hand to the petite woman who took it. Dragged alongside the taller man, Anna swore she hit every fallen branch and tripped over every hidden root. He didn't even look at her, his stern face set in a determined scowl.

"How far is this Keep?" Anna gasped, grabbing at his hand on her arm, though he finally loosened it enough to not feel like it was being yanked from its socket.

"None of your concern," he replied, still not looking at her, "but now we're running late because of you."

Anna made a face, "I didn't do anything," she tripped again over another branch, her feet only covered with socks she put on before bed, "I just want to go home."

The man just grunted, obviously not believing her for one second. Before she could bite out a retort, she smelled something burning and heard the unmistakable sound of voices. He halted, the

43

gloved man held up a hand to his companions, to which they obeyed.

"Why are we stop-"Anna was cut off as the man shoved her indelicately into the angelic person. She gasped as they gripped her shoulders. Their unyielding touch was like steel,.

The winged creature had the masculine body of a man but the feline grace and feminine beauty of a woman. They were stunning and violent at the same time.

"They call me Aramus," the creature said, its wings seemingly moving and flittering on their own accord. She swore she could hear the faint sound of whispering as the feathers rustled and brushed around them. They had a flawless texture to their dark skin with large eyes of gold, and pure white hair cropped close to their head. "I am a seraph, as it seems you are alarmed by my feathered appendages. They won't cause you any harm." Anna was staring, and she knew it was rude. She couldn't find it in herself to stop, but the being named Aramus didn't seem to mind. They seemed to be staring just as interested in her.

"Declan didn't say to talk to her," whispered the other woman, who was now throwing a satchel to her hooded captor, barely gracing her with a glance.

"He did not say not to if we're speaking in absolutes." Retorted Aramus, breaking eye contact with Anna. The man with the gloves scrubbed at his hair with his covered hands, pushing back the dark hair. He pulled over the hood, shading his face and without another word, they followed the man, Declan she presumed.

Finding herself being nudged forward and sensing Aramus's firm and unbreakable grip on her shoulders, she simply complied even as her heart raced and the sounds of a town drew nearer. Slowly the faint trail from the woods transformed into dirt and stone, handmade paths with markers. The aroma of food being cooked hit her, accompanied by the sound of dogs barking and children playing.

Where *was* she?

6

"He's here!" Whipping her head up towards the shout, a town came into view as an older woman stumbled towards them. Her gnarled hands gripped a handmade wooden cane that bent as she leaned on it. The elder woman dressed well, though her face was lined with anxiety.

"Sin Eater, I thank you for coming," She whispered somewhat reverently but hesitant to come much closer to the group. The old woman bobbed her head, not quite meeting the group's eyes. Her gnarled hand waved them to a large structure with iron bars just slightly inside the gates. "I wasn't sure if you would make it. We have our tax for the Reaping."

"Neither did we." Declan declared, "Lead me to the prisoners." His face still shrouded to the crowd he turned slightly in her direction as if pointing her. The old woman looked at Anna curiously, but said nothing. She hobbled alongside them but still at a safe distance.

Anna was hit with the most nauseating smell when they arrived at the building, labored breathing and coughing could be heard from inside.

"I don't want her inside." Her captor said, this time looking at Aramus, avoiding her. "You know I must be present. If you would like,

I can let her go," the seraph replied calmly, dipping their head. "But I fear she would flee."

The man named Declan clenched his fists. Anna attempted to avoid gagging as another breeze carried the smell of decay directly toward her. The structure was lined with tan bricks, an old thatched roof atop its structure. There were no windows and the sound of movement inside made Anna uncomfortable.

Though the day was cool, standing in the path of the sun was unforgiving. Declan turned and nodded to the woman, who took out an old key and fit it in the lock. The sound of bodies moving inside caused Anna to push back against Aramus.

A gate made of bars welcomed them, a foul smell caused Anna to cover her nose and mouth as it washed over her. It was a large room about the size of her apartment, with a lone candle burned by the door, barely casting any visibility inside. A faint smell of incense clouded the room but did little to cover the smell of rot and body odor.

The lack of windows caused the air to be stagnant, this room would be unlivable if it was any warmer. Declan followed the old woman, and Aramus pressed her forward despite her protests. Once inside, it took her a moment for her eyes to adjust to the oppressive darkness. She breathed only through her mouth lest her expensive hibachi dinner make a second appearance.

Once her eyes acclimated, she wished they hadn't. At least four bodies were chained to the wall, and insects buzzed around the buckets of what she was sure contained excrement. The prisoners barely acknowledged their presence, their sunken eyes following the candlelight like moths.

"What's happening?" She whispered, not sure if she wanted to know the answers.

"These prisoners are sentenced to death. We are here to see that through. It is the Reaping." Was all Amarus replied. They were still, reverent and hushed. Their whole body was still and straight beside the hands on her shoulders. Even their wings were quiet now.

"I don't want to see anyone die, please let me wait outside," she pleaded, twisting in the winged creature's grip, her head spinning and stomach churning. Her feet slipped on the disgusting floor. The bugs buzzing by made her skin crawl. Aramus ignored her.

"Do you have it?" He asked, turning to the woman who led them inside. She promptly nodded and dropped a small velvet purse into Declan's gloved hand. The man tossed it lightly as if checking the weight before placing it in his trouser pocket. Then, Declan pushed his hood back, shoving the cloak behind him and carefully removing his black gloves, finger by finger.

That was when one of the prisoners began to mutter, whispering something repeatedly. Another began to sob. The energy shifted around her, and she couldn't help but shrink back into the seraph, their presence the only thing calming her.

Declan looked over at Anna, locking eyes with her. She looked away somehow knowing she should not see what happened next. Declan sank to his knees near the closest prisoner, the old man who had begun muttering as before. His aged face looked at Declan in pure horror and unabashed angst.

Declan tucked the gloves under his arm. Anna couldn't help but gasp when she saw what they had been covering. his sun-touched, scarred skin was stained black from fingertip to forearm, as if ink had crawled along his skin, and made its home there, nestling in every crevice and fingernail bed. Her breath hitched, pressing herself into the being behind her, feeling the wings vibrate against her as she did so, but she couldn't help it. Declan's jaw clenched at her gasp, but he didn't face her.

"I pass judgement on you now," Anna stood still, unable to move or breathe as her captor continued. He placed his ungloved hand on the man's bare chest, right above his heart. "You will know no peace or sanctuary. May Danu forgive you, for I shall not." The last part of the prayer came out gruff and strangled as if it was choked out of him. Declan didn't look up at any of them. His eyes stayed glued to the ground, hair shading his eyes as the man in front of him pleaded for his life, the short chains the only thing holding him to his place.

It was as if all the air had been sucked from the room. Declan ground his teeth together, as the man beneath him heaved upwards as if pulled by an invisible string. Tendrils of inky black seemed to weep from the prisoner's chest and melt into Declan's fingers, working their way up his forearms. The Sin Eater pulled away after the moment, the prisoner sinking as if a string had been cut, his lifeless eyes staring at nothing. His mouth, whispering pleas moments before, was slack as his dead weight hit the back of the dirty wall.

Sweat dripped down his face and Anna could see Declan's jaw working. He said nothing as he stood, chest heaving. It happened over and over again. Black moved from body to body and seating itself in the Sin Eater's arms. She was dizzy. No matter the mantra in her head saying she was in control, that this was all a dream, it became increasingly clear to her that this wasn't a dream and she was not in control.

"Why do you need to be here? You're not doing anything," she whispered angrily to the seraph behind her, whose iron grip hadn't changed since being in the stockade. Tears were burning behind her eyes, partially from fear and the stench in the building. But she refused to let them fall for either purpose.

"I observe the proceedings. I am the Witness." The seraph didn't explain anymore, and Anna didn't press it.

The last man stood, his chains barely giving him leave, and as Anna sank back, the seraph did not move, instead watching with no particular anxiety at the aggressive stance of the prisoner.

"You dare come here as you do to judge me?" The muscled man spat close to Declan's boots. The prisoner's eyes blazed in the dim candlelight, shaved head marked with scabs, and a profoundly crooked nose from what looked like a recently unhealed break.

"We know who you are, Sin Eater, and I don't accept your *judgement*." The prisoner snapped, the last word pointed. He stared eye to eye with the man who had delivered his other companions to their graves just moments ago. Though she could not see him, she could almost hear the smirk that lit the Sin Eater's face as his large hand gripped the man's skull and forced it against the wall. Dirt and stone rained down on them both with the force of the impact.

Startled, the old woman jumped back, causing the large lantern to sway, spinning the dark room into an even more terrifying abyss. Anna strained to hear the words that Declan was muttering into the pinned man's ear, but the last part she heard was his voice strain, raising with his struggles.

"I judge you, you piece of shit, don't you think for a moment that I can't see everything you did to each one of them," the last part punched out of him. Then, the man squirmed, trying to break the seemingly unmovable grip on his skull that seemed to tighten with each syllable.

Declan didn't waste a prayer on this man. He took his other hand and pressed it hard enough over the man's heart that he screamed. The break of bones bowing and snapping filled the room as the heavy, inky blackness left the prisoner's body.

Everything simultaneously came crashing down on her. She felt the blood leaving her face and the whooshing of her heart in her ears. Anna collapsed.

7

A nna woke to the sensation of being carried, a gentle rocking pace, her head swaying with each stride. She hesitated, opening her eyes, allowing the events that had taken place to replay in vivid detail in her mind. She knew, just with the smells around her and the sounds of milling people, that she was still not in her bedroom.

This was not a dream. She should have awoken by now.

"She is awake," came Aramus's melodic voice, confirming that she was being carried by the angelic being. Once her facade was discovered, she opened her eyes, the blue-grey sky greeting her. The prison was just behind them, so she couldn't have been out long. Anna could swear she could still smell the stench of despair; the limp bodies of the prisoners scorched into her mind's eye.

"Set her down," came a gruff reply, and Anna found herself on her shaky feet before Declan, his gloves and cloak, righted upon him. Besides the sheen of sweat on his brow, he appeared the same as before they went into that dark room.

He pointed a gloved finger at her, his eyes fiery, "You stay with us. If you try to escape, you will not like the outcome; I promise you that."

Anna still felt unsteady, her vision swarming and her head pounding from her fainting spell. She had never fainted before and decided she'd like to keep it that way. So she simply nodded.

Anna knew she had no idea where she was and no idea how to get home, and judging by the wide berths the townsfolk were giving them, she assumed this group had some sort of authority or even infamy.

She wasn't someone drawn to danger or the unknown. Dangerous men only had their place in her novels, but Anna had seen how the townsfolk had handed over those prisoners with no trial and no mercy. No one could be trusted here. She wasn't even sure if she trusted herself.

Declan nodded sharply and turned, stalking towards a far-off building his back ramrod straight and his hands in fists. She stumbled slightly as they made their way after him, her feet muddy and cold. She couldn't feel her toes anymore, and the dirty streets stuck to her like glue.

Her grey-washed sweats were thick, but her tee shirt was worn and did little against the breeze that had decidedly turned chillier as the day had progressed. The street was bustling with vibrant life. She wrapped her arms around herself, keeping her head down but her eyes moving, taking in the scenery and anything that could be helpful later.

Various shops and carts lined the cobblestone road, it must have rained recently if the leaking roofs were any indication. Women were beating rugs, and children ran across her path more than once before staring at her captures in a mix of wonder and dread. The crowds seemed to part like the Red Seas when they passed, Declan stalking ahead, giving no quarter to anyone in his path as they quickly made their way for him.

The other woman in their party, petite with untamed curls, seemed to have a presence all her own, though Anna couldn't quite pin it down. She walked with her head held high, her tunic and leggings of a higher quality than the townspeople. Anna noticed more differences between her companions and the townsfolk.

Besides being a bit sweaty from their trek, they seemed clean. Their clothing was orderly, and though nothing flashy besides Aramus's breastplate, it seemed like a status symbol of sorts.

Apart from the people, the buildings seemed old but well-kept. Mud splattered the sides of dark gray stones with signs that displayed pictures instead of words. Declan entered a building, a dark green door with a large iron handle with the sign showcasing a crude carving of a goblet to mark its dwelling.

Anna looked up at Aramus as the other woman followed Declan inside, and they nodded for her to follow. The winged being was constantly at her back, and she knew they were placed there, so she couldn't run.

The establishment that Anna could only assume was a tavern was thankfully better lit than the prison. A grip on her shoulder pushed her in the direction of the seraph's companions, though to be honest, Anna needed no such guide. It was a welcomed change from the chilled outdoors into the warm glow of the small bar.

Though an improvement from the outside, the noise was unsettling. The smell of stale beer permeated the place, the floor tacky as she navigated the room. The atmosphere evoked fond memories of her bar back home, the way her heels clung to the dirty dive bar floor. The laughter of drunk college students echoed in the back of her mind.

The table they approached quickly cleared as the former occupants and their beer withdrew with a surge, their eyes not meeting the dark haired man who stood expectantly at the corner.

"Here," came a soft voice, completely catching her off guard. The petite woman was holding something out to her, her big brown eyes bore into her own as she did so. The woman held a pair of soft shoes in her hands.

"I don't have time to mend a broken toe, and Goddess knows what's on these floors." Anna took them quickly as if she might try to rescind her gift. To be honest, now that she was not running for her life in the forest, all of the pain in her feet hit her at once. The few sticks she stumbled over, and the pebble-strewn street into the village had not been kind.

The shoes were old and slightly cracked, but soft as she pulled them on. Declan removed his hood, sitting at the corner table. He ordered ale for the table and stew, his jaw set, and his mouth pulled into a tight line. Anna sat back, pressed against the farthest end of the booth, as far from the man next to her. She was boxed in, Declan cutting off the exit to her left and a solid wall to her right.

Across from them Aramus and the quiet woman looked comfortable in each other's presence, though not speaking at all.

When the food came, Anna realized quickly how hungry she was. How it had to have been hours since she ate last. The stew was steaming, and chunks of meat floated in a thick broth.

"Eat," Declan all but ordered as he speared a chunk of meat floating in his bowl and shoved it unabashedly in his mouth. She had poised her spoon to do so, but upon his brash words, she set it down sharply, staring at him all the while. The green-eyed man chewed another bite while he looked at her, a small line between his eyes forming as he did so. Even though she wouldn't break her battle of wills with Declan, Anna could feel Aramus and their other companion watching them while they silently battled each other.

"The food is good. We do not seek to harm you," came Aramus's soft voice, their wings vibrating whispers of assent as they did so. Aramus had the feathered appendages tucked in tight. Each of the six wings moved on their own accord, seemingly swaying with an invisible breeze.

"How come you aren't eating then?" Anna shot back, gesturing to their empty place setting. The seraph dipped their head in acknowledgment, "I do not require food as mortals do. Though I do partake when I desire. But the meat of animals is not something I am particularly fond of."

Without warning, Declan growled as he took his fork and speared a piece of carrot in her bowl, almost causing it to tip. He drove it into his lips, chewing viciously. He gestured to his mouth and then to the bowl, "It's not fucking poisoned, so eat. I'm not carrying your ass because you're malnourished while trying to prove a point."

"We're only a few towns away from a Guard's posting, why don't we just drop her there?" The woman beside Aramus asked, her head tilted in confusion.

"Because I don't trust the fucking guards," Declan replied, breaking off a small piece of bread to clean the bottom of his bowl. He glanced towards Aramus with a dip of his head, "Present company excluded, but I want answers now. This is too much of a coincidence." Declan paused and looked in her direction, "We'll rest here for the night, then make our way tomorrow. We can be at the Keep in three days if the weather is good."

The Keep. All Anna could think of was the image of the structure on the high hill, tall points gleaming and piercing a grey sky like daggers, jutting out of the forest like a wound.

Anna tried to shake the image, but the spoonful of soup she had been chewing on fell like a stone in her stomach. She nibbled on some bread instead, though it was stale and best dipped in the soup broth.

"They don't have much on rooms," Admitted Declan, running his hand through his hair. She realized how tired he looked, the lines around his eyes telling his age. "We're taking the two rooms in the cellar. Aramus and Brynn are taking one, and we'll take the other."

Anna's head shot up, "I am not rooming with you!" She exclaimed, probably louder than she had needed. The other patrons in the tavern turned to stare. "Why can't I room with her?" She pointed at the doe eyed woman who had not been forthcoming about her name but was apparently called Brynn.

"Because," growled Declan, leaning closer so that he wasn't heard, "I don't know who you are or why you're following us yet. So you're not leaving my sight until I do."

Anna leaned forward as well, "I am not following you."

"Then explain the bridge last week." Startled, Anna leaned back. And it hit her. Her dream. The woods, the hooded figure chasing her. She had fallen off of the old bridge.

"That was you?"

Declan looked satisfied as he leaned back, "So you do remember seeing us in the woods."

Anna shook her head, still shocked, "You don't understand, that

54

was a dream." Declan shook his head and extended his arms to gesture around them, "This doesn't look like a fucking dream to me."

Her heart beat wildly in her chest, and she gripped the table tightly to stop her breath from coming out in short bursts. She couldn't have a panic attack, not here, not with Declan near.

"Exerting yourself will not help matters," came Aramus's soothing voice. Despite herself, she shot them a deadly look, causing them to simply incline their head toward her as what she suspected was a peace offering.

Declan dropped a couple of thick coins on the table and slapped it, "Let's go. We leave at dawn, we don't have time to waste." He grabbed her arm, pulling her towards him tightly, her food forgotten on the table.

She walked with him, though it wasn't like she had much choice. His grip was solid on her upper arm while the other had snaked around her shoulders. She dug her boots into the sticky tavern floors, causing Declan to pause as she stared at the fireplace. Her dream from the past week came rushing back to her.

The sickest sense of deja vu hit her like a wave, the smell of stale beer, the sounds of people laughing, talking. The whispering. Aramus's wings. The splinter in her finger. She had been here before. Declan pulled her on.

"I do not have a habit of hurting women, but do not run," he whispered, not looking at her. His breath warm on her ear. "You're a threat right now, and until I find otherwise, you will be treated as such. What you saw in the prison is considered a mercy compared to what I am known for."

"You don't scare me." She hissed back, her voice was strong. She tightened the line of her lips to keep the quivering at bay, revealing her nearly unconfined fear.

He huffed a dark laugh as they stopped a door down a few steps towards the back, "That just tells me you have no idea what I am."

"I keep telling you I don't," she insisted, but her fear also made her brass, and she jerked her chin at his still-swollen nose, "You seem to bleed just like anyone else."

Declan said nothing as he inclined his head and nudged her inside the dark room. The moonlight showed through the small, dirty window that barely hovered above street level. A couple of candles lit the small space that was more of a root cellar than a bedroom. Two beds, If you call them that, lay on either side of the room. They were simply straw pallets covered with a course blanket that, upon further inspection, looked somewhat clean. As soon as his grip had left her arm, she scooted away from him onto the pallet farthest away, refusing to kick off her mud-caked boots as he had. She might need them when she had her chance to run. But where would she run to? The only people she knew were the three she was currently traveling with, and she didn't trust them.

Although Aramus had a calm about them, she couldn't let that cause her to doubt that they would hurt her, and who would find her?

Anna achingly missed the comfort of her phone, though she doubted she got service in this place, and if she did, who would come? Who *could* come? Anna found herself distracted from her anxious thoughts as Declan sighed heavily and took off his thick cloak, throwing it over a small three-legged stool in the corner. She watched him sit down with a sigh, rolling his neck as if the strain of the day had finally been thrown off along with the heavy material.

"What did you do?" She finally asked, breaking the eerie silence between them.

"When?" He asked but didn't look up as if he knew exactly what she was referring to as he brushed off the top blanket of the small pallet bed.

"With those people. In that cell." Anna returned, refusing to back down even though he was challenging her.

"Goddess." He spat, rolling his neck with a grimace. "None of your damn business. Go to sleep. We have an early morning." In a fit of either stupidity or trust, he turned his back to her, pulling a thread-bare blanket over himself. So she sat with her arms wrapped around her knees for what seemed like hours, watching his back rise and fall before she decided to move. Anna pushed her boots before her, barely scuffing the ground she stood up as silently as she could.

"Aramus is guarding the door," came Declan's voice, without even the touch of sleep in it, "If you do decide to try to leave." Anna sank back down into the straw with an exasperated sigh. She was stuck here, at least for now. Refusing to turn her back on her captor, she wrapped the blanket around her as the smell of hay tickled her nostrils.

She didn't want to sleep. She couldn't sleep, not that she had to try very hard. The bed was stiff, and her hips ached and screamed at her to turn to her other side, to divide the torment to equal parts of her. But Anna refused to turn away from him. The sound of crickets or something similar outside the small window finally began to lull her. The hay became more habitable, and the blanket less abrasive on her skin, even her feet felt a bit less abused as she tucked them under her tightly as she faded into the darkness.

***

"Anna,"

Her name was being called, but it sounded so far away. *"Anna, can you hear me?"*

There it was again. Anna was so warm. She was drained. A bright light shown in her eyes that startled her. She twitched her fingers to try to remember where she was.

"Where?" Her mouth was dry as she tried to form the words.

"We have her!" Called a voice she didn't recognize. It was then that she noticed the faint beeping noises were louder now and keeping time with her heartbeat. She didn't smell the stale air of the cellar or the hay.

"Where am I?" She asked again, attempting to sit up only to be gently pressed down my gloved hands. Gloves. Latex, not leather. Not her captors.

"You're in the hospital, Anna. Do you know what day it is?" Came the unfamiliar voice once again, light again flashed over her pupils, and she batted it away.

"Thursday?" She replied, not very convinced herself.

"It's Friday morning, Anna. Your coworker found you at your apartment when you didn't show up for work," Stated a female voice, and when Anna finally looked anywhere but the ceiling, she saw a youthful doctor looking at her, checking her vitals.

"Jess?" Anna asked, a mix of relief and disbelief as she sank into the hospital bed.

"Yes, there was glass around you, it looked as if that storm blew your window out, possibly knocked you unconscious," The Doctor explained. Dr. Werth, according to her name tag.

"I've been unconscious?" Anna asked, trying to get everything straight in her head. All she could think of was the tavern. The person with wings. Had it all been a dream?

"For at least 8 hours, we think, but thankfully we haven't found any lasting damage besides a few abrasions from the glass." Dr. Werth explained, setting down the chart and looking at her closely.

"How do you feel?" Anna was silent as she contemplated the question, giving herself a moment to assess how she felt, "Headache. I feel a bit disoriented." She admitted, looking around the hospital room.

Anna didn't want to tell them she had taken a sleeping pill and fell asleep on the floor due to a panic attack. Even if she was prescribed the stupid things. *Something you can see.* Rubbing her fingers over the stiff hospital blanket. *Something you can feel.*

"That's very normal for a head injury, even a small one." Assured the doctor patiently but jotting something on the medical tablet she carried.

"I had," she took a deep breath because she didn't know how to describe it, "A very vivid dream." Dr. Werth nodded, though she did not look up this time but instead glared at her smartwatch as it dinged loudly, bringing her attention away from Anna.

"Mhmm, also very common," she stood up, "I will keep you for a few hours for observation and order a quick MRI to ensure there was no damage we missed. I am confident you'll be ready to go home by this evening."

Anna nodded and watched the doctor walk out the sliding door and close it behind her. *Something you can smell. Something you can taste.*

Leaning back into the bed, she screwed her eyes shut and started over. *Something you can feel.* Anna grimaced as the plastic hospital band tugged at her arm hair.

"Oh, Jesus Christ." Anna tugged the E.R. band down as her heart monitor beeped faster. She tried desperately to control her breathing and pushed the hospital bracelet around the gold chain, still snug around her wrist.

8

J ess scraped the bottom of the pudding with a plastic spoon almost manically, getting every last drop of the butterscotch-flavored snack off the bottom.

"I can't believe you're passing up the butterscotch, these are price-less," her friend stated, tossing the now empty container into the trash. It was safe to say there was nothing left to be gained from the plastic cup.

"You can buy them at the grocery store for like, eighty-eight cents," reasoned Anna, picking at the medical tape covering her I.V. Jess leaned back into the blue vinyl hospital chair, shrugging, "Yeah, but free food tastes better."

"Thank you, by the way," Anna uttered, laying her head back to look at the younger woman. She had bright red hair today. She must have changed it since that last day at work; remnants of it staining her hairline.

"For checking on me. Ian wouldn't have noticed for a couple days."

Jess smiled, "Don't mention it. Besides," she paused, putting her socked feet on the bed and leaning back into the uncomfortable-looking chair, "Let's face it. Eventually, management would've called to remind you were out of sick days or whatever." Anna huffed a laugh, shaking her head at her friend.

A short knock on her room's door alerted her to an older man with a kind smile holding a thick clipboard, "Good evening Ms. Thorne. I'm Dr. Jacobs," he held out his hand to shake hers cordially. He nodded at Jess, who had quickly dropped her feet off the bed as soon as he had entered, feigning propriety. "I was just popping in to tell you that all of your scans came back with no indications of any lasting damage, certainly nothing that needs to be monitored. You're in the clear to go home."

He ripped off a small piece of paper and handed it to her, "Here's a script for some over-the-counter pain medication, just to help with any stiffness or headache." Anna sighed with relief, sinking back into the flat hospital pillows as she did so.

She could go home.

Go to work. Forget this whole thing ever happened. Forget about the being with wings. The girl with the dark eyes. And the man. The man with black hands.

A nurse came in quickly afterwards with a clear bag with the hospital's logo stamped on the side, she smiled at Anna holding out the sack.

"Here are the items you were wearing when we picked you up. Your apartment keys are in there as well," she smiled brightly and set the bag on the end of the hospital bed. Anna thanked her, reaching for the bag, anxious to get out of the scratchy hospital gown. She pulled out her tee shirt and her sweats that were speckled with mud.

Anna dug deeper, feeling the metal keys and something rugged and muddy. She didn't want Jess to see her panic, but she felt the blood drain from her face. She withdrew the worn boots that Brynn gave her. Jess whistled, "Those look vintage as shit, where did you get those?" She asked, genuinely intrigued but the noticeably hand-crafted leather shoes.

Anna swallowed hard, trying to clear the buzzing in her ears as she replied, the lie sour on her tongue. "A thrift store."

When she got home, Anna tossed the shoes in the garbage dump. She had drove barefoot, refusing to put the boots on. The apartment was open, and Anna found her landlord slapping another yard of duct tape over the cardboard to cover the hole where her window had broken. All the glass had been cleaned, and a window repair man called. It would take a couple of days to get the frame needed for such an old space. Nothing had happened except for the ugly box cutting off one of two primary sources of natural light in her bedroom. She thanked her landlord anyway and locked the door behind him as he left. Anna stood there, leaning against the door for a bit, scanning the room. It was just as it was when she left it.

Anna sunk into her bed and sighed in the ecstasy as she sprawled across the linen bedspread and down mattress cover. That hospital bed was doing nothing for her headache and the bright overhead lights of the hospital room didn't help. She was tired. The hospital had not been restful between various tests, I.V.s, and nurses checking on her like a newborn every 5 minutes.

Without bothering to change her clothes, she slipped underneath the covers, burrowing herself underneath the warm layers. Her phone lit up, a cascade of unread text messages bringing her back to reality. She hadn't called her dad since the hospital and promised to call when she got home. Her father was a chronic worrier, and she didn't want to be the reason he couldn't sleep at night, though, she was probably all of the reasons he was anxious. She had always been accident-prone. The car accident had been the icing on the cake.

It rang only twice before her father's voice came across her speaker, "Hey sweet cheeks, how are you feeling?" She smiled at the nickname her grandmother gave her because, let's be honest, she was more than a pudgy baby, and it just stuck. It didn't embarrass her anymore, as you age, those things become less awkward and more endearing.

"Hey dad, I just wanted to let you know I'm home," she said, pulling the covers over her chin and nestling down in her bed.

"Did they fix your window?" Came her dad's voice, hovering between concern and relief that she was well and home. Anna made a humph sound, "I mean, it's covered with duct tape and a cardboard box until the repair guy can come back," she admitted, turning off her bedside lamp.

"That's bullshit," her father replied, "They should've fixed that immediately. It's a safety hazard. Do you have your mace by your bed?"

Anna sighed and rolled her eyes, "I have the mace, the knife, and even the whistle, Dad. Even though I'm unsure how legal a bowie knife is."

"Listen, if someone attacks you, the last thing the police are going to ask is if your knife is the legal length," Her father retorted, sounding matter-of-fact.

"I think that's exactly what the police would do," she laughed, she thought the items were overkill, but her father had insisted, and she humored him. They were deep under some books, a few shiny rocks she had found while hiking, and her flashlight, but they were there.

"Alright, but if they haven't fixed it by Monday, give me his number, and I'll make sure it gets fixed properly." She smiled despite herself. "Ok Dad, I will," they both knew she wouldn't.

"Alright, get some sleep. Love you, kiddo."

"Night, Dad." Anna flipped the alarm button off on her phone since she still had one day left before heading back to work. She figured an employee finding her unconscious in her bedroom was proof enough to management that Anna might need a day or two to recover. She planned to clean-up the apartment. The energy felt off and needed to be cleansed, even with cheap glass cleaner and disinfectant.

She shook out the blankets and lit a candle to let the somewhat stale air come alive with the scent of lemon verbena. A glimmer on the floor caught her attention. She crouched down, a shard barely poking out from underneath her bed. Anna grabbed the remaining pieces of glass and promptly threw them away. Realization hit her, this could have been far worse than blacking out and waking up with a few stitches on her forehead.

The doctors told her her sleep may be disrupted and she could safely continue her sleep pills. She already tucked them back in her cabinet, refusing to use them again. Anna was sure the vivid dreams were a product of the medications and the bump to her head was just her body returning to them. So tea it was, she breathed deeply at the scent of the camomile wafting from her chipped coffee mug.

Her favorite book was left undisturbed on her bedside table, still marked on her favorite chapter. Her night commenced, slow and quiet, with no alarm to wake her in the morning and it filled her with a particular glee. Like a kid knowing there was no school the next day.

Anna felt herself fiddling with the chain around her wrist, pulling again experimentally as if the strong metal would suddenly give. Nothing.

Nothing except a stinging against her skin as it dug into her. She tried desperately to explain it to herself, even after she closed her book and she tossed and turned to sleep.

✳✳✳

Anna had called into work the next day, and they begrudgingly accepted her doctor's note she had emailed them. The day was cold, but the sun shone through two of the three windows in her studio apartment. Anna was just pouring some coffee when a rap on the door startled her, coffee spilling on the countertops.

She glared at the door, who just knocks without calling first? She quickly realized only one person would do that. Despite all of her true crime documentaries screaming in her ear, she swung open the door to see Ian with a ridiculously huge smile on his freckled face, holding some flowers.

"Good morning, sunshine!" He exclaimed, kissing the top of her head and walking in without an explicit invitation. Though, he never really needed one. Ian placed the vase on her crowded counter, the yellow flowers brightening the room.

"How are you feeling?" He asked, and she watched as he finished making her interrupted cup of coffee.

Accepting the offered steaming cup, she took a grateful sip, "Actually pretty good, all things considered." She gestured to the small cut near her hairline, black stitches standing boldly against her pale skin.

64

"Thank you for the flowers." She smiled, her friend's love language was gift-giving, and he always had the best bedside manner.

Ian typically came over for breakfast on her days off, and Matt usually worked early in the mornings, which gave the two time to catch up. Everything else had interrupted their routine, so it was nice to have this schedule back. Ian nodded, smiling and pouring himself a cup of black coffee, she swore nothing could dampen her friend's energy.

"So, what are your plans today?" He asked, sitting back on a barstool. Anna tapped her fingernails on the side of her mug, "I'm going to visit Kate today," she worried her bottom lip. "It's been a bit since I've visited," she admitted remorsefully, guilt gnawing at her empty stomach.

Ian nodded respectfully, he and Kate were also friends. They were always doing things together in high school and were Anna's rock when she split from her ex-husband a year into her marriage. But it was Anna that held them together- their collective love of her and ridiculous bright outlook on life brought Anna back from a very dark place.

But Ian continued living. He moved in with his long-time boyfriend turned husband who was a manager at the same company she worked for, and she knew he was the reason she got the job in the first place. A college drop out with a shoddy job record wasn't exactly a high ranking candidate even for a telecommunications position.

She owed him so much, all she could offer him was her friend-ship and a cheap cup of coffee on the weekdays. But it seemed enough for him.

"Do you want me to go with you?" He asked, resting his arms on the island's countertop. Anna considered it for a split second but shook her head.

"This is my cross to bear."

***

There were fresh peonies every time she visited. Kate's parents must have been by recently. Her mother always said fresh flowers would brighten a room. But it didn't look bright, it was a spot of color in an otherwise colorless room where lay her unresponsive friend. More machines than she remembered were attached to her.

"Hey Kate," she whispered, kissing her cheek and sitting down. "Things are the same but also not." Anna took a deep breath and took her friend's hand, gnawing on her lower lip.

"I have been having these," she paused, trying to think of the best words to describe what had been happening. "Out of body experiences? Or dreams?" She shook her head, feeling silly for unloading this on her unconscious best friend. "I know it's weird to be telling you all this," she whispered, leaning closer, "but I know you would know what to do if you were awake. So, if you could do that, I would appreciate it."

Anna laughed at her stupidity but laid her forehead on Kate's hand. Straightening and clearing her throat, she added to their one-sided conversation, "Ian married Matt. They have a place together, they're talking about adopting, and it's pretty great seeing him so happy. I don't want kids, but I could be a cool rich aunt. Minus the rich part, I suppose." Anna smiled despite herself, pushing a lock of hair behind Kate's ear.

"I miss you, Katie." She murmured. "We all miss you so very much."

9

Anna had little energy, still feeling worn down from her trip to the hospital, and the constant tugging of the stitches on her forehead itched mercilessly. Driving back from her small town home was always the worst part of visiting. The long stretch of toll roads seemed endless, broken up only by small farms or orchards.

Passing several fast food signs, her stomach grumbled, reminding her loudly that she hadn't eaten since the night before her collapse. The coffee she drank earlier was burning a hole in her empty stomach.

Thinking back to the stew she had- no, she hadn't eaten, it had been a wild hallucination brought on by a slight concussion. The siren song of fast food pulled her in, and before she knew it, she was loaded up with a cheeseburger, large fries dripping in oil and salt, and a strawberry shake. Her body craved the grease and tangy sweetness of ice cream. She knew deep down she would crash hard this evening, but she looked forward to it.

She was only a few exits from her turn, sipping the last of her shake, her stomach full and happy. All of a sudden her car swerved hard to the right, her cup forgotten as she took the wheel in both hands to avoid the car next to her.

A blast of strong wind rocked her small car and it pounded across the lanes of traffic, a semi in front of her veered sharply into another blessedly empty lane before coming to a halt as another gust blew against them.

Punching the emergency lights, she slowed her car to a crawl, mimicking the drivers around her. She could see through the dying evening light that they were as confused as she was. A truck ahead of her slammed on its brakes, giving her enough time to swing to the right, narrowly avoiding his bumper.

"Jesus!" She cried as she jerked her car. The truck had rear-ended the small compact car in front of them, and Anna pulled off to the side, utilizing the extended emergency lane to stop her car and look around her. She quickly turned on the radio tuning to the news station, a preprogrammed button her father had made her list "in case of emergencies," which she decided was one.

The sky was brilliant shades of pink and purple as the sun set, yet strangely the wind howled around her like a tornado. Two more people pulled in behind her, hazards flashing, window wipers going though no rain fell from the sky.

"Be advised, that we are tracking a line of straight-line
winds that have cropped up east of the I-44.
Though this looks like a small band, it is strong
but should weaken before it hits too far south
of us-"

Her phone came to life, her father's photo greeting her as she scrambled to grab the device as another powerful gust rocked her car. It was loud, roaring like a train.

"Anna?" Her father's voice came, sounding anxious. She could hear a door slam over the phone. "Dad! Are you getting hit with this too?" She asked, keeping him on speakerphone, the whistling of the wind made it hard for her to hear him.

"Damn thing came out of nowhere while I was mowing," She heard him curse and what sounded like the front door locking before he continued, "Are you still on the road?" Anna nodded before remembering her father couldn't see her.

"Yeah, I'm almost to my exit. I'm pulled over on the side of the road."

"Your hazards are on, right?" Anna laughed, swearing at her father, constantly forgetting she was well into her thirties.

"Yes dad, I'm good, I promise, I'll text when I'm home!" This seemed to appease her father, and once the call was finished, she sent a quick text to Ian and Jess. They immediately responded with the confirmation of their safety, which settled the pit in her stomach. The larger truck quickly got back in his vehicle to clear the highway. Barely anyone was moving, and the large semi-swayed precariously.

The wind finally died down, and the drivers nervously decided it was over and continued on their commutes back home. Though the weather channel assured her that the winds had dissipated, Anna drove quickly and parked sloppily in her assigned parking spot.

She sighed with relief when she was inside. The apartment was unaffected, even the pound of cardboard the landlord put up had held, partly in thanks to practically the entire roll of duct tape. There was only slight anxiety when Anna tried to go to bed, instead she laid down on her overstuffed sofa, her knees drawn up since she couldn't stretch out all the way. Though her apartment was technically one big room, she felt less exposed on the couch this way. She couldn't help but sinking in her stomach and the slight tremble of her hands. The tang of otherworldliness swam around her and deep down, she knew that wasn't just a freak storm. Another part of her knew she had bills to pay and she had promised Kate she would try to live her life.

Anna had work tomorrow and wouldn't be late. The tv droned on as she fell asleep, wrapped in an old quilt that her mother had made. She slept with her shoes on, just in case.

***

Anna opened her eyes slowly, blinking at the alarm on her phone still nestled underneath her arm. She smiled, stretching like a contented feline. It had worked. She was fine. She was here. It was just the concussion. Speaking of which, she touched her stitches gingerly, feeling the stretched skin there, that itched incessantly.

The shower was luxurious and hot, her skin still pink and steaming when she got out. She washed her face with a new cleanser that smelled amazing and Jess had suggested would help her fine lines. She barely wiped off her makeup in her twenties, so now she was doing damage control. Just trying to pamper herself a bit...to make herself feel human. To feel normal.

She wrapped a towel around herself, humming to the music she played from her wireless speaker. Today would be good. Work was in a couple of hours, and her hair was setting nicely from its masque.

The mirror was still laced with condensation. Anna wiped it with her hand in a zig-zag motion, opening the side to reveal a deep medicine cabinet behind it to get her hairdryer. She sat on the toilet seat as she brushed through the tangles with her fingers, the warm air tousling the towel-dried brown locks.

Hair wash day wasn't exactly her favorite, but she had done a conditioning masque and enjoyed how silky her hair felt. The music still filled the air, and the small bathroom was warm and slightly humid from her shower. Anna didn't know when the moment was that she realized the air dryer was blowing her hair one way, but she had the distinct feeling of colder air coming from the other direction.

The smell of rain, damp earth, and campfire smoke assaulted her senses. Anna stilled, her breath began coming out in panicked huffs. This couldn't be happening again. There was no way. She was completely awake and aware.

She pinched her forearm hard, eliciting a red welt and a sharp pain. With trembling fingers, she turned off the blow dryer, her stomach dropping when she still felt her hair moving softly, like a caress. The bathroom had no windows, and her apartment door was closed.

Anna stood on shaky legs, gripped the towel around her, she turned to the mirror. The condensation still dripping from its frame. It no longer held her reflection, but a cobblestone path leading towards a town. Fire lit lamps flickering, and the sound of horses resounded around her. Instantly back peddling in shock, her back made contact with the wall behind her. Wind blew furiously, and the busy sounds of the town growing louder. The sudden scent of smoke overwhelmed her senses. Without thinking, Anna grabbed her phone, slipping on the wet tiles, her hand reaching out to catch herself.

Looking up into the mirror, all that was looking back at her was her own panicked expression.

"Jesus," she gasped, dragging her hand down her face. Stumbling back to the mirror, she wiped it as if she could make the image appear again by will alone. Every hair on her body stood on end as she yanked open her cabinet and fumbled with her medication. Her fast-acting medication was out, and Anna tossed it angrily to the side.

The sleeping pills were beckoning to put her to sleep. Let her think, to rest. She wanted to disappear. Anna didn't want to think or feel.

It would just take one pill. Fifteen minutes. But as the time ticked by after she swallowed her escape it became apparent that the option of blissful unconsciousness was no longer an option, as she was now somewhere else entirely.

✳✳✳

It only took her a moment to recognize the town where the prisoners had been executed. Her feet were sinking into the muddy road, and she didn't want to think about the odor emitting from the mire but judging from the horses ahead, she was sure it wasn't just dirt that was squishing around her feet. She had no shoes on again. Anna pressed her eyes shut when she remembered throwing Brynn's gift into the garbage earlier the day before.

"You lost?" Came a voice behind her. Her heart leapt as she spun around to see three men coming out of the tavern. It only took her a moment to realize it was evening, she was wearing nothing but a towel wrapped around her. Feeling more than exposed, everything in her screamed, every lesson she had learned just by being a woman. Every fear of the dark immediately hit her as she detected the ale rolling off the men like a sick fog. She had no keys between her fingers or cell phone to call for help. She bunched her fingers into a fist, the other holding her towel close to her chest.

"Oh, we're friendly folk, sweetheart," purred the taller man disgustingly. His voice dripped with venom as he took a few steps closer, taking off his cloth hat to reveal a balding head. The third belched wetly, stumbling a bit. His friends roared in raucous laughter, their steps inebriated. They took a few steps towards her, and Anna took several steps back, trying to catch the dim flicker of the lamp-lights on the more open road. The mud sucked at her feet and slowed her movements.

It took only a moment for the men to pounce, and she brought her bawled fists up around her head and fell back. She tried to protect herself and make herself a more challenging target to pull back into the dark corners of the alley.

Meaty fingers grabbed her forearms and pulled her out of the mud, pushing her against the cold stone wall. They laughed and stumbled as they did so.

She kicked. She screamed fire.

But it was dark. People's doors were closed, shutters locked against the cold of the night. She was alone. Her towel was hanging, and she sobbed as she realized it was the only thing between her and these men. Anna kicked out, connecting with the shin of one of them. He hollered and stumbled back, but the other two men still held tight.

"She's feisty, full of spunk, eh?" One laughed in her face, his breath almost enough for her to throw up. As she went to yell, a dirty hand came up to cover her mouth, its width cutting off her airway to her nose in his attempt to shut her up. She thrashed as hard as she could against the attack, but as dots danced before her eyes, the three men went still.

"Get your hands off of her," Came a deep growl, a voice that had been scraped across gravel.

Declan.

"You can have your turn if you get your sword off of my back." Said the one with his hand over her mouth, loosening enough to allow her to breathe more freely.

"It's the Sin Eater," came a disgusting spat from his friend, who let his grip on her go. He backed away from his friends sliding almost next to her. The other man lost his grip and stumbled back, leaving the overly drunk man in front of her, whose eyes widened considerably at his friend's cry. There was still the larger man, his tight grip bruising her arm as she held the towel up desperately, wet hair clinging to her.

"Yes, it is." Declan almost purred dangerously. She could now see his hooded face drawing closer to the man. He could almost whisper in his ear. "Unless you want me any closer, I would let her go and head about your way." Anna nearly collapsed as the force keeping her upright and against the wall fell away. The man nodded and moved to the side with his friend, Declan, backing off, but the glint of a sword was evident in the flickering light.

"We didn't mean any harm," sputtered the taller man." We're just having a bit of fun." He joined his friend and put considerable distance between her and Declan and suddenly found his voice.

The Sin Eater didn't pay attention to him or his ramblings, but to the man that still held Anna. To her surprise, Declan sheathed his sword. The man holding her smiled, his yellow teeth a sight against his grimy skin.

"Changed your mind?" He snickered, the smell of beer clinging to the man like a shadow. Before Anna knew it, Declan had the man by the throat, his feet barely touching the dirty cobblestones as he sucked desperately for air.

She was paralyzed against that wall, watching as Declan removed one hand, lifted the gloves to his mouth, and used his teeth to peel off the thick glove revealing the darkened flesh, rolling and pitching like a living thing. The man's eyes widened, the white of his eyes going bloodshot as Declan squeezed just a bit harder, the drunk sputtering against the wall and the larger man.

Declan leaned closer. In a flurry of stumbled footfalls, his companions had vanished, leaving them alone in the dark alleyway. The only light above them flickered with the breeze, casting shadows around them. She watched him draw a deep breath, blowing it out in the man's face.

"You know I can smell the darkness in others?" His voice was low, deadly, and violent as he waited for the man to nod as much as he could in his current position. "It rolls off people like a musk. It gets more and more disgusting the darker your sins." The held man whimpered, kicking his dangling feet to find his footing.

"And you?" Declan clucked his tongue, shaking his head slowly. "You smell like rot." The last word was punctuated by the tall Sin Eater pressing his hostage roughly against the wall, his head hitting the bricks with a sickening thud. It took Declan only a second to rip the man's shirt open and press his hand across his broad chest.

"I know this township had already had its Reaping, but I don't think the Queen would fault me for just one."

The Sin Eater seemed to revel in the almost soundless moan that emanated from him. Inky darkness leaked from his chest and into Declan's hand, wrapping up his forearms like a viper wrapping around its prey.

Declan was panting as he let the man drop, his body bonelessly crashing against the street. She had an inkling no one would mourn him. Anna turned quickly to run only to find Declan there, the one gloved hand grabbing her upper arm and pressing her back against that wall.

"You're seriously pissing me off," he growled, sweat beading along his brow, his face close to hers. "How the hell did you get out of that room without us seeing you?"

"I'll tell you if you get out of my goddamn face," Anna spat back with what she hoped was just as much venom as he had. But she was still shaking from her attempted attack. "Unless you want another broken nose." Her wrists had been crossed, and his hand covered them both, his grip tight enough for her not to struggle against but not to leave a mark.

She swore she saw his mouth quirk a bit to the side, but Anna was too angry to remark on it. She was cold and covered in mud. Her towel was beginning to slip, doing nothing to keep the feeling of him from her skin. Her hair whipping around her as the wind took up around them. It was damp from mud and condensation of the wall she had just been pressed into.

She felt the towel drop and gasped, only to have his ungloved hand reach out and quickly right the cloth. He let her hands go, and she grabbed at the opening of the towel, his hands away before she could touch him. She shivered despite herself, standing there as he put his glove back on, keeping his eyes on the ground. He huffed, taking off his cloak and holding it at arm's length. Anna stood confused until he shot an angry look at her.

"Take it, or you walk to the camp like that." With that, she wrapped the heavy cloak around herself. It was warm from his body and smelled like the cedar of the woods and campfire. "We are going to have a discussion, and none of us will sleep or let you out of our sight until we do so." Declan ordered, his eyes steeling on hers, his fingers tightening on her biceps. She just nodded because, honestly, Anna didn't know what else she could do. This place was not somewhere where she could stumble around at night, and unfortunately, she knew no one else.

He finally let her go and she wrapped her arms around herself, to protect her from the elements or maintain her modesty. She wasn't sure which one. The wind was biting, and despite the heavy cloak, she broke out in gooseflesh as soon as he pulled away from her.

"We have a camp just outside of town." Declan remarked, not bothering to look in her direction but walking away from the city. "No tavern this time?" She called, still standing in the middle of the road, cloak wrapped around her shoulders.

"We leave at first light!" Shouted Declan, taking a few more steps and then waited on the edge of the woods expectantly. Anna stared past him into the blackness of trees, then behind her to the fading candlelight of the streetlamp that was dancing in the air. She could still hear the raucous laughter of people in their shops and bars.

"I'm in control. This is a dream. I am in control." She stopped her mantra. Whether it was from the stiffness of being pushed against the jutting cold bricks of the building or the continued numbness of her feet, she stopped believing it was a dream. Anna paused and looked back at what appeared to be the only kind of civilization she saw at the moment and then back at the dark woods and the waiting figure of her captor and now savior.

And she followed him.

10

A fire was built and grew quickly thanks to Aramus. Their wings spread out and blocking the wind as Declan had crouched in front of the wood, blowing into the pile of dried leaves and small twigs. Anna had stood frozen next to the group as everyone seemed to have something to do. Anna's father had taken her camping a few times, but it wasn't cold, and they were in an RV, she wasn't even sure if it counted as camping.

Brynn was setting up a structure that Anna hoped would block the wind and if the rumblings of thunder in the distance was any indication, the rain.

"Can you help hang this?" Brynn's voice was monotone and tired, which Anna echoed in spirit. As she walked over she realized her feet had lost all feeling, and wiggling her toes bought them no reprieve. It took longer than she hoped to make a sustainable tent for the night, comprised of thick, waterproof leather hooked through a series of loops in some makeshift poles that offered support after being dug into the cold ground. They hung dividers through the structure, offering extra warmth and possibly privacy.

"Food!" Barked Declan's voice, slightly muffled through the thick tent.

"Here," Came Brynn's own soft voice. Anna couldn't stand in the shallow structure but found Brynn holding out a thick pair of pants that felt like something akin to wool and a tunic that was thicker than the towel currently clinging to her body. Brynn didn't wait for her to say anything and promptly left through the flap, affording Anna some privacy. She quickly dropped the towel and let it hit the floor, kicking it towards the opening.

The pants were a bit scratchy but warm, and the shirt was loose. The attire immediately made her feel better. They were not Brynn's, who was smaller than her in size. The way it hung off her frame as she cinched the pants around her gave her a sinking indication of who the clothing's original owner was. The opening to the tent drew back suddenly, the fire light illuminating the inside briefly before Declan's body blocked it again.

"There's food," he echoed from his previous call. Even in the dim light of the tent, she saw his eyes dart over her, taking in her new attire.

"Brynn," she said, gesturing her oversized clothing. He nodded, noticing his cloak on the ground. He picked it up tossing it back towards a corner before leaving the tent without another word. When the flap drifted open, the smell of food wafted in, causing her stomach to grumble unpleasantly, making her acutely aware of her hunger. She cautiously stepped outside, donning the new clothing that protected against the wind. The night was still frigid so she wrapped her arms around her tired frame. Anna swore she could feel Declan's eyes on her and the feeling of the shirt against her cold skin suddenly grew warmer as a flush crept up to her cheeks. She knew the clothing was his; she swam in it. It smelled like him. God, why did she recognize his scent? The mingling scent of smoke and cedar.

"Eat," Declan all but ordered, gesturing to a bowl set next to Brynn. While not full, it looked hot and smelled appetizing enough. She was too tired to argue with or anger him. There was no spoon, so she did as the others did, sipping the broth and grabbing chunks of vegetables as they rolled to her lips. It was warm and incredibly familiar.

"Is this," she paused, realizing even the bowl was the recognizable. "Is this the stew from the tavern?" That brought a small, rare smile to Brynn's lips.

Declan didn't look up from dipping his fingers into the bowl and fishing out chunks of meat when he said, "Amazing how accommodating people will be when they're terrified of you." There was silence, broken only by the sounds of the night and their eating. Anna looked around at the three, the fire lighting their features. She could see they were also tired and cold.

"How did you find me?" Anna whispered softly, this time looking directly at Declan. Because she knew the answer and wanted to see if he would give it to her straight.

"You have a habit of popping up around us," Declan stated, finally looking up and slamming his now empty bowl on the ground, causing her to jump. "Where did you go? How did you escape?"

"I don't know," she whispered, setting her bowl down as her stomach twisted into knots, "And that's the truth." Silence.

"She's telling the truth Declan," Brynn's soft voice broke the uneasy silence of the night, giving Anna a swell of hope. Maybe they'd believe her.

"Where do you come from?" He asked, brushing off Brynn's revelation, "Because it damn sure isn't here." Anna avoided his gaze, she had no idea how to answer that without possibly giving away some precious information unintentionally. What if they knew something she didn't? About her world?

"Fine," Declan growled. He stood and taking two large steps to close the distance between them and take her arm. "I can't have you running again. Not until I know who you're spying for."

Anna fought the swell of tears in her eyes, blinking them back as she replied in a hushed tone, "I am not a spy."

"You know," he growled, wrenching her arm up and yanking her towards him, his green eyes piercing with anger, "I have heard a lot of spies say that same thing." He glanced her up and down, "But they don't keep to that story for very long around me." Declan dragged her towards the tent, her dinner abandoned by the fire. She earnestly dug her feet into the dirt, pulling against his iron grip.

Declan spun around and snapped, "Do you want to spend the

night outside?" This man had little to no patience, his hair dampening from the slight drizzle that had just begun, chilling her to the bone now that she was away from the fire.

He must have seen her uneasiness because he relented a bit. He leaned forward, his eyes locking on hers so she couldn't look away, "I did not save you from those men to do the same as they would have. Do not run again." She allowed herself to be led inside the tent. She had few other choices.

With lightning reflexes, Declan snapped a golden tether to the chain still around her wrist, trying to pull away as he wrapped the other end around his wrist, securing them with little more than three feet between them. Anna flattened her palm and started to drive it toward his face when he grabbed her wrist before it made contact.

"Leave my fucking nose alone," he muttered, slapping her hand away. "I'll release you in the morning," he said, gesturing to the floor covered in animal skin and thick blankets. "Pick a side."

"I'm not sleeping that close to you," she spat. Anna rubbed her wrist where the link was pulled uncomfortably. It was thin and a brassy color, something that looked like it could be snapped easily but instead held tight no matter how hard she tugged against it.

Declan was in her face in a matter of seconds, causing her to stumble back a step, "Then don't sleep. It makes no matter to me either way." Anna didn't know what to say to that. The taller man grunted triumphantly and gestured to the floor, giving her time to sit before he did so she wouldn't be pulled to the ground. Brynn came in moments later, chunking a bag in front of her and laying down in the corner, resting her curled head on it like a pillow.

"What about Aramus?" Anna asked curiously when they hadn't followed Brynn inside. "They stand watch; they don't require much sleep and very rarely get cold." Declan informed her, taking his pack from the corner and putting it under his head, his cloak wrapped around him tightly.

The skins and blankets did help barricade the chill of the ground but it was still cold and slightly damp in the tent. It instantly made Anna miss her room at home. She wrapped her arms around herself miserably, saying her mantra repeatedly in her head. "You're in a dream. You're in control." Something hit her leg forcefully. She looked down to find a blanket, Declan curling back up in the cocoon of his overcoat.

"This is not a dream. I am not in control..." She had to sleep. That was the only thing that made sense; she slept, came here, slept again, and was home. As she lay there shivering, even under the heavy blanket the foreign sounds of the unfamiliar forest around her, she found it hard to even consider it. When she saw Declan jerk violently, unsure how long she lay there, listening to the fire crackling and the comforting whispers of Aramus's wings.

The chain that held them together tightened as Declan shifted in his sleep, and she gasped as it cinched uncomfortably tighter. She felt uneasy like an unwilling spectator watching him twitch. He keened, his hands coming up to grip the sides of his head as the small sounds turned into an all-out moan, as he began to shake his head from side to side violently. Anna scrambled to her feet, her heart hammering in her chest as she watched her captor thrash. She would've run out of the tent if she could, but the thin chain around her wrist anchored her to him. Her arm outstretched forcefully towards Declan's sleeping figure as he moved in the throes of what appeared to be a nightmare.

Declan was panting, and even in the darkness of the tent, she could see he was bathed in sweat as he licked his dry lips in habit before another moan was ripped from him. "Declan-"

"Don't wake him," came Aramus's voice. Anna started as they appeared in the tent so quietly she hadn't heard them enter. "It would only make it worse."

"Night terrors?"

Aramus moved swiftly to Declan's side. "An unfortunate side effect of his curse." Was all they said before they took his hand and gently placed it on the brunette's forehead, Aramus's eyes closing as they did, their wings trembling and humming. Declan's back arched slightly off the ground, and a pained cry escaped his lips at the contact across his brow before he slumped back. His eyes stopped their sightless wandering underneath his lids, and his breathing slowly returned to normal. The line between his brow did not disappear, only softened.

"His curse?" Anna asked as Aramus stood, their wings drooping slightly. "It is not my story to tell," the seraph walked silently once again to the opening of the tent, stopping briefly to remark, "You should sleep. We have a long road to travel tomorrow." Aramus disappeared from the tent's opening, leaving her again in the dimly lit tent with the other two.

Anna couldn't sleep. She sat up and pulled her knees to her chest, listening to the fire outside. She watched Declan's chest rise and fall, her skin hyper-sensitive to the metal twisted around her wrist. It had slacked now, no longer taunt and jerking with Declan's fits. Anna turned her predicament over in her head. She sleeps; she dreams. And sometimes she ends up here. Is something pulling her here?

Is she doing it somehow, even unconsciously? Her lids were dragging down her eyes, her body slacking more and more as the night seemed to lull her against the day's events. She hated that her arms still hurt from being pushed and dragged by the three men at the bar. Her stomach turned as she thought about what could have happened if Declan hadn't shown up, how wholly unprepared for this world and its dangers.

She fingered the small chain looped around her wrist, the delicate links surprisingly strong, and she wondered why Declan had had it in his pocket, to begin with. Anna laid her head on her knees, the blanket nearly covering her entirely.

She felt warm and bone-crushingly tired.

11

A nna awoke to an incessant jerk on her wrist, her body stiff and
cold, her joints screaming at her as the tug became more
unceasing. She was greeted with the sight of the top of the tent. She
blinked, clearing the sleep from her eyes as she tried to remember
what had happened. She had slept. And she had awoken. Yet she was
still there.

Anna shot up, chest heaving in anxiety as she looked around the
tent, Brynn having already left and Declan stood above her looking
annoyed, his brows furrowed.

"It's time to wake up." He growled. If the dark circles that had
made their home under his green eyes were any indication, his sleep
was not restful. He tugged at her chain again, annoyed this time, she
wrapped the length, connected them, and pulled hard, his arm
jerking towards her.

Declan scowled, and within a moment, he was beside her, grabbing her arms and pulling her to her feet. Lack of proper sleep,
aching joints, and a splitting headache hit her all at once, and she
found her free hand rearing back and to slap the man for all she was
worth. A mixture of pride and terror welled up inside her as Declan's
face jerked back from the force of the slap, a bright red mark standing
out on his skin.

Anna reared back again, but this time, Declan's gloved hand grabbed her wrist, stopping it in its tracks. Before Anna knew what was happening, he used her wrist against her and pulled it across her chest. He pulled her against him and wrenching her shoulder, making it impossible to escape his embrace.

"I don't know what you have against my face," he growled in her ear, "But hit me again, and I'll tie you up so tightly you won't be able to budge until we reach the castle." He jerked her again to check if she heard him.

His voice was full of venom as he gritted, "Do we have an understanding?" Anna ground her teeth and nodded once sharply, gasping as he pushed her away from him, the golden tether between them pulling taut. Anna stumbled back and resisted to urge to lunge at him anyway, her hand still stinging from the force of the slap.

She had never hit someone before, at least never in anger and barely in jest. She had to admit it felt damn good. Declan's angry eyes never left hers as he unclipped the chain from the cuff, the circle still wrapped around her delicate wrist. She scowled at him irately.

"There's a stream just through the tree line. Freshen up. We leave as soon as we're packed." Declan opened the tent's flap and gestured to the bright morning in front of her. Brynn and Aramus were smothering the small fire from the night before, various bags packed and waiting in a small pile.

Blinking against the early morning light, she tucked her arms around her, still cold. Her hips and back ached from the night on the hard forest floor. She envied how the others moved like it was nothing to sleep in a small tent, cramped with a stick stabbing you in the back.

"If you're looking for the stream, it's just through there." Brynn pointed, noticing Anna looking lost. Anna was still furious with the entire morning and stomped past the seraph and woman. Deep down, she knew she was being ridiculous, but she didn't care. Anna was all rage and exhaustion. She was barely through the tree line when she saw the stream, it was small but fed a larger body of water just a few paces deeper.

The one thing she did remember from her time with her father "camping" was to never drink still water and always use the water upstream. So she knelt, wincing at her aching knees, and leaned over the flowing water, allowing her cupped hands to enter the ice cold and brought it to her lips, splashing her face.

Anna felt dirty. She had no hot water, no toothbrush, and certainly no breakfast worth a shit. She knew her anger was bubbling below the surface, so she stood, wiping her damp face on the ends of the tunic. Turning towards the camp, she heard the unmistakable sound of Aramus and Brynn speaking. The sounds of Declan bringing down the base camp.

Then she heard something else. A beeping noise, the rhythmic dinging, immediately had her hands going to her pockets when she remembered she had no cell phone. Her cell phone. She gazed at the sky, trying to judge what time it was.

7 a.m.?

"Do you hear that?" She heard Brynn ask, and she knew she only had seconds, maybe moments, to follow it home. Anna circled, trying to pinpoint the sound. She stopped when she saw the still water floating with what appeared to be lilies and fallen leaves. The water. Of course.

Everything suddenly clicked for Anna, her accident, the bathtub, and the park pond. Just as she turned to run, a large shadow covered the clearing, and she heard Brynn exclaim in surprise. Anna looked up to see a giant, scaly beast fly over, its wings transparent membrane and talons attached to reptilian feet.

"The leviathans are on the move," she heard Aramus utter. She didn't care what they called them; that was a fucking dragon. Before she could think even a moment more about it, she fell silent. They were talking, distracted.

Without thinking, Anna started running. She heard Declan shout behind her, his heavy footballs gaining momentum as he saw her take off through the trees. Anna's heart was pounding, small twigs and branchings scraped past her, grabbing her hair and bits of the rough linen she wore as she pressed on. She ignored the minor abrasions until she stood at the embankment.

"Stop!" Declan tore through the trees wildly, pushing past the large branches and overgrowth. She didn't even think, she ran into the water, swearing as it quickly went to her waist, the icy water bitterly cold against her. She pushed on, feeling the loose mud at the bottom sucking at her feet, slowing her progress. The ringing was louder here as she lost her footing and began to swim to the middle of the pond, trying not to think if there was any wildlife in the area and pushed past the thick underwater brush as she heard Declan crash into the water behind her.

"Anna!" He cried irately, but she had some satisfaction as she heard his quick intake of breath as the cold water hit him as well.

Ding.

Ding.

Ding.

She had been thinking she needed to wake up, but Anna wasn't sleeping. She just needed to get home. A quick look behind her showed Declan only a few strokes away from her, his heavy gear weighing him down as he struggled past the underwater plants that had tangled her own feet only moments before.

Anna took a deep breath and dove underwater, pushing with everything she had to swim down.

Down.

Down.

It was dark and cold under the water, she felt the pull to go deeper and deeper, the sound of her alarm muffled under the water but getting clear the deeper she went. Her ears began to pop, and the water only got colder as the light above her faded. She saw her bedroom floating in front of her, almost as if she was trapped on the ceiling or seeing it through a window. Declan's gloved hand suddenly wrapped around her ankle, trying to pull her back up.

She screamed, bubbles filling her vision. She kicked, connecting with the body above her until the firm grip was released. One more kick, and she felt as if she was being pulled, sucked down into the bottom of the pond, towards her home.

All of a sudden, Anna was lying on her wood floor, gasping for air. She was completely soaked, choking up murky pond water. She looked around, light streaming in through one window, the other blocked by the old cardboard and peeling duct tape. She sat straight up, slapping the floor hard with her hands until they stung from the impact, "Fuck!" She screamed. She was sobbing now, her body flopping back onto the floor as she cried or swore, mostly both. Anna was freezing, had minor cuts adorning her body, and smelled foul.

Anna picked small pieces of underwater weeds wrapped around her ankles, her hair miserably knotted. Anna stood, her feet squelching in her shoes, and she kicking them off as if they had offended her. She spun, her apartment precisely as she had left it. The early morning light streaming in, the sounds of cars outside the red brick apartment building. Before she knew it was heaving. Murky water, the stew from the night before, and bile flooded from her, her knees buckling and slamming into the wooden floor.

She wasn't sure how long she had been kneeling in her own sick. She tried desperately to cleave breaths from her aching lungs, tears streaming down her face. What was happening to her? Anna stumbled up, grabbing a blanket from her bed and wiping her vomit from her chin.

Anna all but stumbled to her bathroom. She turned on the shower as hot as it would go, the ancient pipes moaning as she water rushed through them. She ripped the wet clothes from her frozen body, letting them pile in the corner keeping the covered mirror company.

She finally broke down, her toes tingling at the onslaught of the hot water versus the freezing temperatures they had just been subjected to. Her sobs were loud and broken as she stood, arms wrapped around herself as the steaming water beat on her. Cold. So cold. All she could think about is the sound of her car when it had hit water, the phantom pain in her palm as glass shredded it.

The water ran murky beneath her, bits of tiny leaves and even a twig fell from her hair, and she finally moved enough to smooth shampoo through it. Anna breathed deeply as she ran her loofa over her skin desperately as if trying to scrub what happened off her body, the scent of eucalyptus overpowering the smell of stale water.

She only had a few hours before work, Anna remembered as she settled under the stream of water. How was she supposed to go in?

Pretend everything was ok? That she was ok? But who would she tell? As she ran the sponge over her arms, she stopped. Her eyes were still swollen from crying, but she could still make out a delicate, golden loop encircling her wrist.

Without breathing, she grabbed the end that was supposed to be attached to Declan and pulled hard enough that it bit into her skin but refused to break. "Fuck!"

12

Anna called into work as soon as her hair was dry. Making sure to cough a bit to sweeten the deal. As soon as she hung up she dumped out her purse, emptying her wallet. going through the three credit cards she had. Anna immediately tossed the ones she knew were maxed out, settling on the one with about a thousand dollars left. This was technically her emergency card, but considering where she had been for the past fifteen hours, this constituted an emergency for her.

Anna drew a deep breath, gripping the linoleum countertops. It didn't stop her from shaking. She didn't bother with her mantra anymore. Instead, she took a mixing bowl from her cabinet and filled it with marshmallow, sugary cereal she usually saved for late nights.

A quick knock at the door was the only warning she got before Ian waltzed in, red hair slicked back with some noticeable new highlights.

"Ok, I know it's early, but I couldn't wait for you to see what I did at 3 a.m.!" He said, turning his head for her to view the slightly lighter tresses. Anna was quiet for a beat too long, and he looked her up and down.

"Are you eating out of a salad bowl?" He asked accusingly, his eyes wide as she slumped over the island, practically inhaling the sugary contents.

"Yes, Ian, I am!" she retorted, swallowing before taking another spoonful pointedly. "Because shit is fucked up." Ian's brow furrowed. He looked at the counter, stepping close to her. "Are you going to tell me what's happening, or do I have to ask?" Anna sighed, rubbing her eyes with a mixture of defeat and exhaustion.

"You're going to think I'm crazy." She chewed faster so the wobble in her chin wouldn't be as noticeable. Rolling his eyes, Ian returned, "I already think you're crazy, but we tell each other everything." She hated that he was right. She needed desperately to tell someone before it consumed her.

It only took a second before tears burned behind her lids, and she began crying. The cereal bowl long forgotten as she collapsed on the floor. Ian immediately kneeled, his facade dropping as he held his friend as she cried in his arms. She told him *everything*. About the accident where she first saw the forest, the bathtub, and the pond. She told him about Aramus and Brynn. And then Declan, the man who would kill people with a touch of his cursed black hands.

To his credit, Ian just held her, nodding along at the appropriate times and letting her talk. She finally looked up, red-rimmed eyes pleading for him to believe her.

"Ian, please, please," she sobbed, "I am not losing it, this is happening."

"Anna, I believe you think this is happening-"Anna stopped him, grabbing his forearm hard.

"No, Ian," she all but shouted, "I thought it was in my head, ok? I did, I thought the new meds were fucking me up, but it's not that, and I can prove it!" Anna stood before she realized what she was doing, her socks padding against the floor as she ran to the bathroom, dragging Ian behind her. Picking up the wet clothing, she threw them on the wood floor, showing the trousers and shirt to her befuddled friend.

"Ian," she panted, wringing her hands, "I need someone to believe me." Ian looked at her, clearly torn between concern for his friend and wondering if he should call someone. Anna tensed her jaw and crossed her arms, standing ramrod straight before grabbing Ian's hand and heading back to the bathroom. She tensed, everything in her screaming not to do what she was about to do, less she got sucked in. Though it had never happened before, she didn't want tempt fate.

She held her hand out to her friend, "Just take my hand and trust me, please." She was begging now, she just needed someone to see what she saw. Ian sighed deeply, rolling his eyes and tapping his foot anxiously before reluctantly holding his hand towards her. Anna pulled him into the cramped space, still muggy from her earlier shower.

Anna took a deep breath, mentally preparing herself, her fingertips hovering over the multicolored blanket she had hurriedly draped over the cheap mirror. "Promise you won't let me go?" Anna asked, not daring to look at her friend and see his expression. She felt him nod. So she closed her eyes, inhaled deeply, and allowed the cover to fall to the floor, pooling around the long mirror onto the cold, damp tile. For an agonizing moment, nothing happened.

"Please, please, just this once," she whispered, her voice cracking as she stared into the mirror, looking back at herself, desperately hanging onto Ian's hand. He looked so concerned, his forehead creased with anxiety as he stared back at their reflection.

Ian opened his mouth the speak and then abruptly shut it when a breeze came out of nowhere, brushing his face and causing her towel-dried hair to move. He tightened his grip, pulling her back as their reflections disappeared, replaced with a mirage of a forest and birds filling the tiny space.

Ian hit the wall as moss and vines began to crawl from the frame. Gingerly touching the tile floor experimentally, Anna didn't let go of Ian's hand. But she felt the pull, the siren song of that otherworld. She knelt down carefully, not taking her eyes off the forest as she snatched the heavy blanket off the floor and quickly threw it back over the mirror, instantly stopping the breeze and sounds of woodland creatures.

"Anna, what the actual fuck was that!" Ian screamed, face pale in terror at what he had just witnessed. He didn't wait for her to answer as he pulled her out of the bathroom, slamming the door shut behind them. His chest was heaving as he struggled for breath. He grabbed her to him, crushing her in a hug.

"You saw it? You saw it. You saw it." She sobbed, clutching him as she began to cry, her chest screaming with the force of her sobs. Something finally broke in her like a wave crashing over rocks, since she had been shifting into this other universe, it was like nothing made sense. She had begun questioning everything, even her own mind.

Two hours later, when they both had calmed, Ian had made her food and she told him everything.

"But when did this start?" He finally asked, sipping on his second cup of coffee, his eyes wide and nerves shot. Anna shook her head, scooping another bite of scrambled eggs into her mouth, "I think the first time was the accident, when I died, for that split second I was there. They said I was only technically dead for half a minute," she shook her head in exasperation. "But I swear I was there longer. Ian, it's been getting worse. It went from odd dreams to where I am actually seeing things out of the corner of my eye, my mirror for god's sake."

Ian pursed his lips, thinking, "Have you considered asking your friends in that other place?" He waved his hands vaguely in the direction of the bathroom. Anna scoffed, taking another bite, feeling her hunger gnawing at her.

"They are not my friends, and I don't trust them." Ian nodded, and then his eyes widened with a thought, "Anna, you said you see through the mirrors and water, right? But you don't actually...go through?"

Anna nodded, "Except once, this last time. Its never happened like that before."

"And when you sleep, you can have dreams, but you never cross over, right?" Nodding again, Anna began to wonder where he was going with this.

"Unless," he crossed the small apartment in a few strides, grabbing the orange bottle off her bedside table and shaking the remaining pink pills inside. "You pop one of these?" Anna dropped her fork and sent it clattering on the table before her, grabbing the bottle out of Ian's hand.

"Ian, you're a goddamn genius." She clutched the bottle to her chest, "So maybe, I just don't use these anymore? Maybe it will just, go away?" She opened the drawer below her utensils, threw the offending bottle in, and slammed it shut, practically sobbing in relief.

"But," Ian cautioned, brows set in concern. "I don't know for sure Anna, this is just a guess."

Anna nodded, gnawing on her lower lip. "Then I need to be prepared if it happens again. I won't be pulled back unprepared again." She decided, back straightening in an attempt at bravado. "I need supplies." Her eyes drifted to the credit card she had left abandoned on the counter earlier.

Her friend watched her with barely concealed concern, "Anna, you look like you've barely slept and maybe now is not the best time to rack up debt when you're skipping work?"

Anna rolled her eyes, taking his hand, "Please, I know this is overload for you, but this has been my life for over two weeks now, and I just," she sighed, filling her lungs with air now that she could finally feel like she could breathe.

She heard him sigh in defeat and she squeezed his hand, "I'll get my shoes!"

✳✳✳

Anna shut the door behind Ian, reminding him to keep what she had told him a secret, even from Matt.

She had to figure things out first, but tonight was not that night. Tonight Anna was full of Mexican food and one too many margaritas. She had two bags full of clothing and even a few books Anna decided were necessary.

Ian watched her closely the entire day, the outdoor store wasn't something she visited regularly but she quickly found herself lost among the aisles of survival gear. Anna had found what she was looking for in a glass case, purchasing a pocket knife that was wickedly sharp.

A dozen protein bars, a bottle that filtered water, an emergency kit and a backpack that could camouflage against trees and greenery. Anna shrugged at Ian's look. "Just in case," she whispered, paying for the items, stuffing them all in the backpack. Anna was determined to be prepared next time. If there was a next time.

She slept soundly, knowing the pills were in a drawer far away from her bed. Her bathroom door was shut, and no mirrors or standing water was near her. Anna slept for the first time in over a week with no dreams.

✳✳✳

Living in Tornado Alley most of her life, the sirens were unwelcome visitors every spring and even summer. However, the siren's blaring loud into the late night startled her awake. There had been nothing to indicate an oncoming storm, no rain or clouds. Beautiful 76 degrees while Ian and she paraded around the city, windows down, music blaring.

Branches rattled on her window pane, the sound of leaves and other debris flying around outside made her sit up straight. Fumbling for her phone, she saw the alert on her lock screen. Confused, she opened it to see a disheveled weatherman pointing to a map of her area and various cities around her. Green covered the map, and small red circles dotted it made her stomach sink.

She wasn't the only Oklahoman to stay in bed or even go outside to watch nature's wrath unfold with a beer in hand. This however, felt different, the energy of the usually calm, seasoned weatherman rattled her like never before.

"You need to take shelter, even if you don't hear the alarms. These tornados are appearing at a rapid, previously unthought-of rate with no implications on when they will form. Please, get to safety, a bathtub, away from the outer walls. A closet or hall if you don't have that. This is a strong developing storm-"

Her cell service lagged, small pixels disguising the man's panicked face.

One.

Two.

Three.

Four.

Jesus. A text notification appeared as she grabbed her pillow and blanket.

> Dad: "Take cover NOW!"

Her dad was no alarmist. He was scared. She sent a quick thumbs up as she shut her bathroom door. The antique door was no match for whatever was raging outside, and she knew that. The blankets remained over the glass mirrors, and she held her pillow against her chest in case she needed to block anything quickly.

The porcelain was cold against her skin. She quickly wrapped a blanket around herself and placed a pillow over her head as the wind outside began to howl. Anna could hear the dull thud of objects hitting the building, car alarms going off in the parking lot mingling with the blare of the sirens. And then, silence from outside.

Just the sirens.

Anna could feel her heart thumping in her chest wildly as she clutched her phone, thankful she kept it charged at night. The quiet was the worst. That meant it was here. Like clockwork, the sound like a train coming towards her began. Her ear drums popped at the pressure, and the world outside erupted in breaking glass, the sound of wind and things breaking, hitting the walls all around her.

Anna started counting to herself. She braced her arms over her head, squeezing her eyes shut as her heart pounded in time with the wind's howling.

1. 2. 3. 4. 5... silence. Just as quickly as it had begun, it was finished. Trembling hands touched her phone screen, showing 8 missed calls from her dad and three texts from Jess. She immediately hit her father's number, the pillow over her head tipping back as she sat up.

"Dad?"

"The radar showed it right over you. Are you ok?" He sounded more panicked than she had heard him in a long time. Anna found herself nodding, "I'm ok. I'm fine. I'm in my tub. I think it hit my apartment."

"Do you have shoes on?" Anna glanced down at her legs tucked under her, remembering she had pushed on her slippers as she ran to the bathroom. "Yes. Slippers."

"Good, be very careful when you leave the bathroom. Keep me on the phone." Nodding again, she carefully stepped out of the tub and took a deep breath before opening her door, expecting the worst. Another window had broken. At this rate, she wouldn't have any glass left in her house. Her father told the landlord to cut back that damn tree last time.

There was glass littering her room again, one of her plants had toppled, and the soil scattered on the wood floor. The cardboard that the landlord still hadn't replaced had blown off though, the layers of duct tape finally giving way to the gale force winds. Her bed was now subsequently home to leaves, small branches, and waste from people's garbage cans. But as a whole, everything was here. She was standing, albeit on shaky legs.

"It's ok! Everything's ok." Anna felt if she kept saying that repeatedly, maybe her father would believe her. There was something off about the weather patterns. The ferocity of a tornado in early spring was expected, but how had it turned up? The deep green sky was gradually lighting as the storm continued its destruction west of her.

The sirens could still be heard echoing across the city, bright green flashes of transformers popping, plunging the surrounding neighborhoods and businesses into darkness as the unexpected tornado drew closer to them. She crept closer to the window, mindful of the twigs and litter underfoot, with only her thinning house shoes for cover.

Her phone slipped from her ear as she surveyed the extent of the damage out of the already broken window, seeing a car pushed up against a closed garage door and garbage cans flung from other neighborhoods litter the streets.

A large tree completely blocked off the road to her block and totaled an SUV, an unfortunate casualty of the storm. It took her a moment to realize the sound of her name being called repeatedly as her father, still on the line was wondering where his daughter suddenly went. Anna jumped as a transformer down the street blew, sending the whole road into darkness in an explosion of green sparks and smell of ozone.

"Um, yeah I'm ok, I'm ok," she stammered, stepping back and swearing silently as a small piece of glass pierced her foot. "A transformer blew. It's dark everywhere."

"I need to take care of the chickens outside, please text me if anything changes. Stay inside, be careful of downed power lines." Anna smiled into the phone, forgetting her dad's new obsession with chickens, constantly giving her farm fresh eggs when his four hens decided to lay. Grabbing the broom from the closet, she quickly scooped everything into the bin, pushing the cardboard back over the window sill. Deciding to hell with it, she borrowed a few nails, and pounded the cardboard and an old blanket to keep the wind out. Like the landlord would even notice a few more holes.

Wrapping a robe around herself, she carefully opened her front door, peeking out and walking out into the hallway shared by only her and Ian. She knocked, trying not to be too loud, just in some unusual case that they had slept through the whole thing.

Matt answered, looking disheveled but ushering her in, ensuring she was ok. Ian was gawking out his open window, beckoning her to join her as Matt rolled his eyes and reminded his boyfriend that it was still too dangerous to be leaning on windows and, no, they "couldn't go outside to get a closer look at the damage."

Ian waved his hand in annoyance, remarking about Matt needing to learn how midwesterners handled severe weather since he came from California.

"Ok, but check this out," Matt exclaimed, ignoring his boyfriend's comment and handing over his phone. Ian turned up the volume so they all could hear the newscaster, who looked just as surprised as they did at the rough hour of 3 a.m.

"We have been tagged in this video so many times we had to share it with our late-night or early-morning viewers. This video was taken just east of

96

Tulsa. The user was taking footage of the storm and caught this odd forma-
tion in the clouds, take a look for yourself."

The newscaster looked towards a smaller screen that took over the screen. The shaky footage pointed at the sky, bright lighting and peels of thunder heard as the man exclaimed loudly, someone pointing off camera just as another flash of lightning illuminated the sky to show a giant shadow looming overhead, a flap of what appeared to be wings. Anna felt her heart skip. She grabbed the phone from Ian, rewinding the footage.

She felt herself go cold with recognition of the considerable shadow. The leviathan. The same shadow in the clearing that morning she disappeared.

It was here. It had followed her here.

13

Anna barely slept that night, dozing off on her couch after leaving Ian and Matt. She refused to divulge any more information to her friend, brushing off his concern to his partner. She took the tea they offered and watched the news and weather channel as experts tried desperately to figure out how they missed this weather pattern. Inwardly, Anna knew how. Everything was sinking in, clicking into place like puzzle pieces in her head. She made up her mind before she left her friend's apartment.

Anna hugged Ian a bit longer than usual. The furrow in his brow told her he knew this, but she shut and locked her door before he could ask any questions. The backpack still lay next to her bed, and she filled it with a few more items. Vitamins she rarely remembered to take but seemed important now. A toothbrush, hair brush, and extra clothes.

Anna carefully washed the things Brynn gave her, the laundry detergent making the homemade clothing smell fresher than they probably ever had in that world, and cleaned the remaining mud and stains off the soft leather of the pants. She tucked them inside a waterproof bag that the backpack had come with, along with extra underwear, her new knife, and a water bottle full of purified water.

Anna was about to sling the bag over her shoulder, her hair

pulled back into a neat braid, freshly showered, and she had her morning coffee, breathing rapidly. She knew how to work this now and had to find out why the leviathans were here in her world. Because this obviously wasn't just about her. Anna stepped towards the bathroom, but before she could, a knock was at the door, stilling her hand.

Anna frowned, looking at her phone in confusion. Her days were jumbled, but she was sure it was Sunday, so there were no packages or mail. She pushed the backpack off her shoulder and back on her bed before she went to the door, and quietly tip-toeing to the peek hole. She held her breath so whoever was out there couldn't hear her through the flimsy old wood.

The face that greeted her was an older man with salt and pepper scruff that had grown increasingly grey in the past few months. Her father.

Anna smiled despite herself, hoping she looked decent enough not to cause any suspicion of her mental state. She quickly inspected her tiny apartment. Her unmade bed with the large camping backpack was the only thing that looked out of place. Quickly, Anna stuffed the bag under her bed. She dropped the comforter over it before opening the front door.

"Dad!" She exclaimed, falling quickly into his arms. He smelled like home. Cheap oak-scented aftershave and the lingering hint of peppermint that he always seemed to have in his truck when he drove long distances. He swore it was for his car sickness, but Anna had long thought he was just making up for the fact that he had quit smoking and never wanted to let her know that he had indulged in the habit in the first place.

"How are you, sweet cheeks?" His smile was wide, and his eyes curiously scanned the apartment. She knew he was checking to see how she was without having to ask her.

Anna rolled her eyes, "I'm good dad! Come in, I didn't know you'd be in the city." Bill Thorne stepped through the doorway, looking around quickly. "I like all the plants." He gestured to the few climbing specimens she had perched precariously on her narrow wind sill. She beamed with his praise. Her father had a green thumb and a vegetable garden that caused a fight with their neighbor for years.

"I used that soil mix you told me about. It really makes them pop." Anna admitted, picking up one of the pots and rotating its other side towards the sun, hoping her direction to the other side of the apartment, away from the bed and the sloppily hidden backpack. Her dad nodded and sat as she offered him a seat at her little breakfast table, quickly brushing away crumbs.

"Been working a lot?" He asked, popping a peppermint in his mouth. He was nervous. Shit. Anna passed a smile on her face, as she brought them both a fresh cup of coffee from her morning brew.

"It's a stupid call center, I know, but it pays the bills," she smiled, taking a tentative sip and immediately burning her tongue. Her dad smiled, "It's not stupid. It's a job. And you got an apartment." He looked around, inspecting the room.

"Could use some new weather stripping, and the windows have a small gap around the seal. But I'll get you set up before it gets too hot." Anna bit her tongue mid-chuckle, she knew better than to argue with him. It was his love language, fixing things. She was the one thing he couldn't entirely fix and she knew it gnawed at the older man. Caring for her after her mother had passed. Then Katie. Anna felt heavy with the weight of death that seemed to surround her. She knew, deep down, it weighed on him as well.

"Why are you here, Dad?" Finally getting the nerve to ask, staring at her cup. "Not that I'm not glad you're here!" Bill chuckled, taking a long drink of the coffee in front of him before answering.

"I wanted to swing by after the storm. Seemed pretty tired when we did talk last. Besides," he paused, finishing the cup. "I needed to swing by to see Mom anyway." Anna smiled. Her mother was buried in the most beautiful cemetery in the city, surrounded by mature trees and rolling hills.

"Do you want company?" The words escaped from her lips before she realized she had spoken them. Her time with her mother was quiet. She rarely joined her father on his visits because it always seemed like the same was true for him. But to her surprise, his eyes lit up, and he nodded.

"And I don't mean to hurt your feelings, but this coffee had grounds in it, next ones on me," he stood, placing the mug next to the sink since it was already fairly full. "And lunch. I could use a burger."

✳✳✳

Anna's hands were still greasy when they left the diner, but her stomach was full of steak burgers and thick-cut fries. Her father was true to his word, and he swung by her favorite coffee shop without her mentioning it. It was the coffee shop she loved the most, with $6 cookies that were the size of her outstretched palm and beans roasted inside, so the aroma would surround you.

Fresh latte in hand, Anna and her dad walked the well trim path to her mother's small grey headstone. Nestled below a large oak tree. A family of small squirrels had taken up residence in the aged wood, scattering up the tree as they made their way closer. The birds were singing, and a light breeze stirred her hair as they approached, and she took a large breath. This was the most grounded she had felt in weeks. Maybe longer. But she knew was going to leave again. Just as she felt like her feet were firmly planted here in this plane, on this earth.

Bill set a fresh bouquet of wildflowers at the base of the headstone. Her mother didn't care for roses, but wildflowers with their greenery and assortment of colors always brought her smiles, even in the end. Eventually the cancer had sunk its way too far into her. It claimed her in the early hours of a November morning.

With her gone, they had stopped celebrating Thanksgiving after that. The only reason they had in the first place was her mother and her love for throwing elaborate dinner parties for her friends and family.

"I haven't been up here in a while," Admitted Anna, who carefully pulled an errant weed the gardeners had missed that had jutted up from the manicured lawn. Bill nodded.

"Me either. She loved this time of year, the world just waking up from winter." Anna crooked a smile, put her arm through her dad's, and rested a head on his shoulder.

"Thank you for coming."

Bill nodded. "That's what I'm here for." He dropped Anna off at her door, handing her a small brown bag as he did so.

"What's this?" She asked, peeling back the wrapping to reveal two bags of coffee beans from the shop.

"Dad!" Bill just smiled, "You can't drink the swill you had this morning, I'd be remiss in my job as a parent if I didn't correct that." Anna smiled, kissing her dad's cheek quickly before he left. She held him tighter and longer than necessary, trying not to feel the twinge of guilt that built in her belly at the thought of leaving him. She inhaled the scent of peppermint that clung to him and promised to call.

When the door shut, Anna took out her notepad, taking the time to sit and pen out a letter to Ian to let him know her whereabouts and that she would be safe. Even as she wrote it, she couldn't push pass the sinking feeling that she knew she wouldn't be safe. That she couldn't promise that. She wrote another note, this one stuck on her bedside table, was reserved for her father. Just in case she didn't come back. The gold chain around her wrist caught her eye as she put the envelope on the table. Anna was beginning to like the chain, it was just more evidence that she hadn't lost her mind.

❉❉❉

Anna wasn't sure how long she stared at the bag by her bed. How long had her tea sat before she eventually dumped it out? The burger sat in her stomach like a brick, her indecision warring in her head. She lost count of how many times she watched the leviathan in the video. A few users had uploaded different perspectives. Lightening and thunder rolling around its massive body as it made its way through the thick clouds, never gliding low enough for much more than an ominous shadow.

It was past 11 o'clock before she made up her mind, her legs trembling with anxiety before she finally got up. She double-checked her bag and adding a few more snacks into the inner pouch. She smoothed the lines of the tunic that she had tightened with a belt around the waist, her thick socks padding the leather shoes. She didn't want to stick out this time. And she had to go. Somehow, this was directly tied to her, and the weather patterns were getting worse. Why were there fucking dragons flying through the downtown sky?

Anna knew this wasn't the time to be indecisive or to bury her head in the sand. She had to fight this head on. The longer this continued, the worse it became. Anna stared at the yellow bottle beside the table, pocketing two pink pills into the backpack, before swallowing another two before she could back out.

Her heart was hammering in her chest, she dragged deep breaths through her nose and out her mouth as she felt the warmth of the drug spread over her limbs, allowing her to sag into the armchair. The wind was picking up outside, and she rechecked the forecast. No tornados were predicted, just a spring storm. That wasn't enough to calm her nerves. She still had the nagging question, what would happen if she was in danger or hurt in the otherworld? Could she die there and not here?

She had questions that desperately needed answers and she was determined to find them.

14

Anna didn't even get a chance to turn around before a firm hand grabbed her and threw her against a tree. Her hand went to the pocket knife, but it was slapped out of her grip before she could even raise it. The hooded figure had her pinned and was seething with fury. She swore she could see smoke rising off of him, pitching over his shoulders and around his hands.

Declan ripped down his hood, his teeth bared, "I am getting really fucking sick of chasing you around," he looked her over and noticed her fresh appearance.

"Where did you go?" Anna stared right back at him, the hand he had gripped was still sore and the contents of her pack dug into her back as he gave her no respite. "I went home." She answered honestly, deciding she wouldn't play games with this time.

"Really?" He scoffed, leaning back only a fraction, anger still rolling off him in waves, "You live in the fucking lake?" Anna didn't know how to respond. How could she? Would he even believe her if she told him the truth? Declan didn't give her any more time to mull it over but grabbed her arm, hauling her towards what she could see was a small campfire.

"We're a day away from the castle, Octavia can sort you out."

What Anna did next, she didn't expect, something she would

have never done in real life or even imagined doing. She scooped up her discarded hunting blade and shoved him hard enough to push him off balance, tucking the sharp end underneath his chin. She tried to ignore the fact that her hands were shaking with adrenaline or the way he cocked his head to the side dangerously, his eyes flashing. One side of his mouth almost quirking in poorly disguised amusement.

"This time, I am asking the questions, Declan," she spat his name, pressing the point of her knife against the tender underside of his chin. Aside from a muscle popping in his chin, he didn't move.

"Where are we?" For a second, Declan looked genuinely confused, "We're about a day's walk from the Golden Keep," he said slowly, watching her face as if to see any flash of recognition.

"I don't mean the stupid castle," Anna snapped, closing her eyes tightly in annoyance, "I mean, where is this?" She gestured broadly with her free hand. Declan furrowed his brows, narrowing his eyes to look at her.

"This is Danann, you're in the Silent Forest," he looked exasperated, replying slowly as if trying to explain something to an infant. "And who is Octavia?" Anna asked, trying to think of any information she would need in the future.

Declan ground his teeth, and Anna responded by raising her eyebrows, gripping the knife tighter to make a point, "She is the Queen of Danann, an archipelago in the middle of the Danube Sea. All of which we reside." Anna tried to commit this all to memory. "And what about you-"

Declan relaxed his shoulders, "Ok, enough of this." Within a split second, she was again disarmed, the knife now in his hand, poised against her slender neck. Eyes wide, she met his, not even daring to swallow.

"Next time you point a blade at me," he growled, stepping closer, towering over her shorter frame, "You better be prepared to use it. Trust me when I say if you ever try this shit again, I will not be so forgiving." Anna didn't attempt to nod, no with the knife poised underneath her jaw. The Sin Eater stood momentarily before taking the knife and putting it in his belt.

"That's mine!" She cried, reaching for it without thinking. Declan didn't look at her as he grabbed her wrist and dragged her back towards camp, rummaging through his belt before snapping the other end of the tether to the bracelets once again.

"It *was* yours," he corrected, ignoring her pleas as she dug her heels into the ground. "When you learn to use it, maybe I'll let you have it back. And for now," he whirled around, looking down at her again, "You're not leaving my goddamn sight until we reach the castle."

The fire was crackling as Aramus and Brynn sat around it, looking like they were having a deep conversation before Declan and Anna interrupted them. "Thanks for the help," Declan grumbled at Aramus, pointing to Anna and forcing her to sit with the very small breadth of the tether.

Aramus looked at her and Declan, "You didn't need my help." The being went back to speaking with Brynn, cards spread out between them. Declan huffed, rolling his eyes and shrugging off his cloak. Anna cleared her throat. Declan growled, throwing up his hands, "What now?"

"What time is it?" She asked quietly, looking up at the stars above them. They were so much brighter than the ones in her universe. Confused, Declan just shook his head, "It's about 2 hours until the sun rises."

"So what will we do until we have to leave?" Anna had a full stomach, was clean, and honestly was the first time she had shifted into this reality on her own accord. As much as the man infuriated her, she was glad to have found him and not any others. So far, her times in this Universe had shown her that men could not be trusted in either world.

"You can do whatever you want," he replied gruffly, rolling his cloak into a ball and reclining against the tree behind him, closing his eyes. "Don't go too far." He taunted, the chain connecting them vibrating as he waved his hand. So she sat, Aramus and Brynn still deep in their conversation. Brynn moved her hand between the cards placed in a triangle pattern, flipping over the top one first.

"What are you doing?" Anna asked curiously, scooting closer to the warm fire, the chill of the early morning sinking through her tunic and settling into her skin. She knew better than to try to get away and for the first time, that wasn't her plan. Anna knew she needed more information, this Queen might have it. She just needed to bide her time.

Brynn looked up, her tired eyes taking in Anna as her hands hovered over the cards, the seraph looking at her curiously. The curly-haired girl looked over at the seraph, and something nonverbal passed between them before Brynn regarded Anna again.

"I am in training as a Seer. The cards, they show me the future, the past, just whatever could be useful," she looked at the cards in front of her in frustration, "or not useful at all in this case." Anna immediately became interested, scooting as close as she could being tethered to the man now resting lazily against a tree. She had half a mind to tug until he woke up, but keeping her in their good graces was currently essential. Brynn looked at her curiously, shifting the cards through her hands, shuffling them this way and that, her eyes never leaving Anna's as she held them out.

"Draw a card," she insisted, her eyes bright with interest flickering from the deck to Anna. Anna hesitated. She remembered going to a tarot reader during a fair once before and getting too scared to even draw a card from the old woman. She cleared her throat, smiled like she wasn't nervous, and drew one of the thick, well-worn cards from the stack fanned before her. She turned the card around to face her, a detailed line drawing of a snake winding through some ornate floral background, two heads attached to one body. A chill ran down her spine, and she shoved the card at the smaller woman, eager to return it to its owner.

"What does that mean?" Anna asked, her stomach dropping. It immediately triggered the memory of that night after the bar, the two-headed snake in her path, the night everything started.

"This one means rebirth or duality. A new beginning and closing of another life. It can mean many things." Brynn explained, putting it back in the deck with unhidden anxiety.

Anna swallowed hard, her stomach sick, "What does it mean that

I pulled it?" Brynn hesitated, then looked up at her, her eyes tired, "I asked the cards about you. I'm assuming this is their response."

Anna felt dizzy and reached for the water container she had brought with her, "I saw one," she gulped the water greedily, hoping it would quench the dryness that had suddenly assaulted her mouth. "A two-headed snake before. In my- where I live."

Brynn looked up in amazement, "When?" Anna shook her head, "About a week or two ago." She paused, closing the bottle of fresh water.

"Brynn, what does it mean?" Anna repeated, her stomach in knots. "It means you're in the middle of your rebirth, you're being pulled in two separate ways, but soon you'll have to choose," the younger woman held out the deck again, and Anna pulled another card but paused.

"For your past, present, and future," Brynn explained. This card was odd and depicted stars, stars that she swore she was looking at when she fell asleep. She drew again. This time, it was a skull. Simple and without adornment. "So, are you going to tell me what this means?" Anna asked, setting all three cards down. Brynn took the cards in, holding her hands over them, her wild, curled hair falling around her like a halo.

"Something died in your past. Not you specifically, but a part of you. It's leading to your rebirth. Mind, body, and spirit. Something is pulling you here. Something was written by Danu herself." Anna opened her mouth to ask another question when a branch snapped loudly feet away from their camp. Aramus was up in an instant, wings flared wide against the forest, nearly blocking off one complete side of the camp as they vibrated with energy.

The chain connecting her to the Sin Eater suddenly went taunt as the man stood without preamble, the sound of his sword drawing causing her to retreat closer to the fire. Brynn gathered the cards and carefully wrapped them in a velvet cloth, clutching them to her chest as she stood nearer to the seraph. Anna didn't have much opportunity to talk to the angelic warrior but the pure power and strength radiating off of them at the moment made her realize that whatever was in the forest should be much more frightened of them.

"Jig is up!" Came a laugh followed by a whistle, causing more footfalls to echo through the forest. Anna's eyes flicked to her pack, just out of reach. Her deadlier blade was still being held hostage on Declan's person. She was defenseless and still connected to the dark haired man behind her. The whisper of Declan's blade being drawn added to the sound of footsteps drawing closer to them.

"Show yourselves, cowards," came Declan's growl, the steel sung as he spun the sword, as if it sang for blood. Declan's taunt echoed through the forest and was met in return with the sound of drawing blades. Anna's heart was in her throat, wondering for the eighth time in the past thirty minutes why she had willingly returned to this place.

"Heard you were in town, Sin Eater," a sound of spitting came after that sentence as if the speaker was trying to rid themselves of the title. "You and the Queen's little band, for the Reaping." It took only a second more for the orange-red glow of the fire to illuminate their faces. At least six men surrounded their small campsite, but at the sound of murmuring in the distance suggested more. Anna's head whipped around, keeping her back protected and towards Declan, feeling safer knowing the Sin Eater was there. She would unpack that later.

"Can I ask why you decided to sneak up on us this early hour?" Came Aramus's melodic voice, the steel of anger tinging the words, leaving no room for the listeners to ignore their pointed question.

"I have a feeling that this has something to do with the village prison we visited, Aramus," Declan cut in before the balding man nearest to the group could get his first word out. The bald man smiled, the smirk not reaching his eyes which seemed to gleam with the rage. He sucked on his yellow teeth, shaking his head and pointing his blade toward Declan.

"I told you he wasn't as stupid as people say, boys," his voice was rough and cracked as if he had smoked three packs a day for the past twenty years. "Listen here, that bitch Queen sends you every month, roundin' up our men with nary a trial while you suck them dry, and we all," he waved his free hand to the woods where Anna could see the flash of similar weapons drawn and the murmurs of agreements echoed off the trees. "Have a problem with that."

"You can take that problem up with the Queen's court on a more official level come Autumn," Aramus said, his voice still calm, but his eyes roamed the woods behind the speaking man.

"You hear that?" The man called behind him, the footsteps drawing closer, showing off more men; Anna counted ten. "We can take it up with the Queen!" The balding man took a step closer, spitting on the forest floor. Now closer to the firelight, Anna could see the man's clothing- a white apron over old tunic and leggings. The apron marred with rust-colored stains and some uncomfortably fresh bright red ones.

"I'd rather take it up with you, Sin Eater." Anna looked at Declan, who drew his lips into a cruel smile, cocking his head in thought.

"Who did I take from you, butcher?" Declan also took in the man's appearance, the meaty hands marred with scars and the blood-covered apron. "Your son?" The balding butcher narrowed his eyes, "Your father?" Nothing. "Oh, I see. Your brother."

Anna found herself stepping closer to Declan as the man's eyes widened in rage and pain. She swore if he had the power to summon death at his command, they'd all be in pieces. The bulky man wasted no time. Anna didn't see the small cleaver that whisked by, narrowly missing the Sin Eater's head and instead wedged itself into the tree behind him.

Declan smirked, as he spun his sword in his hand, "Brother it was then." The man leaped, clumsily swiping at the dark-haired man with more emotion than skill, and Declan easily parried the stroke. The butcher's actions spurred the rest of the group into action, screams echoing off the trees and into the morning sky as blade met blade. Anna's wrist was tugged as Declan continued to fight the bald man, easily keeping the man's wild swings at bay.

It was when the man's sword clipped the side of his shoulder, drawing a thin line of blood through Declan's tunic. The Sin Eater snarled and without hesitation, swung his blade so quickly Anna barely saw it move. Suddenly, the sword relieved the bald man of his head, blood spraying almost comically from the body. It stood for a moment before crumpling to the red stained dirt, joining its head once again. Brynn wielded her small paring knife, her dark face unusually pale as she stood back to back with Aramus, whose wings fanned wide when another barrage approached them.

"Aramus!" Screamed Declan, grabbing Anna and throwing her behind him. She was wedged between the tree and his back as a giant man with a butcher knife waving, came barreling from the darkened forest.

"Down!" Yelled the seraph. Declan stuck the large man in the stomach, slicing so his insides spilled before his heart even stopped beating. Anna covered her mouth at the carnage, her heart beginning to thud in her ears. The assailant dropped to his knees, his hands unsuccessfully trying to push his organs back inside. The ringing in her ears was so loud she barely heard Declan cry for her to duck. He pulled her against him, cloak wrapping around her as his gloved hand grabbed her head and pressed her onto the woods' floor.

"Shut your eyes!" Declan cried, his large body curling around hers. It took a moment for his voice to register, for her to see the stream of brilliant, pure light spill through the seams of the cloak before she shut her eyes, the intensity glowing through her closed eyelids. The sounds of screaming were unimaginable. They were quick but loud, guttural, and relayed anguish.

Anna didn't realize she had been holding her breath. Her lungs began to burn, and she quickly brought in a deep breath. She regretted it immediately as the smell of blood, smoke, and burning flesh assaulted her. Declan stood, the chain that bound them yanking her upright. She stood to see a perfect circle of burned forest, charred trees, and near bare skeletons. Some with swords still in hand. And try as she might, Anna couldn't hold in the churning in her stomach as she heaved, turning her back to the gruesome scene. Her retching was the only sound besides the crackle of burned wood and bodies.

"What did you do?" Anna sobbed, her eyes tearing from the combination of throwing up and the sting of the smoke that clung to her that wafted off the burning corpses. Declan looked at her, running his bloodied sword across his cloak, the blood smearing messily across the blade.

"They would've butchered us. And trust me," he kicked the dead man whose head lay smoldering next to him. "This man wouldn't have cared if you what you were to us, he would've done worse than gut you."

Rubbing her burning eyes with her sleeve, she looked at him, lips thinned in a scowl, "And how would you know that?" Declan seemed appeased with the clean blade and sheathed it. He looked at her, the anger behind his green eyes flashing. Once, that would have scared her. Now, it just made her angry. Though the cord that connected them wasn't long, he took a step towards her, gloved finger pointing at the burning bodies.

"Because I remember his brother from the last Reaping. I know what he did, especially to women."

Anna's cocked her head in disbelief, "You expect me to believe you remember these people? The people you kill?" Declan growled as he took another step closer. Close enough to see the specks of blood that had peppered his tan face and the age lines buried around his eyes, "I remember every last fucking one of them," his jaw tightened. He pointed to her this time, "You probably can't remember what you had for breakfast this morning, but I can remember all of these bastards. What they did. How it felt." He spat the last sentence, looking disgusted. With her or with himself, she wasn't sure "So don't tell me what these people are capable of because I get to relive it every fucking night." Quiet descended, save for their heavy breathing, the sound of trees still crackling with the force of whatever Aramus had unleashed.

"Perhaps," came the seraph's ringing voice, breaking the tension between them, her heart still pounding. "We should be moving towards the castle, lest more approach." Declan didn't take his angry eyes off of her. The heat of the ambush still pounded through Anna's blood, and she was sure it echoed in the Sin Eater's. She barely had time to grab her bag before she was pulled, Declan stomping through the forest. Anna took care to step over the smoking bodies underfoot, covering her mouth with her hand. It smelled like cooking meat, and it took everything within to keep what was left in her stomach.

As they found their way back to the trodden down path that Anna glanced back at Aramus, who had taken up the back. Likely more strategic than luck, she realized, cushioning Anna and Brynn in the center.

"What did you do?" Anna asked, marching behind the Sin Eater, who seemed to be doing as much as he could to put the distance between them despite the gold chain tethering them. "To those men I mean, what did you do?" She clarified, when the seraph was silent. It took a beat for the winged being to answer her as if they were mulling over the question in their head before replying.

"The best way to answer is that seraphs have the light of the Goddess inside them, giving us power, giving us life. Even here, in Danann, though it is diminished somewhat, I can call on it in times of great need. Our close relationship to the Universe also imparts upon our feathered appendages as assistance." As if knowing they were being spoken of, the seraph's wings whispered on the breeze. Anna nodded, though it didn't make much sense at the time. It was when the overgrown forest floor turned into a man-made path that Anna looked up from her feet, sweat sticking to her body, and her backpack seemed heavier than before. She stopped, Brynn nearly running into her and Declan all but halting as the tension on his gloved wrist tightened with her halt.

Anna couldn't stop her heart from skipping a beat nor the panting breaths that came from her as she looked up to see the castle from her dreams. Her breath was stolen from her as she viewed the castle again, once just a phantom from her dreams. The slight hill they had been climbing had slopped into a clearing that housed a winding dirt road that crossed an ancient stone bridge. Water cascaded underneath it, crashing down into what looked like a bottomless crevice.

But it was the castle, with its three jutting peaks piercing the morning sky, cresting on top of the mountain, looking over the expanse of the kingdom that grabbed her attention.

"What?" Declan barked, yanking on the chain before she yanked right back, annoyed.

"I've been here before, seen this place," she whispered, more to herself than to him, her eyes still trying to make sense of what she saw, the nauseating weight of deja vu turning her sour stomach.

"Of course you have," Declan pointed to the bridge, "You fell off that damned bridge about a month ago. Yet here you are." Without so much as a warning, he continued, nearly yanking the younger woman off her feet. Her hips ached from the endless walking and sitting on the hard ground.

"We're nearly there now," Brynn whispered, not nearly as breathless as Anna but still looking travel-worn. "I know how it is to be far from home." Brynn was a woman of little words Anna found. She was drawn to her calming presence, and though they said little else the rest of the walk, it was comforting to be next to her. Anna was about to collapse when they finally reached the castle gates. Her feet throbbing in her boots and her water drained almost three miles back.

Declan was walking at a brutal pace and Anna didn't dare ask him to stop because she knew his answer. The dirt road turned to stone, grass pushing through the gaps in the ancient grey rocks. The wind picked up speed as they climbed the steep mountain, loose hair whipped her face as her eyes watered from the wind. The Sin Eater stopped inexplicably by the solid, towering gates that blocked the rest of the world from the courtyard of his Queen. Anna raised her wind-blown face to study the bricks. They were etched with moss and blooming flowers creeping up the tall expanse.

"Declan?" Brynn asked curiously as the man stood, looking at the gates. He barely acknowledged Brynn with a nod and banged on the heavy metal doors, his fists echoing throughout the mountainside. The gates opened, hinges whining as they moved. Seraphs greeted them and looked as if they were barely breaking a sweat despite the heavy white and gold armor they wore. Anna swallowed hard, reminding herself she still had two pills tucked into her bag if anything went awry. She had a way home, but she had to get answers. The sounds of metal footsteps came from the expansive courtyard, empty except for the marching Seraphs in their gleaming gold and white armor, the afternoon sun gleaming off the unmarred metal.

"Sin Eater," came a more feminine voice underneath the shining helmet, eyes shadowed from the sun, only the bottom half of the seraph's face visible. Declan inclined his head, "We're here for an audience with the Queen." Lips twisted in a sneer and a loud sniff.

"You can go through the side gate, clean yourselves up first." Declan stepped forward, "I need to see Octavia now." He all but growled at the tall figure had already turned her back to the man.

The seraph spun around, teeth bared, "And you will see the Queen when you a dressed properly and do not have the odor of death and filth clinging to your skin." The guard turned, wings tucked in tight against her back. Anna noticed the tips of the guard's feathers were tipped in gold. She stole a glance at Aramus's own six wings, feathers barely moving even in the high winds. No gold adorned their feathers, their dark skin glistening in the sun, though not a drop of sweat from their brow.

A tug on her wrist was all the warning that Anna received as they crossed the threshold. She stole a look behind her as the heavy gates slowly closed, sealing her in.

15

The bath looked heavenly. The scented water wafted into the bedroom where she was deposited, Declan in tow. The room was large, afternoon light streaming in through the large glass window. The Sin Eater didn't look impressed, instead dumping his belongings on the floor, mud from his boots marring the ornate rug.

"The Queen takes her callers before the evening meal, so we need to be quick," he jerked his head towards the bath, unwrapping the leather straps from the base of his gloves keeping them tight against the inky depths of his skin. He looked out of place in the lavishly decorated room, polished stones gleaming while the dirt from their travels stained the delicate trappings of the given space, scuff marks decorating the white tiled stone.

She allowed herself to take it in. The lush velvet curtains pooling on the sun-warmed floor, the bed large enough to fill her tiny apartment's whole bedroom. Anna looked pointedly at the cuff around her wrist, raising it to his level. Declan sighed, looking around before taking her arm, unhooking the delicate device with a series of knots and what appeared to be a sort of magic. Before she knew it, the length between them was gone, leaving only the chain circlet. At a glance, it simply looked like a bracelet.

Declan pointed to the bathroom doors. She wrapped her arms

around her and carefully walked into the warm room, inhaling the smell of citrus and warmth like honey that engulfed the room, the chill seeping from her bones. She allowed herself to unclench her jaw for the first time in days.

Declan walked up and slammed the doors behind her with a loud enough thud for her to jump, leaving her alone in the open space. She checked behind the curtains and the closets and even jiggled the handle that led to their bedroom, just in case.

Tentatively she allowed herself to disrobe, the rough linen fabric dragging on day-old sweat and grime, falling to a musty heap around her feet. The sunken tub was large and luxurious and looked as if it was hewn from a giant, pink crystal, utterly smooth at the bottom though the lip of the tub was natural and uncut.

Anna sighed as her tired body was wholly enveloped by the hot water. Flower petals drifted across the surface and rested on her skin and hair as she ducked herself under, feeling the road wash from her. When she emerged, she saw a few bottles resting on a polished part of the tub.

Swimming over, Anna uncorked a few, searching for a label but finding none. Anna looked around and poured a tiny bit on the palm of her hand, the scent of something akin to jasmine immediately filling the air and causing small bubbles when she rubbed her hands together. Anna smoothed the soap into her skin, grimacing as her hands caressed gently over bumps, bruises, and scratches from fallen limbs and grabbing trees.

She saw the dirt trail fall into the water, and it took several dunks in the bath for her hair to wring clear. A loud knock at the door had her ducking into the pool, covering her breasts, but no one entered.

Just Declan's gruff voice demanding "Hurry up in there." Anna resisted the urge to stick out her tongue at the Sin Eater and decided to scrub herself one more time, just to be petty. Anna laid back for a moment, her muscles relaxing as she let herself float for a moment. She ducked under one last time only this time, when she did so, she heard an incessant ringing. Like her phone.

She waited underwater momentarily before shooting out of the tub, looking around her, confused. Taking in a deep breath she ducked under water again, her hair a tangled mess around her as she opened her eyes. Past her toes that currently brushed the bottom of the pink stone tub, her bedroom came into view, her empty bed where she had been before taking the pills. It was shimmering, as if obstructed by fog.

The longer she looked, the more opaque the image became. Anna felt she was so close she could reach out and simply touch it...Before realizing what was happening, something grabbed her arm, wrenching her half out of the water. She sputtered, grabbing at the hand that held her.

"Let go!" She coughed, pushing against her offender. She wrapped her arms over her breasts, and pushing herself to the far side of the tub, trying to move her tendrils of hair out of her eyes while keeping herself covered. She opened her eyes to Declan, his black hand dripping with water. He stumbled back as she screamed, looking just as surprised as she was.

"What the hell are you doing?" She exclaimed, looking around to see it was just them in the room, the water swirling around her, "You weren't answering," Declan ground out, his gaze immediately cutting to the floor as she dipped further into the tub. "I just saw you underwater." He clenched his glove-free hand, almost looking involuntary. He stiffened as soon as her eyes roamed toward the blackened appendage.

Declan's face instantly became a mask once again, his eyes turning cold, "Get out so I have a chance to wash this damn mud off." He stomped off, slamming the doors again as he left her alone. It took Anna several seconds to get her bearings, looking down at her feet to see nothing but the solid pink stone below her again. Her cell phone ringing had stopped, and she was again firmly planted in Danann.

✳✳✳

Anna had smoothed her unruly hair into a simple braid that fell down her back. A dress of pale blue had been set on the bed alongside some velvet slippers, the shoes more of an ornament than to protect her feet. She jumped when the doors to the bath finally opened. Declan coming out, steam chasing him from the warmer bathroom. His hair was slightly damp and dripping and his tunic a soft beige. Such a contrast to the dark colors she had seen him wear so far. He was pulling on a pair of softer black gloves, covering the darkness of his skin beneath soft folds of leather.

"Why didn't you get a room?" Anna asked, trying not to let her eyes wander. The Sin Eater's usually coiled self looked a bit more relaxed in the soft clothing and warm temperature. He looked at her sharply, "I'm here to keep an eye on you," he reminded darkly, wrapping the thin leather straps around the gloves, making a quick fist as if breaking in the gentle leather. "So you don't run or drown, apparently." He looked pointedly at the tub in the other room.

Anna stood from slipping on the delicate slipper, rolling her shoulders back to her full height, "I wasn't drowning,"she argued, barely keeping herself from rolling her eyes.

"Then what were you doing?" He asked, his arms outstretched in an attitude that could be described as sarcastic. Anna paused. She didn't know how to answer his question. She was a terrible liar, always had been. But she couldn't reveal that she knew how to shift between worlds with the little pink pills in her backpack.

So she lifted her chin defiantly, "I was washing my hair." Declan pressed his lip into a thin, irritated line but shook his head, tiny droplets falling from the wavy locks atop his head. He opened his mouth, but before he could speak, a chime filled the room.

"It's time." Before she could complain, he grabbed her wrist and snapped the tether between them again. A sharp knock at the door revealed an elegantly dressed seraph, drenched gold wings pulled tightly against his back, gold lining his eyes.

"The Queen is ready for your audience, Sin Eater." Declan just nodded and gestured to Anna to follow the servant. Anna tried to keep herself reserved, but the elegantly decorated halls with ceilings far above her head and painted with deep, delicate clouds and flowers almost made her stumble for how long she stared.

"Eyes front," barked Declan, straightening before the large oak doors opened. She assumed these led into the palace's throne room or wherever this Queen took her visitors. "And make sure you kneel before Her Majesty." Anna opened her mouth to ask a question, but before she could, the doors swung open, revealing a large throne room. Columns the height of three story high buildings and an all-glass ceiling allowed sun to stream in, bathing the room in light.

Declan grabbed her elbow and steered her towards the throne, which she could only assume was Queen Octavia, who sat upon a crystal throne, her raven hair braided into small braids. The hair was woven through an intricate crown that seemed a part of her, not just a piece of jewelry. Anna's steps began to slow as they approached the raised platform, flanked by armored seraphs, their spears towering over them. Declan dropped into a kneel, forcing her down beside him, her knees connected painfully with the tiled floor.

"So," came the Queen's booming voice, echoing around her chamber, strong and elegant all at once. "This woman has been spying on your party Sin Eater?"

Anna looked up, "I am not spying." She insisted, ignoring Declan's bruising grip on her elbow. The Queen smiled, though Anna noticed it did not reach her eyes. Her eyes were dark and deeply set, while her skin showed barely any age lines. Her eyes had seen much. She was beautiful, cheekbones sharp enough to cut glass, her sharp pointed chin just seemed to extenuate her angular features, her blood-red lips still pursed in a smile.

"I know exactly what you are, my mystery guest," she said, cocking her head a bit, taking Anna in like an animal. "And I know where you come from. So tell me why you are here?" Anna didn't know what to say, she looked toward Declan, but his head remained bowed, but she caught his brow furrowing at the Queen's reveal.

"You know where I am from?" Anna asked, sitting back against her calves, her joints aching against the cold floor. Queen Octavia let out a short chuckle that Anna wasn't sure how to interpret. "My dear, do you think you are our only visitor?" She shook her head, picking at a nail momentarily, her eyes roaming over Anna again as her prisoner shifted again on the cold floor.

The Queen clapped unexpectedly, causing Anna to start before she exclaimed, "Enough of this, let us eat. We can speak there." The Queen stood, and when she did so, Declan swiftly rose to his feet, wrenching Anna up with him. She trembled slightly as the tall woman descended the few steps to meet her face-to-face, pausing a step above her to stare down her nose at her. "You can sit next to me." The Queen glanced at the chain holding Declan and herself tethered together. The Queen's eyes flicking up towards the Sin Eater before waving her hand. The chain dissolved and disappeared before it hit the floor.

Anna grasped her wrist in alarm, the bracelet still around her but the leash gone entirely. Declan stared straight ahead, not a speck of emotion on his face.

"Bring her, Sin Eater. Nicely, this time." Declan looked at Anna, motioning with his chin to follow the Queen and the two gold-painted seraphs that flanked her. Anna didn't realize how hungry she was until that moment, her stomach an empty pit that had only been partially satiated with dry meat and bread that they had shared on the road from the Silent Forest.

A pair of large oval doors opened, the Queen never slowed as her seraphs seemingly anticipated her needs and movements. The long table greeted them with food, meats drenched in honey, pastries still steaming from the ovens, and warm bread. Anna could feel herself salivating but held back, clenching her fists as she sat on the left of Queen Octavia, Declan beside her.

The doors opened again to show Aramus and Brynn, cleaned and in fresh clothing, even Aramus's wings seemed whiter than before without the flecks of mud as they had drooped in exhaustion towards the end of their traveling day.

It was only a moment before they were all gathered together again, the long table having them spread across from each other, a human servant placing plates full of food in front of each of them. Octavia was the first to bite into her dinner, followed by the rest. Anna looked at the sweetmeats, fruits, and vegetables arranged aesthetically on her plate, her stomach grumbling but not touching.

"I hope," Queen Octavia said, her voice breaking the noise of scrapping of cutlery, in the otherwise silent room, "That you do not wish to insult me by suggesting I would poison a guest at my table?" Anna looked up, eyes wide, and shook her head, smiling despite her face going pale. Octavia didn't take her eyes off her as she chewed on her food. Anna took a fork and speared a steaming piece of pale meat into her mouth and chewed pointedly. Octavia smiled, reaching for her glass and taking of generous sip of what Anna could only assume was wine.

"So, Sin Eater," Octavia began, Declan had been working on the solitary piece of bread for well over a minute, his gaze stuck on Anna. "Tell me of your travels. How was the Reaping this quarter?" Declan dropped the bread onto the plate as if he had lost his appetite, his posture changing completely. His spine stiffened and he brushed the crumbs from his gloves before taking a long pull from his wine glass.

"Fine, roads were shit. I collected around 46 along the way this month." Octavia looked satisfied with his answer, focusing again on her food, her wine glass appearing to refill itself without the servant doing so.

It took Anna everything to keep herself from looking around the large dining hall. The place was flooded with light, but besides the few flickering candles sitting on the table, she couldn't quite find the source. Or how the food seemed to stay warm no matter how long it sat on a tray before being served.

The juices of the meat were spiced with something the brunette had never encountered before, and Anna held herself back from appeasing her more feral side and all but shoveling the dinner into her mouth. Octavia must have caught her looking around the room and the way she marveled at the strangely spiced food.

"You must be admiring my work," The Queen said, her chin tilting up minutely. Her wine glass poised in her hand like she was posing for a portrait, her sharp dark eyes dancing about the room following Anna's own. "It is a marvelous work of magic on my part. Each Monarch will take the castle and mold it to his or her choosing, from the colors of the walls," she gestured to the soft green walls with her glass, the wine almost sloshing over the rim but not dripping as if held back by an invisible force. "To the drapes and carpets."

Her eyes held a sparkle for a moment before her jaw worked, and she threw back the rest of the wine. Before she set down her goblet, it was full again of the deep red liquid.

"It's beautiful," Anna agreed, swallowing quickly to give the expected compliment, "Green is my favorite color." Smiling, Octavia clasped her hands together, leaning her elbows on the table, "It was my daughters as well. This was all for her; she lit the place up." Anna sipped the wine in front of her, the acidic drink biting the back of her throat in the best way, warming her bones and giving her more courage than she would typically have.

"You have a daughter?" Anna asked, cutting a piece of red fruit on her plate, "Will she join us?" Anna looked around to see a place set with a chair but no food placed in front of it. Octavia's red lips lined, small creases visible as she did so, the only cracks in her porcelain skin, "No, she passed from this world nearly a year ago." Anna immediately dropped her gaze, putting her fork down,

"I'm, I'm so sorry," she stammered, her heart hammering in her chest at her foolishness. "I lost my mother when I was young. I understand how hard it is." She realized too late that the rest of the party had stopped partaking and simply looked at the Queen as if waiting on bated breath to see how she would react to the statement about her fallen daughter. But the Queen smiled, reaching out a hand and squeezing Anna's, still wrapped around her fork, "Grief is a heavy burden. But it can be a great teacher." Anna just nodded, unsure of what to say.

The sounds of knives and forks resumed, signaling she had adverted disaster with her comment. Despite how welcoming Octavia was, Anna still had an uneasy feeling in her stomach, as if this woman was a viper who could turn at any moment.

"Tell me about your home," The Queen asked suddenly, a small cake from the tray in her fingers as she took delicate bites, looking at Anna with a raised eyebrow. Alarm bells went off in her head, but she didn't know why. She was sitting at this woman's table, drinking and eating her food. So she chewed slowly, taking a long drink before answering the dark-haired woman, the Queen's eyes following her all the while like a lion watching its prey. "It's different than this," she said simply, gesturing around her. "No magic. Not this beautiful." She smiled uncomfortably, hoping this tiny bit of information would appease the Monarch, who thankfully simply nodded and returned to the small cake.

A few more uncomfortable silences passed, the Queen acting as if they weren't there, and honestly, Anna could handle that. She picked apart some vegetables and tried to calm the churning in her stomach from the rich foods.The wine was making her head spin a bit more than expected. She was not a lightweight, but she didn't drink that heavily anymore. Once she hit thirty, her hangovers seemed to last days, the cons had far outweighed the pros.

The Queen set down her wine glass hard, causing the table to rattle and the seraphs at her sides to stand at attention, the tall staffs they held snapped against the tile floor. Anna simply dropped her fork and set her hands in her lap like a child that had been caught doing something they shouldn't have. The Monarch stood and the rest of the table followed, leaving Anna to scramble, her chair scraping across the tile floor loudly.

Octavia turned towards her as she inclined her chin, "Enjoy your stay at my castle, I am sure we will speak more in the coming days." The whole room was quiet, save for the click of the Queen's heels trailing out of the open door, her sentries in tow.

"Well, as lovely as that was, I'm headed to bed," Declan announced, tossing his napkin onto the table, his nearly full plate still steaming and barely touched. Before Anna could say anything, he had stormed off, saying something to the guards on the way out.

Anna looked to Brynn, eyes wide, "I don't remember where my room is." Brynn smiled softly, taking a bright red apple from one of the many bowls overflowing with the fruit, "I can show you." Sighing in relief, she let go of the tension in her shoulders, nodded to Aramus and followed the young Seer, her white linen robes brushing the floors as she walked down the halls.

Anna jogged to catch up, allowing herself to stare at the tapestries and artwork without Declan's brooding presence. "Are you here often? At the palace, I mean." Her companion took another bite of the fruit, nodding, "Every quarter, we go out into the cities and surrounding provinces to collect the soul tax for the Queen. The rest of the time I am in training, Aramus is often called away to smaller missions for the crown, though."

Anna had too many questions from Brynn's short answer, so she just replied, "And Declan?" Brynn looked at her questioningly, "He's Declan. He trains a lot and sometimes helps out with the new sentries."

"The seraphs? He trains them?" Anna asked, surprised, trying not to catch the eyes of the guards as they passed them. "Just the human ones, many are indentured or from poor families. The seraphs train their own, though most come from Hy-Brasil formally trained for the most part." Anna had to walk faster to keep up with the younger woman, the dark passages lighting as they walked down them, darkness behind them. "And, a soul tax?" Brynn frowned, chewing on the fruit for a beat before shrugging, "I know you're not a spy." Anna's eyebrows shot up. She placed her hand on the young woman's arm, stopping her from going further.

"How?" Anna's heart was racing wildly, she looked around only to see a guard a few feet down, standing stoically. "Brynn, what do you know?" Brynn chewed and swallowed, her eyes not leaving Anna's wide ones. "More than I probably should. But honestly, someone from our world wouldn't react to things I say like you do." Brynn placed her hand in her pocket, "The soul tax is necessary, it takes the sinful souls of the realm and puts them to work. This keeps the possibility of demons in check, souls that don't deserve to come back or need to be taught a lesson or two before they rebirth. They fuel our armies. The Kingdom. The Queen herself."

Anna narrowed her eyes, her hand still not leaving Brynn's arm, "What do you mean rebirth?" Brynn looked at her long, sucking on her teeth and shaking her head almost in amusement.The darker woman pointed to the door they had been standing in front of the entire conversation, "This is your room." She pushed it open without breaking eye contact. "Have a good night."

Brynn brushed past her before Anna could protest, the lights following the Seer as she walked, quickly plunging Anna into darkness as the seer walked. Quickly stepping into the warm room, she shut the door against the night that seemed to try to leak into the fire-lit space, the hearth roaring with a few logs crackling across from the bed. Anna never felt more alone, more isolated as she looked out that tall window that had just hours before streamed in such gorgeous evening light now just showed a moonlit bathed sharp drop from the castle's cliff straight into the forest below.

She wrapped her arms around her, staving off the shiver that ran up her spine despite the warmth of the bedroom. She looked longingly at the bathroom, the now empty tub, and then back to her backpack that still sat against the bed, seemingly untouched. In the second small pocket, Anna knew a small plastic bag held two pink pills. Her only way home. Dropping to her knees on the plush carpet, now brushed free of any dirt Declan had left from his afternoon, and rifled through the pack just to satisfy her anxiety that the pills existed. Still tucked away, waiting for her if she needed them.

Part of her itched to swallow a pink pill, to go back to her world. The normalcy, the early mornings and late nights. Her friends. But another, larger part of her was curious. Could she really live her whole life without exploring this place? The thrill of the unknown swept through her, part of her yearned for the comfortable, but the other, louder part of her knew she would never be able to rest without knowing what was going on, why she kept being pulled here. In her childhood, she would clutch these stories to her, reading late at night under a blanket with a flashlight, anticipating other worlds' adventure, peril, and romance. Then Anna grew up, got a job, loved, and lost. She had lost so very much. So Anna pushed the pills back into the bag and placed it under the bed where she could grab it if necessary.

This was her chance, and she wouldn't waste it. Even if she was scared out of her mind, her body ached, and her mind swam with the effects of otherworldly wine. She had stopped being brave the night Katie got hurt. Her therapist kept telling her to try new things. Settling underneath the warm, soft sheets in a strange land, in a castle she couldn't conjure up in her craziest of dreams, and smiled albeit grimly.

She wondered if her therapist would count this as trying new things.

16

～

The sun caressed her skin as she woke, the smell of flowers and citrus perfuming the air. Anna could have stayed there, her body finally not waking up to a stick poking her in the back or her hips aching from the cold, damp forest floor or in a flood of anxiety. The sound of the bedroom door opening had her jolting upright and bringing her comforter to her chest in some puritanical need for modesty though she slept fully clothed.

The woman who opened the door started as Anna sat up, nearly dropping the food-laden tray from her hands, her white hair pulled back into a neat bun and pale eyes wide with shock at Anna's reaction.

"I'm sorry! I thought you were already awake, or I would've waited!" She stammered, turning around to return to the door before Anna interceded.

"No, I am so sorry," Anna apologized, immediately getting out of the large bed, taking the tray from the woman, and setting it down on the table. "Thank you, I should've probably been up hours ago."

The pale girl smiled and gestured to the food tray, "The Queen had me send breakfast up. She said you had had quite a journey, so you'd probably be abed most of the day." Anna's stomach clenched with the smell emanating from the breakfast tray, heaped with thick sausages that looked very close to bacon and pastries with honey drizzled over the flakey crust.

"Thank you again, I appreciate it."

"I'm Ria, if you need anything, you simply need to ask," Ria looked very human, save for her white hair and pale eyebrows. No sign of wings or knives on the woman. The servant turned to leave, and Anna touched her arm, "Actually, I have one question, where is Declan this morning?" Ria drew her eyebrows together, confused, before recognition dawned upon her.

"Oh, the Sin Eater!" Anna nodded for her to continue. "He's in the courtyard, he's been there training most of the morning." Ria turned to leave, and Anna was once again alone and thankful for it. She was alone with the food tray and collapsed in the armchair, trying everything once and then picking through her favorites. The hot mulled drink steaming next to the plate smelled of cinnamon and spice and tasted remarkably like apple cider. After indulging in breakfast she once again grabbed her backpack, checking the small pocket holding the pills.

One.

Two.

Still there, still whole, the backpack still untouched. Anna looked around, wondering if Ria would return to make the bed or anything akin to housekeeping. Carefully, trying to be quiet for no real reason besides the thundering of her heart. She felt as if the whole castle could hear her rifling through the dresser and stuffing her backpack underneath a few spare blankets in the deep bottom drawer.

Anna didn't bother bathing again, because the slight chance that she saw her room again. She didn't have time for that, she needed answers. The drawer was filled with clothing that fit her, she assumed the magic filling the castle had something to do with it. Anna picked a light brown loose shirt with an open collar and soft leggings that put her expensive boutique yoga pants to shame.

Anna pulled on smooth leather shoes. They had more of a outsole than the slippers she had worn last night. Anna needed to find the courtyard, which she could only assume was the large cobblestoned entrance. When they first arrived she remembered seeing a few men and women sparring, it made sense that Declan would probably be there as well. Anna took a deep breath, her heart still pounding as she opened the heavy wooden door, the hinges swinging easily despite its size and her lack of upper body strength.

Anna's stomach rolled as she poked her head out of her room and quietly stepped into the large hallway. The stones were cold, despite her thicker shoes. The guards remained standing ramrod straight as she passed, but she saw their eyes following her as she did so. She stopped on the edge of the stairs, looking to the left and right below her before she finally turned to the Seraph on guard nearest to her.

"Excuse me, can you tell me where the courtyard is?" Though she spoke softly, her voice seemed to echo in the empty hall. The Seraph didn't move but looked to the left of them, wings whispering, *"Down the stairs, to the left. Down the stairs, to the left."* Though it came out as if several whispering voices were trying to say the same thing over one another, Anna got the idea and nodded her thanks before wondering why Aramus's wings were unintelligible when she heard them.

The opening to the courtyard was a wide door, leading to an ample open space with short-cropped green grass surrounding a large dirt area where enormous wooden columns stood, decorated with chunks of wood missing, slices, and gouges. A few seraphs sparred in the adjacent marble-floored court, not dirt that the Sin Eater currently worked in. His long sword sang as he spun it, slicing into the wooden training posts with deadly ease.

His shirtless body glistened in the midmorning sun, sweat beading and rolling between his shoulder blades. Anna stood there for a beat longer than she should have, the wind picking up and whipping her hair around her. As if he could smell her on the breeze, Declan paused and stood still for a moment before he turned to face her.

"Morning." He said gruffly, face wind-beaten and sunburned, but besides the acknowledgment, he didn't put his sword down to greet her. Swinging to hit the training beam. Then another.

"You know," she said, wrapping her arms around her as another blow landed on the pole, "Knowing how to do that would have helped me when those guys ambushed us in the forest." A harsh laugh left the man as a quick swipe through the air rained splinters of wood around him as he dealt a particularly hard blow. The wooden beam would slowly be whittled down to a stick if he continued at this pace. He stopped swinging the sword then, sheathing it, and strode towards her, his powerful body all muscle and violence.

Declan was a foot away from her at most, close enough that she could see the rise and fall of his chest as he struggled to catch his breath. "What are you asking?"

Anna bit her lip, shading her eyes from the sun, wishing she could sound more confident when she asked, "Train me?" Declan knitted his brow, shaking his head as he took the gloves that hung from his belt, slipping them over his stained hands.

"Show me your hands." He ordered, leaving no room for questions or disobedience. Anna's thumb picked at her forefinger, the nail digging into the soft skin it found there before she unwrapped her arms and held her hands to the man. He immediately took the tips of her fingertips and rotated her hands so her palms faced upwards. Her stomach clenched as she saw the evidence of her accident criss-crossed over her palm and wrapping around her finger in brutal red lines and healed staple marks. Perhaps she just made up how feather soft his gloved index finger felt as it brushed against the ugliest of the scars, the deepest across her palm where the windshield had found its home.

"What happened?" A question this time. Not an order. Almost soft.

Anna shifted, looking off as a large bird flew overhead before she looked back at him, "An accident. It took my friend. It took her and left me these. This hand isn't as strong as the other." Declan let go over her fingers, withdrawing slightly. "Make a fist." She did as he asked, her fingers curling into a tight ball. The Sin Eater nodded in approval, "You didn't tuck the thumb." Anna nodded, trying not to feel proud and subsequently sick when she remembered her father at home and how he had taught her the same.

"My dad taught me." Declan nodded, looked at the training arena,

130

and sighed heavily. "Fine, just pay attention, and only for a bit. I still have to finish my routine without you slowing me down." The agreement was curt and edged with annoyance, but Anna smiled despite that, following the man into the center of the dirt area.

The wind was breaking over the open area, her hair blinding her as it constantly whipped around her, standing in front of Declan, nervousness prickling in her stomach. Declan looked at her and sighed, beginning to unwrap the leather straps of his left glove.

"Turn around," he ordered deeply, holding the thin piece of leather in his gloved hands. Anna's brow knitted together, but she did so, on edge as she turned her back to him. She couldn't keep herself from jumping slightly as he gathered her hair in his leathered hands, wrapping it into an intricate knot at the base of her neck, securing it with one of the leather straps of his gloves.

Anna touched the bun gently as he stepped away. He reached into a bin to pick up a wooden staff and tossing it to her. Anna tried not to gasp as the object flew at her, awkwardly catching the heavy item.

"Up," Declan commanded, holding his own staff straight out from him, arms held out far away from his body. Anna did so, her right hand already shaking a bit as she held up the heavy staff, which was probably no more than 10 pounds. Still, she was a sedentary creature of habit, and the gym did not come up in her daily routine often, if not ever. Aside from the required physical therapy to regain some of the mobility in her hand. Though it didn't bother her much now, sometimes, grabbing heavy items required more effort. This was one of those times.

"Keep it straight out, soft bend to the elbows," he instructed, walking around her as she already felt a small trickle of sweat roll down her neck, the sun beating down on her. He touched her shoulders as he pulled them back, straightening her back and making her core strain. Declan sighed in annoyance, grabbing the staff from her hands and wrenching her off balance. "Alright, we start from the beginning."

✳✳✳

Anna didn't know if she had ever been this sore in her entire life. The sun had barely moved in the sky, signaling her worst fear, that she hadn't even been out there very long. As Anna climbed the steps, it seemed more like Everest instead of narrow, marbled steps. She gripped the railing, all but pulling herself up and trying to ignore how the sweat dripped down her back.

"Training?" Came a melodic voice next to her, startling her from her thoughts on whether or not she would lose her breakfast before she made it to her bed chamber. Next to her, Aramus stood, arms crossed, and something like amusement spread across their face as they assessed her exhausted form.

"I think it was torture," she whispered, taking their offered hand as she pulled herself up from her nearly doubled-over position at the top of the staircase. "I've done cross-fit training that hasn't left me this out of breath."

Aramus's brows knitted, and a bemused smile touched their full lips, "May I be of help?"

They offered an elbow as Anna stood at the precipice of the hall-way, her room seeming a daunting ways away. She nodded breath-lessly, taking the offered arm and found it solid and unwavering even as she allowed much of her weight to lean upon the Seraph.

"You know," she whispered, almost limping down the hall with her guide as her calf muscle cramped slightly, "I don't know much about you, Aramus, besides the few times we've spoken."

The Seraph gazed down at her, their beautiful face considering her words before looking ahead again, "What would you like to know?" Smiling, Anna asked softly as they passed a sentry standing guard, "Where do you come from? How do you get here?"

Aramus nodded as if they approved of her question, "Hy-Basil. It's an island off Danann's north-eastern coast, our homeland. Where we are raised and trained to serve. It's a final form for our race, to become one with the universe once our time is up." Anna looked at them, confused, "So, do you have parents? Why servitude?" Aramus shrugged noncommittally, "I honestly don't remember, it was ages ago. When having thousands of years of memories, the older ones start to fade. But to answer the second part of your question, some of us like to come back to assist the population. So I tried for a century or two, picked a form I liked, and was assigned this castle in this timeline."

They were edging closer to her room. Anna was intrigued, purposely slowing her pace for more time with the Seraph. "So you got to pick what you looked like?" That made sense, all the seraph's were all beautiful in their own right, tall, and muscular. Feminine or masculine, or like Aramus, a handsome mixture of both. The Seraph nodded, their gold eyes dancing at the question as if they remembered something in their past, "We're all different with unique tastes and aesthetically drawn features. Some choose from more gentile, feminine forms or masculine dominating ones. But do not let appearances or supposed gender fool you, none is stronger than the other. I couldn't decide as they both were so beautiful to me." They smiled, gazing appreciably at one of the sentries who watched them pass, "So I went with this form. It suited me."

Anna smiled, squeezing the arm of her guide, "I think it does as well." Their dark face smiled at her, and next to them, for a long while, she noticed the spattering of dark freckles dotting their nose, the whispering of white facial hair dusting the flawless skin. A masculine form with feminine grace, poised like a cat but as deadly as an adder.

Her door was in front of her in no time, and she thanked the Seraph for their kindness before she collapsed on the soft bed. She groaned as the door shut behind her, hoping the Seraph didn't hear her. Before she knew it, she was sound asleep.

17

~

"Don't pull yourself up, push the ground away from you," barked Declan, circling her like a predator would his prey. Her legs trembled as she squatted down once again, her thighs screaming as she kept her arms out in front of her, pushing from the balls of her feet, not her toes. Declan nodded, he didn't praise her much when he trained her, but a nod would let her know she didn't fail his instructions.

"Break." He ordered. He threw a towel at her, and she wiped the sweat off her face. Since Anna had been in this world, she had barely any breakouts. Her skin was glowing, and she swore some finer wrinkles looked less noticeable when she gazed in the mirror.

She was flourishing here. Even the air quality was different in this place. No plumes of gas or smoke from exhausts, no trains or buildings. The air was sweeter and tinged with the scent of blossoms, and of course with the smells of horses, who were stabled just a few yards away.

It had been two days since her first training. He had rotated her to cardio the next day, and now she was on legs, her least favorite since muscles twinged and complained heavily. Her body was weaker than she realized.

"Sit," instructed the tall man, sitting on the plain wood bench, taking a deep drag from his water container as the crisp day's sun beat down upon them. Anna collapsed on the bench next to him, taking the offered water, noticing the sweat pooling around the gloves he had secured to his forearms. She gestured to them before gulping the sweet water.

"Why do you wear those? It's hot out." Her task was to gather information while she was here, and so far, the only thing she had learned was that she had a shitty squat form, the food was terrific, and a bit about the seraphs here and there from her conversations with Aramus.

"I wear them for people to ask me stupid questions," came the gruff reply, Anna watched as he took another pull of the canteen.

"Did you just make a joke?" She asked, genuinely smiling. "It kind of sounded like a mean joke, but I think it counts."

"I don't make jokes either," he stood, and Anna tried to pull her eyes away from the thin material of his shirt that rode up deliciously on his stomach, showing the swell of muscles and sun-kissed skin.

"Stand up, we're stretching and done for the day." Anna reluctantly stood, her muscles protesting sharply as she did so, the stretch and pull of her hamstrings caught her off guard as she straightened. Her knee buckled and sent her pitching forward. Anna only had time to gasp as the ground came up to meet, only to be caught by solid gloved hands as she flailed.

Finding herself pressed against the Sin Eaters' chest, she froze. Her heart pounding, and she knew deep down it was not just from the sudden fall. Her biceps were still clutched by his gloved hands, her fingers splayed against his sweaty chest. She was close enough to smell him. Masculine and heady, a mixture of citrus bath oils, sweat, and arena dirt all blended with the lingering blend of smoke to create a scent altogether Declan.

With both pounding heart and head, she dared a glance up, the last time they had been this close, she had broken his nose. Her heart was racing for an altogether different reason this time, and she wasn't sure if she was ready to face that type of awareness, even with herself.

Dear god, his eyes were green with flecks of gold, scars scattered over the beautifully weathered face. He looked so bare right now and she swore, under the touch of her outspread hand, his heart was hammering in his chest. Its rhyme matching her own. She watched his eyes leave hers and settle on the sunlight glittering off the small chains looping around her delicate wrist. Anna swore she felt his heart skip a beat. And all too soon, his eyes steeled, his mouth closed and jaw set, a small muscle in his neck flexing as he gently placed her away from him, the soft leather of his hands leaving her arms.

"Do the stretches I taught you and prepare for dinner, the Queen requests our presence today." And with that, he spun around, grabbing his forgotten water canteen and slamming the door to the palace in his wake. Anna stood there, chest heaving as she tried to figure out what just happened, pushing back her sweat-soaked hair plastered on her brow and taking a deep breath.

"Fuck." She whispered, rolling her shoulders back. A group of seraphs entered the arena, their combined total of wings she couldn't count as she ushered herself away from the dirt pit, waving awkwardly at the tall, gorgeous creatures.

She retreated inside without looking behind her and found getting up the stairs easier though she was still winded. It wasn't as bad as it had been a few days prior. She retreated to her room to do her stretches there, her hamstrings screaming for release as they seized as soon as she lay down against the ground, reaching to touch her toes without the dexterity that Declan seemed to have.

Anna tried to mimic the simple moves the Sin Eater had shown her. Even with his lean muscles, he was pliable in a way she never had been, and she tried unsuccessfully to forget how his chest felt underneath her fingers. Her skin still tingled where he had touched her. Even with his gloved hands, she couldn't forget the feel of gentle pressure, nothing like when he would grab her when she ran.

She groaned into her hands, her hair spilling over her shoulders in defeat. Her therapist could write a damn novel over these clashing feelings inside her. Was this Stockholm syndrome? She would get

Stockholm syndrome, Jesus Christ. Did other kidnappers look as good as Declan? Anna ran her fingers lightly down the back of her tricep, ghosting the place where he had touched her, gently and firmly at the same time, holding her steady.

She now knew his grip could be gentle, but firm. Those hands could hold her down...Anna shook her head, as a burning bloomed in her lower pelvis, making her shoot up from her seated position. She needed a bath. As much as anything under boiling hot water triggered her, she needed a cold one.

***

It was still an hour before dinner when Anna emerged from the bathroom, her body still singing from the workout and the gentle touches of the Sin Eater. She refused to put her head underwater after she started to see the floating image of her bedroom below her.

She had picked a soft pink dress from the dresser. The plunging neckline would have been scandalous to someone with fuller breasts than herself, but she thought it still complimented her. It brushed the floor like a romantic gown in the period dramas she would watch on tv late at night.

Soft slippers were on her feet and she wasn't sure if she could return to her tennis shoes when she got home. Anna couldn't stop the pang of disappointment at the thought of returning. Her home? Her world?

To what, working a 9-5 just to barely pay rent? To do the same mix of things day in and day out? Go to the same restaurants, sleep in her small studio apartment with the crumbling walls and worrisome mold patches? Anna closed her eyes and breathed deeply, remembering why she was there. This wasn't her world and she was here to get information and get home. She needed to figure out why a goddamn leviathan was hiding in the storm clouds of her city.

Anna knelt, reaching into the bottom drawer of the clothing dresser to pull out the hidden backpack and grabbed a small blank book and pen she had stashed there. She needed some answers.

Anna needed help before asking the wrong questions to the wrong people.

The door opened silently as she peeked around the corner, noting only the motionless guards that were always there, monitoring the halls. They seemed more ornament than a threat, and it wasn't like anyone told her she couldn't explore the castle; she just hadn't yet.

With a deep breath, Anna tucked the small hardback in the crook of her arm. Her stomach hollowed as she walked the empty halls, only light by the dying sunset streaming in through oval, color-stained windows. Heavy doors to the left and right of her, she gently jiggled one to find it tightly locked.

She pressed on. Most of the doors were closed, and she assumed since her room was on this level, they were vacant rooms, only opened when needed. Continuing down the corridor, she came to where the hall lay between an opening. Anna tiptoed, finding herself inside a circular glass room. She did everything in her power not to gasp as her gaze danced around the large space.

It was a greenhouse, brightly colored birds flittered about with strange songs leaving their beaks, the smell of flowers and strange fruits was intoxicating, and she couldn't believe this was the first time she had seen this place. Even the air felt different here, warm and a touch humid, despite the somewhat chilly day. It had turned out to be outside as the sunset.

The trees snaked up and melded with the iron that held the glass. Beautiful reds and pinks, dustings of delicate flowers covering the ground as she peered over the edge. A human servant watered a few pots while another poured a large glass vase full of scented oil into a pool of shimmering pale blue water. Anna breathed deeply as the smell of lemons and honey rose from the water that scented the air. She probably would have stayed there longer had not the sound of closing books had grabbed her attention. Rustling come from down the hall across the delicate bridge, her destination all along.

Anna made a mental note to come back here to find the entrance and sit with those plants in the sun. The sunny, warm room disappeared as she crossed the pathway to the other side, her skin rising in goosebumps as the temperature dropped drastically. The large door was opened a crack. Anna gasped when she saw what was inside. The place was filled with stacks of books, spiraling up and around the walls, filling in dark wood bookshelves.

In every corner, there was something. No empty spot could be found. It wasn't messy, but filled with organized chaos that impressed her. Dark green wallpaper with swirls of native plants and animals peeked through the stacks, and a few large crystal-like rocks could be seen balancing on some books haphazardly. It was dizzying and breathtaking at the same time.

"Hello?" Came a cry from behind one of the many rows of free-standing bookshelves, all of which Anna had to crane her head to look to the top.

"Hi?" Anna responded, following the feminine call and walking around the nearest shelf. Sunlight filtering in through large windows between the frames, streams of light illuminated the dust dancing in the air as she walked.

"Come in. I've been expecting you!" Anna rounded the corner, her blank book cradled to her chest, acting as a shield. A tall woman perched precariously upon a high, black iron library ladder, pushing a hefty tome back into its place. Her wild grey hair was in curls around her face, escaping the bun she had placed on her head.

"You've been expecting me?" Anna asked, following the woman with her head as she climbed deftly down the black ladder. The older woman dusted her hands off, the tiny traces of dust floating to join the rest in the air of the musty library before she held out a strong but aged hand. Anna took it, smiling despite herself. She watched with amusement as the woman settled her small glasses back on the bridge of her nose, crooked from her descent.

"Oh, of course, I've heard the buzz around the keep, dear," the woman said, taking her hand in her firm grip and patting it gently. "My name is Sorcha. I have lived in this castle for years and years. Not much happens that I don't know about."

"So you're the librarian?" Anna asked, looking around at the books. Any other time, she would have loved to pour over these volumes and see what secrets and stories they told. A whole world of new novels and knowledge was just sitting here. A bark of laughter stole Anna from her thoughts. Sorcha shook her head and taking a small text from a lower shelf and a large, empty brass bowl.

"Oh, I have been called many things, librarian is one of the nicer ones, though," The grey-haired woman stopped, Anna nearly bumping into her. Sorcha gazed at her in awe, mapping Anna's face with ancient eyes and smiling widely at whatever she found. "Incredible."

"What is?" Anna stammered, unable to break eye contact with the woman.

"Your eyes, dear. So telling!" Anna was suddenly pulled to the table and sat in a chair that was pulled out for her. "You've been on quite the journey, have you not?" Anna nodded, glad to sit for a moment. Had the chair not been there, she would have dropped in surprise at the casualness of the woman's words. Her slightly slouched form walked to the other side of the table, placing the empty brass bowl in the middle, grunting at the object's weight. "When did you appear here?" The woman asked, touching her shoulder gently.

Before she answered the woman's question, Anna responded with one of her own, "Where is here?"

The older woman smiled gently, "You're in the kingdom of Danann, the inner most island nation. We're in the middle of the Danube Ocean." She smiled knowingly, "As a whole, your lore and legend calls this realm the Otherworld." Sorcha paused for a moment, as if searching her brain. "At least, that's what the Celts called it." She waved her hand in dismissal.

Anna swallowed hard against the nervousness bubbling within herself, willing herself to have the strength to ask the question she had been wondering for so long. "Are you all...human? Or something else?"

A raise of white eyebrows answered her question, "You're not in some terrifying afterlife if that's what you're concerned about." Anna let go of a breath she didn't realize she was holding. "But we are not humans like you, our kind is called the Sidhe. But like humans, there are many races."

Anna shook her head, clearing her thoughts and remembering

the original question the old woman had asked. She answered all of hers, and she was overflowing with even more questions at this point.

"The accident, I was in an accident." Sorcha closed her eyes and nodded, like everything made sense, though Anna was anxious to see if she deemed it pertinent to share with her. Anna waited for her to explain, but when she didn't, Anna leaned forward, her arms resting on the dusty table. "I don't understand, ma'am. Why am I here?"

The older woman leaned forward as well, a smile pursing her lips as she sat her wizened hands on the younger woman's.

"Sorcha, dear." The older woman reminded before looking around the large room, "Your world is so much different than this one, but even your world, there is myth and lore." Sorcha tapped the top of her hand before releasing them, grabbing a handful of colorful stones before setting them on the table, the sound echoing around them in the still room,

"When you think of the world and time, many think of it like this," she set down a singular stone, pushing the others out the way so it laid by itself. "But it is more like this," she moved the stones together, touching each other somehow. "They touch, sometimes very faintly. Creating lay lines of power and magic where they do so. I am sure you have apples where you are from?" Anna just nodded, staying silent so the woman would continue.

Sorcha dipped her head towards the stones, "Some things are different, some are the same. And time," she chuckled, shaking her head like it was the funniest joke in the world, "Time is happening, for everyone, simultaneously across all of these worlds and dimensions. " Anna was silent, taking in the information. "We are incarnations of a grander being, learning and growing with each life."

Anna leaned forward suddenly, tapping the table. "You mean like reincarnation?"

Sorcha smiled toothily, patting her hand encouragingly. "Exactly, my dear. I love that your world has such a lovely word for it!"

Leaning back into the stiff chair, Anna's head was a whirl of thoughts and fears, but everything began to click into place.

"Why am I shifting back and forth?" She asked, suddenly finding her voice, "It started after I had an accident last year." Nodding, the old woman stood, moving towards a large ceramic pitcher and bringing it over the table, pouring water into the brass bowl that had sat neglected, the water splashing onto the wooden table as she did so.

"You died, I assume. Even briefly?" Asked the woman, setting the heavy water pitcher down on the floor with a clump and a sigh. Anna nodded, "A little less than a minute, they said before they revived me." Sorcha looked at Anna again for a long moment before beckoning Anna to stand beside her. Anna wasn't very tall, but she towered over the hunched older woman, who moved quite well for her unknown age.

"This just a bowl. With plain drinking water. Mirrors and water can allow certain people to see through the veil of death and time itself," she explained, drawing it nearer without spilling a single drop. "Children are very apt at this game as their souls are so new to their time. But if you stare long enough into them, you begin to see. Sometimes, just out of the corner of your eye." She gently placed Anna in front of the antique bowl, smiling knowingly. "But I think you figured that out already?"

"How do I stop coming here? And why water?" Anna whispered, not giving the older woman an answer. She suddenly felt conscious of the gold chain on her wrist, the silky light fabric wrapped around her frame, everything was still there while she played dress up in a world that wasn't hers.

Sorcha's brows knitted in concern and patted her hand, "Anna, you are always in control. You are being tugged in two directions, and the universe or the Goddess isn't sure what to do with you. That's why you shift."

"Why does it bring me here?" She demanded, her ruined hands balling into fists as her voice rose. "Why am I brought to him every time?" The old woman flittered her eyes to her wrist that the gold chain wrapped around, opening her mouth for a moment before she froze, her eyes shutting gently.

Anna felt the movement before she saw it, someone nearing and the scuff of boots on the polished marble. Within a moment of the door opening, the old woman pushed the polished stones off the table, letting them scatter off in a clatter. Declan stood in the doorway, looking around the empty library, save the two women at the table.

"Sorcha," he dipped a head in greeting, reverently but somewhat mistrusting, watching her under squinted eyes.

"Sin Eater," Sorcha did not mimic his movement but stood as straight as her curved back allowed, chin high. Her eyes behind her spectacles that balanced her thin nose looked watery.

Declan looked past her to where Anna sat.

"It's time for dinner," he stated, making it very plain that he would not be leaving the library without her. Anna looked at Sorcha as she stood, gently placing a hand over the old woman's, a silent assurance that she would return. Anna followed Declan through the large door, only daring to look back once at the towering books and the only woman who Anna knew could get her out of this mess.

She *would* be back.

She just had to be careful.

18

Dinner was uneventful. That's the easiest way to describe how Anna felt as she returned to her room that night, full but unsatisfied. Part of her wanted to sneak down the darkened hallways, find the library past the greenhouse, and see if Sorcha was there. But she knew that was too risky, walking around a guarded castle in open rooms during the day looked like curiosity. Creeping out of her bedroom at night looked like espionage, the very thing that Declan accused her of in the first place.

She was growing too close to her goal to get sloppy now. She brushed out her wind-blown hair, her fingers pushing past the small tangles and knots they found. A brush of something fell from her hair, startling her back to see the thin leather strip that Declan used to hold her long hair back at training that morning.

Gingerly she picked it up, rolling the slim, tanned leather between her fingers. She thought about tossing it into a drawer, but something wouldn't let her. Anna chewed her bottom lip for a moment before setting the strand of leather reverently on the small vanity top, plaiting her hair into a loose braid, securing the ends with the length. Not knowing how long she sat there, staring at the damn string, a heavy thud at her door startled her. As she jumped from her chair, its delicate old legs scraping loudly against the floor.

"Who is it?" She hated that her voice seemed unsure and unsteady. Honestly, what would she do if someone came bursting through the door?

"It's me," came a soft, deep voice. Declan. He sounded almost as unsure as she did. Anna tossed a glance at the window, at the fading sun as it crested over the mountain.

It was dark, and the castle was quiet. Would the guards come if she needed them? Or where they are loyal to their Sin Eater? Anna shook her head because deep down, she knew Declan wouldn't hurt her.

She took a deep breath, all but tip-toeing to her door, and tried to calm her beating heart before she unlatched the door chain and opened the door slowly. Declan stood there, eyes downcast as light flooded his shadowed features.

He was dressed in the most casual outfit she'd ever seen, soft linen pants and a white shirt that dipped below his color bone, showing off a deep scar that disappeared into the tunic.

Declan smelled like lemongrass, the scent stronger now than in the arena, his hair soft and unmated from the day, presumably from a bath. She stared longer than she should have. He raised his eyebrows at her and she shook her head, stepping back and allowing the imposing man into the room.

He looked around as if to see anything had changed from the day he had brought her here. He held out his hand to her, something clutched in his fist. Anna stared at him, they still hadn't said a word to each other. Something was on the tip of her tongue, but she fought back against it thinking the words would be as ridiculous as this pounding in her chest.

"Here. It's to help with training," he explained, pushing his hand closer toward her. Anna licked her lips, fighting a smile as she held out her hand, his large one dwarfing hers. Declan dropped a small, blue-colored ball in her palm. Anna rolled the soft item between her fingers, it was smooth and not made of plastic but something pliable.

"A ball?" She asked, confused but not wanting to seem rude. Declan seemed unnerved for the first time in her presence, his usually brash and aggressive attitude seemingly washed away in his bath, leaving him softer and unguarded. Aside from his ever-present gloves that nearly went to his elbows.

"It's soft, I use it for my fighters to strengthen their grip," he gestured to her scarred hand, "That one is weaker than the other. Squeeze hard ten times, rest, and do it again. About three sets a day should help."

Anna was speechless for a moment, rolling the round object in her hand, gripping it gently, and feeling the soft material give around her fist and recoiling as she released. It was like a stress ball. She had used these many times during physical therapy and, to be honest should have been using it this past year to keep building her strength. Still, her yellow stress ball, stamped with her physician's logo, sat untouched in her bedside drawer, another reminder of how her life had changed.

Declan shifted his weight from one side to the other, clearly uncomfortable. Anna lifted her head with a smile, "Thank you, Declan. I appreciate it." The Sin Eater dipped his head turning to go. His gloved hand gripped the doorknob and he paused, looking back at her. His gaze shifting to the length of leather wrapped around the end of the braid slung over Anna's shoulder. Before Anna could explain, even though she wasn't sure what she was embarrassed about, the man had given it to her. Practically.

"You can have it," she stammered, inches closer and going to unknot the leather.

"No," Declan said low and rough, "No," he repeated, this time softer, "You, uh, can have it. I have others."

Without another word, he left the room, the only sound was the click of the doorknob as it shut gently.

A flutter in her stomach traveled into a flush to her face. She blew out a breath, pressing her hands to her blazing hot face, knowing instinctively that her ears were bright red. Anna placed her hands on the vanity, looking at herself in the mirror, the evidence of her embarrassment coloring her cheeks and tips of her ears.

"What the hell was that?" She asked herself exasperatedly, covering her hands over her face before groaning. She grabbed the ball from the table and climbed into bed. She cocooned herself in the pillowy softness of the comforters and overstuffed down pillows.

Shit.

✳✳✳

The training yard was full today. A few dozen seraphs, all in various states of dress and fatigue, worked around the training field, sweat glistening off of rigid bodies and different shades of wings. One in particular, a tall seraph almost meeting Declan in height, spoke to the Sin Eater as he wrapped his fists, bare chested, dark wings shading him from the day's sun.

Anna walked cautiously up to the two, fidgeting with her thumbs. She tried not to look intimidated by the two or the group of well-trained warriors that danced around each other, tossing spears and swinging swords or fledging arrows in their pack. Both male and female were training, and the different shades of their wings were the first thing Anna noticed. From white to grey, brown, and even a few black wings speckled their ranks. It was a sharp contrast to the seraph guards she had seen around the castle, their ivory wings pure and gold tipped at the edges.

Declan jutted his chin towards her, "Anna," the Sin Eater acknowledged her, breaking his conversation with the tall seraph when he noticed her presence. "This is Ararmus's Lieutenant, Titus. Aramus's second in command of the 26th Garrison." Anna smiled, holding her hand to the seraph, "It's nice to meet you, Titus," she replied politely, not surprised by the firm grip that met her hand.

Titus inclined his head to her, grey eyes glittering, "How is this one treating you? He can be a bit intense on the newbies." Shading her eyes from the sun, a smile tugged at her lips as she rotated her palm to him, showing off the impressive callouses that had not graced her once soft hands.

"It's harder than any other workout regiment I've done." Titus caught her, looking at the dark wings as he lifted them slightly, her hand following as the sun's glare disappeared at his actions.

"Our wings look different from the soldiers you've seen, I

147

assume," He grinned cheekily as she looked away, slightly embarrassed for being caught staring. With the seraph's wings shading her from the sun, she could also make out a few tattoos etched into his outer bicep, strange markings that she noticed on the rest of the group.

Declan dipped to scoop up a training sword from the dirt, flipping it a few times and brushing off the bruised wood. "Aramus and their team are second seraphs, an aerial unit. These seraphs are trained and built for speed and flight, they can turn the tide in a battle. They're also the only garrison allowed flight by her royal Majesty."

Leaning forward, the sandy haired seraph shot a glance at the standing guard in their glittering armor, still as statues, "We aren't just for ornaments, you see." He winked at her, and Declan cleared his throat while Anna caught herself almost in a blush.

"Ok, Titus, you're dismissed. Check in with Aramus before you're finished for the day." Titus dipped a head at the Sin Eater, his expression immediately schooled but graciously bowed before Anna as he left, the dimple in his cheek showing off at the crooked smile as he retreated at Declan's bark.

The day was overcast and chilly, but she felt she would be sweating regardless of the weather. Declan, who had been out for a while, was already covered in sheen and cursing as he dropped his sword onto the earth.

"Rough morning?" Anna asked, wrapping her arms around herself as soon as they were alone, trying to look everywhere but him and failing miserably. Declan turned quickly, shaking out his hand, a curse on his lips. He stalked past her without a word, mood as dark as the clouds forming overhead. Anna watched as he pulled his right hand out of his glove, bright red marring his black skin and leaking out of the leather.

"Declan!" Anna gasped, her steps toward him faster than anticipated, anxiety pouring through her words. "Did you cut yourself?"

She went to take his hand in hers to inspect the damage, but she halted when he jerked back and barked, "Don't!" Anna's fingers froze mid-air, and she took a cautious step, her eyes not leaving his stormy ones even as he swore again. Declan shook his hand again before reaching into a small sack next to the bench, unrolling some gauze and wrapping the injury, using his teeth to tighten the bandage.

"I just jammed it,'" he said, his voice less tight as he looked over his shoulder at her. He looked more angry than hurt, so Anna went back to rubbing her bare arms against a particularly stiff wind.

Declan jerked his head to the arena, "Laps, hug the corners. I don't want to see you cutting through the middle." Anna fought everything in her to not stick her tongue out at the man. She was nearing thirty-four years old and not sixteen, but this felt like gym class.

However, the motion warmed her as she lapped, trying to breath steady as he had taught her, Anna completely ignored him as he sat on the bench. Declan was watching her form, critiquing if she strayed too far into the arena, cutting the length even a bit.

The breeze was making the jog more enjoyable than previous days, but Anna would be the first to admit that she missed her wireless headphones. Anna crossed lap five, going stronger than days before when she doubled over at the pain in her side, and the knowledge made her smile a little. Lost in thought as she circled again, she suddenly realized the soft breeze as her back had turned aggressive, pulling at her braid and tugging at her clothing. Just as she slowed, the dust around her began to rush up upon her, pushing dirt and grit into her eyes as the wind whirled around her.

"Anna!" She heard, but her heels pressed into her eyes, trying to rub the grit out, a roaring sound that was almost deafening. Anna stopped, her stomach sinking as she went utterly still, it sounded like a train was bearing down on them. The sound of a tornado.

"Oh my god," she whispered, keeping her watering eyes screwed tightly shut as she hit the ground quickly, dragging herself over the dirt, keeping her body as small as possible as heavier things began to fly through the air. She heard the frantic cries of the horses in the stables and the flapping of dozens of wings as the recruits tried to weather the wind. In her gut, Anna knew it wasn't just a simple storm.

Digging her fingers into the dirt, she felt the grass twisting in-between her fingers as something heavy flew over. Debris spun around her, something heavy striking her hard in the hip. Anna cried out, getting to her knees just to get to safety. Her ears were ringing, popping as the tornado came closer, so loud she could feel the vibrations in her chest.

She screwed her eyes shut, covering her head with her arms as she was pelted with flying objects. Anna felt a solid form wrap around her, strong arms dragging her until they hit a wall, cleaving themselves into the side.

Anna opened her watering eyes and she realized it was Declan. His body covered hers, back to the wind, and his leathered shielded hand keeping her head down, protecting it. She looked around, noticing the training nook, the weighted staffs and prop swords heaved and pitched in their corner as several of the 26th huddled. Their different hued wings flared out like a shell against anything that flew against them. Anna couldn't even hear the wings whisper over the howling of the wind.

Declan grunted, his body jerking against hers as something flew at him. Anna tried to twist to check on him, but his grip was unyielding as he pinned her to the ground. It felt like hours, but it was probably only a couple minutes before the winds began to calm. The sounds of trees being ripped from their roots as the tornado continued to tear its way through the forest, away from the castle.

Declan finally moved, standing up and surveying the damage, holding out a hand and helping Anna to her feet. Her hip twanging as the growing bruise became known. "Sin Eater, were we attacked?" Came a slighter build woman, her wings trembling as they whispered in a panicked hush, eyes roaming the terrain in curiosity and fear. Declan looked around, shaking his head.

"I don't think so," He replied, and Anna noticed the wince he tried to swallow as he turned back towards the herd of seraphs. "I think it was a storm." Anna held her tongue, looking around at the destruction. The castle looked unharmed, save the door to the Golden Keep's lower levels was ripped off its heavy metal hinges. Broken branches littered the ground, and the horses were stamping nervously in their stables.The clouds were shifting as Anna watched the tornado break apart when it hit the shores of what looked like an ocean glinting far across the mountains.

"Everyone clean up, you and you," Declan pointed to the two closest seraphs, "Take to the skies, see if anyone needs assistance nearby, and report back on the southern village." He turned to Anna, looking her up and down, his eyes noticing how she was favoring her left leg, and flickered up to her in question.

"Just a bruise. I'm fine." She assured. Declan paused and opened his mouth as if to say something but nodded instead. "I have to talk to the Queen, go back inside." Anna nodded, his voice leaving no room for arguments. As she walked towards the castle door currently held on by a singular hinge, a crunch stopped her in her tracks. Anna moved her booted toe to the side.

When she saw the colorful packaging, she covered it again quickly. Anna looked around to see no one, not even Declan paying attention to her as they cleared the arena and checked on the livestock. Quick as Anna could, she grabbed the packaging, stuffing it inside her shirt, and crossed her arms before ducking inside; she bypassed guards running down the stairs, panicked and confused as their wings all but buzzed with excitement.

Anna was back in her room, the latch secure against the wood frame before she pulled the packaging from her fist, her heart racing wildly in her chest as she pressed it to the wood vanity.

She stared at it for the longest time before she swore violently, clenching the colorful chip bag before she paced her room. It was getting worse. Things were getting blown here. Was the tornado from Tulsa? Was it a bad one?

Fuck.

Fuck.

Anna stopped pacing and grabbed the wrapper, smoothing it and folding it into the tiniest piece possible. She shoved it into her boot, the latch to her door screeching as she opened and then slammed her door, no longer worrying about the possibility of being watched.

She had questions that needed answers *now*. Following her path from the day before, she passed the greenhouse without pause, all but running to the massive library door. Anna breathed a sigh of relief as Sorcha sat at the table, her back to her as she shut the door firmly behind them. There was no lock, but it was heavy enough to make noise if someone entered.

"Some storm, wasn't it?" Sorcha pipped up, still not turning to face Anna as she jogged towards the woman, her hip twinging. Anna raced around the table, almost knocking over the adjoining chair as she sat down. She pulled out the wrapper from her boot and slamming it on the table.

"Sorcha, I'm running out of time," she whispered desperately, "Please tell me what is happening." The old woman slowly took her glasses off her nose, cleaning them with her robe before setting them back upon her face. Her wrinkled hands took the package from the table and scrutinized it carefully.

"Hmm. Interesting." Anna stared at her, eyes wide, "How is this interesting, Sorcha?" She pleaded, "Please, something is happening, and it's not just happening to me, but everywhere around me. And now," she pointed to Sorcha's orange piece of litter. "It's happening here."

The woman sighed and set it down, looking at Anna in earnest this time, no hint of amusement or joking left in her eyes. "Anna, my dear," she said carefully, pausing to find the right words. "The universe doesn't know what to do with you, my girl." She broke off, taking a steadying sip from a goblet near her. "When you died, your soul came here, ready for its new dawn. New life. But I believe you were brought back by intervention, much to the Universe's surprise. So here you are," she placed two stones on the table, side by side. Sorcha took a piece of string, lying abandoned on the table, and put it over the two stones. "You are straddling both worlds."

Anna sat back with a thud against the back of the chair, as she bit nervously on the nail there, a habit she kicked when she was in her teens but had resurfaced after her accident. "Is this my fault? The weather? People are getting hurt, Sorcha." She found her eyes starting to fill with tears, but she swallowed them back. There was no time for anxiety attacks. Sorcha shushed her, leaning forward again,

"You did not start this, even the Goddess can get confused, so many souls. With so many universes and timelines, it is bound to happen." Something raced through Anna, settling in her stomach uncomfortably.

"Sorcha, how do you know this? How do you not even blink at what I've told you? Or shown you?" She pointed to the wrapper in a crumbled mess for an example.

The older woman sighed, "As I said, I've been around for a while, my dear. I've seen many things, done many things. I grew up in this castle. My mother told me stories," she smiled, her eyes unfocused momentarily at the memory that word produced. "Ancient whispers and children's stories. About a woman who straddled the fates line and had to choose where her heart lay." Sorcha shook her head, her untamed grey hair coming more untangled from her bun.

"But no, it's not your fault, Anna something has caused this much bigger fracture. Something stronger than your death, I'm afraid."

Anna's slumped, "In the stories," She made a motion with her hand, "The ones your mother told you. The woman made a choice? And it stopped?"

Sorcha nodded, smiling tightly. "A choice must be made, I'm afraid, one cannot straddle two worlds for too long. Your soul, it gets tired."

Anna felt that tiredness now, the tightness in her chest that threatened to spill out, the bone-deep exhaustion from her mind at war with itself. "How do I choose? None of this makes sense." Sorcha chuckled, shaking her head, before patting Anna's hand and becoming somber once again. "The woman, in the story that is, aided the universe but cut her life short so that her soul may continue on its natural path, towards the desired place." Anna froze at the woman's words, drawing back in horror.

"She died?"

Sorcha's gaze was mournful, "Death of the physical body. Your soul, unlike others who die, already has a tether attached to it, so it will," the old woman clapped her hands together, the sound reverberating through the large room,

"Snap back to its place. On the rare occasions this does happen, it can drive the poor person mad when they do not understand what's happening. After their natural demise, it is settled, and their soul's path continues normally."

"After the first few times," Anna swallowed, unsure if she wanted to know the answer, "I had been shifting only to this one pond, right outside the castle."

"Yes, water is a natural magic in itself. The pond outside the Silent Forest is on a very powerful lay line." The old woman replied and motioned for her to continue. Anna lowered her voice as if they weren't the only two in the room. She leaned forward on her elbows, the pitted wood of the table digging into her skin.

"I keep shifting to Decl-the Sin Eater. It's like I am drawn to him. Them, I mean, his group." Sorcha's mouth thinned as her weathered hands reached a few inches towards the chain around Anna's wrist, touching it.

"You know they place these around prisoners," Sorcha replied softly, "It is powerful magic. Binding the prisoner and the guard, so they could never really get far, the two twin metals called to its companion piece. If I had any guess, when he placed this one on you, it acted as a beacon. Pulling you towards him when you shifted." Letting that settle, she twirled the simple chain around her wrist.

"Will the storms stop?"

Sorcha opened her mouth and cocked her head to one side as if listening to something only she could hear. "Oh, I believe that's enough for today. But you can come back tomorrow."

"But-"

"Tomorrow," The old woman commanded firmly but patted her hand. "You should ask your Sin Eater for answers. He knows more than he lets on."

"He's not *my* Sin Eater." She whispered as she turned to leave, crumbled chip wrapper prickling the inside of her foot as she shoved it far into her boot.

"Hmph." Was all she heard as she shut the library door behind her.

154

19

～

Dinner was another grand affair. Ria had brought up a yellow gown. It was soft and whimsical, cut low and cinched at the waist. Anna felt a little ridiculous putting it on but another part of her felt as if she was living a childhood fantasy. Ria pushed a few hair pins into her freshly brushed hair, the pearled pieces securing her thick hair in a stylish way. Anna looked at herself in the large mirror, smoothing the soft bodice.

It wasn't long until there was a knock at the door and upon opening it, she saw Brynn. She wearing a simple but dazzling black dress, high in the neck and lace wrapped around her arms now to her fingers.

"You look beautiful, Brynn," Anna whispered, smiling at the woman. Brynn dipped in thanks. "I have to ask, what's the occasion for this? I mean, this is so elegant." Anna gestured to the gown she was wearing, and was grateful to see the other woman before she went downstairs, afraid she was too overdressed.

Brynn looked somber, her eyes slightly red as if she had been crying.

"It's the anniversary of her daughter's death day. She's holding a day of remembrance." Anna folded her hands, picking at her cuticle. "I'm sorry, I didn't know." Brynn shrugged, taking her arm and leading her out of the bedroom and into the lightened hallway.

"How could you? It's a light affair, just don't bring it up. I think this is how she grieves." Nodding, Anna noticed the purple ribbons hung from the seraphs staff as they passed, "Was she very young?" Asked Anna, "When she died, I mean?"

Brynn smiled sadly in memory, "It depends on how you track age. Royal bloodlines age very slowly, giving them time to train to become good leaders. She was around 50, but she looked about your age." Before Anna could ask more questions, they found themselves at the entrance to the dining hall, the grand table was decorated with peonies of all colors and varieties, lush greenery tucked between the stems and sending a luscious sent throughout the room, mixing with the smells of food and wine.

"Ah, welcome! My lovely guest, come and sit next to me." The Queen was dressed in dark purple velvet, dainty flowers laced through her long raven hair that spun around her head in delicate braids, tucking the flowers between the strands in the crown.

"That color of yellow suits you." Anna dipped her head, not knowing if curtsying was appropriate here, but since no one else did, she assumed she was safe. "The flowers are beautiful, your majesty," Anna remarked, sinking into the padded chair, her dress fanning around and covering her slippered feet.

The food in front of her was delicious, and was similar to a roast with a carrot glaze and root vegetables. She hoped it tasted just as good as it smelled. The morning's excitement made her forget anything about lunch. She had poured over her scribblings after she left Sorcha's, making sure she remembered everything the old woman had told her.

The Queen smiled at the compliment, looking longingly at the colorful peonies, touching one absentmindedly in her hair, "Yes, they were the princess's favorite." Anna opened her mouth to speak, but before she could, the doors to the hall opened with a whine. Aramus and Declan entered, and Anna felt herself melt into the chair.

He looked uncomfortable in the tailored finery, dark green cape draped over his left shoulder. Aside from that deep green and poppy on his lapel, he wore all black. From his tunic, his breeches and even his leather gloves.

Anna tried not to stare. She felt like all her breath had been struck from her. She shook her head minutely as he sat down. It had been a stressful few weeks, and she knew that people can form attractions to people in hard times. That's all this was.

Aramus had entered a beat later, wearing a white gown with a small crown of peonies set into their short white hair, their wings gracefully dusting the ground behind them. A few other people were sat at the table across from them. Judging from their airs and attire, she could only assume they were people of importance, and though she didn't quite understand how their political system worked, she could imagine they were somehow connected to the Queen and her reign.

The long table was already overflowing with conversation and people, the most notable was the tall, sharp chinned Seraph, who Aramus was in deep, reverent conversation with. Atop the seraph's black hair sat a golden headpiece affix across his forehead and wings a dazzling grey that shimmered in the candle light. If Anna had seen him in a painting, she would think it was a halo.

A leaner older man, with a greying beard and sharp eyes sat across from the Queen. He smelled like the sea and had a deep, rich laugh.

The conversation was light and easy, though Anna couldn't shake the feeling of melancholy, which made sense given the occasion. The loss of a child is hard for anyone, and though she never had children, she had seen her friends go through losses. She sat and ate respectfully, only speaking when addressed, sipping lightly on the wine.

"That storm we had was quite a spectacle!" Said the bearded man. She noticed his clothing seemed lighter than the heavier materials everyone else wore. The Queen only nodded slightly, as if the tornado was simply a passing cloud and not something that tore through her castle and the nearby towns.

"Any issues in the village?" Asked a fair-haired woman, sipping long on the goblet of deep red wine, her tone light and conversational. The woman was tall and regal, her entire presence screamed that she was someone of consequence.

"You can ask my Sin Eater. He coordinated the search from the sky after our slight damages in the courtyard." The Queen redirected, pointing her knife lazily at Declan, who ignored his plate of food completely, only sipping on the dark colored wine.

The blond woman looked over at Declan, cutting into her meat without actually looking at him, "A few casualties and a few prisoners tried to escape as the cells were torn apart. I had the seraphs lock them in the dungeon of the castle." The woman shook her head at the news, "Such ghastly business."

"You, sir," the grey-bearded man said, jutting his chin at Declan, who only stared at him dangerously. "I am interested in your role. I know it's only been barely a year from the start of your position. Can you indulge me as your role to the Crown?" Declan shoved back his plate, leaning forwards on his elbows, his fists clenched in the soft leather gloves. Anna watched, her fork poised above her plate, waiting on his answer, and so was the other nobles.

"King Bellam asked you a question." The Queen commanded icily. Anna froze at the reprimand, like one scolding an errant child, not a seasoned warrior. She didn't miss the slight swirling smoke that leaked from Declan's gloves, wrapping around his elbows as his jaw clenched.

"Of course," he bit out, his jaw working so hard she was surprised she didn't hear the snapping of teeth. "I serve the Crown by assisting in the execution and removal of guilty parties. Their souls will serve the Queen in her armies for their crimes if the need arises." The blond woman lowered her wine glass to glance at the Monarch, "Such an army you must have amassed." Octavia only smiled, feline and predatory.

"It's more of a safeguard. After the murder of my daughter, I felt it was my duty to make sure my Kingdom was safe. On all fronts." No one spoke for a while, Aramus began to chat with the general of Bellam's army, military talk Anna didn't quite follow. The rest was polite conversation, clinking of glasses and silverware. Towards the end, the Queen stood, and Anna scrambled to stand with the rest of the guests, drink in hand.

"As you know, today is the day my dear Nona left this world. We celebrate her life today. For we will be reunited in the afterlife if Danu allows." Everyone raised their glasses, and a few 'here, here's' rang from around the table. Anna glanced at Declan, who presented the glass and drained it completely, setting it down hard on the table. He remained standing as everyone else sat again.

"Your Majesty, I have matters to attend to in the lower levels," he bowed, and at his Monarch's wave of her hand, he all but stalked out of the dining hall. Anna mingled a few moments longer, but as soon as the Queen dismissed them all, she caught up with Brynn who was walking down the aisle with Aramus, arm in arm.

"Brynn!" She called, jogging to catch up with the pair, who immediately stalled so she could walk with them. "Sorry, I think I had too much to drink tonight." She said, the lie falling off her tongue as she giggled, keeping up the charade.

Aramus smiled, their golden eyes twinkling, "The wine is a specialty here, it is hard not to overindulge." They walked silently for a moment, and Anna cautiously asked, "Did the Queen have any more children? I'm not sure how this monarchy works."

Brynn glanced at her, "No, Monarch's only has one offspring in their time. Nona was next in line for the throne." Anna nodded like she understood, silently storing away that information to write down in her notebook. "So the King and she only had one? What happens for the next in line?" Brynn raised a brow at her question, "Monarchs here are chosen by the Goddess, only one rule. Most do not marry. For obvious reasons, they have their consorts."

Brynn looked down the darkened halls around her before lowering her voice, "We have three neighboring kingdoms, Anna, up north, a larger series of Islands with their own sovereigns. Danann is considered blessed by the Goddess Danu for many reasons, but most of all, for the power given to their rulers. It is dangerous to them to have someone who could strip that from them."

Anna raised her eyebrows, about to ask another question before remembering that she was supposed to be tipsy. She feigned a slight trip and was dropped off at her door, waving at them from the safety of her room before locking the door. She immediately freed herself from the beautiful, yet restrictive dress.

It had to have been well over an hour later before she rose from her bed. Sleep evaded her as she poured over her scribbles, anxious for the time to come when she would meet with Sorcha again. King Bellam, from what she gathered, came from an Isle with a more tropical climate. It was smaller and exported fruit and coffee to the nearby regions.

Lady Uma was in charge of a Port. Most of what they spoke of was trade agreements and privateers. She weighed the pros and cons of slipping out into the night-bathed halls and going through the books. If Anna was going to sneak into the library it would be tonight. The guards more at ease with the wine-soaked party that even the servants and sentries indulged in.

Anna wrapped a dark green robe around her, the high neck and long sleeves giving her the warmth she needed to go out into the cool halls. She pulled the soft slippers on her feet, hoping that it would help hide her footfalls. With her heart pounding, Anna crept out of her warm room and into the bitter, dark halls of the castle of the Golden Keep. She swore that the halls grew longer as she walked, barely daring to breathe as she passed corner after corner, door after closed door.

The greenhouse area was warm, the temperature difference hitting her quickly as she jogged over the small bridge into the open library. Anna placed both hands on the door, quietly begging it to shut silently and willing the old hinges not to scream as soon as they were closed. She waited silently as the door swung shut, her heart hammering in her chest for a crash of guards or something equally alarming. But nothing came, just silence and the thudding of her pulse in her ears.

It was dark outside. Night had crept over the kingdom hours ago, but the large moon showed through the grand windows, bathing the bookcases. In a muted light it was enough for her to read the spines of the old books. Anna didn't even know what she was looking for, only that she would know when she found it. Realistically she knew that was a terrible way to ascertain information, but this was all she had, and time was running out.

"The Hierarchy of the Monarchy" stood out to her as she slipped the book from the shelf, thanking Danu, the stars, or whatever else was in the heavens that it was nowhere near as large a book as some of the others pushed between the shelves.

Anna placed the book under her arm and was about to leave when she saw another, smaller text wedged between two large ones, dull gold letters glinting in the pale moonlight. She grabbed it, not bothering to look at the title, just set it on top of her hefty tome.

Anna could make it.

She was going to make it.

Tiptoeing down the dark halls, she passed each closed room, some with a light still spilling underneath the doors, some dark and silent. As she passed one on her right, she heard something that made her pause. A cough. Retching.

Anna's lips formed a tight line, biting her lip as a sharp curse word followed. Declan. She shook her head and moved to finish the path to her room when she heard something hard hit the ground. Now it was Anna's turn to swear, looking around to find a plush, decorative armchair around the corner. They were placed strategically around the castle for some reason, but for tonight that reason was for hiding books. So she took the dusty cushion and placed the tomes carefully underneath before putting them back atop them.

Anna stood, wincing at the pains in her knees from the last training session. She took a deep breath and pushed at the door where she heard the noise. To her surprise, the door opened easily, and no lock or chain forbade her entrance.

Anna gasped, closing behind her as she saw his crumbled form next to the bed, shirt thrown off into a puddle in the corner. Declan's bare, black hands and arms were wrapped over his head as if shielding himself from some unknown assailant.

"Declan," she breathed, barely over a whisper, as she dropped to her knees beside him. He began shaking his head, putting his hand out. Pushing her away without touching her.

"Please, I just want to help," she reached out to take his hand, but before her fingers even brushed his, Declan unraveled, pressing himself back to the bed. His eyes were wild and face pale and Anna drew back in surprise. Declan had become a cornered animal, teeth bared, and fists clenched.

"Do. Not. Touch. Me." He ground out between gritted teeth before his whole face contoured in a wince. Declan stumbled to the corner where the water pail sat and emptied the entire contents of his stomach into it.

Anna grabbed a towel from the bathroom, sidestepping him as she went, giving him a wide berth. No one wants people to see them when they are sick. She knew that just from her college days alone. Though this seemed more severe than simple overindulgence. As soon as her steps neared him, his hands blocked her access.

"I won't touch you," she said softly, keeping her voice barely above a whisper. She showed the rag that she dampened into Declan's field of vision. "But for the love of god, let me help you." He stood against the corner wall, one hand bracing him up while the other fell limply, allowing her to kneel next to him.

Anna offered the rag again, closer but far enough away that he didn't feel trapped.

Declan shook his head but took the damp cloth, carefully avoiding touching her with his hands. She had the chance to see them, something he kept so carefully hidden. It felt wrong to stare, the inky flesh in stark contrast with his sun-weathered skin, as if they were singed, rolling up his forearm.

Crawling, devouring.

"Go ahead," came his rough voice, even deeper than usual after retching. "Ask me." Anna looked away, embarrassed, anxiously worrying about her nails.

"Ask you what?" She whispered, pressing the cold rag to his forehead. He chuckled without humor, shaking his already bowed head and lifting his hand around the rag.

"Ask me about them." Anna stood her ground, if he wanted to play that, she would too. What did she have left to lose?

"What happened?" She finally asked.

Declan laughed lowly, taking the damp rag from her and wiping the back of his neck and mouth. He spat into the pail before stumbling a few paces and lowering himself to the floor, not quite making it to the bed.

Anna sat on the high-piled rug, crossing her legs far enough from him that he didn't feel she was a threat.

Part of her wondered why she was here when her week was running out, and she had books that could help her find out how to stop this from happening again. But Sorcha's words rang in her head, *"She made a choice."*

Anna couldn't help this, deep down, she did not know why this universe or Goddess kept bringing her to him. Or to the Queen. Either way, she had to know. And she waited as Declan took a glass from the bedside table, reaching up and swiping it, drinking a gulp with a wince. When he didn't answer her still, she shifted, allowing herself to look at the marks in the flickering firelight.

"You've seen what I do," he whispered, face emotionless as he looked at the black hands. Anna blinked, shaking her head, "Declan, I've seen you kill people. That's what I've seen."

Declan stared back at her, "I don't just kill them, Anna," he whispered gruffly, "I take them, their souls that were bound for hell or wherever assholes actually go. The worst of the worst. And we use their souls to power and stock an army." Anna listened, turning over what he was saying in her before pointing behind her, "Declan, she has an army, it trains near us daily and guards the halls."

Declan chuckled, shaking his head, "Those seraphs? They have morals. They're...enlightened. Demons, however," he looked at his hands for a second more before dropping them over his knees. "They are another thing." Her heart was racing, this time in terror. Until this moment, she hadn't known how entirely over her head she was. How absolutely fucked.

"So why are you like this? Were you born this way?" Her eyes were wide and her skin pale, but she needed these answers.

"I'm cursed, Anna." His eyes hardened, and his jaw worked as he swallowed what looked like another opportunity to be sick. "This position I now have is more punishment than occupation." He paused, his eyes hollow. "I can see, feel, and relive everything these people have done." He gestured to the corner where the bucket sat, the evidence. Anna's hands balled into a fist, and she swallowed hard, ears pounding.

"So why you?"

Declan leaned back, pinching his nose at the bridge and sighing, "That's a story for another time." It took a moment of her sitting there before she realized he had passed out, hand still over his eyes. His body was lax, and his breathing came easier.

"When he takes souls in, it drains him very quickly." Anna was to her feet instantly, nearly tripping over herself as she turned to see Aramus in the doorway.

"How did you-"

Aramus shrugged, "Seraphs are very good at being quiet when we need to be." Anna slowed her breathing to look at the unconscious Sin Eater.

"Aramus," Anna whispered, not aware if she wanted to know or why she felt she needed to know. Aramus hummed in acknowledgment, still standing in the doorway, wings tucked tightly in. "What did he do to get cursed?"

The seraph's wings fluttered with whispers and excitement, and Aramus shushed them quietly as they spoke to her all at once. "Declan was a royal guard, the one assigned to Princess Nona the day she passed."

They gestured to the peony buds still woven through their hair, "As you can imagine, he failed in that duty."

"So, the Queen?" Aramus just nodded. Anna looked again at the sleeping man and then back to the seraph, "I guess I'll just go back to my room, he seems settled now."

Aramus nodded in agreement, holding their arm to her, "Allow me to escort you." Pasting a smile on her face and hoping they couldn't hear how her breathing hitched, she took their arm and quietly shut the door to Declan's room. She chanced a look at the chair behind her before staring ahead, counting the entries as they walked.

One door.

Two doors.

Three.

The pair turned a corner, Anna could feel Aramus's wings brushing her shoulders as if they also reminded her they were there.

Four.

Five.

And her door was six. She smiled at the seraph, thanking them for the escort. Pushing open the heavy door, she was met with the roar of the fireplace.

She paused as Aramus held out something, moving it towards her, their glinting gold eyes not leaving hers. "Be careful in the castle after hours," They whispered, their wings rustling though no wind could be found in the dark corridor. "Strange things happen on the lower levels."

Anna found her books placed gently in her hands, and before she could even stammer out an excuse, the seraph turned and disappeared around a corner. With trembling hands, Anna slammed the door shut, locking the bolt. Though she knew realistically that small piece of metal would be like snapping a toothpick to the guards.

It was a facade of safety. Anna was beginning to think this whole place was as well.

20

~

Anna skipped training that day to pour over the books she stole from the library the night before. Brynn hadn't been lying about the one heir-born thing. From what she gathered there was always a monarch and one heir in all Royal Bloodline archives. The book ended with the 6th Age, showing the branches for Octavia and Nona. The units split again, but all blank spaces were awaiting the next heir. Anna closed the heavy tome, dust flying from its ancient pages, and tucked it next to her backpack.

Anna popped two pain relievers for the body aches her training had given her over the past six days. Her breakfast tray was largely untouched, her stomach in knots from last night. Aramus hadn't appeared or said anything more about the books, or the fact she was in Declan's room last night. She wasn't sure what was worse, them not saying anything or waiting for them to say something.

Tomorrow would be her last day. She planned on taking the sleeping pill tonight and return home, possibly forever. Depending on how this last meeting with Sorcha goes. Anna waited impatiently for Ria to bring in the lunch tray, pretending to be reading one of the novels on the bookshelf in her room when she entered. She thanked her for the food and waited until she knew she would be down the hall. Everyone should be occupied with their lunchtime meals, so she thought she would be ready to leave this time.

Taking a deep breath, Anna passed the halls and headed down to the library, all but barging through the doors into Sorcha's domain. The old woman was arranging a few texts when she saw the large one Anna laid on the table.

"I knew I was missing one," she tutted, walking over and placing the book exactly where it was supposed to go on the shelf.

"Sorcha," Anna began, a bit breathless from her near sprint to the library, anxiety filling her to the brim. "Sorcha, this is my last day here."

The old woman smiled knowingly, "Of course, dear, you couldn't stay forever," she paused, fixing her glasses. "Unless you wanted to, of course."

Anna crossed her arms tightly over her chest, "That's the thing, I need to know everything you can tell me," she whispered, taking the old woman by the hands and sitting them at the table, "Please, you're the only one who can help me right now."

Sorcha sighed heavily, "What do you need to know, Anna?" She grinned and opened her book full of notes, hand-drawn maps around the castle, and stock from what she brought in her backpack.

"Why does it happen when I sleep?" Anna tapped the page nervously, awaiting the answer plaguing her. Sorcha squinted at her, "Does it happen when you sleep?" Anna nodded, "I mean, I dream of it. I don't come over."

Sorcha grinned slightly, "If you really think about it, isn't sleep the time when we are most vulnerable? Open? Perhaps even to the Goddess herself."

So Anna sighed, scribbling something in her notepad before looking up again, "Why is everything happening with the weather? Why am I finding Leviathan in my world and junk food wrappers in yours?" She scooted closer, pointing to the windows just as the rain began to come down outside, pelting the glass ceiling of the library.

"Why did you get your first tornado while I was here?" When she asked this, Sorcha took her glasses off and rubbed the bridge of her nose like she was suddenly very tired. Anna waited for the woman to speak, as patiently as she could, taking a deep breath while listening to the sounds of the rain on the glass.

"When the Queen lost her daughter, she knew she had to find her. Her monarchy and the royal line depended on it. If she did not produce her heir before she passed, the kingdom would fall to another family, who sat with her at dinner. Or even perhaps to an invader." Anna's mind immediately conjured up the man with the grey beard. "So she decided to look elsewhere for her dead heir, including..."

A loud bang echoed through the room, and though the old woman did not turn, Anna stood in a panic, grabbing her notebook and tucking it underneath her arm.

"That will be enough, Sorcha," Came the booming, silky voice of Queen Octavia. "I thought we had an agreement." Then, Sorcha stood unsteadily to her feet, glancing up at the menacing monarch with a smile, "I think we both know who started this, Octavia." The Queen gave a curt nod, as one of the seraph guards took Sorcha by the arm and all but dragged the old woman away.

Anna couldn't believe what was happening, her voice catching in her throat as Sorcha only smiled at her as she was drug out the large library doors.

"Majesty, Sorcha didn't do anything wrong!" Anna exclaimed finally, running from around the table to stand in front of the Queen, only to be held back by two guards who came quickly from behind the Queen.

"I am afraid I don't agree." Octavia sneered, looking down her nose at the smaller woman. It was the first time Anna thought of the woman was frightening. Imposing? Always, but there was something new that crackled like raw energy around the monarch, and it made Anna's mouth go dry. The Queen took a step closer, taking her chin in her grip, her long silver nails scraping Anna's skin as she did.

"Now, you aren't my daughter. How upsetting."

Anna looked at the woman, confused, "How could I be your daughter? Nona died?" She didn't even have time to react to the slap across the face. The pain erupted only after she had realized what had happened, blood dripping from the Queen's nails.

"She is but lost, and I will find her," she roared, shaking her hand from the impact, spraying droplets of Anna's blood on the tile floor. "I will restore my regency as soon as I find her soul's alter!"

Sagging in the guard's vice-like grip, Anna shook her head, "Octavia, I didn't know you thought-" The Queen scoffed, "You think you were the first? No, you are but many in a line of women who died on the 4th day of the 4th month." Before she could say anything else, the Queen turned promptly, stalking out of the room and spouting orders at the seraphs as she did so, "Take her to lower levels."

She knew. This whole time the Queen knew everything. Anna's legs felt weak as the soldiers walked her down the halls, turning right instead of going over the bridge to the greenhouse. Anna had never made it this far. Her stomach churned as she tried to count the doors, but they were going too fast, wings whispering quickly as their grips never let up, even as she stumbled down the stairs.

"Please, please let me go. I won't say anything," Anna stammered to no avail, the seraph's faces emotionless under their helmets, their eyes fixed forward. The stairs spiraled down.

Down.

Down. The lights of windows ceased after their third turn, and the smell of wet stagnation, mildew, and ice-cold air greeted her as they made their way down the last turn of tight, dizzying spiraled stairs. The steps underneath her feet grew slimy, and she fought to keep her balance as she descended.

She was so fucked.

They ended up in a dark tunnel, singular candles posted to the walls barely allowed enough light to illuminate the hallway. She couldn't help the whimper that passed her lips as she saw rows and rows of cells greeting her.

"Please, please, no," she begged, turning once again to the sentries, but their bruising grips only got tighter as she struggled. One opened a metal door and pushed her inside, Anna immediately threw herself at the metal bars. Its not as if she could stand against two armed seraphs, but she would not make this easy.

"Open this door, you fucks!" She screamed, rattling the iron bars as they began to walk away. "You can't keep me here you feathery pricks!"

A door opened and locked behind them. And there was silence.

A scream ripped from Anna's throat as she repeatedly pounded the metal bars before collapsing against the stone wall, wrapping her arms around herself. Her light morning dress did nothing for the damp chill of the dungeon.

Taking sputtering deep breaths, Anna surveyed her surroundings. The cell was no more than a 10x10 room, barred on all sides except the damp, leaking stone wall at the end, the bars meeting and delving deep into the stone ceiling and floor. The old bucket in a corner made her gag as she realized its purpose. A pile of dirty blankets lay in the corner, but they reeked of mildew and sick.

It wasn't until Anna's eyes adjusted to the dim lighting of the flickering candles that she could see into the next cell. She didn't have time to reach the bucket as she retched in horror at what she saw. There was nothing but a pile of bones, evidence of a long-dead prisoner. But what the prisoner was wearing made her scream until she was sick, her stomach emptying itself of its meager breakfast this morning.

The skeleton, still curled in the corner of the cell, wore jeans.

***

Time was nonexistent in her cell. There were no windows or cracks in the heavy stone. It was impossible to know if she had been curled in the middle of her cell, arms wrapped around her legs for minutes or hours. Anna couldn't keep herself from shivering. Her thin dress was tented over her legs, and she rested her tear-stained face on her knees. Anna knew she was probably in shock. Everything had happened so fast.

Anna was about to go home. Anna's eyes flooded with tears as she sucked in a breath, thinking of home, her father, Ian and Matt, Jess. Katie. They would never know what happened to her. They'd live their entire lives without her and never have any peace. And it was all her fault. That hurt the most, not that she would probably die in this dark, cold place but she followed the siren's call of it. She played dress up, ate their food, and laughed with them.

Her fingernails dug crescent shapes into her palm as she cried, sobs wrenching deep in her gut. It took a while, but her butt began to grow numb from sitting on the cold floor. She refused to go near the reeking blankets, so she scooted far away from the corpse in the other cell and leaned against the adjacent bars.

Her eyes watched the candle flame as they flickered, the tapers never moving in size despite being lit for as long as she had been down here. Anna finally closed her burning eyes, taking a deep breath. Reciting the exercises her therapist taught her, whose appointments seemed so long ago.

Something she could see. A candle.

Something she could hear. Dripping water.

Something she could smell. Anna skipped that one.

Something you can taste. The blood from where Anna bit her lip from throwing up.

Something you can feel. The iron bars. Anna kept her eyes closed and started over.

Something she could see. Something she could hear.

***

The opening of the large door that she entered woke her from her uneasy slumber. Her head pounded from leaning against the bars for so long, and the lack of food was starting to get to her. Hearing the rattling of the keys locking the door again, Anna stood on shaky feet and nearly collapsed when she saw Aramus observing her.

"Aramus," she whispered, running to the door's bars. Before she knew it, tears were streaming down her face again. "Aramus, please help me. I have to get home."

The seraph looked around before coming closer, their wings unfurling to reveal a large cup of water and a cloth napkin with bread, cheese, and a slice of ham. Anna's mouth was dry and tasted like sick. Despite any concerns about poison, she drank it through the bars and greedily before handing them back the empty glass they stored in their pocket. The food was next, and Anna grasped Aramus's hand as they gave it to her.

"Aramus," she whispered, blinking back another flood of tears that would do her no good. "Aramus, I didn't do anything wrong. I shouldn't be here."

"There have been others," they whispered, their gaze dropping to the cell beside her. "We weren't aware at first. That she had been stealing the others." Anna nodded, not caring if they were lying or not.

"Please, I need to get home." Aramus looked confused, "I don't know everything, Anna; you must help me. I have only just begun to unravel this heresy." Anna nodded, and she told them. Everything. About the night she died and the dreams, she had had since that day. That she thought she had been going crazy this entire time. The seraph seemed to be piecing it all together. She didn't realize today was April 4th, the exact day of her accident.

Anna squeezed the seraph's dark hand, "I don't belong here." Aramus looked at her intensely. "Are you so sure?" Anna paused, her hand still clutching theirs. For a moment she realized didn't know how to answer that.

"Please, my backpack, it's in the bottom drawer of my dresser. If you can bring it to me, I can leave." The seraph looked torn, disobedience didn't come naturally to the seraph's kind. Aramus had their time for disobedience and growing as a human soul. Their gold eyes seemed to glow brighter momentarily, and they nodded, squeezing her hand in return.

"Give me time. Be patient. I will return." Anna just nodded, bringing their knuckles to her lips in gratitude. She couldn't help the tears that fell when that door shut and locked again, signaling their exit. Anna collapsed on the cell floor, dirt and grime smearing her skin, the cold biting through her.

She dug into the food regardless, afraid if the guards returned anytime soon, they would wonder where she got it. Her anxious stomach rolled as Anna introduced food to the gnawing pit, but she knew she needed her strength, and she had no idea how long

Aramus would take. She tried not to dampen the flicker of hope that was building in her chest, even though she trusted the seraph. She didn't even know why. In this entire place, it seemed the world was just as full of untrusting people, dangerous criminals, and cruel politicians in the same way her world was.

Minutes turned to hours, the food finally settling in her stomach, and the trembling from lack of nutrition ceased after a bit. She sat there, knees pulled up around her arms holding them tight while her head rested on the rusted bars. After a while, she didn't even notice the smell. Anna dozed in and out, her cold and aching body constantly waking her, her hips screaming at her crouched position and her neck tight from her leaning.

The sound of a key and the door scraping pushed against the dirty stone floor as it opened.

Anna stood, pressing down the pain and aching deep within her as she did so, her fists balling as she took a steadying breath for whoever came through that door. A seraph guard entered, and Anna's spirits fell as she attempted to hold back the barrage of tears that were flooding her.

Anna jumped as the guard crumbled to the floor before he made it past her, wings screeching and going silent as the sentry fell in a heap, his helmet thudding on the floor. Running towards the door of the cell, she looked to see Declan tossing the stone he had used to disarm the sentry.

"Declan!" Anna cried, pressing her face to the bars, her fists gripping the them until her knuckles were white with urgency. The Sin Eater whipped his head in her direction, running towards her, the backpack slung over his shoulder. Tears streaked down her face as she realized she would be going home. She wouldn't die here. Her cell door opened with a flick of a key. Anna flew through the opening quickly, breathing in as the suffocating blackness of the cell was behind her.

"Aramus said you needed this," Declan said, looking behind him, his face lined in anxiety. Anna's heart raced as she dug through the bag, breathing a sigh of relief as she found the pills. Looking back at the blackness of her cell, her stomach was in knots as she realized what she had to do. Pressing a tablet underneath her tongue, she returned to the cell door.

"Lock me back in."

Declan looked as if she had gone mad, "Do you know what I had to do to get here?"

Anna nodded, "Yes, but I can go now, if you put me back, I can leave without them thinking you or Aramus had anything to do with it." The Sin Eater looked at her dubiously, glancing between her and the dark cell.

"Are you sure?" He asked and Anna just nodded, her stomach in knots, and this time she walked back into the cell of her own accord, shutting the door behind her as Declan locked it. They lingered there for a moment, not saying anything, Declan opening his mouth and then closing it before softly saying, "I didn't know."

Anna took a deep breath, the tang of the pill settling underneath her tongue. "Declan-"

"No goodbyes." He interrupted, his gloved hand gripping the bars before he slowly turned the key, locking her back in. Smiling softly, Anna just nodded, sitting down, backpack behind her as she was already starting to feel the effects of the drug.

If she could just keep breathing, pushing away the damp cell and the smell of rot and death that clung to that place like a shroud. She would be home. So close. Anna's head rested heavily on the grate, her breathing slowing as her muscles melted into the bars, the slightly fuzzy feeling buzzing around her brain.

Her breathing slowed. It couldn't have been more than ten minutes before she heard a commotion at the cell doors, her heavy eyes barely opening as a crash sounded, accompanied by the cracking of splintering wood. Anna lifted her head as much as she could, already feeling herself starting to sink as her vision blurred.

She could only see Declan's unconscious form being dragged across the floor. A moan of protest slipped past her lips until she felt herself floating.

And she was gone.

21

She woke in her bed. Anna could sense the soft down comforter and the aroma of her wax melt lingering in the air. It smelled clean, comfortable, and safe. Still, Anna sat straight up and looked around in confusion. Her stomach rolled as she barely made it to the bathroom before she lost the meager meal Aramus had brought her in the dungeon.

Dungeon.

She looked down at her trembling hands, dirt and grime fixed underneath them. Anna lowered herself to the cool bathroom tile, gasping for air as she gripped her head, it took everything in herself not to scream. She had been locked in a dungeon.

What could have happened if Aramus hadn't helped? If Declan- Her stomach was in knots thinking of him, the image of his unconscious body being dragged across the stone floor seared into her brain. She shook her head. Anna couldn't go back, not after what happened.

It was Declan. He would be fine. She wrestled with that, her stomach churning. Outside, thunder rumbled. Anna glanced at the clock to see it was 8 a.m. Almost 7 days had passed since she had shifted into the Otherworld.

With trembling legs, she went for her phone, the object seeming foreign in her hands after so long without it.There were a few missed calls and texts, but it seemed like everyone had gotten her message that Anna was "detoxing" from her phone and relaxing at the urging of her therapist for some self-care. Anna almost laughed as she rolled her shoulders, the tight muscles screaming in protest as she did so.

Suddenly a clap of thunder shook the room. She grasped her bedspread and realized it was still shaking, the walls were trembling and books began to fall from the shelves.

An earthquake.

Anna knew she should get under a door frame or a table but instead she sat, frozen in the middle of the apartment, until the trembling of her building ceased. While not unheard of, it was a big earthquake for Oklahoma, more impressive than the small ones they barely felt daily. These minor quakes were not an uncommon occurrence, but they happened just as she came back. This couldn't be a coincidence. The clouds outside swirled like nothing Anna had ever seen before, not producing a tornado as the ground still tremored with aftershocks. It wasn't stopping. The storms were coming and only going to keep getting more intense.

What had Sorcha said? Anna quickly grabbed her backpack, once brand new now stained with the grime of the cells. Her notebook was still there, untouched. Anna felt something in her release with relief as she flipped through the notes. There were her crude drawings of the castle, and the small hand-drawn map from her explorations in the night.

One soul could not live two lives. Anna sank to the floor. She has to sever the tie, making it impossible to shift anymore. Closing her eyes, let herself sit there, head resting on the soft mattress, inhaling the linen spray that had lingered on her bedspread. And she cried.

***

The shower's heat had reddened her skin, accompanied by the rough scrubbing she gave it. She felt limp as she got out of the damp heat. Anna felt the smoothness of her legs as she dried her skin, using the sugar scrub she hadn't even opened then, and shaved her outgrown leg hairs.

It hadn't bothered her over in Danann, but back with the tighter, rougher fabrics, she seemed to feel everything on her body. The feeling of the seraph's grip on her elbow as he pushed her into the cell, the bite of the cold, dirty stone as she fell into it. If Aramus and Declan hadn't interceded, she would have met the same fate as her companion in the separate cell. Anna breathed deeply, compartmentalizing everything that happened. It was the best way Anna knew to keep from breaking down. She had work this evening, and Anna had to find a way to make it impossible to shift again without returning.

The first thing she did was call her dad, text Ian, and video call Jess. She let them know she was alive and well and had a wonderful self-care week. She felt bad for lying. For one reason she was terrible at it, and everyone knew that, and that these were the people Anna trusted most in the world. She still couldn't trust them with this because, until recently, she couldn't trust herself.

Despite the small chain still dangling around her wrist and the dirt she brushed from under her nails, she wanted to believe it was a dream. Anna couldn't fool herself any longer though. She had felt more alive, more awake than she had in her life there.

After the accident, her mind had been a very dark place. An unfamiliar darkness had lingered over her, and over time, that numbness had become a familiar and safe place that she nestled into when she couldn't process what had happened. During that time, she couldn't trust herself, her mind, her thoughts, or even her sleep. Anna had come so far since then, and she felt as if she had started to grasp normalcy, only for it to get ripped out from under her once again. As Anna glanced into the mirror, rinsing the dirt-covered nail brush, and saw herself. Truly saw herself. It wasn't just her muscles that had grown and been pushed to the limit. But she had. She wasn't sure if she could return to who she was. Part of her missed- No. Anna shook her head, barely glancing at the mirror to not glance anything she didn't want to see.

The humidity hit her as soon as she opened her apartment door. Sticky on her recently scrubbed skin, the smell of fresh rain mixed with the smell of car exhaust. The sounds of honking horns and loud TVs blaring from open windows around her. It was almost over-whelming after being in a place like Danann.

"Excuse me, miss," Anna was ripped from her overstimulated reverie by the mailman, trying with undisguised difficulty to place her new mail in her already overfilled mail slot.

"I'll take that, thank you," she whispered, taking the mail with a thin, embarrassed smile before rushing down the stairs, opening her car door, and throwing the mail in the backseat. Her car smelled unused, and the leftover takeout she had left the day before she shifted filled the car with the scent of over-salted french fries. Despite it all, she drove to work, turning on the radio to drown out the noise in her head. *"More storms on the way for Green Country as we hit a stag-gering 7 days of rainfall and thunderstorms, though not uncommon for this time of year, we are still seeing some very out-of-character storm fronts-"* Anna had never been more thankful to pull up to her job, the drab grey building that took over the out-of-business department store well over a year ago.

"Oh my god, finally!" Jess cried as soon as she entered the build-ing, scanning her badge at the clock-in counter. The golden-haired girl threw her arms around her in excitement. "I have so much to tell you! How was 'vacation'?" She said, using air quotes.

Anna rolled her eyes and fought a smile, "It was fine, I'm much more relaxed now." Lying was getting easier, and she wasn't sure if she liked that. Concentrating on work was difficult, and the seemingly endless phone calls from frustrated people with mundane problems. Anna couldn't find it in herself to care, not that she had before, but she at least pretended for the paycheck. She was on autopilot and doing her best to get through until clock out. The best part of the day. Was this what she really wanted?

It was sprinkling as she walked out to her car, the sun had set long ago, and the nighttime chill cut through her thin cardigan. As she pulled her keys out of her pocket, she felt a hand on her elbow. Panic swept through her as she jumped, keys slipping between her knuckles on instinct.

"Jesus Anna, calm down!" Jess exclaimed, raising her hands in defense. "You're jumpy for being on a self-care week." Anna's heart continued to hammer in her chest as she forced a smile, pretending though even the light pressure had gripped the bruise from the dungeons, making it throb incessantly.

"I want you to come to get dinner with me," Jess continued, her hands folded in a pleading gesture as Anna laughed. "We can go wherever you want!" Anna mulled it over momentarily before nodding in assent, giving in to her friend's pitiful entreaty.

"Fine, but I want steak." Anna replied as Jess immediately grabbed her hand and pulled her towards her car before tossing over her shoulder, "And you're buying my drinks since you scared the shit out of me." Anna smiled and nodded in agreement, her smile feeling fake.

The voicemail icon blinked on her phone. Her therapist called to schedule her next appointment.

Anna ignored it and Jess blasted music and rolled down the windows despite the cold night air and misting rain. Anna's anxiety was still stirring, a crawling beast under her skin as she forced a smile at Jess, who sang along with the radio. She had more energy than Anna would know what to do with, and it did not come from a prescription bottle.

At the restaurant Anna ordered her steak, loaded with mashed potatoes, and drank through three sodas. While her body was firmly here, her mind was elsewhere.

Still in that forest. Still in that dungeon. Still with Declan.

Anna tried to remind herself this was what she was meant for. This was HER world. Her timeline. She couldn't help how her stomach flipped every time the gold chain settled around her wrist.

"Cute bracelet!" Jess cooed, following Anna's gaze to the links. "Where'd you get it?"

Anna's throat caught before she made herself smile tightly, "A friend. A friend gave it to me."

***

Her apartment was cold when she came home later that evening, Anna pulled her cardigan around herself tighter as she turned up the thermostat, feeling slightly ill after such a rich meal and sodas. Not bothering with a shower, she pulled on her pajamas, she felt something catch as she pulled the old shirt over her head. The gold chain was snagged on an errant string of the shirt. Carefully unraveling it, Anna caught herself just staring at it. What it represented. The tether and link to Declan. To Danann.

"Fuck this," she whispered to herself, stomping to the kitchenette and grabbing her wire cutters from the junk drawer. Biting her lip, she stood momentarily, mulling over her actions with the clippers cradling the delicate chain.

Steeling her jaw, she pressed the handles down hard around the metal, squeezing with all her might as she didn't hear anything besides the grind of the two clipper blades as they clasped down on the seemingly indestructible metal.

"Son of a bitch!" she breathed, tossing the cutters down, now with a sizable dent where the chain refused to give. Anna collapsed on her bed, everything hitting her at once. The stress of the dungeon. Work. Faking everything, even around her friends. She was so, very tired.

Anna fell asleep quickly, floating in a sea of blankets until she finally succumbing to the darkness beckoning her.

***

It was dark. So damn dark. Anna was floating, observing only, not shifting. She had a view from the ceiling, no feeling, no smell, just sight and sound. The dungeons where they had kept her came into view as she continued to float. The jangling of chains and low, deep moans broke through the darkness.

Black hands in balled fists, chained together, and a muscular body that was pulled taunt. All but hanging from a hook in the stone ceiling. The Sin Eater spat. Blood and spit hit the red-tinged floor, his booted feet barely standing upright, slipping in his own blood.

"Tell us where the bitch went." Came a demanding voice, a seraph, glittering armor, two red slashes over the breastplate instead of the one. Someone important then. A General? His markings matched Aramus's own.

"I told you," Declan growled as the seraph knit his fingers through his sweat-matted hair, "I don't know where she went." A thud of knuckles on flesh, the sound of splintering bones as Declan doubled over as much as the chains allowed, coughing wetly in the aftermath.

The general got close enough to Declan that their noses nearly touched, "You disgust me," the interrogator spat on the ground in distaste, "You're nothing, your mere presence here is an abomination, and I have no idea why our great Queen allows you to live."

Declan smiled, his teeth tinged red, "Maybe because your brigade can't get the shit done that I can, Angus." A glint of steel flips dangerously in Angus's hand. A swipe.

Anna winced, or at least she cringed inside herself. She couldn't move try as she might. She was glued there, an unwilling voyeur as Declan's blood drip from numerous cuts all over his chest.

Angus growled, bearing his teeth, as he brought the knife to sit near the waistband of Declan's pants, "You know, I could just take the one thing you lower Sidhe seem to have such a fondness for. Watch you bleed out like a stuck pig."

Declan chuckled, his head lolling to the side to rest on one of his raised arms, "Your mother would miss it so much." He grinned, blood marring the white of his teeth. "Do you guys remember your parents? Or have you shitheads been recycled so many times you can't remember anything but your blind loyalty?"

Angus gritted his teeth so hard that Anna swore she heard one snap as the general pointed the blade underneath Declan's chin, their eyes meeting in a battle of wills as the point pierced the skin, blood rolling slowly down the edge.

"General," whispered a younger seraph, no red lines decorated his breastplate. "We are instructed not to kill or dangerously maim the Sin Eater."

"I know my orders!" Barked Angus angrily, the blond seraph flipped the knife with the blade pointing towards the ground, the red still painting the metal.

"Yeah," whispered Declan, he winced as soon as the seraph went around his back. "Heel boy."

"Declan, stop!" She screamed though she knew he couldn't hear her. No sound came out of her, but it was like in any dream when your mouth is open, you're screaming with all your might, but nothing comes from it.

Declan's brows furrowed, and he looked around the room momentarily. His eyes screwed shut, and his teeth grit suddenly, Angus at his back, dragging the knife down his bare back like a paintbrush to an empty canvas.

The seraph sneered, "Let's start with the back now. I'm running out of room everywhere else." And the screaming began.

Anna was screaming. Tears streaming down her face, her feet tangled in her sweat-soaked bedsheets as she stumbled out of bed just before reaching her toilet. She swore she could still smell the copper scent of blood, feel the clammy coldness of that cellar. Splashing water on her face, she stood staring at her reflection just long enough to see a vine twisting around her mirror frame.

Anna stumbled back and left the bathroom, her stomach still rolling as she slammed the door behind her. That was more than a dream. A sob broke free from her chest. He did that for her. Guilt ripped through her, her stomach a hollow cavern, her skin rising as she felt the panic attack settle in her chest. Why her? She didn't ask for this.

"Fuck!" She screamed, throwing her lamp and watching it bounce off the wall and shatter, spraying the room with ceramic fragments. Anna was panting, chewing her nail as she paced. She had to go back. She had to save Declan. This was her fault.

Anna grabbed her backpack, still sitting in the middle of the room where she had dropped it when she shifted back. She dumped the contents on the bed. Her pain reliever bounced off, her pen rolled, and her new snacks and first aid piled on the crumpled comforter. A weighted feeling in the pack made Anna pause, again shaking the pack onto the bed. A small, unassuming book fell out of the bottom of the bag. Anna stared at it momentarily before remembering the tomes she had stolen from the library. It was the small book she had grabbed at the last minute before running back to her room.

Fumbling, Anna turned on the other lamp across her room, bathing the small space in an orange glow as she opened the small text. Unlike the other book, which was more of record keeping, this one was filled with words, handwritten in tight neat lines.

"This book is my only solace, my only company in this place. They took my baby from me, still covered in my blood and screaming. Healthy lungs, with tiny hands, already balled into fists. A fighter. I didn't get to hold him. They cut the cord that bound us, leaving me with swollen breasts and an empty belly. It didn't matter how loud I screamed or how much I cried. Niamh's head still hangs on the pike out of my dungeon's window. The smell of rot rolls in with every breeze. When my milk finally dried up, and my throat was too ruined to scream any longer, my sister finally deemed it time to move me to one of the upper rooms in the unused portion of the castle."

Anna picked herself up from the floor, folding her legs underneath her as she pulled the covers over her. Rubbing her thumb over the discoloration at the beginning of the page, she realized quickly whoever had written this had cried, smearing the ink as they had brushed away the salty tears.

"I was then told she allowed the newborn to live. And the price for his life was my silence. My obedience. My death, in a way. Though no one knew about me, not really. The second born, a living heresy to the monarchy. Mother had quickly killed the midwives and guards that had attended our birth, and I was whisked away to be raised as the firstborn's servant and play-mate. Never sister. Never equal. The only reason I know this to be true is my mother's deathbed confession, spurning much hate from Octavia on her ceremony day. We became pregnant the same day. Her through duty and magic, and me? Through love."

Anna felt her skin begin to crawl as she turned the page, like suddenly things were starting to make sense. Something was being put together in front of her, just out of her grasp.

"Niamh. Niamh. Niamh. I knew we were meant to be when we first met. The man was sunshine in such bleakness. Green eyes sparkled when he laughed. They drug him from me the moment my stomach began to swell. Just as they did with our son. So here I sit, in a large room, finely furnished with books I've reread a million times, bars on the windows, and only one seraph that knows I exist. Magic has sworn them to never reveal me or my son in name or writing. My name will surely be lost to history, but I hope to be remembered on these pages. As will my son. Out of girlhood affection and possibly some tug of sisterly love deep inside her dark heart, Octavia allowed me to name the baby. He will train as a protector for her daughter, Nona. Though I never held him, I will forever carry him in my heart. My little Declan."

Anna almost dropped the book in surprise, her heart racing. But her hand covered her mouth in astonishment as she finally found the writer's identity. It all made sense now.

Signed, Sorcha.

22

～

Anna didn't realize a tear had rolled down her cheek as she opened one more page to only see a scribbling of a family lineage. One long line with smaller lines branching off, two at a time. A mother and two daughters.

It was so similar to the one in the tome, except next to Octavia's name was connected by a small thin dash, neat handwriting that scrolled Sorcha. Besides, her name was her lover, Niamh, and their son below them, nestled next to Nona's name. Declan. Born the same day. In the same castle. Under vastly different circumstances.

It took a minute for Anna to grapple with why this journal had been hidden, most likely by Sorcha herself. Why was Declan taken from her? Why was Octavia so scared and trying to find her daughters alter? The monarchy will not be destroyed or wasted, but the magic will be passed on to Declan when her reign ends. Giving him her powers, her near immortality. His birthright. Something tugged in her when she realized that Declan was meant to be king. A king born out of love, not duty or supernatural powers. And he was currently being tortured in a cell because he saved her life.

Putting the book back into her bag, she repacked, throwing off her work uniform and replacing it was dark leggings and a black hoodie. Running shoes. Her knife. She shot her phone a look, the voicemail from her therapist still blinking, reminding her of the problems that this world held as well. Anna looked in the small bag at her last sleeping pill, stuffing it deep into her pocket. That was for emergencies only.

Slinging the backpack over her back, her stomach fluttered, but the knife was a comforting weight in her hoodie pocket as she opened the bathroom door, revealing the large mirror propped in the corner of the small bathroom. Deep breaths. Anna stepped up, kneeling in front of the mirror with purpose this time.

Reaching out a timid hand towards the glass, concentrating this time, holding her gaze, thinking about Danann, the Silent Forest. About Declan. A breeze wafted through the mirror, her fingers still brushing the solid glass, caressing it like a lover, coaxing the magic to do her bidding, begging the universe to help her this time.

A forest, the lush green so vibrant it almost hurt her eyes, the sound of the night's rustling and the smell of dew-laden grass came at her, closing her eyes as it stroked her cheeks. Anna embraced it, allowing the feeling of otherworldliness to swirl around her.

The forest was so close, it was as if she could reach out and touch it. Another caress, another whispered prayer to whoever was listening. The view of the forest firmly in her mind and swirling in the reflection in front of her, Anna took one of the few pills she had left and waited.

✳✳✳

The forest was dark. Creatures that Anna couldn't see skittered around the forest floor, some large enough to make Anna crouch against a tree, closing her eyes. She had to get into the castle. Getting close enough to the large rock wall that enclosed the fortress, she searched for any imperfections in the stone, any grates.

A branch snapped behind her and Anna froze, a chill running down her spine as she felt something watching her. Carefully, slowly, she reached into her hoodie pocket with cold, numb fingers and quietly withdrew the knife. The hard metal biting through the numbness of her fingers as the crunch of a footstep fell behind her, closer this time. She took a breath and swung around, knife raised.

A white flash of wings and gold armor, a firm hand gripping her wrist that knocked the knife out of her hand before she could do anything more. White hair and a grin, "So you found her journal?" Anna gasped in surprise and hope, her body going slack in their grip, loosening immediately as she let her arm down.

"You knew?" She spat accusingly, dipping down to pick up her knife from the dirt and returning it to her pocket. "You're his friend, and you didn't tell him!" Aramus drew closer to her, their wings flaring as the insult made them whisper in anger. The being still towered over her, ducking down to see eye to eye.

"Why do you think I asked for the position of Witness? It is a position beneath my training, and I am bound by my magic to keep my oath to the Queen. But then I found the journals. Made other discoveries...." They trailed off, shadows deepening in their eyes. "I knew I had to do something." Anna was silent, the whispers of the forest the only sound.

Aramus fixed their eyes on her, "Are you afraid of heights?" Anna looked around her, the dark of the woods seemed to close in around her, the sounds of animals weaving through the night causing her skin to crawl.

"No," she replied softly, looking up at the tall being. "Why?"

They reached out their hand, "I need to show you something."

Deep in her gut, she knew she could trust this seraph. Whether it was from the resolution in their gold eyes or that they risked everything to free her. To get her home.

So Anna took their hand in hers. Before she could object, she was picked up by the strong General and they gave a mighty sweep of their wings, shooting into the sky. Wind grasped at her as she shut her eyes against the leaking tears from the cold gusts, her stomach dropping as they climbed so high that the castle was no longer visible in the thick, low cloud cover.

Anna didn't trust herself to speak as she finally allowed herself to open her eyes. The clouds broke and the large moon shone across the kingdom's hills and valleys. With a gasp, she reminded herself to breathe as she stared at the views from this height. The seraph inclined their chin, gesturing to a small clearing far away from the chimney smoke of the small village in the distance.

"There." Aramus's melodic voice was grave as they began their descent, Anna trying hard not to dig her fingernails into the seraph's shoulders as she held her breath. She fought the urge to scream as they descended, the seraph's feet dropping underneath them as they landed. The white-winged seraph set her down gently, her shoes sinking in the lush, green grass of the meadow as she straightened her backpack. Anna looked around, seeing nothing besides the occasional firefly.

"What are we looking for?" Aramus put a finger to their lips and tucked their wings in tightly to their body, making themselves as small as possible.

"They are frightened easily," they whispered, the white feathers of their wings moving as if in agreement.

"What are-" She stopped, her heartbeat thundering in her chest as they crept around a large tree to see the creatures they had motioned to. Anna blinked, dropping a knee beside the seraph, the tall grass hiding most of them. She had never seen so many, definitely not this close without some sort of fence.

"We do not know what they are called or their purpose," The seraph breathed, their eyes not leaving the massive creatures. "But they arrived a few months before you did." Anna nudged closer, resting her hand on the immense tree trunk.

"Buffalo," she gasped, counting at least twelve either sleeping or grazing on the ample grass. "Aramus, those are buffalo." The seraph mouthed the words as if testing them on their tongue before nodding.

"I was inclined to believe they were native to your world." Anna dragged her stare from the large creatures to scowl at the seraph.

"How long?" She whispered vehemently, suddenly feeling stupid to allow the seraph to take her so far away from the castle. "Longer than I am comfortable admitting," Aramus didn't shy away from her accusatory glare but instead mirrored the emotion. Anna relaxed when she saw their face drawn in shame as they looked back at the lazy beasts.

"There is still much I do not know, much that I believe Declan and even Brynn know. About the Queen. About the night that Nona was murdered." They paused, fixing Anna with their sorrowful eyes. "Please believe me, when I started finding things like these..." they pointed to the herd. "I dug as much as I could with limited resources and without raising any attention." Anna swallowed back any judgment at the deep supplication in the General's face.

"Does Octavia know these are here?" A nod.

"I was instructed to bring them here, my aerial unit watches them from afar. We are in the middle of the changing shifts, so we don't have much time." The tall seraph stood, dark skin glowing in the moonlight as they softly walked away from the mammals. Anna put a hand on Aramus's arm, her eyes not leaving their gold ones.

"Why now?" She asked softly.

Aramus drew back, their eyes sweeping the ground and his wings drooping slightly.

"Not many know of Sorcha. The ones who do are dead or have even heavier magic upon them. I only know because I found Sorcha's journal. I am the one who left it to be found. It was only the first volume. My soul has known no rest since that discovery."

Anna looked at the commander of the Queen's aerial force, the flawless skin and golden eyes were present but deeper still. She saw it. As someone who knew deep sorrow, grief, and regret. Anna saw it reflected in their gold eyes. As the seraph retook her hand, situating her in their arms, Anna finally asked the question that had been churning inside her the moment she stepped back into this realm. A shattering in her, her arms tightening around Aramus in anticipation.

"Is Declan..." She started, but Aramus quickly shook their head.

"He lives." The seraph scanned the sky, "We can save him. There is still time." With a steady gaze that begged her to trust them, Anna tightened her grip, and before she could protest leaves around her flew as she was lifted into the air. The feeling of the powerful feathered wings pushing against the air was exciting and terrifying at the same time. It wasn't until her feet touched the ground that she let go of a breath she had been holding, despite reminding herself to breath.

"Where's Brynn?" At the mention of the Seer's name, Aramus's lips tightened into a thin line, and they simply shook their head. Anna's heart sank, she enjoyed the woman's company and knew the dark-haired woman was powerful. She knew how much Aramus loved her. Anna shook it off, "We need to get down to the dungeon."

"Anna, before you see-" But Anna had already turned and stopped, her knees locking as she hit ground before Aramus could warn her. A scream was smothered as Aramus covered her mouth, muffling the horror that was clawing through her.

Her ears were buzzing too loud to hear if they said anything, the world tilting on its axis as his wings vibrated behind him. Before her, on a pike in the middle of the courtyard, was the head of Sorcha. The forgotten sister of Queen Octavia and the mother of Declan the Sin Eater.

The old woman's eyes were still open, staring off into nothing. Her mouth frozen in an endless, silent scream. Blood was congealing around the pole, still dripping from what was left of her neck. The only thing that saved Anna from throwing up was knowing that any noise would bring guards, so she swallowed her horror and grief. Aramus removed their hand as Anna nodded, showing them they would be silent. The seraph took her hand as they went around towards the stables, allowing her to viciously wipe at the tears.

"I'm going to kill her," became her mantra echoing in her head as she leaned on the seraph, her stomach rolling and eyes still burning. The stables were ahead of them, Aramus keeping her close. All of a sudden all Anna could see were feathers as she found herself pressed against them, the seraph's wings flaring protectively.

"General," gasped the deep voice of Titus in surprise as the soldier tucked his wings in tight and stood at attention to the senior officer. Anna delved closer to Aramus as if she could disappear into the taller seraph's form.

"Lieutenant," Aramus straightened as well, their hand going across Anna as if they could shield her from the other seraph's sharp eyes. When no one else spoke, she dared to look at the younger seraph, his jawline tense as grey eyes flicked to his commander and Anna.

"General-" But he looked towards the castle, his eyes stopping at Sorcha's head, still dripping blood as his voice lowered. "What can I do, General?" Anna let go of a breath she had been holding, her eyes going to Aramus as the seraph's wings relaxed.

"Guard the grate, we will return through it." Titus nodded, jerking his chin. "Understood, General." She smiled at the seraph in gratitude as Aramus rushed her toward the back of the barn.

"Where are we going?" Anna whispered, her voice soft even though the only beings around them were the horses, their large bodies shifting in their stalls, their armor hung on the doors. Gleaming sharp horns glinting in the moonlight streaming through the barn windows.

"There is a water runoff beneath the stables, it runs the length of the castle," Aramus led her to an empty stall, discarded tack, and dented armor thrown about, almost covering the grate where Anna could hear the slight sound of trickling water. With barely any effort, Aramus lifted the heavy iron grate, setting the rusted thing to the side and holding their hand, "I'll let you down first and cover it." Anna hesitated, looking at the drop and the darkness below, the only sound of running water.

Aramus moved their hand, "I will not leave you, Anna." She looked at their face and squared her jaw, giving them her hand. Her running shoes were immediately submerged in water as she was carefully dropped below. Anna let go of the seraph's hand reluctantly, moving to give them space and only then remembering she had packed a flashlight this time around. She could have cried when she rummaged through her pack and felt the cool plastic casing of her small emergency flashlight.

The tunnel was immediately illuminated, as water runoff tunnels go, it was fairly clean, but the bottom felt slick with algae. A splash echoed behind Anna as Aramus dropped down, tall enough to scoot the grate back over the entrance, keeping their secret for as long as possible. The seraph looked at her flashlight in amazement but seemed to remember their quest and pointed her down the long, dark hall.

As they passed down the dank tunnel, she could see patches of light where the grates littered the palace. The kitchen was quiet but still with the lingering smell of food. She dimmed the light with the palm of her hand each time they came close to the grates in case any sentries were about. It grew colder as they walked, the tunnel growing increasingly damp. The musty smell of mold immediately brought her back to her cell.

They were close. Aramus drew closer to her as the last grate came into view, flickering candlelight showing overhead. The smell of rust, copper, and mold was almost overwhelming.

Aramus grabbed the flashlight quickly as footsteps echoed overhead, and they pulled her back away from the light, hand lightly pressed against their lips. They waited for what seemed like forever when she saw the shadow of one seraph accompanied by two guards and the sound of a cell door opening. Her stomach sank. Angus and his seraphs.

A loud moan issued from that cell echoing around the pair. She didn't realize her knife was in her hand until she had flipped it open. The air was sickeningly heavy with blood and sweat. Declan's blood.

Anna's teeth set, a fury in her chest she couldn't explain as she gripped the hilt of her knife as the men laughed at something Angus had said, eliciting another cry from the Sin Eater. It felt like forever as they taunted him, drawing hoarse screams for the bound man.

Finally the seraphs returned through the door, their shadows darkening the flowing water under the grate as they crossed over them.

Aramus and Anna waited on bated breath until the door shut and the resounding click of the lock sounded. Aramus held her back for a few more beats, their head tilted towards the ceiling, listening. There was silence beside the heavy breathing coming from the cell above them.

It was their only chance and they knew it as they looked at each other. As silently as they could, Aramus drew themselves up to full height, their wings vibrating to keep them hovering over the water as they pushed the heavy grate aside. Anna held her breath as the seraph pulled themselves through the opening, their wings curved to their body as they barely fit, their hand coming down and bringing her behind them.

Anna found herself again in the dungeon, the hazy light from candles illuminating the curved ceiling. Aramus looked over at the cell, their hand reaching out and cracking the lock with a crushing grip. Before she knew it, Anna was ripping the door open, finding a flickering torch lighting the small space. Anna's knife nearly fell from her hand as she took in Declan, hanging by the wrists from a pole strung from the hook in the ceiling.

Her vision tunneled as everything in her dream came into focus, as she saw them with her waking eyes. His clothing and gloves were strewn to the side, and his torso was a map of knife marks. Nothing too deep but enough to cause his blood to flow and inflict the maximum pain without killing him.

Bruises were beginning to bloom on his chest which heaved with every breath as his toes struggled to keep him upright. He was going to suffocate. Quickly bringing over a bench, she stood on it and found herself face-to-face with the captured man.

"Declan," she gasped, running to his side, pushing a piece of dark hair away from his sweat-soaked face. The one eye that wasn't swollen shut squinted at her in confusion.

"You?" He gasped, chapped lips barely moving. The green of his eyes was striking against the molten bruising. "Yeah, you're welcome." she breathed, trying to ignore the swell of emotion, pushing tears to the brim of her eyes. Aramus was suddenly at her side, their helping hands going for the knots, cutting off the circulation around his swollen wrists.

"Don't," he gasped, shaking his head, and one eye widening. "Don't touch me, please."

"Declan..." Anna started, staring at him incredulously, but her hands hovered at his black wrists.

"Please." It wasn't a question, it wasn't a request, it was a plea he nearly choked on. Anna held her hands just inches away from his, burning to touch and get him off of the accursed rope. Swearing,

Anna grabbed her blade, wiping the blood on her tunic before grabbing the bonds and beginning to saw away.

"Be ready then," She snapped at him, and Anna stepped back as his arm was free and immediately went to his abused ribs. Aramus grabbed their friend's side, keeping the pressure off his ribs as Anna's grasped the rope above his blackened fingers, not touching the skin. And she sawed.

He collapsed against Aramus in a gasp, curling up for a moment and breathing in gasps of air as he was finally able to. The dirty cobblestones that lined the cell were damp and sticky with the Sin Eater's blood. A click at the door made them all freeze, Aramus still holding Declan steady as he tried to stumble to his feet, wheezing as standing seemed impossible. Anna looked at Aramus in alarm. The seraph looked as panicked as she felt, their wings trembling. One sheltering the injured sin eater and the other flared out in alarm.

"What's going on here!" Came a cry, and the slow footfalls became running as they must have encountered the opened grate. The seraph rounded on them, coming to a stop before drawing her sword and stalking towards them, Declan still hanging limp between them, Anna's knife ready in her hand.

"Stop right there- "Anna looked at the seraph in horror as the guard's mouth gaped open, but nothing came through. A knives point sticking through their throat, blood gurgling out the seraph's mouth as she tried to draw a breath. Anna started as the guard dropped. Standing behind the sentry was a pale, shaking Brynn.

"Brynn!" Despite her horrified appearance, Anna couldn't help but cry out, feeling joy welling up in her chest at seeing the young Seer.

"Brynn," whispered Aramus, holding out their hand as she ran to them, "Are you sure?" The dark-haired woman didn't answer, just pushed the grate over.

"I owed him." She nodded at the man, "Let's get him out of here."

Aramus looked at her for a long moment before Declan groaned, spurning him to action.

"I can stand," mumbled Declan, his arm wrapped around his

middle, all but leaning on the wall across from the drainage entrance. "Yeah, I can see that," whispered Anna, "You get down there first."

Declan shook his head, "I'm not leaving you up here alone." Shaking her head, Anna reached out but stopped as soon as the man flinched back, watching her hands floating in between the space between them.

"I'll be right behind you, I promise." But his gaze was unflinching, flickering to the sewer.

"Ladies first," he grumbled, trying to sound blasé but failing miserable, a short cough racked his weakened frame. Rolling her eyes, trying to give him the energy he desperately needed, sat on the edge of the opening before dropping in. Anna could finally breathe when he dropped down, Aramus almost carrying him down, their wings vibrating to keep them hovering long enough to help their weakened friend.

Anna raced down the pipe, careful around the openings as Aramus held up Declan, their pace increasing as they heard yelling echoing down the tunnel from the dungeon.

They had found the murdered guard.

Trying not to slip on the algae, Anna picked up the pace, her breath coming out in short bursts. She was so afraid she didn't even notice the smell anymore.

"Anna, ahead!" Aramus softly cried, jerking their head towards the soft light spilling through from the stables, the smell of fresh straw mingling with the musty scent of the tunnel. Her heart swelled, she waited for Aramus to reach up with their considerable height difference to set the grate aside for them.

The barn was still dark, the sound of moving horses surrounded her. They had made it.

23

As soon as the group was free of the tunnel, the sound of a deep, thunderous horn pierced through the quiet night. Horses tossing their heads as Anna spun around, trying to find the source.

"General," Titus said from around the corner, bringing one of the mares already saddled and ready. "I think you may need this." Aramus clapped the soldier on his back, taking the reins from the younger soldier.

"Now, back to barracks, do not say a word." Titus ducked his head, his gaze brushing over the group before disappearing into the night. Another horn bellow rang through the night, the horses stamping nervously. Aramus swore under their breath, "They found the dungeon, we need to move now!" Declan said something, so quiet like he couldn't quite get the words out. His cuts reopening from the movement, blood slowly rolling down his bare back and chest.

"Leave me." He repeated louder, looking directly at Anna when he said this. "Leave me and run." Something jolted through her at his soft plea, causing her spine to stiffen and her jaw to set.

"No one gets left behind, especially you." Anna ground out, throwing open the stable door. "We need the horse." The Seraph nodded, bringing the sizable dapple mare, large hooves stamping the floor. The horn continued to blare, alerting everyone in the castle and surrounding areas that something was wrong.

"Let's get his ass on that horse, take Brynn in the air. Tell me where to meet you." Anna snapped, grabbing a horse blanket from another peg, shaking the loose straw from its woven fibers, and throwing it over Declan's shoulders, trying to ignore the way the man winced as it made contact with his abused flesh. Aramus nodded in agreement,

"There's a town, a night's ride through the west part of the forest, known as a haven for those who wish not to be found. Follow the stream, cross it. It will throw off the scent and tracks." Brynn took the reigns, the creature's ears pinned back against its head in trepidation.

"Meet us at Grey Mountain Inn," Brynn whispered, handing the reigns to Anna. Declan was behind her, swinging his leg over the horse, a hiss escaping his lips. "Brynn, I've never ridden a horse," she admitted, now next to the enormous creature. The seer rolled her eyes and kneeled, patting her leg for Anna to boost up. Declan sat behind her, "Use your thighs and hang on, don't let him fall."

Declan's black, swollen hands held the reigns shakily as he wrapped his arms around her and whispered in her ear, his voice full of pain and rough from screaming, "I won't let you fall."

Before Anna knew it, Brynn whistled, slapping the rump of the large animal, spurring it into action as Aramus drew open the doors just as seraphs began to pour out of the castle. Anna saw a flash of white as Aramus wrapped Brynn in their arms and took to the sky, and burst through the courtyard gate, giving them the way out. Anna squeezed with all her might, the giant horse shaking its mighty head as Declan kicked it into action, galloping out of the busted gates, the seraphs behind them still scrambling for their weapons behind them. Anna saw a few take to the skies behind her.

The night was chilled, and the wind made it even worst. The cold air piercing through the hoodie she wore and she knew that Declan was trying to stay quiet as they tore through the thick forest. Trusting the horse to weave around obstacles, she felt Declan pulling her against him. His body was a furnace and he didn't let her move from her spot as he shared his body heat, even as he tried to stifle the hiss as her back came into contact with the mangled flesh. The trees barely allowed any moonlight to filter through, but the thick trees saved them in the end. The flying seraphs couldn't fly through the narrow gaps, and taking to the sky in the inky darkness was just as futile. They crossed a river, waiting until it bottlenecked to allow them to cross without being pulled into the fast-moving current. The darkness was oppressive, folding in on them with the sounds of the local wildlife. Every snap of a branch had Anna whipping around, Declan's arm tight around her middle, keeping her seated even as the horse jumped over obstacles.

She wasn't sure how long they had been traveling, but the grip around her middle had begun to loosen ever so slightly, the chest at her back rising in stuttering breaths as they continued. Anna leaned forward, squinting her eyes in the dark, and blinked a few times before knowing what she saw was real. The flickering of lamp light.

The town.

Anna had never ridden a horse, but she had watched movies, so she clucked her tongue and squeezed with her heels, urging the horse faster towards the light.

"Hold on, Declan, we're here," she whispered, her own voice foreign in her ears; they hadn't spoken the entire ride, too frightened of the seraphs circling overhead. The crashing of trees and branches that had followed their trail for far too long during their escape, the sound of the horn becoming more distant until it disappeared entirely. Declan only hummed in response, his breath hot on her neck, his forehead leaning on the back of her head as if he hadn't the strength to hold it up. The grip around her waist loosened even more, the strong hand slipping slowly until she grabbed him. She wrapped his arm and held it to her, his breathing quickening as she did so.

"Anna?" Came a loud whisper, breaking the silence of the woods as they found themselves out of the woods and onto a dirt path leading up to the town. "Aramus! Over here!" Anna cried softly, nudging the tired animal carrying her forward, the jolting pace bruising her tailbone. They barely had stopped when Declan slumped forward, Aramus running to grab the falling man, throwing their arm around him.

Anna dismounted the massive beast, almost falling herself but took the reigns, following Aramus as they all but drug Declan towards the town. Tucking a wing over the injured Sin Eater the Seraph pulled him into an alley, Anna following, looking around the streets down the way that were full of milling people. Drinking, fucking, and dancing. Despite the late hour, they were full of revelry. The general energy made Anna uneasy, so she followed the Seraph quietly through the dirty alley, the poor horse barely fitting down the narrow space between buildings.

"Third door, Brynn will mind the horse." Anna was eager to hand over the reigns to Brynn. Still, before she could follow the Aramus through the door, Brynn touched her elbow, "Here," the seer whispered, pushing a small clay pot in her direction; it was full of a fragrant poultice. It smelled of rosemary and citrus. "It's for his wounds, only use a thin amount, it goes a long way." Anna quickly shook her head, trying to push the jar back at the woman, "Why can't you-" Brynn interrupted, "I don't like blood." That was all she said, and she turned away. Anna remembered how she looked at the guard's throat she had slit and how her wide her eyes got at the pooling, deep red spurting from the seraph's neck by her small blade.

Pushing over the heavy old door, Anna was greeted by a warm hearth in a spare storage room. The dusty room hadn't been used in a while by the looks of it. She was just thankful it was warm, away from the raucous crowd. Besides the dust it was reasonably clean. Anna hurriedly shook off an old tarp covering some barrels, rolling it up as thick as possible before placing it on the floor next to the crackling hearth Brynn had conjured.

Declan was awake now, his face screwed in a mask of pain as he sat down on the pad that Anna had set up. The Seraph pushing a tankard of water at the man. He had greedily drunk, laying back with a contented sigh as Anna was sure it filled his empty stomach, though he refused the food Aramus had laid out. The sight of him illuminated in the bright firelight made her stomach lurch, his already scarred skin was bruised and bloody. The way he winced almost invisibly when he thought she wasn't looking.

She turned, nervously opening the jar that Brynn had supplied and looked at the injured man. Declan was propped up by a barrel as the fire's warmth licked his bare skin as it attempted to pacify the shivering. Aramus sat near the fire, their wings tucked to their back, almost hiding while they vibrated. Aramus looked as if in a trance, like they were recharging.

Anna cleared her throat and willed her trembling hands to still while she sat next to him. A wave of worry sweeping over her as she saw his goose-pebbled skin even in the warm enclosure of the room. She pulled down the blankets to reveal his chest, crisscrossed in shallow wounds that she was glad to see, though they looked painful, would heal quickly.

"What are you doing?" He grumbled, his eyes still closed, one by choice and the other having been punished by someone's fist. She didn't meet his gaze, just scooped some sweet-smelling ointment onto her fingers, "Brynn gave me this for your wounds, so just stay still."

Anna kept her touch feather-light as she applied it to the first wound, trying to ignore how his skin felt under her fingers. Feeling him draw away from her, she stopped, "I know you can't stand me touching you, but just let me do this," she mumbled, touching the next one.

His good eye opened at this, "I don't." It was barely a whisper. Anna pretended she didn't hear it and quickly worked on the more minor cuts over his abdominal muscles. "Just hold still." She looked up to see his good eye staring at her, deeper green than she remembered. They were silent as the larger man allowed her fingers to ghost over the painful wounds. She tried to blink away the memory of the sight of him, strung up, being cut into because of what he did for her.

"Why did you do it?" She finally asked quietly, breaking the tense silence between them. She kept her voice just above a whisper, conscious of the seraph meditating in the corner. More silence met her question, her fingers skimming over a particularly deep wound near his side, and he pulled away minutely. The muscles in his jaw tense as she worked as gently as she could.

Anna sighed, "Declan, why did you save me?" Firmer this time. "Don't mention it." He growled, spitting a congealed wad of blood into the fire, his tongue moving over his teeth, looking for breaks.

"I am mentioning it. Right now, in fact." She spat back, leaning forward, the fire warming her suddenly angry, flushed face. "You have been hell-bent on either throwing me over bridges or throwing me to your Queen, and you become a white knight? You knew they would do this, yet you helped me anyway." Declan fished inside his mouth; he was undoubtedly feeling a welt that she could see swollen from the outside. Wincing, leaning back against the barrel, fixing her with a solid gaze from his one good eye. "What I do or do not do is none of your concern."

Anna scoffed, "It is, especially if it directly concerns me!" He laughed darkly, shaking his head. "This had nothing to do with you."

"It sure as hell felt like it did," she retorted, pointing at his bandages. "You've been tortured. Because of me." She hated that her voice broke on that last sentence.

Declan set his jaw firmly, "How many times do I have to tell you that I am a bad person, Anna? What I did wasn't out of any sort of goodwill or affection, I can assure you." Anna kept her eyes on him for a beat before grabbing the jar and tossing it to him.

"I could be wrong, but I don't think many bad people have to spend so much time convincing everyone that they're a bad person." He didn't reply, and she took that as a sign she had won this round. Without another word, she headed off into the night to find Brynn. The night air was a calming balm on her heated skin as she leaned against the wall. She took a deep breath and closed her eyes.

"Are you going to leave us?" It was Brynn, wiping her hands on her tunic, smelling of fresh hay. "You shift when you sleep. Is that not right?"

"I don't know. I hadn't planned to come back."

"Do you want to leave?" The seer asked directly.

That question gave her pause, and she considered that she hadn't thought about work, her father, or her friends. And that worried her. "I don't know." Was all she said, her fingers coming down to the gold cord around her wrist, reminding her that this was not her world, not her fight, but she felt like she was supposed to be here.

"He won't talk to me, Brynn," she blurted out, embarrassed as soon as she said it. Brynn leaned against the wall, her dark eyes curious. The sound of the town around them echoed through the alley, but the night air was cool and refreshing as they left the confines of the room to talk.

"What do you mean?"

Anna rubbed her face, the smell of the fire still thick in her nostrils, "I don't know what to do, I mean. I'm confused. I'm tired. Brynn, I'm not supposed to be here." Brynn nodded, her lips pressed into a thin line as her eyes roamed Anna's face and dropped to take her hand.

Before Anna could react, Brynn brushed a soft finger over the scar she found there, smiling gently. "Do you want to know what I think?" She whispered, inching a bit closer. "I think that your world was never big enough for you. I think you've always felt this pull. And that terrifies you." The seer smiled, letting her hand go and disappearing into the room where the Sin Eater slept. Anna stood back against the wall looking up at the sky.

She realized how startlingly similar they look to her own back home.

24

~

It was the scream that woke her, a gut-wrenching scream that stole her sleep. In an instant, Anna was awake and her knife in her hand. Sleep still thick in her vision, she realized quickly that it was Brynn, kneeling on her bedroll, hands gripped into claws, pawing at her face leaving red welts as she dragged her blunt nails down her dark skin.

Anna could barely blink before Aramus was at the woman's side, grabbing her hands, pulling her into their chest, and rocking slightly. Brynn's body was wracked with sobs as she melted into the seraph's embrace, her once brilliant dark eyes now a milky white, staring right through Anna as if she wasn't there at all.

"Aramus-"

"There's always a price," it was Declan, his bruised face looking crestfallen, his gaze on the seer cradled in the seraph's arms. "For betraying Octavia." The sight of the woman in Aramus's arms shaking with sobs made a lump in Anna's throat. She didn't know what to do. Or how to help.

She went to kneel beside them, but Declan beat her to it, wincing as he went down on his knees in front of the inconsolable Brynn. The forces of her sobs shook her petite frame as Aramus's wings folded around her, the feathers almost caressing her skin as they comforted her.

Declan carefully tucked his hand under Brynn's chin, his voice softer than Anna had ever heard it before, "Thank you, Brynn," he said calmly and evenly, "I promise you, I will not forget this." Brynn nodded, unseeing eyes staring right through the Sin Eater.

"I will stay with her," Aramus said as Declan stood, trying to hide the grunt of pain that the movement put on his still-healing wounds. Declan dipped his head in acknowledgment and drooped as he approached the smoldering fire.

"We can't stay here another night, we need to move fast," Declan said to no one in particular, searching through the pack Brynn had thought to bring for a shirt, contented with what he found.

"We can find lodging in town, but tomorrow we need to move."

"Where will you go?" Anna asked softly, standing from her post at Brynn's side, dusting the dirt off her knees as she did. Her stomach was hollow, and it wasn't just hunger. Declan stopped, the shirt wrapped around his arms as he inhaled deeply as soon as his arms lifted. She realized his ligaments and muscles must be at least strained, if not outright torn, after hanging for so long. Anna shook her head to rid her mind of that vision. Of him dangling there.

"Here," she said softly, gesturing for him to raise his arms as high as he could. Declan stood there frozen, his eyes wide, darting to his arms, the gloves barely covering the creeping darkness.

"I won't get handsy." She smiled, trying to defuse the tension. His lips thinned as he nodded minutely, raising his arms until he gave a wince, staying still as she slowly and gently pulled the soft linen over his beaten chest, careful not to roughly pull the tender skin. Anna moved away as soon as she got past his navel, trying not to focus on the unnatural heat radiating from his skin. The shirt was blessedly black, and the few oozing cuts would not show any evidence. His eye, however, was a different story.

"What about your eye?" Anna gestured, though the swelling had dissipated slightly, it was still vibrant black and purple, the broken vessels almost completely overpowering the white of his eye.

Declan shrugged slightly, "We are in an area where someone with a black eye or even a stab wound is fairly common. People don't come here leisurely. They come to hide." He pointed to the wall, facing west, "There are ports on the other side, easy to charter a ship to leave Danann." Anna stood, her backpack still sitting near where she had eventually fallen asleep, tucked inside was the small diary of his mother, Sorcha.

"Declan," she whispered nervously, "I need to speak to you." Declan looked at her, brows furrowed as he carefully wrapped an old cloak around his shoulders, his face paling as he did so.

"Can it wait until we have a room?" Anna looked again at the bag, at the secrets it kept within, and nodded reluctantly. It didn't make any difference where she told him, just that he needed to be said, so she could go back to her world, and he could remain in his. That Aramus and Brynn could have a chance. Because she realized, deep down for the first time, that these people had become her friends. She couldn't leave them behind without knowing they would be safe.

Dipping his chin in acknowledgment, Declan's eyes rested on her arm, specifically the chain still wrapped around it. It was just for a moment before he left, closing the door against the chill of the morning. Stomach in knots, Anna turned to Brynn, watching Aramus rock her softly as the woman seemed out of tears to shed, her milky white eyes screwed tight. Anna was terrible at comforting people in pain or sadness. It wasn't that she couldn't empathize; she empathized too much, felt everything too deeply, and had no idea how to help. Twisting her hands, she knelt slowly so as not to startle the blind seer and took Brynn's clenched hand in her own.

"I know something about loss," she whispered, her voice catching in her throat and her eyes beginning to burn as emotions threatened to overwhelm her. "You are so strong, Brynn. I want you to know that. Sometimes what is meant to break us makes us so much stronger."

Anna shook her head softly, starting at the dirt floor, "I know that doesn't help now. But we're here. We're not leaving you." Aramus's wings softly brushed her shoulder like the seraph was thanking or comforting her. Brynn's dark hand was still enclosed in her own before the woman squeezed it slightly as she moved, resting her head on Aramus's chest. Releasing her hold only momentarily, Anna brought the seer some water, which she reluctantly drank.

"Everything is so bright," Whispered Brynn, her voice edged in a rasp from her cries as she screwed her eyes shut again. "So bright." Aramus looked confused at Anna but said nothing until they fished in their small white leather bag at their side, pulling out a red silk scarf from its depths.

"I was training when I realized Anna had arrived," The seraph explained, running the soft material between their fingers, "This is to block our vision, to heighten our senses when training for aerial combat. It is light blocking." With such gentleness, the seraph pushed back her dark mess of curls and instructed her to keep her eyes closed as they wrapped the scarf around her eyes and tied it securely behind her head. With a trembling touch, Brynn lifted her fingers to feel the soft material, nodding as she did so.

"Thank you," she whispered, choking back another sob, "It helps."

The door opened, bringing a flood of cold morning air as Declan stiffly made his way inside, looking at the group still on the floor. "I have our rooms, they're not much, but it will work for tonight." He nodded to Aramus, who helped Brynn stand on unsteady feet, her hands clenching his own as she fought to maintain her balance without using her sight. Anna grabbed her backpack, the bag's weight flooding her with anxiety with the knowledge she would have to give the Sin Eater.

"A ship leaves tomorrow evening on the tide," Declan explained, leaning down to scoop up the bags left near the smoldering fire. Aramus raised their head, "We're leaving?" They asked, holding on tight to Brynn, her hands clutching their larger ones. Declan dipped his head, "We need to put as much distance between us and Octavia until she cools down." He didn't say anything else, leaving the door open as he strode out of it, the others following behind him, Aramus bringing up the rear as they slowly helped Brynn.

They trudged along the town's dirty streets. The other cities Anna had visited had been small but, for the most part, clean, save the alleys and more bawdy elements of the town. This was mayhem. Slouched individuals littered the roadways, either dead or drunk, there was no distinction. The streets had no pavement, no rocks, just loose mud dipped with horse hooves and wagon wheels pooling stagnant water, leaving a putrid smell lingering as they walked.

The Inn was a building crammed between two others, the door solid but marked with splinters and rusted hardware. Inside, Anna was pleasantly surprised by how warm it was compared to their last lodgings, the sticky floor pulling at her footwear as she followed close behind the Sin Eater. He adjusted his hood to cover his face in shadows.

"We'll take those rooms," Declan snapped at the ruddy-faced Innkeeper, who was tossing a half-full tankard of ale into a bucket. "Hmm," the man replied, bulging eyes flittering over the group, lingering long over Brynn and her wrapped eyes. "Seems to me as if you're lying low. That'll cost you." Behind the hood, the only part not hidden by the shadow of his hood, Declan crooked a smile, digging into the hidden pocket in his coat and tossing a few uneven gold coins onto the bar.

"I would expect nothing less," he pushed them forward towards the man's hungry gaze, "For your discretion." The coins were swiped from the gummy bar top before any of the equally shady patrons could see what he held. The Innkeeper pushed his chin to the right, "Last two, top floor up the stairs."

Declan steeled his jaw, "I asked for three." The stout man leaned on the counter, now more emboldened as the gold stirred in his pockets. "And you'll get two. The third got swiped up, take it or leave it." Clenched glove fists, the slight smell of smoke Anna swore drifted past her until the Sin Eater simply nodded, jerking his head to the group as they filed behind him, keeping our eyes down as they drifted through the Inn's tavern.

They were almost to the stairs before a beefy man, smelling of stale beer and unwashed clothes, stepped in front of Declan, his gait slightly unsteady as he pointed past him to Anna.

"Seems to me, I've heard talk of you four," his red-stained eyes locked on Aramus and Brynn but settling on Anna. "You girl, you have a mighty bounty on your head." A step towards her was all he got before Declan's gloved fist came out from under his cloak, grabbing the man's meaty throat and pressing up against his windpipe.

"And you'll be missing yours if you don't step away from her." Her heart pounded as the Sin Eater didn't let up. Declan pressed harder on the man's throat until his eyes bulged, and his feet collapsed underneath him. Declan dropped him, no one in the bar looking in their direction. Anna could thank the packed, rowdy crowd for that. A small bar fight was an everyday occurrence here. So she and the others stepped over his unconscious body and quickly up the darkened stairs. She felt the way Declan's hand went to the small of her back, hovering there as he put her in front of him.

Aramus took the unsteady seer into the room adjacent to the one Declan stood in front of, closing the door behind them without looking at the pair. The room was bigger than Anna had expected, with two beds across from each other. Anna sat down, wincing as the bed sank considerably on worn ropes holding up a thin mattress pad.

"Will she be ok?" She asked, her fingernail picking at her skin. Declan had slowly removed his cloak, the lines on his forehead deepening as he moved his shoulders, the black shirt dotted with rust-colored blood. Anna averted her eyes as he peeled it off. The hundreds of cuts in various stages of healing, some still weeping from the rip of the cloth, others beginning to knit on their own.

"Why did you come back?"

Anna's head shot up at the clipped tone of the man across from her, still not looking in her direction but fisting the shirt he had just taken off like he wasn't sure what else to do with his hands or eyes. "What do you mean-" The shirt was thrown to the ground, Anna jumping a bit as it hit the floor, and the Sin Eater turned,

"Why the fuck did you come back?" He all but growled, his face tight and his gloved hands clenched, his body trembling as he held himself back. For a moment, Anna was stunned, and tears filled her eyes unbidden. But something happened that never had for her, instead of shrinking back, she stood with her fists clenched, rage filling her. Billowing and pushing like a fire. "

"How about a thank you?" She cried, wiping a tear that trailed down her red cheek. Anna hated that she cried anytime she was angry, and she captured her trembling lip in her teeth. "I risked *everything* to get you out!"

"Exactly why you shouldn't have!" Roared Declan, turning towards her, his face a storm of passion, and she didn't miss the thin wisps of smoke escaping the top of his gloved hands. "I knew what the fuck I was doing when I got you out, do you?" Anna crossed her arms, her brows furrowing as she stared up at the taller man. "I knew I couldn't let you fucking rot!" Gnawing on her lower lip, she shook her head, "When I saw you hanging there with Angus...."

Declan stopped, his head tilting in questioning. "What do you mean, saw me?" He stepped closer, the space between alive and crackling with the energy. "How did you know what happened?"

"I saw you," she admitted, gesturing to the bed. "In my dreams. It was like I was above you. I watched it all." The Sin Eater was speechless, his face blank and slightly colorless. Anna took this opportunity to step closer, ignoring the heat rising from the man, "So don't tell me I shouldn't have done anything or that I didn't know what I was doing!"

With a mighty burst of emotion, Anna pushed against Declan's bare chest, barely moving the man, but the look of surprise, as he rocked back gave her the satisfaction she was craving.

"Don't you tell me what I can or cannot do! I'm not a fucking asshole just to leave you like that!" She pushed him again, and he rocked back easier that time, like he expected the blow.

"I didn't ask you to come back, Anna!" Bellowed Declan, and she swore the floor vibrated with his shout, taking a step towards her, closing the space between them she had just created. Her heart thrummed so loudly in her ears that she could barely hear what she sobbed out next.

"I couldn't let someone else pay for something I did," She cried, her chest so tight she felt her lungs constrict. "Not again." Anna's voice broke at the end, but instead of collapsing as her body begged her to, she reared up again, pushing him. Her hand came up to push his chest, but his gloved one grabbed her wrists before she could make contact, the warm leather-clad fingers enveloping her. Declan's eyes were on hers, searching her tear-flooded hazel eyes and flushed cheeks. She stared right back.

"Why did you come back, Anna?"

Anna released her teeth grip on her bottom lip, "To save your ass. You could say thank you." She spat, wrenching her hands in his clutch to no avail.

"Is that what you want?" He replied, a tilt of his head, cocky, but at the same time, something lingered in his eyes she couldn't quite place. "Is for me to say thank you?"

Raising her chin, she stared him dead in the eye, "That would be nice." The Sin Eater was silent then he hesitated. "Thank you." He whispered, his voice so soft she almost missed it, her attention on his eyes, the way they seemed to look right through her. To touch her.

"Why did you help me?" Anna asked, breaking the silence between them, the air thick with every word unspoken. Declan didn't reply, but his tongue darted out, wetting his dry lips, his gaze dropping to her parted ones.

"Anna-"

"Why, Declan?" God, her heart. It was going to beat through her chest.

"I can't."

Anna's body moved on its own accord, leaning in. His towering one looking down at her as she refused to break their stare. It was then that she noticed the way his chest was heaving, his breathing coming out in soft breaths. He smelled like rosemary, a lingering after scent of the ointment she had smoothed over his wounds. Like fire and smoke, fresh dirt and blood.

The grip released her and her hands hovered in that electric space between their two bodies, her fingertips itching to touch him again. Declan gave a sharp intake of breath as she gave into her urges and let her hands rest lightly on his chest, careful of the healing wounds that decorated the skin. He didn't take her touch away this time.

Just for a moment. Just their breathing between them, as a wounded soul touched an injured body. Anna clenched her eyes shut, her lips trembling as she tried to keep the tears at bay. She went to step back, her fingers not even having the chance to leave his skin, by a soft touch on her chin. Her breath seized in her chest.

A knife through the heart would have been less surprising than that feather-soft touch. Testing, lingering, and lifting her dewy-eyed face to his. He was so goddamn beautiful. The gloved hand pushed her limp hair behind her ear, the touch electrifying and sending a jolt through her as she felt herself lean into it.

"Declan,'" Anna whispered, not knowing why she even spoke. What she was asking. Her face. Her eyes. Her lips. That's where Declan's gaze stopped, fixated.

"Tell me to stop," Declan whispered, his voice wrecked, his body trembling as his lips parted sinfully.

Anna shook her head, "No."

It was like a band had snapped between them, the air alive with their wanting, with their restraint finally broke as Declan surged towards her. Their lips connected in a fury, a wave washing over them as Anna wrapped her arms behind his neck, pulling him even closer as he bent to meet her in turn. They pressed together as Declan wrapped his arms around her waist and pulled her unfathomably closer, their bodies meeting flush.

Anna gasped, Declan taking the opportunity to run his tongue along her bottom lip, asking, *pleading* for the entrance which she freely gave. The Sin Eater tasted like tendrils of smoke, like the aftermath of a fire. Biting and altogether intoxicating. He kissed like a drowning man, and she was that last breath of air. His tongue massaging hers, swallowing her moan as Declan's glove hand caressed her jaw, asking her to deepen the kiss.

Anna was spinning, and all she knew was she needed him closer, his fingers knitting through her hair. Their heartbeats matching rhyme as their bodies entwined. It could have been moments. It could have been years. Time didn't matter because, at that moment, it was just them.

It was Declan that finally broke them apart, that static between them swirling and pulling. The Sin Eater's gloves were still tangled in her hair, their noses bumping as they looked at each other, lips swollen and blushed with the friction.

"You're leaving tonight," he whispered, his eyes closing, his gloved hands tracing patterns behind her neck. Her skin was on aflame in their midst. "Aren't you?"

Anna bit her lip, leaning her head back against the wall to give him access to her neck as he nipped and peppered her exposed neckline and collarbone, eliciting a soft moan from the woman.

"I have to," she whispered, feeling a swell of emotion as she responded. Something like loss. "I don't belong here." The Sin Eater carefully nudged aside her shirt, kissing every spare inch of skin he revealed. Anna was careful with her own hands, resting them on his shoulders, loosely wrapped around his neck as it was some of the few spots of unmarred skin left on his upper body. Anna let them wrap into the hair along his neckline, his kisses lulling her to lean back further into the wall.

"Stay with me," he whispered into the nape of her neck, his breath warm on her skin. "Just tonight. Please."

Anna pulled away, her hand going to cup his cheek and looking at the taller man, pupils blown and lips swollen. He looked wrecked. He looked sinful. She wanted nothing more than to stay with him.

So she nodded, "For a bit. Until we fall asleep." Something caught in her throat. Something she forced down. Declan scooped her up, a gasp forcing its way from her as her stomach flipped, feeling the strong arms lift her as if she was nothing.

"Declan, you're hurt-" The Sin Eater silenced her with a kiss, swallowing her protests as he walked her to the small bed in the corner.

"I don't care." The bed was thin and flimsy, their combined weight stretching the ropes holding the mattress pad to groan as he nestled her against the corner, giving him the view of the locked door. Anna dug in her pocket, pulling out her singular sleeping pill. The last one she had left, her prescription had run out, and this was her final chance. She placed it under her tongue, conscious of the Sin Eater's eyes on her every movement.

"The chain," Declan said suddenly like he didn't want to say the words he was about to speak. "It's magic to draw you to me. It's a simple spell that many sentries use when transporting prisoners." He paused, his gloved hand fingering the thin metal links. "I think that's why you have been shifting to me now. But I wanted you to know, and I wanted you to know that I can take it off." Anna was momentarily silent, her head pillowed on Declan's bicep, watching the Sin Eater touch the thin metal band. That same chain that had kept her sane through all of this.

Reminded her, grounding her. Telling her that she wasn't unraveling.

That this was real. He was real.

"Don't." Whispered Anna, "Do you still have yours?"

Declan shifted uncomfortably before nodding. "Can I see?" The Sin Eater was silent, his fingers stopping their petting of her wrist, and his whole body stiffened. She waited, knowing without anyone ever really having to say that Declan's hands were a sore subject for him. The way he wore the gloves, no matter the heat or the condition.

Declan cleared his throat, his brows knitting as if in pain as he lifted the hand that wasn't pillowing her head. "Anna," he sighed, "I'm not proud of these." She was starting to feel the effect of the sleeping pill, her heart caught in her throat as she looked at him under heavy eyelids. The sparse dusting of freckles that danced over his nose, the deep green in his tired eyes, the one grey hair hidden in his dark scruff.

"Please." She whispered. He finally met her gaze and, without breaking it, took the glove's index finger in his teeth, slowly pulling back the worn leather to reveal the marked skin, the gold of the chain standing out against the inky blackness. She nestled closer to him, their foreheads nearly touching, and she lifted her hand, observing him as she floated. She was waiting for permission.

Declan swallowed, his chest heaving, "It's not good, Anna," he stated, his hand now a mere inches away from her own, his index finger twitching towards her as if pulled. "I'm...marked. They took me apart, piece by piece until this was what was left. I don't want this staining you too."

Anna hummed, the sleeping pill emboldening her, "I'm not too terribly concerned about that, Declan." And she softly let her finger brush the tip of his, a feather-light touch that sent shockwaves through her as Declan all but gasped at the contact. Anna stared at him, letting him off the hook, and pressed her lips against his, her movements slow and her brain fuzzy as she fought off the sleep.

"I don't want to go," she admitted, screwing her eyes shut at the verbalization of her inner voice. Declan let loose a breath. Somehow, the glove was back in his hands as he pushed her hair away from her tired eyes.

"I don't want you to go." A pause. "But it's not safe." Suddenly, she remembered what she needed to tell him about Sorcha. About him. Everything.

Everything was fuzzy, but she took his gloved hand and squeezed, "My bag, by the door. Read the journal. Please." The man looked confused but nodded. "I promise." She felt herself deflate, her work was done, he would know. He could get Brynn and Aramus to safety. He could rule.

So she pressed up against him, the small bed creaking at her movement as she slung a leg over his hip, bringing their bodies closer, Declan's hand gripping her tighter.

"I wish," she breathed, a tear slipping past her clenched eyelids. "I wish we had more time." She was floating. She felt so heavy. "Maybe," she heard a gruff sorrowful voice against her ear, a soft brush of leather against her lower back. "Maybe in another life." She hummed. "Declan..."

"No goodbyes, Anna."

25

~

The birds were singing just outside her window.

Anna's eyes lifted, and the sun streaming through her blinds illuminated the small room. She slowly ran her hand over the spot of the bed next to her, and her breath caught in her throat as only a cold comforter met her search. A cry broke out of her, her body seizing with the force of her sobs as she pulled her pillow close to her, a cheap imitation of the body that had been next to her. She knew he was right. It was dangerous. Her friends and her family-they were all here. But it didn't heal the break in her heart as she gripped that pillow tighter, muffling her cries into the soft surface.

Anna stayed curled there for over an hour, letting the sun track through the room until it hit her bed. Her dehydrated body unable to cry anymore. The chain was heavy on her wrist, and she swore she could feel him touching it. Touching her.

Her phone rang, startling her out of her reverie. The anxious scuttle to find the device ended with her seeing her therapist's number flashing on her screen.

Fuck.

Anna cleared her throat before answering, "Hello." Her voice was rough from crying and sleep.

"Yes, Anna. Dr. Warner wanted to schedule your visit today as she has had a cancelation. Are you free at 11:35?" Anna stared at the phone, her mind still so far in Danann that she had to remember where she was, the chipper voice of the receptionist on the other line waiting for her response.

That was in less than an hour. She knew she didn't have any pills left. A part of her didn't want to give up the option of going back. Anna didn't wait to talk herself out of it before she sat up and replied "Yeah, I can be there."

✳✳✳

"So, how are those dreams of yours?" Asked the therapist, her pen hovering over her yellow paper pad expectantly. "How's your sleep?" Anna took the offered paper cup of water, tipping it back and draining it quickly.

"Just dream stuff," She started, closing her eyes and visually mapping out her dreams. She swore she could smell the fresh air. Anna's brow furrowed at the thought of Declan. "Sleep is getting better," she paused. She still needed the prescription, so Anna hastily added, "Some days, but other nights I hardly sleep."

Dr. Warner hummed, writing a few things on her pad, the pen scraping the thick paper. Anna picked her nails nervously. The clock ticked in the otherwise quiet room, putting her on edge.

"These dreams sounded so vivid," Dr. Warner followed up, owl eyes staring at her unblinking behind her thick glasses. "Anna, perhaps tell me about the forest again." Anna summoned the Silent Forest quickly in her mind's eyes, opening her mouth to describe the beauty of the place when she stopped.

It was sudden, like cold water being dumped on her, pouring over her as she stilled instantly. "Dr. Warner," she whispered, picking at the hem of her hoodie, eyes looking over to the solid window, rain beating on it. She looked to the door that had been shut behind her when she entered. "I don't remember talking about a forest."

217

The therapist looked flustered for a moment, the pen scraping on the paper as she hummed, then cleared her throat, fixing her glasses on her hooked nose.

"I'm sure you mentioned it in another session," she waved her hand dismissively.

"I think I would have remembered bringing that up," Anna replied, her voice tight, her eyes fluttering to the door.

Dr. Warner sighed deeply, taking off her glasses before rubbing at the space between her eyes annoyingly. "My dear, you have a severe sleep-deprived mind and anxiety perpetuated by post-traumatic stress. I don't think I would trust your memory over mine." She chuckled as if it was a joke.

"I would have remembered," Anna insisted, standing quickly, taking her bag, and slowly walking towards the door. "Anna, you should sit," Dr. Warner pleaded evenly, gesturing to the now deserted green sofa.

Anna shook her head as she insisted, "I never mentioned that." Her hand was on the doorknob. She wasn't quite sure what had happened next because, at one point, the aged Doctor was sitting in her ergonomic chair. The next, she was next to Anna, knobby knuckled hand pressed firmly enough on the metal door that the slight opening Anna had provided for her escape. It was quickly shut down as the door closed again. Anna looked up as the woman's eyes peered at her, blinking at her with a tight smile on her thin lips.

"I think it's time for you to rest, my dear." The Doctor said confidently, nodding as she spoke.

"What do you mean?" Anna asked, her voice edging in suspicion as she pulled against the door to no avail. The old woman was much too strong for her frame. She felt so weak.

"Who are you?" Dr. Warner clucked disapprovingly, shaking her head. "My dear, I am just like you." By this point, Anna had found herself pressed against the adjoining wall, her phone buzzing in her pocket. She hoped beyond hope she had pressed the accept button and that the person on the other end was someone she could trust.

"What are you talking about?" Anna whispered, her heart beating so fast it skipped a beat. The old woman before her seemed to shudder as if her irritation was physical.

"You think you're the only one?" She spat, her glasses nearly slipping as she stepped forward toward Anna. "That you were the only one in history to go there?"

"Go where?" Anna all but choked out, her hands balled into fists. The Doctor laughed darkly, "You're more stupid than I had first believed, so closed off by your perception that you can't see what's directly in front of you, what is touching you." The older woman grabbed her arm, and at the chain still wrapped around her delicate wrist. Anna shook her head, unsuccessfully pulling her arm away from the oddly strong woman. Dr. Warner hissed at her, her grip stronger than Anna imagined,

"I have been trying to get back there for years. I have dedicated my life to getting back."

"I don't know what you mean-"

"Stop lying, Anna!" The Doctor screamed. Pulling back her thick sweater, she revealed three deep scars running parallel on her upper arm. "That was from one of the beasts there, the only reminder I had when I woke that I wasn't dreaming." She had a far-off look in her eye as if what she was describing had just happened. Like she could still see it. "What makes you so special? That you can go back and forth at will?"

Shaking her head, Anna tore her eyes away from the raised marks and confidently said, "I am nothing special."

The Doctor hummed, smiling and putting her sleeve down, patting Anna's cheek a bit too roughly. "I think you're wrong about that," she stepped back, clasping her hands together neatly in front of her. "I think you just need some time. To relax."

"I'm going home," Anna said, taking a step only to realize the world began to tip violently. Anna grabbed the wall as the room spun around her, and her knees locked. "What did you do?"

Dr. Warner raised, "Don't worry, the drug isn't that potent. Not strong at all. Just a nice nap. It's good for my patients who seem too traumatized to be released into society." Anna found herself kneeling on the thin carpet, forehead pressed to the rough fibers as she swallowed hard around the bile billowing in her stomach as her head pounded behind her eyes.

"You can't do this," she was slurring her words, they seemed too loud yet not loud enough. It was nothing like the sweet whisper of her sleeping pills. Her brain was fuzzy, her body disconnecting from her altogether as she tried to move.

"Oh, Anna," the old lady crouched beside her, her voice closer. "That little intake paper you signed months ago said I can. Sometimes this is a necessary form of therapy for any patient that might be a threat to themselves or others."

"I'm not a threat," she mumbled as a cold sweat broke out all over her body as she pulled her knees to her chest, her stomach threatening mutiny as it rolled inside her. The woman tutted her tongue, standing.

"You are more of a threat than you realize, my dear." Anna's vision began to blur around the edges. Still, she looked up just in time to see a security officer enter, bringing a wheelchair before she succumbed to the effects of whatever the Doctor had placed in her water.

✷✷✷

Anna didn't know when she woke up. She had no inkling of the time, the place, or the date. Her head was throbbing, pulsing against the back of her eyes, and her mouth was like sandpaper as Anna licked her dry lips. She attempted to raise her hands to rub at her temples only to find them fastened to the bed, a soft lining disguising steel cuffs that trapped her. Everything returned to her in a wave, and she pulled desperately at her fastenings, the bed was secured to the floor and did not move despite her fevered attempts. Anna's ankles raised as much as they could, the restraints at the end of the bed holding tight.

"Help!" She screamed, closing her eyes at a wave of nausea threatening to overtake her as her voice rang around the empty, white room. "Please!" She couldn't even wipe the tears that had spilled over, catching on her lashes and rolling uncomfortably to the lining of her neck.

A door opened to the right of her, and she strained her head to look at a nurse who held a tray of what looked like pills and a glass of water. She licked her lips, her throat dry and sore. "Please," she pleaded, straining against her bonds as the woman came closer to set the tray next to her. Everything was white and soft blue. Clean and sterile. A hospital?

"Good morning Anna." The woman greeted brightly, opening the blinds to a small window with crisscrossing bars against the glass. Definitely a hospital.

"Where am I?" Anna asked despite knowing the answer but still afraid to hear it confirmed. The nurse smiled, but it didn't quite reach her eyes, "You're at Morning View Hospital, Anna," the nurse's voice was low and neutral like she was speaking to a wounded animal, trying not to get bit. "Your therapist, Dr. Warner, felt like it was the best course of action after assessing your mental state at your last session." Anna shook her head vehemently.

"I don't consent to this. I need to go home." The nurse smiled sympathetically but the smile of an older person to a young child. A smile that said precisely what Anna was afraid of.

"Ms. Thorne, your Doctor does have permission in these cases to administer treatment. I understand you have undergone a lot of trauma. It's ok to rest." Anna closed her eyes and gritted her teeth.

"I don't need to rest. I need to get home."

"We'll see what the doctors say when they make their rounds. For now, I have some over-the-counter pain reliever," The nurse, her name tag read Haley, showed her the small cup where two white pills rattled. "And some water. I heard you passed out, headaches are terrible after something like that."

"I didn't pass out! Warner drugged me," Anna tried, knowing how she sounded, especially for being where she was. The nurse just pushed a small button, lifting the top part of the bed and sitting Anna up. She decided the threat of a migraine was more than she could stand at the moment and took the offered medication, gratefully drinking the water.

"Thank you," Anna said sincerely. The water stung going down. She felt it coat her throat and dampen her dry tongue. Haley nodded and took the tray, placing a small remote in Anna's left hand that held three buttons.

"Top is to raise the bed, the bottom is to lower, and the middle is to call me if you need anything." She smiled, her auburn hair tied into a perky ponytail, and the blue scrubs matched the blue of her manicured nails. Anna just nodded. She wasn't going to get any help from her. Then it hit her, her phone. She had answered a call.

"Excuse me?" Asked Anna as Haley went to open the door. The sound of doctors and nurses talking, patients yelling, and the ever-present beeping of machines flooded in as soon as the door was cracked. Haley stopped and turned around, almost looking annoyed for a split second but masking it quickly. "My phone? I had it on me before I..." she swallowed the lie that Warner had perpetuated, "before I passed out. Can I get it back?" The nurse smiled softly, shaking her head.

"All your belongings were taken to holding, and you'll get them back when you are discharged. Don't worry, though. They're safe." And with that, the nurse was gone, the door locking with a loud click as she left. The noise from the hall quickly tampered out. Anna leaned back on the pillow, closing her eyes and taking a deep breath against the welling panic within her.

"Shit," she whispered between gritted teeth, a sob bubbling and breaking free, and with it, she broke.

***

Anna drifted in and out of an uneasy sleep. Her only dreams were jumbled and incoherent. She woke up each time Haley did her rounds, each time asking when she would see a doctor, and each time she was urged to be patient. She took to counting the cracks in the ceiling, then muttering to herself that she wasn't crazy, which in retrospect, was probably exactly what someone who was having a mental breakdown and delusions would say. Time was nonexistent there. She wasn't sure how many hours had passed, unsure if it was morning or evening, the sun barely spilling into the room.

That was when the door opened, and her red-rimmed eyes

looked up to find Warner in the doorway, clipboard and stupidly thick glasses perched upon her nose like she didn't just drug her and lock her away.

"You bitch!" Anna screamed, pulling against the restraints even though she knew that was futile. Dr. Warner just smiled and stepped closer, viewing her chart and smiling at Anna absurdly.

"So Anna, since you've had a little time here, can you remember any little details you've been leaving out of our sessions?" The older woman pulled up a chair, the metal scraping noisily across the tile floor, grating on Anna's nerves.

"I'm not telling you anything," she ground out, her eyes following the woman's every movement until she finally sat down, adjusting her sweater. Dr. Warner took out her pen and opened her notepad expectantly. Anna stopped pulling against the restraints, her muscles screaming at the abuse, and laid her head back against the pillow, exhausted.

"Who are you?" She finally asked quietly, looking at the woman before her. Warner smiled and put down her pen, folding her arms neatly over the paper pad.

"Now you're asking the right questions, my dear," she sighed deeply as if delving back into her memory was a physical activity she was about to undertake. "My name is Amelia Warner, and I disappeared for 24 hours in the summer of 1971."

Anna remained quiet, hands still balled into fists.

"Now, we didn't have all the fancy alerts in the' 70s," Amelia Warner explained pointedly. "So when a 12-year-old girl goes missing swimming in a lake, it's up to the local police and park authority to see what they can find."

Dr. Amelia Warner was quiet again, her eyes unfocused, lost in the past. "So," she cleared her throat, returning after a moment of silence. "That day, I was swimming in the lake with some friends when I went down and didn't return. At least, I didn't resurface." Anna sat up more this time, eyes narrowed. Dr. Warner nodded to Anna's unspoken question. "Yes, I came up in what I now know many have called the Otherworld." The older woman sighed, pressing her hand to her lips. "It was beautiful, you know. I was an only child and prone to fits of imagination, but even this was beyond me! Even the air smelled different."

Anna knew. The fragrant smell of the forest, the trickling sound of the lake she had emerged in. The sound of the various species of birds seemed to sing in rhythm with each other.

"I wandered that forest, at first very disoriented. Scared. I stayed by that pond, waiting for someone to fetch me. But, of course, they never did. It wasn't until nightfall when I began to grow cold, and the sounds of the forest were louder and more sinister at night," she paused, giving Anna a knowing look. "But of course, you know that." Anna didn't respond.

Sighing annoyingly, Dr. Warner sighed and continued, "A large beast, beady red eyes and smelled something awful came from the trees. Eyes dark as night and mouth just," here the old woman paused, grimacing her eyes. "Gaping. I screamed, and it lunged at me, giving me that souvenir I showed you earlier. I ran into the pond to escape, dove deep down as the creature tried to follow me." Amelia took a sip of her water bottle set at her feet, giving Anna an annoyingly long pause to her story.

"So I swam, deeper and deeper but never reaching the bottom. My lungs were burning, but I kept going. Until finally, I saw moonlight overhead and pop! There I was, it had to be around three or four in the morning when I surfaced. I could hear people still calling my name, boats on the river with nets and hooks looking for my body." So she wasn't the only one who had been to Otherworld. It sounded as if Amelia encountered a demon from what Anna had gleaned from the pages of the Golden Keep's library.

Dr. Warner clapped her hands silently, "We'll, of course, no one believed me. Thought I had run off or quite honestly gone insane. I went to Doctor after Doctor, and from hospital to hospital." She poked at the soft-covered restraints at Anna's wrists. "The hospitals then weren't as comfortable as they are now, I'm sure you understand."

Anna wanted to scream. She was angry and disturbingly understanding of this woman's plight because she knew what it was like. To feel like they were going insane. "So I learned to shut my mouth and to learn all I could about the world I had visited in my youth because, even fleetingly, it had placed its spell on me," The Doctor picked up her pen once again, making lazy circles on the page. "I realized becoming a therapist specializing in delusional fantasies and trauma would be the best way to find out who else had been touched by that place. Who's life had been ruined by that little jump between universes. And then?" she smiled, her crooked teeth on display, and pointed the ballpoint pen in Anna's direction, "You came along. With your nose dive into the same lake. But you kept going back, didn't you?" The older woman had leaned closer, excitement dancing in her eyes. "You can control it, can't you? You've been more than once." Again Anna remained quiet, her heart racing as the woman leaned closer still.

"No need to be shy, my dear," The pen now gripped in her gnarled hand, "We know each other's secrets now, don't we?" Anna leaned back as far as the restraints would allow, the old woman's smile becoming a tight frown. The antique-looking pen was suddenly at her arm, a tiny bit of ink dripping onto her skin before the woman pushed. Anna gasped as the nib pierced her skin and found the alarmingly gleeful eyes of the old woman staring at her as she drug the office utensil down inch by agonizing inch. Anna screamed, throwing her head back but unable to move.

Dr. Warner laughed softly, "Go ahead and scream, my dear. It makes no difference to me and not to anyone else here," she gestured to the door with a jerk of her head, "It's just another Tuesday for them." Anna sagged against the bed as the woman leaned back, taking her instrument of torture with her, the end swirling with black ink and blood. She dared a look at the long, jagged line that deco-rated her skin.

Dr. Warner tutted, grabbing a handkerchief from her purse and wiping the blood before it could be caught by the bed sheets and pressed hard, staunching the flow as Anna gasped against the pres-sure. "Now, we can be friends, and you can walk through that door and back to your life," Warner pressed harder on the wound, eliciting a gasp from her charge. "Or you can stay here. A day. A month. What

I say goes, Ms. Thorne." Anna pressed her eyes together, trying to staunch the tears spilling through her lashes.

"I can't control it." She whispered, wincing as the old woman pulled the now blood-stained cloth off of her wound and pulled down her gown sleeve away from the prying eyes of the staff. "I can't take you there."

Dr. Warner looked angrier than she had seen her yet, her grey eyes flashing. Anna sat up against the bed, straightening as well as she could, "Why would you want to go back? You were attacked! You're lucky you're alive!"

"Exactly!" The old woman cried, throwing up her arms and gesturing around her. "That day I spent in those woods with the animals and the birds. The fruit that dripped from the trees. That, THAT was the first and only time I had felt alive in this miserable life. I returned to drab colors, the smell of gasoline, and the sound of motor cars. The stars," she stopped, gasping and clutching at her breast, "Oh Anna, those stars!"

Anna knew. She knew what she meant. But she shook her head. "What happened? To the others that you found?" She had to know, even if her voice shook. Dr. Warner frowned, waving a hand at her. "Useless creatures. Probably dribbling out of buckets at craft time at some University hospital." She chuckled, shaking her head. "They just don't let you use shock therapy like they used to." This admission caused Anna to choke and lay back on the pillow as a sob caught in her throat.

"So, are we going to be friends, Anna?" The therapist picked up her notepad and bloodied pen, tucking it in her bag before slinging it over her shoulder. When Anna didn't reply, she shrugged and walked towards the door. "I'll come back tomorrow. See if spending a night here changes your tune. Stay away from the chicken noodle soup. Shit is awful if you ask me." And with that, the woman left and shut the door behind her.

Once again, Anna was alone.

✳✳✳

It was early morning and the light streamed through the grid-lined window. Anna barely acknowledged it, she was in a steady stream of anti-psychotics, broth, and foods she couldn't choke on. Her days had fogged together.

Dr. Warner had been in twice just to tell her that she had already spoken to her job, not to worry, she wouldn't lose it. Anna broke down again, repeating that she couldn't control herself when she shifted. Again she was met with a stab of an ink pen and a closed door. Her arm had begun to throb incessantly, but she knew it wasn't infected yet because the good doctor that Warner was made sure to disinfect them each time. She knew deep down she couldn't tell her about the sleeping pills. That if Anna did, something terrible could happen. Just from speaking to Brynn, she was aware that even her shifting needed to be kept secret, that was so dangerous that it was ripping a hole in her universe.

What would happen if Warner got to it?

A door opened, the sound muffled from the static in her ears, "I told you, I can't control it." She whispered, her voice dull and her mouth dry.

"Anna?" The voice made something in her stir to look with attention at the tall figure at the door.

"Ian?" Anna choked out, reaching out her arms to him only to be pulled back by the ties on the bed. He ran to her, looking for the clasp on the restraints, "We need to get you out of here. I heard everything on the phone. Jess is waiting in the car," he swore as he couldn't find the clasp to either one of the restraints on her.

"You believe me?" Anna said softly, her tired eyes following him as he wound around the bed frame, throwing back the thin blanket that covered her.

Ian looked up at her incredulously, "Of course, I believe you." He said it so simply, so honestly, like there was no other way to think. As her friend swore again, Anna seemed to come to her senses. "Wait, Ian!" She whispered loudly, "I need sleeping pills."

He looked at her for a beat, "I don't understand. Isn't that the last thing you need?"

"It'll get me free. If we run out of here, there will be cameras and questions. They will drag me back here, Ian."

Ian crossed his arms, "So, the sleeping pills will help?" Anna looked over his shoulder towards the door as if Warner could come in at the moment like she was waiting at the door to find her secrets. "You were right. They help me shift," she reminded him in a hushed tone, barely loud enough to hear. "I can leave here, they'll have no idea how I escaped, but they'll bury it without video. They wouldn't want this to get out, Ian."

The man waited momentarily, then took out his phone, "Tell me what they're called and how many you need."

26

It was all Anna could do to stay calm. Visiting hours were strict and depended on how the doctors felt that day and how coherent their patients were. Anna did her best to seem unsuspecting. To be dulled and dazed by the pills they gave her every morning. The nurse had gotten used to her and was careless. She didn't check under her tongue this time as she swallowed the pills with the offered orange juice. She shuffled her body to hide the spat out, melting medication underneath her.

Anna kept her eyes on the door, every time she heard footsteps, she leaned up and braced against the restraints, only to sink back into the bed when they drifted further away. She times the rotations of the nurses now, so it was 3 p.m.

Still no Ian.

What if he changed his mind? No, he wouldn't do that. He wouldn't.

Steps. This time they drew closer and stopped at Anna's door.

The handle moved and Ian rushed in, shutting the door firmly behind him.

"Ian! Did you get them?" She cried, pushing up from her propped-up position. He nodded as if there was any question about him not getting him. "Where did you find them?"

He rolled his eyes, "It's sleeping pills, not an controlled substance Anna, we just have to assume this kind will work."

"How did you get them passed intake?" She asked as he pulled a water bottle from his book bag.

He rolled his eyes, "Please, like I can't sneak drugs passed a middle-aged front desk attendant? Brought back memories from high school."

Anna rolled her eyes and sat up, "Put them under my tongue and get out of here."

"Two, right? Are you sure that's not too much? We're not twenty anymore." She looked at him and opened her mouth. The medicine settled under her tongue, dissolving nearly instantly, the sickly sweet flavor trying and failing to mask the bitter taste of the medication as it ran down her throat.

Then, the door was flung open, and the flustered form of Dr. Warner appeared in the room, clutching her clipboard to her chest and breathing as if she had just sprinted down the hall. She straightened immediately when she saw Ian standing next to her bed, the mask of a concerned physician slipping over her face all too easily for Anna's liking.

"Ah yes, Mr. Smith, the receptionist told me our Anna had a visitor!" She said this brightly as if this was a welcomed event in her plan.

Ian straightened as well, looking the therapist up and down, "Yes, it is visiting hours right?"

Dr. Warner's smile faltered slightly, "Absolutely, of course! it's just that I'm on rotation for this ward, and it's my turn to see Ms.Thorne for her daily therapy and counseling session."

Ian turned, crossing his arms, "And how are those going?" The older woman decided to look grave at this question, eyes looking over at Anna sadly, like a dog that needed to be put down.

"I think she would benefit from further treatment, but she is making small improvements every day she is here!"

Ian squinted at the woman, and Anna was already starting to feel the effects of the drugs, "Thank you for coming, Ian." She said, ensuring she conveyed that she needed him to go so Warner would leave sooner rather than later. Ian kissed her forehead, staring at the therapist as he went.

Dr. Warner smiled out the hall as she shut the door, turning on her ward as soon as the lock clicked on the metal door. "So," she said, her tone losing all of its merriness that had filled her tone when Ian was in the room. "You having a little visitor?"

"He's my friend. He was worried about me," she tried her best to remain non-combative, her mind already going fuzzy. These pills tasted different, and her head was spinning.

She needed her to leave.

Now.

Dr. Warner settled into the metal chair that had become her home at her bedside. She tapped the paper pad with the end of her pen.

Tap. Tap. Tap.

The rhyme of the pen was putting her to sleep too quickly, a single dose already working in about fifteen minutes, but the double amount she asked Ian for was already putting her down.

"So tell me, how are you feeling today, Ms.Thorne?" Dr. Warner, asked all business.

"I'm fine." She mumbled, trying hard not to slur her words as she did so, feeling her lids closing and widening her eyes to keep them half-lidded.

"You're lying about something. What did he give you?" Warner hissed, her pen gripped like a weapon, menacingly leaning towards the bed. "Tell me how you shift, this can all be a bad dream!" Anna huffed a laugh, the medication lowering her inhibitions.

"I wish I was in my dreams." She whispered, feeling a tear roll down her cheek. Stabbing pain, she groaned as the pen pierced too close to another sore wound. Anna arched off the bed, trying vainly to move away.

"Tell me, Anna!"

More pain. The feeling of blood trickling down her arm. Anna was sure that it had reached the sheets. There would be some explaining on Warner's part when she was gone, and all that was left was a bloodied bed and locked restraints. She thought she had screamed, though it sounded more like a groan being dragged from her throat. And then blessedly, the smell of the hospital was gone.

✳✳✳

Everything was black for a moment. No new pain but the throbbing in her arm from where the pen had made its home in her flesh. Anna was still moaning in pain when she tried to sit up on the forest floor and she immediately put pressure on her wound. Anna winced at her stiff muscles and joints that protested the movement after being restrained for so long. Anna hissed as she pulled out the pen that still stuck in her arm, throwing it away with shaking hands.

She looked around trembling, and recognized the forest immediately. She laughed, her voice scaring a few roosting birds next to her. It was the one just outside the town that they had brought Declan.

"There!" She heard Brynn's voice and closed her eyes, but tears still made their way through, a sob ripping from her throat. Brynn was kneeling next to her, the red sash still around her eyes, Aramus next to her as the seer's fingers danced over Anna.

"Oh goddess, what happened to you?" Brynn asked, pushing a piece of limp brown hair out of Anna's face. Anna embraced the other woman tightly.

"You found me," she just kept saying over and over. She was weak from the light meals she had been fed, her muscle so tired from being restrained she stood on shaky legs.

"Brynn!" Anna heard being called from the thick forest, a deep voice echoing off the trees. "Aramus!"

Her heart skipped a bit when she saw Declan move through the trees like a storm, pushing off a large stump when he saw her. Brynn ensured she was standing on her feet before stepping away, Aramus pulling her back, giving Declan space. She stood, clad only in a hospital gown, shaking in the cold morning while gripping her bloody arm. His green eyes looked her up and down, his brows furrowed, and that small vein in his forehead became more pronounced as he took her in.

"What happened?" His voice sounded like he was holding back, a hard edge to his tone."Who did this?" Anna didn't say anything but took a step forward where her knees locked, and she fell into Declan, who wrapped her in his arms and swept her feet up until she was situated against his chest.

A blanket was tucked around her and she let herself be carried through the forest. The heat from Declan warming her enough that the trembling had subsided, but the throbbing in her arm persisted. Anna wasn't sure how long they had been walking, but it couldn't have been very long before his smooth gate lulled her into an uneasy sleep.

✳✳✳

A crackling fire was the first thing she noticed when she began to wake, the second was a gentle grip on her injured arm which then turned into something that was being smoothed over her injuries. She hissed, sitting up and trying to pull away from the soft restraints on her wrist, which caused her breath to hitch. Was she back? Did she shift?

"Shh," came a soft, deep voice, and she opened her eyes to see Declan there, a rag in his gloved hand, carefully dipping and wiping away the blood and dirt in her wounds. The skin was red and inflamed. Infection had set in, which is probably why her arm throbbed so severely this entire time.

"Hold still. Brynn had a salve for this." Nodding, Anna sat still as he painstakingly rinsed and cleaned until her skin was free of days-old dried blood. His leather-covered thumb rubbed the crease of her wrist where the skin had been rubbed raw from her constant thrashing against the hospital bonds.

"Who, Anna?" He rumbled, the question seemed to come from deep in his chest. His forehead creased in anger and sadness. Brynn sat down beside her suddenly, smiling gently and holding a small bowl full of fragrant cream.

"This might sting a little." Brynn's delicate fingers were quick and gentle as she smoothed the clear cream over the wounds. It smelled tangy, like antiseptic, and began to sting like one. Anna noticed how much better the woman was moving with the sash still sitting around her head. The seraph standing in the corner, a silent guard and their gaze tumultuous. Anna sat up straighter and hissed, nearly pulling her arm out of Declan's soft hold, but he instead took her hand, his thumb gently making circles. She wasn't sure if he even realized he was doing it, he wasn't even looking at her but the fire. She could see the anger pulsing through him.

"A doctor," she gasped, trying to distract herself from the stinging pain. "Warner. She had been here before. She's been trying to find a way back."

Declan looked at her then, "Someone else who had been here?" Anna nodded, breathing a bit heavier as another layer was already added to the other, melting into her skin. "When she was young. They put me away in a hospital. They tried to make it look like I had lost my mind." She caught his eye. Anna knew she was on the verge of crying again, everything seeming to hit her all at once. "I haven't lost my mind," she gasped, looking between the Sin Eater and seer. "This is real." Anna was nodding to herself, "It's real."

She gasped as Declan took her chin, stopping her motions. His green eyes looked directly into hers, unwavering. "This is real." He declared as he squeezed her chin a bit before he let go, a soft gasp escaped her lips as his grip left her.

Brynn cleared her throat, "These will heal, they're too far gone for us to close. I wouldn't want to reopen the wounds by stitching." The younger woman wrapped Anna's injured arm in a soft black cloth, tying it just below her elbow.

"Thank you, Brynn." Declan stood from his kneeling position, his knees popping as he stood. "Get some sleep." Was all he said, disappearing into another part of the tent. Brynn smiled at Anna, putting another blanket on her. Anna took Brynn's arm as she turned to leave, "What if I leave again in my sleep?" Her heart raced just thinking of waking up in that hospital, on that bed.

Brynn settled her hand over Anna's tight grip, "I can't see into every future, but I have a feeling you'll be here when we wake." Anna nodded, biting her lip to stop a sob from breaking through, and let go of Brynn's delicate wrist and settled against the bed roll. "I'm here. I'm safe." She whispered to herself. Over and over.

Until she finally fell asleep.

***

Anna did wake up there, in the tent. Everything was too cold, yet she felt so hot. Sweat poured all over her body, and Anna curled into a tight ball under the thin blankets, shaking. Her dreams had been filled with fire and burning, giant dragons and screaming people. God, the people were on fire. She swore she could smell burning flesh.

"She's burning up," she heard Brynn say. The blankets pushed further down, and Anna grasped at the frayed edges trying to keep the heat in her cocoon. "Declan, get me her arm."

The voices were in and out. Anna could hear her teeth chattering, and the deep pulsing in her head made her stomach lurch as morning light hit her closed eyelids. She felt his gloved hands on her injured arm and she gasped, pulling back against him and cradling the throbbing appendage. Again a pull, more insistent this time, a large hand had her arm in a grasp, and she curled up tighter. Goosebumps rising over her skin as the cool air hit it.

"Shit," she heard a deep voice mutter as her bandages were unwound. "Hold on, I'll make a poultice," Brynn stammered. Anna didn't care what they were doing, everything hurt, and she just wanted to sleep. Anna moaned, and a particularly piercing stab behind her eyes caused her head to explode. Lights dancing behind her closed eyelids. A tentative soft touch pushed her sweat-drenched hair plastered to her forehead away and out of her eyes.

The cool, soft leather was a godsend to her flushed and heated skin, and Anna leaned into it only for it to be taken away hurriedly. "See if we can get her to drink this," Brynn said again. A floral smell filled the small space and water was poured into a cup.

"Where the *fuck* is Aramus?" spat Declan, she could feel him trembling even through the thick gloves. Brynn said something quietly, and Anna smelled the floral notes again, this time under her nose. It

235

was attempting to mask a more bitter taste, she could smell it just on the water's edge.

"Drink, Anna," Came Brynn's soft, insistent voice. "This will help." Anna shook her head, her stomach pitching. The next thing she knew, the cover had been thrown off her, and she was propped up against Declan's chest. He had no cloak this time, no leathers. Just a soft shirt as she sank into him, trying to stave off from the chill. A covered hand on her chin stopped her from rolling her head away.

"Drink," she could hear it in his chest, vibrating against her. His heart was beating so fast. Why was it beating so fast? The tea, if it had the gull to be called that, was bitter and she immediately tried to spit it up. Declan's hand quickly covered her mouth, "Swallow it, Anna."

Everything was cold and hot and painful. Anna's arm burned, and she cried out as warm water hit the raised wounds, an arm coming around to hold her to his chest. A soothing humming that she could feel more than hear.

"Please, it hurts," she sobbed, tears soaking her hospital gown she still wore and Declan's shirt.

"Hang on, Anna." Came Declan's soothing voice. She had never heard him speak like this before to anyone. His usual deep baritone was replaced with a soft, gentle voice. Anna was shaking, trembling so hard now her teeth wouldn't stop chattering together, her eyes burned, and her head was pounding against her skull. She just wanted it all to stop.

"Her fever Declan-" Arguing, Anna couldn't make it out anymore as her body convulsed against Declan's gentle embrace. She was so hot, so cold. She just wanted to sleep, but the dreams pounding at her head when she did so made her heart race. More tea was poured down her throat, new coverings on her wound. She was still being cradled in Declan's arms. At least, she thought. She was still floating in and out of consciousness, trying only to escape back into that dark abyss as soon as she awoke.

She wasn't sure how many hours, minutes, or days had passed while she was in his arms, but she remembered being picked up. Crying out against the jolting, the pain in her arm started to dull, but her body was aflame. Her mind a sea of fever. Anna heard birds, and the morning sunlight streaming through the trees hit her sweat-soaked body, no longer covered by a blanket but only the thin blue hospital gown. Her head lolled against the warm chest, and shivers accosted her body. She had only remembered being this sick once, she had the flu when she was ten years old and had ended up in the hospital. Her father had never left her side.

She smiled despite herself, her burning eyes pouring tears. Anna was being moved around and sat down, only to be picked up again. The sound of water filled her ears as Declan walked with her in his arms.

"Declan?" She slurred, opening her eyes slightly to see his worried face over her, her wrapped arm against his bare chest. Anna closed them immediately as the world spun around her. She screamed as the cold water hit her bare legs and back. They were in a river. The water was ice cold, and even Declan hissed as it hit above his thighs, but he kept going until he was waist-deep. Anna struggled, clawing at his chest, wrapping her arms around his neck as he made comforting noises, holding her in the cold water.

"What are you doing!" She cried, her hot skin cooling in the icy water, her teeth chattering. Declan looked fierce as he looked at her, his skin rising in gooseflesh, his lips a thin tight line. "Hold your breath," he whispered, and before she could protest, he dunked himself and her into the cold depths. It was only a moment. A baptism to ward off the fever, and as they rose, Anna clung to him. Her body exposed to the elements as the paper-thin gowned was pasted on her.

Declan didn't look at her, his eyes averted ahead of them where Brynn stood on the shore with a large blanket. He kept her there for a few moments, holding her to him as the heat was leeched from her body by the cold waters. Her head wasn't pounding, and her eyes didn't feel as tight and hot. A sweat had broken out all over her, and it seemed to please Brynn as she wrapped her in a blanket, still cradled in Declan's arms.

"Let's get her inside," Declan ordered and he trudged to the tent, where Anna was greeted with a fire and what smelled like soup. Anna awkwardly unwound herself from the man as he placed her gently on a cushion near the fire, and she pulled the blanket more firmly around herself, realizing her near nudity. Brynn's hand pressed against her brow, and she sighed deeply.

"You're fever broke, thank the Goddess," she whispered, walking over to the fire and spooning some thick stew into a clay bowl, placing a butt of bread into the mixture to serve as an appetizer and utensil.

"Thank you," Anna said, the warm bowl comforting between her hands, "I haven't eaten in days." She tried not to look over in the corner as Declan peeled off his soaked breeches and hung them on the line near the fire. She tried and failed not to look at his bare back, muscles rippling under his skin, scars marring the flesh. One particularly nasty one curving from his ribs and disappearing into the waistband of his thin, very see-through underthings. Declan turned around, and Anna immediately dropped her gaze to the stew, chiding herself. Declan took an offered blanket from Brynn and sat across the fire, gratefully spooning the stew with his bread.

"He hasn't eaten much since you took sick," Brynn whispered at her side, only looking half apologetic when Declan shot her a look across the way.

"How are you feeling?" He asked, not looking at Anna but at his food. Anna swallowed the hot soup, chewing on the fresh bread with so much happiness she couldn't quite put it into words. All the food she had eaten at the hospital had been tasteless mush. This was alive with spices and vegetables, thick broth that softened the tougher bread.

"Better," she said truthfully, her voice a bit rough from the screaming she did earlier. "Thank you. Thank you both for doing what you did." Neither said anything, but Brynn smiled. Declan just continued eating and took seconds. Anna pressed her fingers to her temple as her head gave a sharp stab.

"Are you ok?" Brynn asked alarmed, setting down her bowl. Anna nodded, "Just lingering headache. I still feel off." The other woman said nothing but stood and pulled the bed roll she had been lying on before closer to the fire.

Upon closer inspection, Anna noticed the sweat and blood-covered blankets had been replaced with new ones, though these looked a little worse for wear. They didn't have many provisions, and Anna's heart filled when she realized how much they were doing just for her and sacrificing for their comfort so she could be safe.

Brynn motioned to the bed, "You should rest, just because we broke your fever doesn't mean the infection is through with you." Anna realized how tired she was, the fever dreams didn't allow her a peaceful sleep, and the naps she got at the hospital weren't exactly restful. It felt unnatural to lay down while her companions were still awake. Someone was always on guard, but most of that time, it was Aramus since he didn't need conventional sleep. But just the three of them, still eating and chatting lowly, she slowly realized how comforting it was.

Anna had been on edge thinking of sleeping again with her fever dreams still fresh, but the thought of them awake settled her a bit. She laid back into the rough blankets, her thin gown dried by now, and while not incredibly comfortable, she was still too weak to want to redress.

As she settled, Anna caught Declan's eye, but he quickly returned to his meal. Anna turned her back to the fire, the blanket wrapped around her in a cocoon. Anna shut her eyes and was immediately thrown back to the vision of Declan's unclothed body. Her hands tightened into a fist when she remembered how his corded muscles felt under her hands as he cradled her, walking her back from the ice-cold waters and into the tent. She vaguely remembered him covering her mouth with a large hand, pulling her back against him. Fire bloomed in her belly, but she internally shook her head. He was trying to save her life, and she shouldn't be objectifying him like this.

After that night in the inn something had happened between. Something they had been dancing around for months. His touch. His scent. Anna could remember the way he tasted and how he sounded as he had moaned against her mouth. Was he a friend? Lover? Her past captor? Anna wasn't quite sure of anything anymore.

27

"Get your hands off of me!" Anna's eyes immediately flew open, and she sat up straight, her pulse pounding so hard she could hear the drumming in her ears. She felt sick. That voice.

"Anna, it's ok, it's just someone-" Brynn stopped when she saw the look on Anna's face, which had lost all trace of color. "Anna, what's wrong?"

"It's her," she whispered, swinging her feet around and out of the safety of the covers. "Oh god, she figured it out." Brynn took her shoulders, the red sash still firmly around her eyes, "Anna, who figured what out?"

Anna took a deep breath, "Dr. Warner. The one who took me to that hospital. She figured out how to get here." Everything was swirling around her, and she felt unsteady, "Oh god, what did I do?"

"I'm sure you didn't do anything-"Anna didn't wait to listen to Brynn as she stumbled out of the large tent, wincing against the late morning sun. Aramus was there, with one hand holding the arm of a very pissed off looking Amelia Warner. She had a gash across her forehead, but aside from that looked no worse for wear. She looked jubilant, her eyes sparkling as she absorbed the world around her.

Declan was there, his arms crossed. He was regrettably dressed, even his dark leather cloak was flung around him.

As she lurched out of the warmth of the tent, Declan glanced over at her and quickly looked away. Anna realized too late that her gown was barely on her, untied from sleep and barely covering her, but Brynn was behind her, wrapping around a blanket like a cloak and covering her immodesty. The old woman in the Seraph's grip barked a laugh, "I knew I'd see you here," she laughed, pointing at the younger woman. "You thought you could outsmart me?"

Anna gritted her teeth, "How did you find out?"

Dr. Amelia Warner scoffed, "When you disappeared, I knew something new had to have been introduced to your system. And the way you were fighting to stay awake? Just a process of elimination. Especially since I prescribed you the pills to begin with! Never thought they would do this!" She waved her free arm around her.

Declan's eyes narrowed at the old woman's speech, and they looked at Anna. "Is this the woman?"

Anna pulled the blanket around her tighter and nodded. It felt like a moment from when Anna nodded to when Declan shed his cloak and ripped off his thick gloves with his teeth, revealing his dark hands underneath. The Sin Eater stalked towards the older woman menacingly.

"Declan..." Brynn started and moved forward but immediately halted when the Sin Eater raised his hand and cut her off with a dark look that had overtaken his features. He stood in front of the woman, who, to her credit, had the forbearance to cower in his presence, her haughty disposition disappearing at the sight of the large man with black crawling up to his elbows. "I found her around the northern side of the tree line, she was making quite a racket," Aramus stated, looking none too pleased with the woman in their custody.

"I belong here, you beast!" Warner hissed, spitting at the seraph who didn't so much as stir at her insult.

Declan moved closer, barely a foot from the physician, and clenched his fists, "You see, madam, I do not believe you do." He looked her up and down. "How did you get here?"

The older woman sneered, a flash of bravado as she straightened,

"I've been looking to return to this place since my youth. I belong here." She all but stamped a foot.

Declan leaned closer so he was nearly nose-to-nose with the shorter woman and lifted a hand to show her. The dark skin and nails in full view of the awestruck woman, he closed his fist, and the veins pulsed, moving like a sentient being.

"What-" The doctor began but was cut off as Declan covered her mouth with his hand, her eyes widening. Anna moved forward, scared, but every bit of her was roaring in anger at the damage this woman had caused. The things she had told her. She had trusted her.

"You don't know what I am, so let me tell you," Declan growled, his voice a thundering boom in the quiet clearing. Even the birds had stopped singing. "I am the Sin Eater, and I can smell your sins from miles away, old woman." He breathed in, cocking his head to the side like he was listening, his brow furrowing now and then. It was only a second, but when Declan opened his eyes, they were filled with rage.

"How many people?" He cried, her face still underneath his hand. He didn't want her to answer. He wanted her to listen. "How mean people did you break? Did you put away in white rooms to get your answers?" The woman struggled underneath, cries of protests muffled under his hand. Declan pushed off the woman, wiping his hand on his tunic as if she had sullied it.

"They served a greater purpose!" Warner boomed, her lipstick smudged by the Sin Eater's hand. "It was my destiny to be here!" Declan talked to her again, his finger pointed at her, "It was your purpose to help people. If you were supposed to be here, you would!" Warner looked over at Anna and pushed up her nose as if she smelled something rotten, "And her? Last I saw her, life was in my world." She argued back, and one thing Anna could say for the woman was that she had the balls to contend with a man such as Declan.

"She was pulled here," he said lowly, his gaze darkening. "You pushed." Anna was close to him, her bandaged arm given them all. He pointed a black finger at her arm, taking the woman's chin in hand so she couldn't look away.

"Was that your handy work healer?" He spat the last part,

Aramus's grip tightened on the woman's shoulder as she appeared to want to bolt. When she didn't answer, he drew his sword and Aramus forcing the woman to her knees. "And that is why you die today." Anna didn't realize she was running until she was at Declan's side, grabbing his bicep and carefully avoiding the black snaking up his arms.

"No! Declan, I don't want this!" Anna realized, somewhere dark and deep in her that she did want this. That wanted that woman's blood spilling the earth, her body fertilizing the ground she had so hoped to walk on at the expense of so many people. Anna remembered the screams down the halls at night, how many of those patients had she brought there? Tortured and twisted until their lives were only drugged-up days and lonely, terrifying nights. She was shaking, the part of her knowing that she had only to ask Declan, and he would gratefully dispatch the doctor's head from her body.

There were no police here, no punishment for her actions that would roll over into the real world. Her world. Declan seemed to sense the war inside, but he stilled as if waiting for her word as the woman below him cowered and stammered excuses over excuses as to why she did nothing wrong.

"Shut up!" Anna screamed, her rage taking over, hearing the old woman spew lies at the end of a blade. "You know what you did was wrong, and you didn't care." She sniffed, using the blanket to wipe away an errant tear. "You've ruined people's lives to get here. Was it worth it?"

The old woman looked at her and straightened, "Every second." She hissed back, leaning towards her. "Anything to get back here." Anna kneeled on the cold ground, inches from the slender older woman. "You know, had you just asked me, told me your story? Made me not feel so alone and dosed me with all of those pills, I probably would've helped you," Anna shrugged, biting her lip, "This happening to me was not the gift you seem to think it was; I have struggled, Amelia." With that, Anna stood. "I could've used a friend."

Declan raised his sword slightly, and Anna cried, "But I am not you. And will not kill or hurt someone just because I feel like it." Declan barely nodded and though reluctantly, he sheathed the blade.

His hands clenched around the hilt as if he was still considering his actions.

"Perhaps," Aramus interrupted their voice, a melodious break in the screaming that had been taking place. "A better punishment can be had." Declan gestured to the Seraph to continue, the physician kneeling, awaiting their judgment. The Seraph turned towards the woman, looking down at her and allowing their six wings to uncurl and stretch out, peering down. Their whispers rampant only drowned out by the terrified doctors' cries.

"You will be marked." And with that, the Seraph placed a thumb on the woman's head. A small sigil appeared and disappeared so quickly it was barely seen at all, "You will not be able to ever visit this realm again, but instead I will send you back where you will be driven mad with the knowledge of what you have experienced. No one will believe you. And in those white halls that you sent others so gleefully to is where you will stay for the duration of your short life." Dr. Amelia Warner screamed in rage, fighting against the Seraph. Aramus pulled her to her feet, and she lashed out, swinging wildly for Anna. Stepping back quickly, Anna missed that flaying fist by inches, and within moments, Declan's knife was out and pressed to the woman's throat. Stopping her raging as the blade pressed against her throat. "You touch her again, old woman, and there is no beast, seraph, or even her who can stop my blade," his eyes darkened as he whispered, "Had I had my way, I would have marked your soul for the hell lands, ripped open the earth itself and let their demons carry your soul away. Just for the satisfaction of witnessing it." He spat the last part and pushed the woman into Aramus's grip. The Seraph reached into the woman's jacket pocket and pulled out a bag of small pink pills. Anna gasped in recognition. The sleeping pills.

"No!" The doctor cried, seeing the bag being handed to Declan. "You have no right!" Anna looked at Declan as he inspected the transparent bag, somewhat confused.

"Two," she said, her voice sounding far away. "Two, that will send her back quick."

Dr. Warner stuttered, her hands curled into claws, "You bitch!" Declan opened the bag, took out two small pills and stalked towards the woman, who immediately clamped her mouth shut. Declan wasted no time squeezing her chin, covering her nose until the woman gasped for breath and allowed the Sin Eater to throw the pills into her mouth, immediately covering it with his hand.

The woman collapsed on the ground, the Seraph next to her close enough to know that if she ran, they were quicker. The old woman clawed at the ground, yelling until she grew quiet and collapsing on the green earth. Anna was holding her breath. She had never seen shifting done secondhand. She blinked and Warner was there, and then she wasn't. The grass was still indented with the weight of her body. "She's gone?" Anna asked Aramus, her heart still racing. Aramus nodded, "She will forever be unable to return." Anna didn't smile, she didn't cry. She wasn't sure what she felt now other than numb and cold. Declan was at her side, pulling on his gloves and staring at her strangely.

Once his hands were covered, he took hers and gently placed the medication in her hand, curling her hand around it.

✳✳✳

That night, they had laid out in the field, her body wrapped in a warm blanket as she lay against his chest. The clearing was quiet save for the sounds of the nightly stirring of the forest that surrounded them, the damp chill of the night air settling around them, but she felt safe and warm.

"You know," Anna said, breaking the silence between them. "The stars, they look the same where I am from." Declan hmmed his acknowledgment but said nothing in response. "They're brighter here, though, so much easier to see without all the light pollution." She finished, pushing a stray lock of hair out of her eyes, still looking up.

"That's comforting if you think about it," Declan responded, and she could feel his gaze on her as she looked up. "What is?" She finally rolled over, turning on her side and tucking her hands underneath her head to cushion them.

"The stars," he said, his eyes flicking up towards the night sky,

"Even if you're not here. It's still the same sky. The same stars." Anna smiled softly, "Like we're looking at the same ones. Even if I am at home." Declan nodded, his dark eyes turning from the sky to meet hers. He took a gloved hand and carefully moved the stray hair that had once again drifted across her face.

"No matter what," he said, his voice deep with emotion. "We have these stars." Anna leaned forward, eliminating the space between them, kissing the man softly under those stars.

"No goodbyes," she murmured, playing with the stubble on the end of his chin.

"No goodbyes," he agreed. And she fell asleep in his arms.

28

The sound of thunder woke her. Her eyes shot open, and she sat up quickly, her heart hammering in her chest so hard she could swear she was able to hear each beat. Anna found herself alone in the clearing, Declan gone from her side.

It wasn't thunder. It was hooves, horse hooves. And they were all around, their riders yelling and screaming obscenities, some laughing as they hooted and swung broadswords around them.

"Where are you?" She whispered to herself, laying low as the ground shook with the force of the animal's hooves.

"Come out, Sin Eater!" Came a shout from a seraph, his 6 wings tipped in solid gold, glinting in the afternoon sun. "Your Queen demands it!" The red marks painted on his breastplate showed off his rank. Octavia had sent Angus.

She crouched down, taking in the scene before her as a mix between man and seraph circled the field and roamed into the tightly knit grove of trees around them. The horses were huge, similar to the one they stole from the stables on their escape. Their coats were in varying shades of grey and black with manes long and waved as if someone had spent hours styling them. But the most unique thing was the horns in the center of their heads; not attached, not a unicorn from her children's book but a headpiece attached to their bridle. It didn't look like it was for decoration but used more as a spear. Covering her mouth with her hand to keep herself from getting sick as she realized that one of the horses had congealed blood and tangled hair wrapped around the ivory-white spiraled piece.

Their backs were to her, she couldn't stay there. She was exposed and could be trampled at any moment or end up as a brutal decoration of one of the horses' lances. She didn't like either option. Most of the group, which seemed to be around six, the ones closer seemed preoccupied with scanning the forest line.

It was now or never. Gathering her strength and willpower, she took a few heaving breaths and darted to the trees, a spot that looked tangled and tight that would be harder for those soldiers and their hell horses to follow. Anna got a good few strides in before she spotted, definitely sooner than expected.

"There!" Came a frantic scream from behind her, and she only dared to look for a moment as she sprinted across the open field and pushed herself to go faster. The sounds of hoof beats spurned her to hasten her gait, the woods closing in. But her concentration was broken as whirring came past her ear. She stumbled in alarm as an arrow embedded itself into the ground where she had just been.

"Stop where you are!" Came the voice holding the bow.

"Absolutely not," she gasped to herself, going around the arrow and taking off once again, the woods were just a few paces now. The sound of the horse's hooves where drawing closer, and her body seized, anticipating the impact of heavy hooves or the sting of the arrow. But instead, she felt someone grab her wrist and pull her into a tight embrace. She looked up to see Declan, having run out of the safety of the tangled branches, and he held her close. He spun, his grip on her so tight she could barely breathe. He whirled around, putting his back to the soldiers and running into the woods. She looked up to see his green eyes widen as he viewed the sentries.

"They cut me off at the river," he explained in a hushed tone, seeing the hurt in her eyes. "Stay close." She found herself nodding as he pushed her towards the woods. Anna grabbed his gloved forearm, pulling him with her as the forest swallowed them.

"Here!" Came shouts of the other seraphs calling them to their location, and they stumbled and tripped through the overgrowth of the trees.

"Declan!" Came a cry. Brynn. She emerged from behind a tree, knife gripped tightly in her hands, her snowy eyes wide and panicked, pressed against the large trunk.

"Brynn!" Anna cried, trying not to cry out as Aramus dropped suddenly from the sky, their feet living a cavity in the ground where they made an impact. "There is a city a day's ride to the south of us," Aramus panted, their face unnaturally tight and lined with anxiety. "I believe if we can cross the riverbed, we can lose them. The trees are thicker and uncut across the channel."

"We need horses," Declan panted, his hand wrapped around her wrist as if he was afraid she would disappear if he didn't. Brynn stopped and grabbed her bandana-type wrap around her neck, and placed it around her eyes. "What are you -" But Aramus held up his hand to silence Anna. Brynn took a few quick, deep breaths and put her hands to her head, fingers splayed across her face and temples.

"Hurry, Brynn," ground Declan, leaning on the tree beside him. Anna looked at him in confusion, "What is happening?"

"I'm trying," Brynn breathed anxiously, until suddenly she went utterly rigid, her teeth grinding loud enough for Anna to wince. It was probably less than a minute, but she swore she watched Brynn for hours until she gasped, ripping down her neck guard. "

"A grey horse, seraph rider. He'll dismount in," she looked at the trees as if listening to them, "One minute. That's our mount." Aramus nodded to Declan, "Get to the river." The seraph held out his hand to Brynn, who looked in Anna's direction before taking it and jumping as Aramus took off into the sky. Brynn was wrapped around them like a child.

"Let's go," rasped Declan, the sound of frenzied footsteps where they had just come in through startling Anna out of her astonishment at seeing Aramus fly away with the Seer.

"Keep close. Keep quiet." He said, grabbing her hand and pulling her in the direction that Brynn had pointed out. It took only a moment to find where the woods parted into a clearing again, and to her surprise, she saw a monstrous stallion nibbling at the grass as his rider followed his comrades to where they had entered the thicket. Declan put his gloved finger to his mouth, silencing any words she would have said as they waited. The sounds of crashing in the brush were getting closer and closer to them.

Louder.

Closer.

Closer.

"Now," he whispered breathily, grabbing her hand and pulling her towards the horse, whose head whipped up as they crashed into the clearing. Declan let go of her hand and grabbed the pommel of the intricate golden saddle with surprising speed, and soared on the back of the large steed. "Declan-"

"In the clearing!" So she grabbed his hand and yelped as she was hoisted to the horse, mirroring the grunt dragged out of Declan. Before she knew it, she was pressed against him, her legs stretched around the huge gelding. Anna swore she was only being held in place by Declan's grip on her waist with his other hand gripping the reins. He kicked the horse quicker, the wind whipping her hair around her. She would have closed her eyes because everything was jarring and fast as the horse ran through the clearings and dodged branches, but she heard the beat of wings and saw a shadow over them.

Anna looked up to see Aramus above them. Brynn clung to them, their arms around her with their six wings beating in unison. She looked behind them to see the soldiers gaining, their swords drawn and the arrows whizzing by them. Anna waited for the impact of any one of the them at any moment.

"The river!" Anna yelled, pointing ahead to the large body of water, white caps, as it flowed faster than she would have liked.

"I see it!" He cried, spurring the horse quicker, using the reins to keep it faster, getting the gelding to ignore its instinct to avoid the rushing water ahead.

"Hold on!" This was not a yell but a plea whispered roughly into her ear. She grabbed the Sin Eater's arm, which had tightened considerably against her as the horse leaped into the rushing water. Anna didn't even have a chance to scream as the waves rushed up around, clogging her mouth and filling her lungs. Her legs gripping the saddle as tightly as she could through the white caps that seemed hell-bent on ripping her from Declan's arms. Looking back, she saw the other mounts and their passengers bucking wildly at the water's edge, refusing to follow their pasture mate into the jaws of certain death.

"You're dead, Sin Eater! You and those bastards!" Anna heard screaming from the bank as the horse finally lost footing on the loose, rocky river bed. She felt their mount lifting and being tossed with the waves. The water. The sound of the rushing. The feeling of floating. It was all coming back to her, and she clawed at the hands holding her in place, she swore she could feel the glass tearing at her palms and fingers. She could hear Katie screaming next to her.

"I have you!" Came Declan near scream in her ear as the rushing water sounded louder than anything around them. The water was all around them, lapping at her shoulders. "I have to guide the horse, he won't last with us on him."

"I can't," she sobbed, shaking her head and gulping more water than air as she tried to breathe. It was all coming too fast, and her heart would surely beat out of her chest. "I can't, please!"

"You can," he replied, wrapping the reins around his hand. Anna could feel him tense with every movement of that arm. "Trust me." He begged, heartbreakingly pleading. She knew she had no choice, she could see the shore now, where Aramus had just landed with Brynn. Aramus was kneeling on the ground like they were exhausted or hurt. God, she hoped they hadn't been hit. So she nodded, praying to the god she didn't believe in to give her the strength to do this. Because she hadn't had it in her the last time.

Feeling Declan push her forward, she used everything for swimming along and fighting the current. It was intense, the waves going over her over and over. She went under again, and she could see the hospital room. The bed. The straps lay empty with no prisoner to hold. Her head breached the water again, and she was dazed, looking around and seeing Brynn pacing on the shore only feet away. The poor horse had its snout above water, the whites of his eyes visible and straining against the undertow. Then Declan was there, pulling the creature ahead by the horned helmet and pushing her forward, alternating between swimming and pushing.

Her head went under and there she was again, the sick white of the hospital room making her nauseous at the sight. Then her feet hit loose gravel, and a large hand pushed her forward. She found herself sputtering and heaving herself to the bank where Brynn had run blindly into the water to grab her and help her to shore where Aramus had still sat, looking on the brink of collapse on the sandy beach.

The Seer had her head tilted the entire time as if absorbing every sound. She turned back, grabbing the hand that had been pressing her forward the entire time and. This time she guided him to solid ground. The soldiers on the other sides were pacing back and forth before sending one of them plunging into the icy water. "We have to run," gasped Anna, stumbling up, still not having caught her breath.

"They won't make it," Brynn said confidently, not moving as the wind picked up her curly brown hair blowing around her like a halo. She stared blankly at the man struggling in the water, his wings flapping, and they just seemed to pull him under faster.

"Why doesn't he fly?" She asked, looking over at Aramus. Despite their still ethereal ambiance, seemed more drawn than usual. "They clip their wings," Aramus sighed, shaking their head as if in pain. "The gold isn't decoration. When that is clipped onto the wings, it disables them. Keeps them in line and obedient. After training, it's the ritual. A sacrifice is always needed."

"Most have never flown," confessed Brynn somewhat sadly, "Aramus is one of the few allowed due to their station." Then, a vast swell swept the seraph off his mount, the water swallowing them in the next blink. Anna turned her attention away from the water, the rushing waves bringing back the pit in her stomach. Like the nightmares she couldn't shake after the accident. The roaring always seemed to be present.

It filled her ears, her memories, and now it was in front of her. Her mind couldn't work around it. Declan was next to her, the horse at his hip.

"We need to get into the woods," Declan stated, gesturing to the tangle of trees a few hundred yards away. "I know where we can go."

29

Aramus was exhausted. The weight of another body for such a flight seemed to drain the young Seraph, who finally took the offer of riding atop the horse that Anna had affectionately called Rosie. She tried to distract herself with the feeling of the wet clothes on her body as they walked, tripping over roots and branches tugging at her as they navigated the forest.

"Where are we going, Declan?" Brynn asked finally, the sounds of the roaring river long behind them now. "The town ahead," the Sin Eater answered, pointing to the billowing smoke in the distance. "I have a contact. A safe house."

"Safe from Octavia?" Aramus asked, wings dragging the ground as Rosie trudged along, water still dripping from her braided mane.

Declan shrugged, "Maybe the word hasn't reached him yet," but he didn't seem too optimistic. Anna sagged with relief when they came into the town, Aramus dismounting with the seer who pulled her hood well over her sightless eyes, her fingers threaded through Aramus's as they walked.

It was a busy morning, filled with townspeople, a child darting in front of them at one point. The war horse didn't even flinch at the movement. "Let's hope he's in a hospitable mood," the Sin Eater sighed, walking down the street past taverns, shops, and a blacksmith. It was the last home on the end of a long stretch of street, Anna's water-filled shoes rubbing blisters into her heels as they stopped in front of the dark blue door. Declan nodded to Aramus, who took hold of Rosie as he took his fist and pounded on the thick wood, the door rattling on its hinges.

"Fuck off!" Came a gruff voice from inside. "I said I don't want what you're selling!" Declan smirked slightly, kicking the door lightly with his mud-covered boot.

"It's Declan, you shit." Silence. The sound of another expletive before the sound of footfalls followed it. Anna stepped back as the door opened a crack. An older man's face peered out, piercing grey eyes matching his short grey beard.

"Sin Eater?" The plump man asked in astonishment.

Declan just nodded roughly, "I have my company. We'd hope you can spare a room for the day."

A humph came from the man's mouth, "Can't refuse the Queen's envoy, can I?" Anna tried not to let the relief show on her face. He hadn't heard. The door swung open, the warmth of the home meeting them as it did so.

"Take the beast to the stable, try not to spear my stable hand, they're hard to find." The old man said, gesturing to the horned bridle still atop Rosie's head. They entered the spacious house, clean and meticulously decorated, everything with a place. Maps hung on the walls with ornate frames around the curling parchment.

"Oran," Declan greeted, grasping the old man's outstretched hand.

"You look good." The older man named Oran huffed a laugh, "That's because I stay out of trouble," he looked at Declan up and down, at the barely dry clothing and the weary look on his face. "Can't say the same for you, I'm afraid." He nodded, gesturing to the vast hall, past a roaring fireplace chasing off the chill. "Rooms are down the way, I'll let you show them. I'm finishing a project that needs completing before the ink dries."

Declan nodded, clapping the man on the back as he passed Aramus back from the stables, their wings tucked in to fit through the door. The group followed Declan, each of them in a small room.

Anna looked at the Sin Eater as he pushed open the last entry, revealing a plush bed in the confined space and an adjoining door to the room adjacent.

"I'll be in that room," he gestured to the door, joining them. "If you need me." Her body seemed to follow him as he left her, her hand reaching out to the empty air as he entered the other room. Anna felt a flood of embarrassment as he left, the wet clothing was rough against her skin. She gratefully shed the layers, leaving them in a pile. Silently berating herself for the butterflies in her stomach. Her smooth hand ran over her ruined one as she paced the room.

A preliminary search found a plain blue dress hung in the simple dresser, it was a bit large for her frame and hung off her shoulders, but it was warm and soft. A quick knock at the door, soft and light. Brynn stood on the other side, her unseeing eyes focusing on the floor as she smiled when she heard the door open at her request.

"Brynn! Come in," Anna pulled the door open wider, Brynn's hand reaching out to feel the door frame as she entered. Anna took the opportunity to take the brown-haired woman's hand and lead her to a chair as she sat across the bed. The seer's hands were twisting in her lap as she sat.

Anna sighed, "What's happened since I've been gone?" She closed her eyes, searching her memory. "How long have I been gone? It was hard to track time where I was."

Brynn dipped her head in understanding, "It's been a bit over a week." She paused as if trying to figure out what to say next. "You've - well, things have changed since you left."

Anna tugged at the hangnail on her thumb, "He found the journal?" Brynn nodded, staring unseeingly out the window as she closed her eyes, letting the warm sun bathe her skin for a moment. "How did he take it?"

Brynn raised her eyebrows, turning away from the window, "The room at the inn took the brut of the abuse. After he was worn out, he was...in a mood."

Anna winced, "I had to tell him." The seer nodded. "We know. So did he. But I just wanted to tell you we didn't go to the Port. That's why we're still in Danann."

Anna could only wait, the other woman looked worried, making her stomach churn. "Brynn, what's going on?" The seer sighed deeply, "There is a way," she cleared her throat. "For Declan to claim his power." Anna's heart leaped, and she leaned forward, remembering that Brynn couldn't see her. "To get rid of the curse?"

Brynn shook her head, "There's nothing that can undo that. It's a mark on his soul, Anna. Blood magic. But his power, though it is great, is capped. So he can't become too powerful. Not while Octavia is Monarch."

"And you can help him?"

"Anna, you still don't understand the laws here. They're not of man but also of magic. The magic, it's thicker here." Anna knew she looked confused and stayed silent, and even without her sight, Brynn took her hand as she continued.

"Monarchs only have one child, their power is tied to each other in a way. No one person should have too much for too long. The Queen or King is nearly immortal. But once their child begins their 50th year, their power begins to thin."

"So, it's like they are growing older?"

Brynn nodded, "In a sense," the seer's brows furrowed in sorrow, "When Nona passed, Octavia had no clear heir."

"Except Declan, he's her nephew…"

Brynn nodded, "Yes, but she won't allow Declan to arrive at his power willingly. And he will not be recognized by the Goddess or the people without it."

"So, is there a way to get him to that power? I don't understand?"

"Anna, she is pulling life from the demonic souls." She replied simply, "She's still in power because of Declan." The room seemed to buzz around her, and she felt the blood drain from her face, her fingers clenching on the bedspread.

"Why?" She whispered, her chest tight, "Why would he do that? What is he gaining by doing that?"

"He didn't know." She whispered, her eyes closing, pressing tightly together in grief. "Because the magic that helped her tie herself to them…" The seer paused, taking a deep breath.

"Brynn-" The seer leaned forward, her fingers reaching out towards Anna, who grasped them in her own.

"Anna." The dark-haired woman opened her mouth to say something but instead whispered, "Let me just show you something," Brynn gripped Anna's hands tighter. "It will be startling, but with the loss of my physical sight, my other sight... Aramus has been trying to help me amplify it." Anna kept her hand in Brynn's, still not understanding. "It'll be a memory of mine, I just need to show you why this is important."

Brynn closed her eyes, her brow furrowing and nose wrinkling in concentration as she gripped Anna's hand harder, and just as Anna was about to say something, everything went dark and just like before in her dream when she saw Declan, everything became a tunnel.

The palace was glittering and new, the throne room came into view. A crumpled figure was on the ground, her screams echoed off the palace walls. Anna's heart hurt hearing the wailing because she knew the sound so very well. It was the sound of losing someone.

"Where were you?" Came an accusatory shout as Queen Octavia stood, the body of a young woman laying still and limp at her feet, blood pooling around her head. And Anna could see Declan kneeling, not like before, but with both knees, his hands clenched as if he could dig his fingers into the marble.

"Majesty, I was outside her chambers. There was an explosion-" The Queen spun, seeing two beautiful young seraphs, blood staining their clothing, wrapped in chains held by armored guards.

In her rage, the Queen, with tears running down her face, grabbed the sword from her sentry, yielding it as if it weighed nothing, and held it under the first one's throat. Her hand trembling, but the blade remained fixed.

"Why?" She asked, her voice quivering. "Why her?" The Seraph looked at her, spitting on the ground.

"We know what you've been doing in the darkness of the Keep, pooling into dark magic. Demons to strengthen-" The Seraph didn't finish his sentence as the blade cut through sinew, muscle, and throat before lodging

in his spine, the Monarch dropping the sword and the Seraph it was attached to.

Octavia spun on Declan, leaning down to grab a fistful of his hair, pulling him to his feet. He didn't utter a word of protest, his eyes locked on Octavia's. "Majesty, I'm sorry-"

"I don't want your pity!" She reared back, her ring catching his cheek, ripping his skin, and spraying blood as his head jerked to the side. Still, he didn't protest.

"Aramus!" She called and strode to the Seraph Anna knew so well, glittering and new, their armors gleaming in the firelight as they approached the Queen. They simply stood, waiting for their orders. "From this moment on, your station will be this man. To aid his mission."

Aramus stood ramrod straight, but their white brows furrowed slightly, "And what mission is that, Majesty?" Viciously releasing Declan's hair, she spun on the Seraph, "I want an army so mighty that no one will think to rise against me. Disobey me." She looked around at her mix of human and seraph sentries. "I will never have royal blood spilled again."

Her eyes were screwed shut as she looked at the crumpled body of her daughter lying in her congealing blood. "I hear you have power, Aramus, training to become a Seraphic seer to aid the royal court," her tears had dried, and an edge had replaced the cracking voice. The Seraph nodded simply and quickly. "Then you can look beyond," the Queen stared at them, pointing to Nona's body. "To bring her back to me. Restore order."

Aramus finally brought their eyes to the Queen, shaking their head lightly. "Majesty, no one can reach behind the veil of death. It is heresy."

The Queen laughed, "This," she shook her finger again at the prone figure, "This is heresy! I ask not for her soul but her other one. Her alter. It has been done before."

The Seraph looked stricken, "Majesty, while it is possible, the fracture it would cause in our universes could be so damaging." Octavia grabbed the Seraph's chin, forcing them to look at her, "Do I look like I care about the consequences? Or that I could not handle them?" Aramus said nothing, the grip on their chin only getting stronger. "You have your orders." The Monarch spat, releasing the Seraph and clenched her fists so tightly that blood dripped from where her fingernails had pierced the soft skin of her palms.

Taking the blood, she returned to Declan, pulling him up again, his eyes full of anguish as she forced him to look upon the very body he had carefully set before her only moments before. Nona's blood still fresh upon his tunic.

"And you, Declan." She spat his name, "I only spared your life as an infant out of foolish girlhood affection for your mother. And as that blood oath stands, I will let you live." Octavia's face screwed, the angry mask breaking as fresh tears poured down the mother's face. "But you will help me build my army so when my daughter is returned to me, nothing shall touch her or her future children. You will live with the weight of your sins and your negligence for the rest of your unnaturally long life. For your punishment will be long life in service to me until I deem it time for your cursed soul to be sent to the Underlands." Shaking fingers gathered the blood pooling at her feet, a hand once again gripping Declan's dark hair bending him back until it looked as if his back would break, his knees crashing back into the marble floor. She pressed her thumb to his forehead, her long nail swirling, dragging and pulling a mark into his skin.

"Majesty!" Came a yell from Aramus, but she brought forth a small knife from the belt around her waist. Before Declan or anyone could react, she drove it into the man's neck, his eyes widening as the blood sprayed around the delicate blade. She let him collapse, tossing the knife to the ground as he choked on his life source, chest heaving as everyone stood frozen as the Princess's guard died next to his charge, their blood mingling on the white floor...

Shaking, Anna went to let go of Brynn's hand, but the seer squeezed. "It's not finished."

Declan's body seized, his back arching off the floor as his hands clawed at the ground, a guttural scream coming from his lips. The sentries, human and seraphs took steps back as the white marble floor seemed to vein black from underneath the shaking Monarch and flow into the fallen man. Declan's fingertips sizzling, and Anna could smell the odor of human flesh burning. The black snaked up the man's arms just above the wrist. "I invoke," cried the Queen, circling her prey. "The order of the Sin Eater, as it will now be written, in on my 156th year as Regent. A descendant of Queen

260

Oona, the first of us. You will reap the souls of the damned that the Under-
land has claimed, and I will store them until they are needed." Anna
focused on Declan, who was writhing on the floor, every vein protruding as
he struggled to breathe through the dark pushing through him, working
through his veins and skin. His neck wound healed, and a small scar was
all that was left of any of Octavia's wounds.

"You," she heard the Queen say to Aramus, who was stunned and still
looking at Declan. "Take that girl seer with you, go through every timeline,
every universe, and find my daughters alter."

The last thing Anna heard was Declan's panting breaths. Brynn let go, and Anna collapsed, her knees giving out beneath her. She lifted her hand to feel hot tears streaming down her face.

"After that, Octavia made it a crime for seraphs to be allowed to fly. She melted gold to their flight feathers, only Aramus and a 26th aerial legion are allowed the privilege. She crushed any rebellion that night."

"Is that what's happening?" She choked out, pointing outside. "The weather, the leviathan, me?" Brynn nodded, "Every time the Queen sends the envoy to scout for Nona, the fracture gets wider. Her power grows weaker and more unstable. She's barely holding things together. She has had us watching fracture points for over a year, and you? You're the closest we've felt to Nona's soul. She's there. She knows you or at least has come in close contact with you."

"So wait, I know Nona's alter?" Shrugging slightly, the seer continued, "It could be a teacher, a salesperson you see regularly. Anna, all we know that you're the closest we have gotten. Octavia has had us working on a beacon to send back. That will alert us to Nona's exact location. We'd get one shot at it, the fracture would be unstable." Brynn bit her lip, "She doesn't want Nona to alter back to restore her to the throne anymore."

Anna stared at the woman, "I don't understand. I thought that's what all this had been about?"

"It started that way, but as time passed, the Queen delved more and more into the thought that she could siphon Nona's alter's power if she was brought into our realm. The magic would hit her slowly, you see. But the Queen knows the alter isn't HER daughter. So she wants to take her power, extending her reign by another few hundred years." Brynn grasped her hands tighter this time, her face filled with anxiety. "Anna, if she figures out who the alter is, she could do this for every timeline, siphoning her power repeatedly. Her reign could be endless."

"Why hasn't Declan told me about this?" Anna asked, horrified.

Brynn's gaze shifted downwards, "We didn't think you'd be back. But when you returned, you were so injured. I think," she paused, chewing her lip. "I think he just wanted more time."

A sinking realization hit her. "So it would close. I wouldn't be able to return at all, would I?"

Brynn shook her head, silent for a moment. "The Queen's power is becoming unstable. But Declan might not have the royal power, but he has the royal bloodline. But by sending you, we would close the rift between our worlds. There is something wrong with Nona's link, Anna. It is so unstable we aren't sure if she is alive or dead. But either way, if we close your fracture, she wouldn't be able to get to her. She'd be safe." Anna was silent.

Brynn touched her hand to reassure her the woman was still across from her. "We must close the source of the portal. The lay line. It's in the Silent Forest, the pond you began with. With the fracture closed and Octavia dead, the blood spell will unbind itself. It will put things right."

Anna shook her head, "But what does that have to do with Declan? Could he rule?"

"There is something called the Right of Champions-." A firm knock at the door caused them both to jump as the Sin Eater's voice came through the wooden door, "Dinner is ready."

Anna moved to stand, but Brynn's hand held her fast, "Don't tell him that I told you." Anna bobbed her head, remembering that the seer couldn't see her, "I promise, Brynn." Her head was swimming with everything she had witnessed second-hand through the seer, and she knew she was pale as she led the woman down the hall towards the sound of the voices of their companions and the smell of food.

Her stomach grumbled despite herself, and she realized she had barely had anything to eat since her stint in the hospital, her collarbone more pronounced than usual, and her body weakened by the week strapped to that bed. Declan's eyes followed her as she sat Brynn next to the Seraph, who held out a chair for her. Anna taking her place next to the Sin Eater.

"Are you alright?" He whispered as she sat, pouring her a glass of water. Anna forced a tight smile, "Yeah, just hungry." He didn't look entirely convinced but didn't ask any more questions. Oran was a large man, not only taking up space physically, but his presence was that of someone with a prominent personality, and it seemed like even a larger appetite as he loaded his plate.

"So my friend, tell me what you have been about," he said, waving a piece of bread in the Sin Eater's direction as he took a healthy bite. "It's been nearly a year since you humbled my home with your presence."

Declan smiled, biting a piece of steaming meat from his plate before responding, "Just on business, my companions and I caught some bad weather on our way to the Gorge."

Oran grimaced, "Nasty place that. Guess it seems like a paradise for you, I expect! Good eating of sorts, I suppose." The heavy man winked at Declan. The Sin Eater didn't respond at first but took a deep pull off his mug.

"Yes, I suppose it is." Replied Declan, forcing a smile.

From picking at the vegetables, Anna looked up, "I'm sorry, what's The Gorge?" Their host looked surprised, wiping his mouth on his napkin, his beard drenched in the juices of his drumstick.

"Surely you've heard of The Gorge? The island penal colony? A nasty place, but I think a Sin Eater would have no hard time finding supple Underbound souls there, believe me. The leviathan that come from there are most spectacular though."

"Thank you for your hospitality Oran; I will make sure the Queen is told of your loyalty." Aramus quipped, changing the subject, sipping from their wine glass. Oran beamed, Anna's stomach-turning slightly as another hunk of gleaming meat joined his plate.

"Of course, always happy to help the crown." Anna forced herself to look away from the man's eating as she slowly finished her plate, making sure she did so because she needed her strength. This was no place to be weak. The Gorge, though? Is that where the group had been headed when she had shifted? Why was he still gathering souls for Octavia if he was escaping her? Nothing made sense, and her head hurt.

"I hope you find your rooms accommodating," belched the man, standing suddenly. "I must retire for the night, but if you need anything, my servants are at your command." He dipped his head, bidding them goodnight.

Anna caught Brynn tapping Aramus's arm, who nodded, "I will escort Brynn to her chambers. We will reconvene in the morning." The dining hall was silent, a few servants dipping in and out to clear the table as Anna and Declan sat alone. Him nursing his ale as she pushed around a few last bites of food she refused to finish as her stomach began to turn.

"The Gorge? When were you going to tell me?" She whispered, setting the fork down and finally turning to the man beside her.

Declan raised an eyebrow, his mug halted midair. "I'm sorry I didn't get to tell you my intricate plans while we were being hunted."

Anna slapped the table as she stood, "I'm going to bed." She declared sharply and as she turned, she felt a grip on her wrist, the chain around it pressing into her skin with the pressure.

"Did I say something wrong? Did something happen?" Asked the Sin Eater, mug abandoned. Anna didn't turn towards him but shook her head.

"No, I'm just tired." She tugged her wrist and he let go, and it took everything in her not to run but walk to her room. Someone had lit a fire, the small room warm and glowing into the late night. Anna moved to the bed, sitting on the soft mattress, her mind millions of miles away.

She was going to lose him. Anna couldn't stay here, she had to close the fracture. There was no choice. Not that she could stay, she had her father. Her friends. Anna swallowed a sob that welled up in her but refused to cry anymore. Her tears wouldn't change anything. She wasn't sure how long she sat on that bed staring at the flickering fire, her fingernails ruined where she had picked them to the quick in her anxious motions.

Footsteps echoed down the hall and stopped at her door. Anna waited for a knock, a whisper. Anything. But there was nothing until a moment later, the steps resumed, the door next to hers opening and closing. The lock click sounding down the hall.

The sound of walking in the room next to her stilled her breathing, footsteps as it sounded like the Sin Eater was pacing for a moment, then taking off his shoes the next. But despite his lack of footwear, she heard the soft padding of his feet, the shadows stopping in front of the door that connected his room to hers.

Anna swallowed hard, standing as quietly as possible before stepping at the door, their shadows mimicking each other. She placed a hand on it, resting her head on the cool wood door, breathing in the smell of the fireplace. She looked down, seeing his shadow hadn't moved either. The thin wood was all that stood between them. She could feel him, his presence just on the other side.

This could be it.

Anna started this by giving him the journal, she didn't regret that. But she couldn't keep risking her life to fight this battle that wasn't hers. At least, not in that way. Anna would save them by leaving and closing that portal behind her.

The shadow below the door started to move, and before Anna knew what she was doing, she took the door handle in both hands and wrenched it open. On the other side stood Declan, his shoes off, his shirt slightly agape.

"Anna," his voice was rough, like the first time they met. But instead of hostility, it was filled with something else.

Something like longing.

30

He was hovering, just close enough but far enough where he filled the small space between them, the air between them electric. Carefully, slowly as if one was to approach a wounded animal, Anna lifted her hand, and his breath came faster, almost panting. Declan closed his eyes in an almost wince. She lingered there, watching him trembling with anticipation while her own heartbeat was so loud and hard she was surprised he couldn't hear it, could feel it thrum against her skin as her blood flowed quicker.

Anna waited, Declan's gloved hand bracing the doorway over her. The other was clenched in a fist as if he was holding back from touching her. From scooping her into his arms.

"Declan,' she whispered, breathy and needy. Anna took her fingers and lightly stroked his brow to the edge of his sharp jaw, her fingertips dancing over his skin that raised in goosebumps in her wake. His eyes opened, pupils were blown wide, and faster than she could follow he enveloped her. His large arms wrapped around her, cradling the back of her head. Breathing each other in as their lips almost met as he pulled her into his room.

"Say this is ok," he cracked, his voice breaking, husky and worn. "Say you want this." Her eyes, which had been closed, opened, looking into his own.

Wetting her lips, she leaned in a fraction closer, "Please, Declan." Declan moaned and surged forward, his arm going to brace the wall behind them as he pressed her into it, their bodies allowing for no room as his knee went between her legs, pinning her there. She tried not to think about the whine that left her lips as he ground his leg up, grabbing the collar of his shirt that he still wore despite the very thin dress that she was clothed in.

The hand that was wrapped around her waist came to take her chin, forcing her to look at him, and he leaned in, but she pressed back suddenly. Declan stopped immediately and looked at her in confusion as if he had misread the situation.

"I want you," Anna clarified, pushing back his coat from his shoulders, and he obeyed, letting it drop to the ground. "All of you," she continued, unbuttoning the shirt button by button, her eyes taking in each bit of skin bared to her. Declan moved so the fabric joined the worn leather coat at his feet. He moved to unlace his trousers when she stayed them with his still-gloved hands. "Everything, Declan." She illuminated, his eyes flying to hers.

"Anna, you can't want..." She cut him off with a small shake of her head, replacing his hands on the laces that currently his need was straining against. Letting out a shaky breath, Anna finished unlacing the front and was currently tracing the plunge of his hip bones, keeping the pants where they were.

"I do, Declan." Anna said, finally replied looking up at the taller man. Even with his boots off, he was still pleasantly towering over her, enclosing her into him. "You're not a bad man. And you don't scare me. They," her gaze flickered to his gloved hands. "Don't scare me." She could see the indecision on his face, the battle he was waging in his head as she allowed her fingers to dance over his now bare chest. The tanned skin was a constellation of scars and still healing bruises. Beautiful, graceful and lean. The muscles rippling through the flesh with each heaving breath he took. Anna never remembered ever having any interaction like this one.

Never this intimate. Never been this passionate.

Her heart hadn't stopped pounding in her ears, and it felt like her blood was on fire. All she wanted was him. Declan locked his jaw, the small muscles there moving as he made up his mind. The same tell showed when he was stressed or angry. But he was neither at this moment. His large gloved hand moved from where it was, drawing circles on her back to hold up in front of her. Anna waited, her hands on his gloved fingers, the tiny, almost unnoticeable nod from him. Slowly, he closed his eyes as she peeled the glove back, the worn but thick black leather slipping free, revealing the black stained skin.

Upon closer inspection, she could see the hairs on his arm, the lines on his palms, cracks in his knuckles, and fingerprints. It was as if he had plunged his hand and forearm into a vat of ink, which wouldn't scrub off.

"You know what this means, Anna," he whispered, "Everything I've done with them. They aren't meant for tenderness." Anna smiled softly, guiding his elbow to maneuver his hand closer to her. A pause until she lowered her face to be cradled in the large hand.

"I'm not afraid of you, Declan." Declan took two steps forward, his fingers pushing through her hair, his wide palms cupping her face so delicately as if she would break. He didn't blink but removed the other glove with his teeth, letting it fall. Both hands carefully sheltering her, he leaned down, nearly letting out a whine as she put her hand over his, keeping his hands where they were. She hadn't realized how much he must have needed this, how he had been so abused, neglected, and shunned. The only touch he had had in years had been at the hands of his enemies or the criminals he was cursed to punish. Never tenderness.

When their lips met, it was as if a spark had caught. The fire between them raged as he pressed her harder against the wall, his grip moving from her face to her hips, where he lifted her as if she weighed nothing. Her legs immediately wrapping around his naked waist, the pants he was wearing riding down enough where she could feel his heat and growing need. Anna's thin night dress slipped down one shoulder, the buttons straining at their insistency. Her touch was all over him, blessing every scar and bruise.

Declan grabbed the front of the pale shift and bent towards her breast, biting on the top button of the dress as his other hand was holding her ass against him.

He spits the glass button out, looking at her with a lopsided grin, "I'll get you another dress."

Anna huffed a laugh, "Fuck the dress." It was all the encouragement the dark-haired man needed, and his hand ripped the remaining few buttons, freeing her from the confines of the muslin. He immediately went to kiss her neck, her head hitting the wood wall behind her. A moan escaped her lips as his mouth nipped, licked, and sucked on the hollow of her collarbone. His bare hand cupping her breast.

"Declan, please," was all she could manage. She needed to be closer; she needed him. She needed more. The Sin Eater was more than happy to oblige, holding her closer, legs still locked around him and his lips moving from her neck to her mouth as he teased her. He ran his tongue along her bottom lip as if begging entrance, which Anna enthusiastically granted. He swallowed her moan, his tongue tenderly stroking her own. Before Anna knew it, she was on her back on a soft surface. He had walked them over to the bed that Oran had provided.

As far as beds go, she was surprised at how soft it was as her body sagged into it. Declan had crawling over her, claiming her mouth again, soothing and stoking the fire of her need. He pulled away, and Anna was embarrassed by how her body followed him, the sounds she made when they were separated.

"It's been," Declan swallowed, smiling embarrassingly. "It's been awhile." Anna shared his shy smile, running her fingers through his unruly hair.

"Me too." He was looking at her as one who was admiring a piece of art, mapping her hair, her eyes, her lips. Declan's gaze settled on her opened mouth. He stroked her cheek, looking admiringly as she leaned into his touch. Declan's thumb stroked, ghosting her lower lip. Anna stared at him, almost surprised at her own gull, as she lowered her lips to his thumb, bringing it into her wet mouth, sucking lightly on the digit.

Declan hips thrust on what seemed like their own accord, his large body covering her, burying his face in the crook of her neck as

269

he moaned. Anna's body was responding, her breasts screaming to be touched, the place between her legs wet and needing him.

More than anyone she had ever been with. This wasn't just sex, and the thought thrilled and terrified her, but she was too far gone to be thinking logically at that moment. And she didn't want to. She had thought everything through her entire life, weighing the pros and cons, always taking the safe way. Never taking risks. But she wanted this. This was a risk worth taking. Anna could feel it in her bones that this was different. She wouldn't let this be on her growing list of regrets she had had in her life.

"I'm stronger than you," he whispered, his face still hidden from her, her own hands clasping the back of his head, urging him closer as he licked the shell of her ear. "I don't want to hurt you." With that statement, he pulled back, face flushed, pupils were blown in such urgent need.

"I won't break," she replied, pulling him down for a chaste kiss as she went to the drawstrings of his pants again. "I trust you." She reached between them, going to pull down his pants, when he grabbed her wrist, stopping her in her tracks.

"I trust you too." He said it with more meaning than she had ever heard anything uttered from his mouth. Something in her swelled and broke, releasing more emotion than she was comfortable with. Declan let go of her wrist and performed the rest of the job for her, lowering himself down as she spread her legs to accommodate his muscular form. Declan's tanned body encased her smaller one, his weight was comfortable on top of her. Drawing one of her legs up, he was able to curl closer to her. His hands were everywhere, like he couldn't get enough of touching her, feeling her. Every atom of her body was alive and responding to his delicate touch. She no longer softened her moans as he took control, pinning her arms above her head as he ravaged her breasts with his tongue, sucking bruises into her delicate skin. Claiming her as his own.

"Please, Declan," she whispered, bucking her hips into his own. Anna could feel him smile into her skin as he traced his tongue from her sensitive nipples to her navel. His hands left their task of pressing her wrists into the mattress, instead, the black-stained fingers gripped her hips, pinning her in place. He kept making his downward descent, Anna bringing her knees up, giving him access to the center of her. With her free hands, she bit down on her thumb as he tenderly kissed her inner thigh. Declan bit gently on the spot he had just lavished with kisses, causing her to look down at him.

"I don't want you to hold back," he all but commanded, his voice like gravel, and it took everything in her not to climax right there at the dark look in his eyes. But she didn't have time to even think as he began licking at her most intimate part, his tongue lavishing her, opening her for him. Anna's fingers dug into his hair, twinning in through the brown tresses, his fingers dragging her closer to him, pulling her down the bed with him.

It could have been minutes, it could've been years, she had lost all sense of time, and she was floating in the sensations, her heart skipping a beat as he found her center.

"Please, Declan," she whimpered, actually whimpered his name repeatedly until he crawled up the bed to her, claiming her mouth. Tasting herself on his tongue. He kissed her forehead, a surprisingly chaste act considering what his mouth had just been occupied moments before.

"Are you sure? Are you sure you want me?" She took his chin firmly until his eyes met hers, "I'm more sure of this than anything in my life." It was all he needed, taking her wrist from his chin and kissing her scarred hand with such tenderness her heart ached. He set himself against her, and with his other hand, he intertwined their fingers as he entered her.

Anna threw her head back as her body made room for his length, a welcomed ache as he filled her. "Fuck," she whined, grasping him close to her, and he seated himself deep within her.

"Are you ok?" He whispered low in her ear, almost gasping as his body trembled like he was doing everything in his power to hold back, to not move until she was ready. "Please say you're ok."

"Move Declan, for god's sake," she replied with a huff, tilting her hips up in invitation. There was a dark moan against the hollow of her throat as he drove into her, his hips snapping against her thighs with a force that exacted a gasp in her surprise at the passion. Declan was reserved, with such a force that his energy trembled to be unleashed, but he held everything back, everything was controlled.

Not now. Not with her. And she knew it.

Anna could feel his restraint slipping as he moved, sweat building up between their bodies, each stroke hitting something primal in her as she howled in unison with his movements. Anna felt the build-up in the pit of her belly, but she wasn't ready to go so soon.

"Put me on top," she commanded breathily in his ear, feeling his own build-up coming. She wasn't ready for this to end. Anna had wanted this for much too long. She was going to savor this. Savor him. Declan cocked an eyebrow but complied immediately without complaint, and Anna felt her body leave the bed. Without leaving her, she was seated firmly with him still inside her, a perfect view of his body, his heaving, scarred chest, and his blown wide eyes. He was panting, looking up at her like a saint in rapturous prayer. Taking advantage of his brief surprise, she snapped her hips, rocking back and forth and watching with undisguised glee as Declan's head pitched back, his Adam's apple moving as he swallowed hard. Gasping and trying to catch his breath as she moved.

Hands still clutching her hips, pushing himself as deeply as he could into her, she grabbed one of the bruising grips and watched his face as she took two of his fingers deep into her mouth, sucking and teasing the digits with her teeth.

"Anna!" He growled in warning, his thrusts starting to become erratic, and he gasped around her neck, just scrambling for purchase as he bucked into her. He became a feral beast, flipping them once again so he was on top, burying himself so deep inside her she wasn't sure if they hadn't merged into one person in the process. Declan grabbed her chin, forcing her to look at him, and that sight alone would have been enough, but between gritted teeth, he ground out,

"Look at me," he thrust again, "Finish for me. Just for me." Jesus. It was all it took, and the building pressure in her abdomen came to a crescendo, her heart pounding in her ears and her throat allowing for a strangled scream as she clenched around him. She opened her eyes just in time to see Declan's face contort in pleasure as he shuddered, his stomach muscle coiled tight as he moved in her once, twice before collapsing on top of her in a sweaty mess.

Anna's body was tingling, waking from her nearly an hour of lovemaking. Love making? Sex? Whatever it was, her body was singing out, her muscles feeling deliciously rung out in a way she had never experienced.

They stayed there, connected, his fingers making small circles on her hips as he fought to control his breathing in the crook of her neck. Her fingers were still tangled in the nape of his hair when he kissed her, long and lavishly. Declan slid out of her with a whine, rolling off of her. Anna was still riding the wave of ecstasy when Declan ran a hand down his face, and in that instant, Anna felt he was miles away.

"You can't stay," came his voice, a bit harsher given their amorous cries. "Can you?" The room seemed sucked of all of the energy that it had once had. Anna turned, one hand twisted in a blanket covering her nakedness as she sat up next to him, laying her head on his chest, closing her eyes as she focused on his breathing. And she swore, she could feel her heart breaking.

"No," she breathed, her eyes burning. "No, I can't."

Declan shook his head, "Shit," he murmured, running a hand over his face. Anna knelt, sinking into the soft mattress as she faced him.

"Declan-" The Sin Eater smiled softly. God, he was so beautiful when he smiled and drew her into his arms, her blanket falling away as he wrapped his arms around her. "Can we just have tonight?" Came his grave voice, nestled into her neck, his hands making languid strokes down her back.

Anna couldn't help herself from sniffing, "I would give you more than one night if I had it. I hope you know that." They didn't talk the rest of the evening, he laid her down, stroking her, kissing her. Cursed hands against her skin, wringing pleasure out of her deep into the night. Anna kissed every scar, mapping his hands and arms with her lips and tongue until he was shaking on top of her. She couldn't let him go without him knowing how much she wanted him. And he held her with more care than anyone had ever thought to before.

They slept there, tangled together. And Declan or Anna's dreams did not plague them that night.

31

B ang. Bang. Bang.
The metal bearing rattling at the force of the blows from
their bedroom door was what awoke them.

"Open up, Sin Eater!" Came the growl of Angus, his voice low and
deadly. "Or we will tear this house down and burn you all the cinders,
damn my orders." The door was splintered before Declan could
stand, revealing Oran standing there, behind the guards, his face
unreadable as a large purse was pushed into his hands.

"For your work here." Stated the General, grabbing Declan and
loosening a chain to wrap around his neck.

"Oran, you fuck!" Cried Declan, but Angus pushed him down,
black hands bound and a leash attached to his neck. "You know I
serve the Queen," Spat Oran, though his eyes looked unsettled, he
shifted from foot to foot. "As you did, old friend." Anna screamed as
one of the guards grabbed her, and the next thing she saw was a
rising fist. And then darkness fell over her.

Rattling woke Anna, wood pressed into her back, her heart
pounding against her ribcage. Something warm and sticky covered
her face and eyes, and it took her a moment to open them and adjust
to the dark wooden wagon she was placed inside. She felt cold steel
around her hands and feet. Declan was in the corner, eyes trained on

her as she looked around. Aramus's wings were bound painfully, their face strained as the wagon jolted. Brynn was unconscious next to her.

"Declan?" She whispered, not wanting to talk louder than that, her head throbbing and bile rising in her throat. "I'm here." he replied, his eye swollen and his arms wrapped around his ribs. "Where are you hurt?"

Anna winced as she tried to rise, "Just my head, I think. Is Brynn ok?"

Aramus was the one who answered, "She lives, they hit her harder than necessary." Their voice was steely, their eyes trained on the downed Seer. The cart halted before Anna could say anything else, and doors swung open. Light flooded the dark hold. Anna blinked against the sun, her stomach churning.

They were drug out, Brynn limp as they carried her unceremoniously over a human guard's shoulder. Aramus's wings buzzed beneath the chains as they walked towards the castle, swords drawn around them.

"Take the seer and seraph to the lower levels." Barked Angus, Anna looking helplessly as they moved Aramus away from her and Declan, Brynn still limp in the sentries grip.

"Take them to the throne room. The Queen will be there soon. She has asked that they do not speak to each other." Angus gestured to Anna and Declan. Smirking, a seraph pulled something from his belt. A gag was pushed into Declan's mouth, his eyes throwing daggers at the General, who only chuckled as he secured it behind his head, doing the same to Anna. She heaved, the old rag pressing down on her tongue, and between the pounding in her head and the taste in her mouth, she was surprised she hadn't thrown up yet.

Anna's knees slammed into the thin carpet covering the cobble-stoned floor with a crunch, and she barely contained a wince at the contact, the firm hands of the seraphs gripping into her shoulders with no point of relief. She heard Declan's growl behind her as he moved to intercept, but from the sound of the rattling chains, to no avail except to irritate his captors.

It felt like hours they sat there, kneeling on the stone floor, her legs and feet numb. Anna leaned towards Declan, his green eyes wide and taking in everything around them, focusing on Anna as if asking her if she was ok. She wasn't. Then, Anna looked around the palace, once so welcoming and bright. The stones seemed dimmer and darker, and clouds overhead cut the sun's light from the glass ceiling. The once floral blooming vines woven around the windows were drooping and limp. The doors swung open and Octavia strode in, flanked by seraph guards, gold gleaming and swords drawn. She stood in front of their kneeling forms, looking down at them in distain.

"All of this for her?" The Queen said, her eyes waving over Anna like she was an insect that she was about to step on. The Queen's black hair fell long past her waistline, displayed in intricate knots and pins, a long ivory piece as ornament through the top knot with small trinkets hanging from either end. She stepped down from the platform of her throne, the long, narrow steps in solid grey marble that Anna remembered to be white when she was first brought here.

Before she realized it, the Queen was over her, tall and imposing, her back ramrod straight as she surveyed her from hooded eyes, her red lips curved in distaste. "Not much of a thing to be causing much trouble, is she?" The Monarch sneered, "I don't know how I thought she could be the holder of Nona's soul. Slip of a thing."

With a flick of her wrist, Octavia motioned to the guards, and Anna was relieved as the gags were pushed away around her neck, Declan spitting on the floor as he was pushed down.

Anna turned to look at Declan, but the Queen's fingers shot out and gripped her chin in a bruising force, "Don't look at him. I am the one you need to plead with. For I am the only one who can spare your life." Rolling her jaw as the Queen released her, she kept her eyes on the woman. Nothing was left of the Monarch who had welcomed her to her court when she thought there was a possibility of her being her long-lost daughter. The Queen yanked the gag out of Declan's mouth. "You have anything to say for yourself Sin Eater?"

"Octavia, I know everything," snarled Declan, and she couldn't stop herself from looking back at him, her heart sinking as she saw him wrapped in chains, his arms secured tightly to the sides of him.

He looked desperate, a caged animal. Queen Octavia snapped her attention to him, her pale blue eyes a stark contrast to her dark hair, and they were full of rage, anguish, and absolute fury. All directed at the man Anna desperately loved. "

You know nothing!" She screamed back, all but charging at the kneeling man, grabbing his face, her fingers covered in spiked silver rings piercing the delicate skin on his jaw as she did so. "You destroyed everything of mine, and now you are reaping those consequences."

"I have been reaping my consequences for longer than you have mourned," he spat back, his eyes holding as many flames as she did as they stared each other down. Neither paying any attention to the blood running down the Queen's wrist from Declan's wounds.

"You have given nothing," the Queen's voice broke at these words, and Anna was surprised to see tears welling in the other woman's eyes.

The rage in Declan's own faded a touch, "You know I loved her too." With those words, the Queen slapped his face hard enough for it to whip sharply to the side, but Declan didn't make a sound.

"You know nothing of love!" She sobbed, "You know nothing of loss."

Declan's eyes flittered over to Anna so briefly that she wasn't sure if she had imagined it. But Octavia had caught it. The older woman looked at Anna in stunned silence and then barked a hollow laugh, angry tears streaming down her face as she did so.

"Or maybe?" She whispered, pointing to Anna and glaring daggers at Declan, still kneeling only now with fear in his eyes that had replaced the rage. "You do. Or you will." Before she knew it, Anna was on her feet, being held up by her hair that was cruelly tangled in the Queen's fist. Her silver nails digging into her skull, causing her to cry out despite herself.

"Octavia, please-" Started Declan, only to be pulled to his feet roughly by the guards as she turned to face him.

"It's Your Majesty, you filth!" The Queen was trembling, Anna could feel it as the woman held her in her grip. Trembling from rage or from loss. She couldn't tell.

"Your Majesty," Declan rephrased, gritting out the words as if they were being pulled from him, his pained eyes following Anna's movements as she was stumbling to keep up with the Queen's pace as she stepped towards the throne. "I know who I am now. Who Sorcha was." He whispered Sorcha's name in reverence. Octavia choked out a laugh, and Anna's heart sank.

"Your mother was nothing but filth, just like you," She lifted her chin, leaving the tears to go trails in her pale makeup. "And you are nothing. No royal power flows through you, and you know it." Octavia looked over at Anna pointedly, shaking her hand still fisted in Anna's hair, "You think you can close it? Take my daughter from me?"

"It's not your daughter you want anymore, is it Octavia?" Declan spat, causing the seraphs to look uneasily at each other. "Your Highness!" The Queen bellowed, her fury nearly ripping Anna's hair from its root as she shook her again. Octavia set her down, leaned over her kneeling form, and looked her dead in the eye, "He's been running his seraph and Seer ragged, looking at every nook and cranny of the kingdom. Asking every hack job for incantations and lore to help in his foolish cause," she ran the one hand not currently holding her head back at a neck-breaking angle and took a clawed finger a ran it across her jawline leaving a red welt in its wake.

Anna opened her eyes, which had been screwed shut, and looked over at Declan. He looked deflated, his body no longer fighting the chains but sagging against them, leaning back on his heels. "I know." She whispered, barely feeling the sting of the bleeding cut along her skin.

"Anna-"

"No one speaking to you, Sin Eater," the Queen purred, letting Anna's hair loose, taking her face between her fingers, and forcing the kneeling woman to look at her lover in all his defeat. "I think we should end this now." Anna's heart leapt as Aramus and Brynn were brought in, the Seer awake, but an angry bruise blooming over her temple. Aramus looked pulled and drawn. Brynn was brought forward, yanked from Aramus's grip as the seraph choked out a bark of protest, the dark-haired woman pushed into a kneel beside Declan.

Her scarf had been ripped from her, her eyes screwed shut against the light of the palace.

"Brynn was kind enough to tell me everything." The Queen simpered, looking down at the kneeling woman. "Brynn?" Anna choked out again, her bound hands reaching for the other woman.

"They threatened Aramus," she whispered, tears tracking down her dark cheeks.

"Wings are so significant to their kind," whispered the Queen, looking so triumphant she was nearly glowing at the Seer's pain. "The loss of their wings can drive a seraph completely mad." She stopped, her eyes shining. "I've only seen it happen once." The seraphs that had murdered her daughter. Anna's blood ran cold.

The whispers of Aramus's wings rose with the word the Queen uttered as if outraged. "You see, Anna, all you need to do to close this fracture to your world is to leave through the portal you came through a year ago. It's obvious my daughter is not in your world. A silly mistake. You'll have your world. I'll continue to look for my daughter. Elsewhere." Anna looked up at the Queen in shock. "Yes, so simple, isn't it? The little pond in the Silent Forest is just a short ride outside the castle walls." Anna steeled herself, blinking back tears.

"Now, Anna," Queen Octavia vibrated, "You can save your world. You know what's happening over there. The hurricanes, the flooding, the disasters around every corner." She motioned to the windows. "You simply need to slip away, forget all of this. Like a dream. I will close it behind you." The Monarch gestured to the injured Seer at her side,

"We'll restore everything. Everything will go back to normal for everyone." Anna closed her eyes, the feeling of defeat setting in her bones. The Queen smiled. If she hadn't known any better, Anna would have thought it might be genuine.

Anna flinched as the other woman cupped her chin, this time delicately, avoiding the wound she had inflicted.

"You know, deep down, that you don't belong here." Anna shut her eyes as a vision of her father came to her, of Jess. She thought of her stupid half-dead houseplants. Ian and Matt. Anna felt like she was being pulled in two different directions, her stomach lurching.

"Will it stop this?" She spoke the words before she realized they had left her lips. A stroke of the Queen's thumb against her cheek.

"Yes. I know what that Seer told you. But my magic is stable for this, I only want my daughter. And you can stop ripping your world apart each time you shift." The Monarch tempted, pushing against the guilt she felt inside her.

"And them?" Anna looked over at Declan who was kneeling miserably. While Brynn leaned on Aramus, their wings whispering as she did so. A smile cracked against the Queen's face, despite her age, she barely had a line gracing her alabaster skin, but it showed in her eyes. The Queen snapped with her silver tipped fingers, and the guards holding Declan forced the man up, the chains binding him clanking together.

"Anna, no-" A sound of a fist connecting with flesh as a seraph stopped the Sin Eater's pleading. A sword rang out as it was held to the base of Aramus's wings. The seraph rising straight, closing their eyes against the threat, their wings shivering. The Queen smoothed Anna's hair, and a few pieces of brunette locks still clung to the seams of the metal rings she wore.

"I will spare them. If you don't, I will gut them and watch their entrails spill on my floor without a moment's hesitation." At her words, the guards holding her friends unsheathed their swords, holding them at their throats.

"Anna, *no*," Declan whispered, his eyes welling. Deep down, she knew she had to return but thought she had time. That she had a choice. This was no real choice. But it was one she had to make.

"Take me to the pond."

"Anna!" Declan cried, his head wrenched back, exposing his vulnerable neck as the sword nicked the delicate skin. "It's ok, Declan." She whispered, her voice strangled.

"Yes, Declan," mocked the Queen. "It will be right after this is all finished." They were all loaded onto horses, Brynn's arm secured to her chest as she sat in front of Aramus, their wings surrounding her. Declan was being pulled behind her horse, secured by a long chain, his bare hands swollen and bleeding at the pinching chains. She went to look back at him until the Queen's manacled hands grabbed her head, pushing it forward.

"Best not to look behind you dear, so much better to look ahead." But it was Aramus who was walking beside her, wings shackled so they couldn't extend. But they whispered so low that Anna first thought the wind was playing with her imagination. But Brynn, her scarf returned to her face, was also tilting her head to the side.

Listening.

So Anna took a deep breath and listened. *"She's lying, Anna. Nona's alter is in your world."* Anna waited, the hundreds of soft voices coming together to form the sentence. She tilted her head slightly, trying to signal Aramus that she heard them. *"You will be given a beacon, something small. It will follow you. Leading the Queen to your timeline."* She blinked hard, hoping that the seraph understood. *"The beacon won't be able to make it through the shifting if the host is no longer alive."* Anna tried not to look at the seraph in shock as the words registered. *"You'll be safe in your time. Trust Brynn."*

Anna tried desperately to swipe the tear away from her eyes with her bound hands at the seraph's words, Aramus looked pained as they walked. There was silence as they finished the few twists and turns to the old pond where she had first found herself in the Otherworld. Danann.

It was shorter than she remembered, maybe it was because she was taking everything in, everything she had tried so hard to forget. To medicate away. The way the trees whispered in the wind, the vibrant green of this alien world.

The giant horse she was currently perched upon, gleaming horn pointing ahead like a compass dial. The woods opened to the meadow where she had first arrived over a year ago, broken and dying in her own world.

The Queen gestured her to dismount, the seraphs taking the chains and holding her there. Like she would run while her friends were being held at knifepoint. So she walked towards the pool, the glittering water looking inviting, even though she knew this would be the place of her death. Why was it always water? But then again... She looked up at the staggering ceiling of overhanging trees, exotic flora, and small tittering birds that clung to the foliage.

It was a beautiful place to die.

"Unchain her," The Queen cocked her head as if she was enjoying watching the emotions flickering over Anna's face as the dark-haired man was placed in front of her.

"Anna," Declan looked gutted, and as soon as the chains fell to the ground in a heap, she was to him, wrapping her arms around him. He clung himself to the smaller woman.

"I'm sorry." She whispered, and he looked at her, face a mask of confusion. "We should have had more time," she whispered, intertwining her fingers with his, keeping them close to her cheek. "But maybe, maybe in another life."

He freed his hand from her grasp and took her chin delicately between chained, black hands.

"I would find you anywhere. I will find you." His blackened fingers touched the gold chain on her wrist. Anna smiled through tears, "No goodbyes right, Sin Eater?"

Declan swallowed hard, "Anna-" A sharp clap behind them broke their goodbyes like a bucket of cold water. "Enough of this!" The Queen declared, motioning to the pool. "Seer!" Brynn was taken down from her mount, withdrawing a blue stone from her bag, waves and swirling beneath the hard surface like an entire universe was trapped inside the small enclosed stone. It was heavy, about the size of her fist.

"Just hold this as you shift." Brynn's hands pushed the stone into her hands. Something hard dug into her palm as the stone was placed there. A tear escaped the red cloth around the Seer's face. Oh, Brynn.

"Thank you, Brynn," she whispered, stroking the thumb of the woman. "I'm so glad to have met you. Take care of them."

"Majesty, please-" the seraph holding Declan yanked on the chains pushing him to the ground.

"Before we let you through, perhaps a test," Octavia pursed her lips, snapping her fingers behind her, and Anna froze. She couldn't breathe, oh God, she couldn't breathe when she saw the group of bound seraphs coming around the thick forest bend.

Aramus's wings flared in anger, the blade against them pressing into the feathers as their jaw clenched at the sight of his legion, all twenty five of them. Titus, with his head held high, his blond cropped hair clumped with blood, a bruise blooming over his face, the rest of the aerial team looking none the better.

"See what happens?" The Queen purred, flicking her wrist towards the group, addressing Aramus this time. Her silver-capped nails dug into Titus's face, leaving a long slash down his cheek and over his lips as she smiled at the blood that sprung forth. The hate bloomed in the man's eyes, and to his credit, he barely flinched. His once soft and sweet eyes murderous as he beheld his Queen.

"You did this. You're responsible for all of this suffering. You're a traitor, and you will be treated as such," She all but cooed. The Queen snapped again. This time, her gold wing-tipped guards brought them to the water's edge where Anna stood, feet sinking in the soft mud. "And I don't abide traitors. Seer," Octavia barked, "Open it."

Brynn stammered, her bound hands wringing against the rough rope. "I don't know where they'll end up. There's no beacon, no tether-" The Queen rolled her eyes, "Did I ask where they would go? Open. It." A knife glinted against Brynn's throat, her deep swallow against the glinting blade the only tell that she felt it against her skin.

Brynn was muttering, her fingers trembling as she pointed towards the water as it began to swirl and toss, becoming a torrent of waves, the pond's ground disappearing as flashes of light and dark, lightening and sounds of roaring and crashing echoed throughout the air. Anna stumbled back as the pond's ground gave way to open air. A city? Glimpses of life and sounds of car horns, blurry and focusing in and out, just as if she was looking through her mirror in the bathroom. She tried not to widen her eyes as something small fell from Brynn's hands into the swirling waves, as she muttered and moved her hands in intricate movements. Anna didn't scream, only could look on in horror as the twenty five seraphs were pushed into a swirling mess. Titus was the last as he watched his friends, his soldiers, fall into the abyss.

Then they were gone, Brynn heaving as the portal closed, the leaves that had been flung around so carelessly earlier falling to the floor as the wind died down. It never looked like that when she shifted.

Where had they gone? They were trapped. Forever.

"You're next." The Queen gritted out. Aramus looked shattered, their wings low. They fell into the soft earth, bound hands bracing on their knees as they choked on their emotion. Their legion. Their friends. She knew too well that guilt.

Anna wished she could comfort him. To tell the seraph that she shared the blame. But Anna waded into the pond, her toes sinking into the soft, warm mud at the bank. Her dress floated around her as the sun-warmed water lapped at her. The stone was gripped in her hand, a small knife that Brynn had nestled into her palms dug into the sensitive skin.

It was so small, it must have been the one Brynn had kept in her boot. That she had only used once when defending Declan. As she was to her waist, Anna turned to see her friends, still bound in chains looking at her mournfully. And Declan. God, the look on his face. She mapped it, memorizing every line, every scar. The way he looked at her after they had shared that night, the way he tasted. The weight of him.

"I'm so sorry, Declan." The Queen went to say something, but as she opened her mouth Anna threw the stone onto the bank at the Queen's feet. They wouldn't follow her this time. The knife now revealed as she quickly brought it to her throat, pressing deep into her artery. It would be the quickest way.

Behind the muffled thrumming of her, she heard shouting, screams, and a loud blinding light as Aramus's wings unfurled. The Queen's mouth was open. That must have been the scream. Or was it Declan's, whose whole body was fighting against one of the human guards, pulling him back as Anna drifted below the surface?

The sky was beautiful. And clouds were rolling by, and a bird flittered over her. So colorful. The water entered her ears as she began to sink. When her head went under, she looked up, but the water was murky with her blood and the sun was disappearing as she sank. Her lungs burned as water entered them, but she was so close to the end it didn't matter anymore. So she closed her eyes. She focused on her apartment, sunlight streaming through the windows. Her unmade bed.

Anna had one more thought, breaking through the burning in her lungs and the pain in her neck. She had wished she could have told him she loved him. But she didn't have the time. And now she never would.

And for the final time, Anna slipped away.

32

6 MONTHS LATER

~

Matt and Ian smiled as Anna opened the envelope at dinner. Her father and Jess all sat around the casual restaurant, glasses full and hearts light. "A baby?" She cried, seeing the ultrasound and the circled mass in the middle. Ian smiled so wide, Matt leaning on him. "She's due in 3 months. It was last minute, we got a call last week." Ian explained, and Anna could barely contain her glee as she wrapped her arms around her friend, her father clapping Matt on the back in congratulations.

"More margaritas!" Jess cried, waving over the waiter with jubilance. Anna's heart was so full, her friends nestled around the table, celebrating. Being together. She had ended up with a scar when she had shifted back over, right where the knife had pierced through the vein. But no more dreams. No more mirrored glimpses of other worlds. She was here. Jess and Bill got along great, but Jess got along with everyone. She had this innate sense of what to say to make people feel at ease, she could chameleon herself to whatever situation was given to her. Anna knew it was from the years of customer service jobs from retail to now a call center, which made it even harder to read people and judge their situation with sometimes tens of thousands of miles between them. Her dad laughed at one of Jess's very inappropriate jokes that seemed just right for her retired firefighter father to laugh at until the tips of his ears turned red.

She saw her father wave for the check, "Dad, I can get it! We invited you out!" Her father huffed, taking the small black tablet before her hands could interfere, scribbling his information casually.

"I'm just glad we both had a day off, and I get to see you and meet your friends." She smiled a genuine smile. Anna had felt so hollow, leaving them the way she did. "And getting to celebrate with Ian! My god, it's been at least a year since we last saw each other!" Her father clapped on Ian's back, shaking Matt's hand in congratulations. Anna smiled, bringing her glass to her lips, her eyes flickering to the chain around her wrist. Declan. Her heart pinged at the thought of him, and she knew her eyebrows drew together in pain because Jess gave her an odd look, and she quickly smoothed her features, tapping her margarita glass as if to explain any oddness in her behavior.

"Lightweight," mouthed the blond girl, rolling her eyes humorously before finishing the small bit in her glass. Looking at her father and Jess interacting, the taste of tacos and margaritas. The smell of fresh tortillas being made while the sound of the latest pop song filtered in between it all.

Anna smiled. She could do all of that with ease. She was where she was supposed to be. Aramus had assured her that they could take it from there. She knew Brynn would explain. Declan would arrive at his power and rule Danann as it should be.

He would be happy. He would be free.

But it didn't help the months as she lay in bed, the sounds of his screams as she had plunged a knife into her neck. The way her blood had felt as it had run down and mingled in the pond water. The way he touched her, kissed her. She knew he was a once-in-a-lifetime for her. That no one would replace him. And she knew that it had only been a few months, but she wasn't sure she wanted to ever try again.

"Ready?" Bill asked, smiling as he placed his napkin over his near-empty plate. Anna smiled and, upon standing, was quickly pressed back into her chair as the ground beneath her shook violently. A siren rang out.

"Earthquake!" Cried Jess, grabbing Anna's shoulder. Everyone in the building froze, waiting for the shaking to subside. But it only grew stronger. "We need to get out of the building!" Her father leapt into action after twenty years as a firefighter. Emergencies triggered a muscle memory, they ran out the door, other patrons following and stumbling over each other as the shaking didn't stop but only intensified. The large plate glass windows shattering with a particularly nasty jolt. They pressed through the group of pedestrians and onto the road, where cars were swerving or standing still as the buildings swayed overhead.

A truck ran into a stalled car, the sound of bending metals and shattering glass exploding around them as they continued to run. Her ankle gave an agonizing twist, and she cried out as her boot protected it from what she was sure would've been a break.

Anna pressed on, her ankle shooting stabbing pains as she did, and looked over to see Jess's forehead adorned with blood, a jagged cut running nastily on her brow, red pooling even as the other woman wiped it away. Bill pushed his daughter quicker, Anna's hands flung over her head as debris rained above her as buildings and apartments shook from their foundations. Jess's blood-soaked hand was clasped so hard in hers that she was convinced if they held each other any tighter, her bones would break. Ian and Matt ran behind them, dodging another car that careened towards them as the street cracked underneath.

There was so much screaming. The salon Anna had her hair done had an SUV through the front glass, sirens from cars jostled so hard that their alarm systems triggered, and alarms echoed downtown, bouncing off the buildings. She couldn't remember how often she had heard the downtown alarm system activated. This was out of a horror movie.

"Keep going, we need to get away from the buildings!" Yelled Bill, tugging her hand to move faster, grasping his as tight as she could. There was a scream as they entered the only clearing without a building jutting directly above them for blocks, all turning around to find the source.

Anna looked up. "Oh, my god." She whispered, horrified. The

parking garage. Its seven stories of vehicles swayed as the earthquake continued, unlike any other one Anna had ever experienced here. They only got a few, barely triggering the scale or being newsworthy. This was different. And deep down, she knew why. But she left. She closed the fracture by leaving. Her breath was coming in short pants, everything sense overwhelmed with sound, smell, the very earth beneath her feet coming apart underneath her.

"Oh god," she heard her dad swear and followed his gaze. A woman, carrying a screaming toddler, was running down the stairs of the parking garage, falling with each jolt as she did so. Before she knew it, her dad was running across the street, narrowly being missed by a speeding motorcyclist escaping the city's trembling structures.

"Dad, no!" She went to chase after him, but Jess grabbed her arm, pulling her back.

"You, stay back!" He yelled back in a tone that nearly stopped her in their tracks at the pleading note it gave.

"You won't make that!" Jess screamed, pulling her away from the road as a major split erupted underneath her, steam shooting up from the broken sewer line.

"What the fuck is that?" She'd never heard Jess's voice like that. The sound of wings above, beating. The whoosh. The low thrumming hum and whine. Anna's blood froze, and she looked up, knowing exactly what she would find there. There was nothing through the smoke, clouds, and rain until a clap of lightning illuminated the sky to outline the leviathan that loomed within.

"No."

She breathed, the wind whipping around her, tugging her hair with each beat of its mighty wings.

"DAD!" Anna screamed as she saw the figure of her father with the woman running from underneath the last level. Anna yelled for him to run, and the earth stilled for half a second before it shattered around her, throwing them both down to the ground. They scrambled to find purchase in the rain-soaked grass as thunder joined the jolt of lighting. A roar from above them was loud enough for her to scream alongside it, but she knew that no one would see the monster because no one would be looking to the sky in an earthquake.

A second sound louder than the thunder, more deafening than the screaming, sirens, or leviathan. The sound of concrete snapping and iron rods buckling as the structure in front of them began the domino of collapsing. Anna couldn't scream. She couldn't cry. All Anna could do was kneel there, fingers twisted in damp weeds and knees sinking in the mud. As she saw the greying-haired man push the woman and child into the street, he disappeared into a cloud of concrete dust, twisted metal, and seven floors of cars.

She thought she heard Jess scream, she felt her grab her around her shoulders, supporting her as Anna's arms gave out, clutching at the other woman and the world wet grey with dust. Her ears were ringing, Anna could barely make out the sirens anymore, there was too much screaming. She couldn't differentiate between Jess, the survivors, or her own.

He was gone, just like that. And the world dared to still be spinning on its axis like it didn't even matter.

This was all her fault. She was supposed to fix all of this. She had given everything. Everything. The beat of the wings above them, more screaming. People were looking up as the ground stopped shaking.

Anna looked around, Jess was on the ground crying, and the warbled beeping of car alarms from beneath the rubble wailed in time for the emergency sirens that still vibrated around them.

No. Anger so hot and fresh she could taste it. Anna stood on shaky limbs, her ruined ankle making itself known as she did so, Jess pulling on her arm to stop her assent.

"Let go, Jess," she whispered, her voice empty and hollow, her eyes on the rubble before her.

"You can't do anything, Anna!" The blond replied, her voice cracking and coughing on the lingering dust that seemed never-ending. Ian and Matt grabbed at her, but she pushed them away. Anna pulled her dad's keys from her back pocket and crouched, ignoring the agonizing pain radiating through her leg. Anna grabbed Jess around her shoulders and pulled her into a crushing hug. She looked at Ian, whose face had drained of any color. Because he knew. The only one she had told.

"Anna-" He started but she shook her head. "I'm going to fix this." Without another look back, she stood, ignoring Jess's pleas, and took off towards the parked blue truck that had been mercifully untouched in the carnage, her gait lurching as she ran, almost being thrown to the ground again as a sudden aftershock shook the city streets. But she didn't stop, not as the pale police officer with blood running down his face tried to pull her back to the safety of the park clearing, not when a woman walked down the middle of the road with a dazed look on her face, her steps tottering with only one red high heel on. Blood running down her face and into her unblinking eyes.

Anna swallowed the vomit that threatened to push past her lips and yanked open the truck's stiff driver's door, yelling in pain as she leaped into the tall vehicle, pulling herself in and tugging the seat belt around her. The street shifted the car around again with another shake. How long could this go on? Anna realized she didn't have the time to find out as the leviathan above her took off, its shadows eclipsing the sun and casting its entire expanse on the road in front of her as she drove, swerving around a corner, clipping the ornamental traffic lights, her teeth set as she pushed the old truck faster and catching air over the uneven road.

"Fuck!" She screamed, smacking the steering wheel hard enough that her hands rang out in protest. The overpass had collapsed, the ruined pile of unfortunate cars twisted in between asphalt and mangled rebar, the lucky individuals that made it out sitting in confusion on the side of the roads. She was only minutes away from her apartment. The roads were caved in, their foundations ripped apart, roots sticking out from the crumbling dark pavement. Anna drove with intent, almost with tunnel vision.

Deftly weaving between stalled vehicles, panicked pedestrians, and screaming emergency vehicles. Pulling the break and not even caring when the engine gave a screaming protest as she had barely stopped it before she jumped out, cursing again as her boot was the only thing keeping her ankle steady.

"The building is coming down!" Came the voice of her neighbor. He looked so scared. She pushed past him, the door to the entrance hanging off of one hinge, and she took the steps two at a time until she made it to her unit. Her keys fumbling in her hands while the building rocked heavily.

Inside, she was met with her apartment in shambles, broken pottery from her plants and dirt strewn everywhere. She grabbed her book bag and stuffed a few items inside. Bandages, medication, and underwear. The earth stopped shaking momentarily, and she used the opportunity to her advantage, limping to the bathroom and opening her medicine cabinet. The orange bottle with the small, pink sleeping pills was next to her face wash, and she looked at them only for a moment before deciding to grab the entire bottle and shove it in her jacket pocket. Anna's memories flickered back to that time at the pond as she kept looking at her wrist.

The tether. The reason Declan and Anna had been pulled together when she shifted. The fracture was still opened, somehow. The lay line still alive.

A roar. A sound she could never get out of her head as it vibrated the room and made her eardrums ache. There were two of them now. The fracture was never closed. Octavia had found a way. Anna looked at her apartment one more time, hand stilled on the brass door knob, a sharp ache in her chest. The panicked screams outside caused her to draw herself up and steeled her jaw, scrubbing at her face and running down the stairs as fast as she could. Tears swam in her vision as she put the aging truck in drive, peeling away from her home in the one direction she never wanted to go. The roads were a congested mess, cars abandoned, and people fleeing from the more dense part of the city as the buildings around her pelted the pedestrians with debris or collapsed altogether.

Swearing loudly, she swerved around a van that suddenly was swallowed as a sinkhole opened up under them. She didn't realize she was crying until she reached the overpass and pulled the emergency break at the last minute, the truck fishtailing before stopping in a slew of smoke and the smell of burned rubber.

"You can do this. You can fix this." She muttered to herself, her shaking hands making opening the tiny, childproof bottle nearly impossible.

One. She took three of the small pink pills, just in case.

Two. A stale soda washed it down, and she gripped the steering wheel, feeling the sun-warmed cracked leather. The same one she had learned to drive with the first time.

Three. A sob ripped free from Anna. Her father laughed as she struggled with her parallel parking.

Four. Declan. Tears were clouding her vision as she felt her brain start to static.

Five.

Declan.

Declan.

Declan. The parking brake was released. Something she could feel. The steering wheel. Something she could taste. The after-wash of the sleeping pills. Something she could hear. The ringing in her ears. Something she could see. The bridge. That fucking bridge. A large shadow overhead followed her.

"Come on, you fucking bastard." She gritted out, watching the leviathan circle overhead, following her. A roar that reminded her she didn't have much time. Octavia was going to rip apart all their worlds. Anna let out her breath and pushed the gas pedal, the truck struggling to accept the new command and weaving before straightening. Careening towards the edge of the broken bridge where the structure had begun to fail.

The sound that came from her was foreign to her, the cry of anguish, relief, and panic all at the same time as the truck sailed from the safety of the road and into the air. She was floating. The sound of beating wings overhead and the roar of the leviathan chasing her vehicle as it careened off the bridge. Her hands were simply placed on the steering wheel. She wouldn't be fighting this time.

As the water rushed to meet her, she closed her eyes. The chain around her wrist gleamed as the sunlight hit it, and her hands left the steering wheel and wrapped around the small, simple chain. Please work.

Declan. Declan.

The last thing Anna saw was blue.

Declan.

It wasn't the woods this time. It wasn't the castle. Anna struggled to open her eyes, her head heavy. Water lapped around her, but she was on solid ground. The sound of roaring, bellowing as the leviathan struggled in the water.

Anna pushed herself up to her elbows, seeing the floating truck and the winged beast pushing itself to the opposite shore. She looked up, the wind still pushing the clouds, the trees swaying.

It worked.

And for the first time since the day she had died, even as she choked on the lake's water, Anna felt like she could breathe. She sat there. Stunned, taking deep gulping breaths, the sky spiraling as the wind whipped around her. Her trembling limbs struggling to right themselves.

She was shaking, but her heart thudded calmly in her chest. It was as if the two parts of her finally came together.

As the sky above her whirled in dazzling pinks and purples of storms, wind pulling at her hair and wet clothing, she went shakily to her knees. She no longer felt a pull. She felt seated and firm, like she was were she was supposed to be.

And Anna stood.

EPILOGUE

Beep. Beep. Beep.

"We need to get these people stabilized!" A doctor yells. More beeping, more praying, and screaming as the building shakes again. The hospital beds moves from side to side as it lulls in time with the earthquake. Tubes are stretched, IVs are pulled taunt as nurses and doctors scramble to stabilize the patients.

A roar of something in the distance, something stirring in her. Like walking past a stranger and smelling your mother's perfume, instantly jolting your memory. A pull at her chest. Deep, like something tugging. A slight movement of her finger.

The beeps got more persistent. More put together. Another rattle of the building. A light bulb exploded somewhere in the hallway with a loud pop. Someone was sobbing, trying to be quiet.

No more shaking. No more roaring. Silence. Then came a burning inside of her, something screaming at her.

Wake up.

And Kate opened her eyes.

CONTINUE TO READ THE PROLOGUE OF THE
SECOND INSTALLMENT OF THE
OTHERWORLD ANTHOLOGY

the sum of our faults

THEIR STORY CONTINUES. COMING SOON

A GLIMPSE FROM A SUM OF OUR FAULTS

~

Titus was falling.

There was a roaring in his ears that drowned the other sounds around him, the wind ripping at his clothes and feathers as he plummeted. Titus heard the screams of his fellow aerial legion as they all seemed to regain consciousness at the same moment. The seraph struggled to right himself, even as his body was tossed around through hazy, night sky. The stars were dimmer here, the air thick and smelled so strange. But he didn't have time to think about it as they broke through thick cloud cover, and the below them the land was lit with thousands of lights and towers piercing the sky.

"Wings!" Titus shouted over the rushing wind and the beating of his own heart in his ears. "Glide!"

Titus breathed out through his nose, tightening his core and neck as he braced himself. All six of his wings spread, cutting the air in half and jerking him from his free fall and he couldn't stop the scream that ripped itself from his throat as his muscles strained.

The beating of wings and yells from his fellow aerialist had him looking up, to see a few dozen of his brigade steading as the terrifying buildings and lights came into sight.

"We need a place to land!" Cried Cleo, her black hair whipping around her. Titus jerked his head in agreement, turning every which way to find a place to land that wasn't covered by buildings or blinding beams of yellow lights.

"Lieutenant! On your right!" Titus barely had a chance to bring his wings in tight, dropping him quickly towards the ground to maneuver out of the path of a huge, green metal object.

"What are those?!" Screamed another soldier, their wings beatings quickly to join the other as the giant metal beasts all but surrounded them. There were things inside them. Goddess, where were they?

It was Adrian, the youngest and newest recruit that broke formation, falling rapidly through the sky as another beast came at them, spinning incredibly fast.

"Adrian! Formation!" Titus screamed, his head pounding as his lungs repeatedly pulled at the thin air. "Stay with the squadron!"

It happened so fast; one minute Adrian was there, the next there was a flurry of orange pulses that ripped through the young soldier, his silver wings and body all but disintegrating into the night sky.

Titus's chest tightened as his mighty wings beat against the wind and rage swarming through him.

"Formation!" The seraph cried, looking up as rain began beating down from above. Their visibility was now cut in half, however the large metal beasts seemed immune to the downpour.

Back to back, wing to powerful wings, the 26th Aerial Brigade tightened their ranks. No seraph was left with an inch of space as their massive appendages beat in unison, their vulnerable backs kept towards the center. Titus had no blade, no arrows.

He had no plan.

More beasts flew around them for what seemed like forever while he blinked away rain and prayed to Danu that the flashing lightening did not strike one of them.

It was a flash of lightening that filled the air, the hair on his arms standing on end. It obstructed his vision long enough to hear a seraph to his right yell, "Lieutenant!"

They were hit hard, something catapulted from one of the green demons. They were falling.

Screams and cries of pain echoed around him as thick cable cut into his face and his wings. he futilely ripped at the thick strands as the winds ripped around them. He wasn't sure how long they fell but it came to a sudden, colossal stop. He heard a pop before he felt the blinding pain of his middle wing ripping from its socket, deep in his back. Titus had the feeling of floating, the loud noise of a thousand grinding gears and being carried through the storm.

Titus felt everything all at once, then nothing at all.

CONTINUED IN THE SUM OF OUR FAULTS...

ACKNOWLEDGMENTS

~

You wouldn't be reading this story without the constant encouragement from my sister, Chrissi. I sent her chapters from when I first started my very first draft and got really in my head about it. Chrissi insisted she wanted to know what happened, so I continued. And I am so glad I did. This work took me over 2 years to finish and quickly took over my life. These characters are so dear to me, and I am glad to finally be able to tell their story.

To my husband Ryan, who didn't even ask questions when I was shut in our bedroom for hours, asked weird questions about geography and bought me candy for my "reading time." He's a gem.

To my cousin Meagan, who was just a fantastic beta reader and so helpful. Her notes and advice really made this story much more concise.

To Elizabeth, you're absolutely amazing. Thank you so much for helping me make my story more readable.

For my fantastic friend Angela, who lives literally over 4,000 miles away from me and has become such a good friend, Her beta reading and notes made me laugh so hard. They made me feel so great about my characters.

To Ashley, girl. You're a rockstar. She helped me immensely in this process, and I adore her forever.

To my mother Margaret, who instilled my love of reading at an early age and would take me to the library up to twice a week to get new books. I wouldn't be here, writing this without you.

Thank you. Thank you. Thank you.

ABOUT THE AUTHOR

Heather Dubree lives in Oklahoma with her husband Ryan, son and animal companions who kept her company while writing this book. Heather is a photographer by trade and a creative by nature.

Ever since her mother Margaret introduced her to Little Women, she knew she had to become an author like Jo March.

She's obsessed with medium roast coffee, enemies to lovers, sleeping in and romanizing her life as much as possible.

HEADSHOT BY HALEY McELROY

Made in the USA
Middletown, DE
25 March 2024

51739889R00187